Good
GAME

Editor: Katie Krasne
Cover Designer: Cat at TRC Designs (@trcdesignsbycat)
Formatting: Alyssa at Uplifting Author Services
Interior Art: Alina Alilyushka

MADISON FOX

To Me.
You did it, babe.

For everyone dreaming of a stupidly hot gamer boyfriend.

13 songs • 43 min 26sec • by MADISON FOX

GOOD
GAME

2:13   1.07

♡   ⏮ ⏵ ⏭   ⊕

Reading Playlist

Name of the song	Time	Artist
Game On	**2:50**	**Club Danger**
Detonate	2:47	G2, Jeris Johnson, YONAKA
Champagne & Sunshine	3:16	PLVTINUM, Tarro
Red Lights (Bang Chan, Hyunjin)	3:09	Stray Kids
Superfan	2:22	Bohnes
Fire Again	3:37	VALORANT, Ashnikko
Lone Wolf	3:30	Egzod, Waslu
Devil In A Dress	1:51	Rhea Raj
Freefalling	2:33	Facading
Waiting	3:30	KUURO, Bianca
As They Bloom	3:57	Unlike Pluto
Red	3:27	BEAUZ
Only One King	3:30	Tommee Profitt, Jung Youth
Back One Day (Outro Song)	3:52	TheFatRat, NEFEX

GAMING GLOSSARY

Camping – staying in one place, normally a secure location, and not roaming the map.

Cozy Games – a genre of games that are designed to be relaxing and feel good. Typically, they are non-violent.

DLC – downloadable content. Refers to extra content that can be downloaded for the game that is separate from the main storyline.

Easter eggs – hidden messages or features in a game.

FPS/TPS – first-person shooter and third-person shooter. Shooters are games that focus on the character using a weapon, typically a firearm, to defeat an enemy. First vs third refers to the viewpoint of the character.

Gamertag – a player's in-game screen name. Players often go by their gamertag instead of their real names.

Ganking – when a group of high-ranking players gang up to kill a lone lower-level player. An unfair kill.

Good Game – what players say to each other after finishing a match/game, sometimes abbreviated as "GG."

K/D – "kill-to-death" ratio. This is used to measure performance in a video game.

Lag – a delay between the input of an action and when the action is completed. Commonly, when you are lagging, your character will glitch.

Lobby – an in-game waiting room.

MMO – massively multiplayer online. An online game in which many players play together on the same server.

Mod – a modification that is player-made to a game. Not by the game developer.

Noob – refers to someone who is new at a game or lacks skill.

OP – overpowered.

Permadeath – a game mode where the player has one life. Should they die, all their progress is deleted, and they must restart the game from the beginning.

PvP – player versus player. A game where people play against each other (no computer-controlled opponents).

RP – role-playing. The act of playing an in-game character within the backstory you've assigned to them.

RPG – role-playing game. You create a character that you then level up through experience points.

Sandbox – refers to a game that is an open-ended world with non-linear gameplay. It allows freedom for the player to explore however they wish.

Speedrun – the act of completing a game as fast as possible.

Swatting – the act of calling emergency services with a fake scenario to dispatch a large number of officers (ideally, a SWAT team) to an address. In streaming, people will swat streamers while they are live streaming as a form of cyber harassment.

Troll – a person who posts content online with the aim of harassing, irritating, and/or provoking others.

VOD – video on demand. In streaming, this refers to storing a stream on another platform for people to watch after the stream has ended.

Chapter ONE

ALEKS

He's right where I want him.

I round the corner, ready to take the enemy down. Rifle raised, finger on the trigger. Until a grenade launches through the window and the guy explodes in front of me.

"Boom, baby." Parker's posh London accent chimes over my headset.

"Asshole," I huff into the mic.

Damn it. I wanted that kill.

"Hey, there's a guy left on the roof," Jackson's deep voice swoops in.

Mine.

With only a few seconds left on the clock, I race up the stairs, reloading my ammo as I go. I'm cutting it close as I push through the door and onto the roof.

Ten, nine...

The enemy spins around, throwing out a flash bang. But he's not quick enough.

Eight, seven...

My bullets rain down on him.

Five, four...

The confirmed kill pops up just as the grenade hits, assaulting me with a fuzzy white light.

Two, one...

I smirk as the word VICTORY splashes across the screen, followed by my match statistics.

31 Kills, 4 Deaths, 15 Assists. Not bad. Scanning the rest of my team, I silently groan when I see that Parker got three more kills than me. He is going to be such a little shit about it.

Parker and Jackson switch on their webcams, their respective blue and green masks popping up on my right monitor. Sighing, I tug off my headset and grab my red LED mask. Once it's secured over my face, I position my mic closer and turn on my own webcam.

"I just want to say I owned you all that round." Parker gloats.

"First, we're on a team, so we all won. Second, you died fifteen times, which kind of cancels you out."

"Aw, come on. Can't you give me a little credit?"

"Nope."

My eyes flick to my third monitor, turned vertically so I can better track the chat board while I stream. Most of the comments are babying the hell out of Parker right now. Typical.

I stretch my arms over my head, leaning back in my

chair. We've been streaming for six hours now, and the edge of exhaustion is starting to bleed into my stiff muscles. I feel a slight breeze and realize the bottom of my shirt has ridden up. Fuck. My eyes dart back to the chat, and I tug the top back down before shaking a finger at my webcam.

"You guys should know better than to ask me to strip for free."

Suddenly a donation for two hundred dollars pops up with the message "take it off."

"You asked for that," Jackson chuckles. I roll my eyes knowing no one can see it through the mask. Whatever. I'm more than used to it at this point; it comes with the territory.

"Anyway, thanks for joining The System tonight everyone. We'll see you next Sunday." I watch various versions of the sad face emoji fill the chat. Every time they act like this, as if we don't stream forty hours a week. "Come on, you know I'll be on tomorrow night. We have to continue my current *Death Valley 5* role-play; can't forget about that nurse I kidnapped Friday night." Our moderator drops the link to my latest solo stream into the chat. "Alright, Blade out."

I click the END STREAM button and switch off my webcam without hesitation, leaving Parker and Jackson to do whatever they want. The three of us spend the first thirty minutes chatting before we start playing, so I don't see the need to stick around any longer when we end.

I let out a sigh as I tug the mask back off and set it next to my keyboard. Over the course of the stream, I had a total of 239,450 viewers on my channel, which is pretty average for our joined streams as The System. The numbers always rank a little higher when we are together—probably because my viewers know it's the only time I show my "face."

Pushing away from my setup, I stand and stretch out my legs just as Sydney, our publicist, comes barreling into my room.

"I would be congratulating you on having a good stream and for keeping it tame for the sponsor if not for the fact that I found out you haven't officially RSVP'd to the Vazer Stream Awards after-party."

"Syd, I already agreed to go to the VSA itself, isn't that enough?"

Her brow twitches slightly as she levels me with a look.

"Aleks, you had to agree because you're winning a damned award."

I groan, falling back into my chair. Ah, yes. Nothing like being the lucky recipient of this year's Golden Vazer Award—an award given to a veteran streamer who has significantly impacted and influenced the gaming and streaming community. It's a sick award and I'm proud of it, but it's a pain in the ass that I have to physically receive it on stage. Well, technically I don't have to, but Sydney would sooner drug my ass and drag it there than let me skip out.

"I don't care. You know we can't drink or eat with the masks on. The after-party isn't happening, Syd." I fold my arms and stare at her. She purses her lips, holding my gaze for a solid few seconds before letting out a huff.

"Fine," she pops a hand on her hip and points a single manicured finger at me, "but you have to promise to actually play nice with Davis Monroe." I let out another groan, one that borders on a whine, at hearing the name of the Vice President of Vazer. "Nu-uh, Aleks. You blew him off at the last gala. This one's in his name, so you can't pull the same shit."

Saying I blew him off is putting it kindly given the fact that I told him I would rather eat glass than sit through another conversation of him trying to kiss my ass. He was probably too humiliated to give Sydney the exact wording. Which means that there's a good chance that I *could* pull the same shit.

"I'll promise you a single civil conversation with the man." I reach out my hand, and she narrows her gaze, turning the words over before meeting me in a firm shake.

"Deal. I left your new suit in the living room with the others. And before you whine, yes, Aleksander, you have to do the yellow carpet." She spins on her heels to leave, but her tiny body smacks right into the naked chest of my roommate as he comes jogging into my streaming room. She recoils, falling right onto her ass, and glares up at him.

"Whoa, sorry, Syd." Parker reaches out a hand to pull her up, and she rolls her eyes before taking it.

"What is it, Parker?"

"Just wanted to see if I could switch out that shirt you put out for me to wear on Saturday for this one." There is an electric blue dress shirt in his hand that he holds up with a wide grin. Knowing Parker, it's probably a limited-edition shirt from some exclusive European designer that costs a stupid amount of money. Parker is the heir to the Covington Hotel conglomerate, a chain of high-end hotels throughout Europe that has recently expanded to the United States. The number of people he knows, and the depth of his bank account, has no end.

"No. We agreed on all black for everyone."

Parker places his free hand on her shoulder and leans in with a sneaky smile.

"Come on. Just think how good I'll look. Blue mask. Blue shirt. Perfectly styled hair. I'll be a walking PR wet dream for the cameras."

"Parker, no. I—"

"Thanks, Syd. Love ya, babes." His accent thickens on the last words before he sprints back out of the room.

She rubs the bridge of her nose muttering, "You boys are the reason I have preventative Botox at the age of twenty-seven."

"It's a good thing we pay you the big bucks, then." I stand up and ruffle her hair before dipping out into the living room.

Parker, Jackson, and I all live in a six-bedroom penthouse apartment with a large wraparound balcony. Three of the rooms we sleep in, three we converted into soundproof streaming rooms. The place has an open floorplan and is pretty minimalistic, just decked out with a lot of neon signs and limited-edition gaming memorabilia. There's even an obnoxious poster of the three of us on the wall next to the black leather couch, which sits in front of a sweet ninety-inch TV with surround sound. There are floor-to-ceiling windows lining the east side of the room, where the kitchen is, and the south side, leading to the balcony. The windows and outdoor space were the main things Parker wanted when we picked an apartment, and the twenty-four-hour gym and sauna were the main things Jackson wanted. I just wanted enough rooms so we could stream and sleep in the same place but in separate rooms. We owned a warehouse a couple of years back where we streamed and edited, but it was annoying to travel back and forth each day to sleep when we were streaming for hours on end. Half the time we ended up crashing on a shitty couch, which was killer on our backs.

I swipe a water from the kitchen fridge, chugging it as Sydney comes to rest on the island.

"I'm serious, Aleks. Don't pull the same shit you did at the Streamzies awards, okay? Wear the outfit I put out, please."

"That leather jacket cost two thousand dollars, Sydney."

"It was a black-tie event, Aleksander."

I sigh and grab her hands, looking her directly in the eye.

"I, Aleksander Knight, promise you, Sydney Lake, that I will not only have one civil conversation with Davis Monroe, but I will also wear the exact outfit you have requested with only minimal changes."

"No changes."

"I'm wearing my necklace."

"Fine. Minimal changes."

I let go of her hands with a chuckle and circle back to the fridge. It's almost midnight, and I'm starving. The nights where I stream, dinner falls to the back of my mind. It's not until I finish that my body begins to register the hunger.

I pull out one of tonight's servings of dinner that has been prepared by our chef, Alicia. Sydney hired her two years ago when she noticed that Parker and I were surviving off packets upon packets of two-minute ramen as dinner after our late-night streams. She said the sodium would kill us one day. Syd is a cross between an annoying little sister and a mother hen. You never really know which one you're going to get on a given day, but we love her all the same.

"Can you heat one for me?" Jackson's deep voice rumbles into the room as he drops himself onto one of the island barstools.

"Fine. But only because of that triple kill you got in the last three minutes." I pop the lids off two containers, inhaling the smell of homemade lasagna, before shoving them both in the microwave for a few minutes.

"Alright, I'm heading home. I expect pictures before you leave for the event. And please don't screw anyone in the bathrooms." Sydney pauses right before entering the elevator and spins back around. "Scratch that, please don't attempt any sexual acts with anyone at the VSAs. I hate the media fallout from streamer drama. Okay, thanks." The elevator door closes on her tense grin.

"She's still pissed about that time you finger banged that chick at the Streamzies," Jackson chuckles.

"That's because she said no fucking. Fingering didn't count."

The event was over a year ago, but Syd still uses it as leverage. The girl, some stream bunny, had gone around bragging to all of her friends after our little rendezvous. The news spread faster than an STI in a nursing home, and I was a trending hashtag, again. Everyone was talking about how, even after all these years of streaming, I hadn't grown out of my bad boy ways. And yet these same people wonder why I stopped going to events. Why I drew back from the toxic limelight.

I wonder just how much trouble I would get in if I sent a body double in my place to the VSAs…

The microwave beeps, jarring me out of my spiraling thoughts. I toss a set of forks on the island before pulling the lasagnas out and taking a seat next to Jackson. The food is piping hot, but my starving body inhales it anyway. All the while, I plan for some way to make this upcoming ceremony a little more exciting.

Chapter TWO

STEVIE

"Damn, Stevie. You're going to put the rest of us out of our jobs."

I smirk, admiring myself in the mirror.

"Hey, you're the one who called asking for an emergency set of extra hands," I smooth down my black mini dress and re-cup my boobs, "and you know I always bring my A-game."

"Mmm," Deanna hums, "more like your dick game."

I swat her arm with a flick of my wrist before grabbing my name tag and pinning it to my chest. I look at myself again, assessing the length of my dress and tugging on the hem. Damn it, is it too short? My ass is as round as a deflated balloon, so I didn't think it mattered if the dress was a little on the shorter side. Whatever, it's cute and I don't have a change of clothes.

"Speaking of your dick game, have you heard from Chase?"

As if she spoke him into existence, my phone buzzes and I see a new text from said ex-boyfriend. I know that if I were to unlock it, the series of unread texts he has sent me over the last three days would glare back at me. All one hundred and fifteen of them. This is the third time I've broken up with Chase and the fifth time I have caught him cheating on me over the last five years. Which makes me seem like a bit of a dumbass because who goes back to a guy after he cheats on her a second time?

Me. Clearly.

"I'll take that as a yes."

"He's been sending gifts to my place, and I'm five minutes away from moving."

"You would sooner sell your kidney than move apartments, Stevie."

I sigh because she's right. I received the apartment from my yiayia's will along with a hefty inheritance that goes into effect once I turn thirty. I love my parents, but it was my yiayia who spent the most time with me as a child, who gave me a place to turn to when the only people at home were nannies and butlers. The apartment is everything to me. Which means that even though Chase could literally sit in the lobby and greet me every morning if he wanted to, I wouldn't move.

"I'm sorry, I didn't mean to down your mood." I turn back to Deanna as she gathers me in a bear hug, the familiar scent of her coconut body lotion grounding me.

"It's fine. I'll just focus on the free booze we'll get to take after the shift."

"And the fine men we will be serving."

"Dee, half the men in there are vampires who flinch at the sight of sunlight."

"And the other half are guys who are only popular because they're hot."

"Fair."

"And just imagine the kinky shit they are probably into."

She bumps her hip into me, and I smile at the prospect. While Chase may have cheated on me multiple times, I remained woefully faithful to him. Which meant five years of sex that consisted mostly of reverse cowgirl.

I hate reverse cowgirl.

With each breakup, I became more bitter. Each time he cheated on me, my resolve strengthened. After nursing a killer hangover yesterday, I came to the conclusion that this time Chase and I were done. For good. I'm not wasting the rest of my twenties on him.

"Alright, ladies, let's get you all lined up and I'll go over the rules for tonight." Deanna's aunt Lia strides through the door in a pair of silver Iriza Louboutin heels and a striking all-white pantsuit that is stark against her dark skin. Dee tugs on my hand, and we fall in line with the other women working tonight. "The VSA is a platinum event." She props a hand on her hip. "We have five champagne carts posted across the floor; you should already know if you are stationed there. Everyone else, you will begin making the rounds with the champagne, and you can restock at the carts. Pay attention to the tables with white tablecloths, those are streamers and VIP guests. If they want a drink, you get them that drink. No matter their questions, the answers are always yes. Tables without white tablecloths do not get table service. I don't care if they want water, they can get up and get it themselves; you are not being paid to cater to them." She claps her hands. "You head out in five. Grab a gold tray by the door, make sure your bags are stocked, and smile."

It's been an hour and my smile already aches.

"Miss." I see a hand snap out of the corner of my eye and twist to walk over to a woman in a tight orange dress that is most definitely not her color. Before I can open my mouth, she plucks two flutes off my tray and walks away. *Lovely.*

Sighing, I turn back around and scan the room for any holes.

My eyes lock on a white-clothed table that is empty save for three men. I pause for a few seconds, observing the way everyone is trying–and failing–to sneak glances. All three men are in masks. They're those LED purge-looking masks, with X's for eyes and stitched mouths. As far as masks go, they're pretty hot. I know faceless stream-ers have been a thing for years, but I didn't realize they actually attended events.

How do they plan on eating or drinking anything?

As if feeling my stare, the guy in the red mask turns to look at me. Well, I can't exactly see where he is staring, but I am eighty percent sure he is staring in my general direction. Give or take a few feet. I slap an easy smile on my face and stride over.

They are all in black suits, but the guy in the blue mask has a bright blue shirt to match. Blue mask has platinum hair, almost white, and up close I can see two small cartilage hoops in his left ear that he is playing with. The guy in the green mask is absolutely massive, his shoulders straining his suit jacket, and his black hair is tied in a bun at the nape of his neck. The guy in the red mask has brown hair that, even with the mask on, has that just-had-sex kind of wave to it. It matches the vibe of his half-unbuttoned black dress shirt and thick silver chain necklace. They are just three men, and yet it feels like the entire event orbits around them.

"Good evening, can I offer you any champagne?"

"To get through this night? You can offer me several," a British accent filters out from Blue Mask. I smile, placing three flutes in front of him before turning my attention to the other two.

"Champagne, or can I get you something else?"

"Whiskey, neat," Red Mask says before turning his attention away. Disappointment bubbles at his easy dismissal.

Green Mask leans back in his chair, crossing his arms. "Cosmo," his deep voice rasps out. Before I can help it, my right eyebrow twitches up at his request, and his mask tilts in response. "Don't judge, sweetheart, it's not nice."

"No, of course not." My cheeks flame. I have to get out of here. "I'll be right back with your drinks."

I swivel on my heels, only to feel a hard body knock into me from behind. I hear the tray fall, along with the gut-wrenching sound of the two remaining champagne flutes smashing on the ground, followed by a loud gasp. But instead of landing in a wet pile of broken glass, a hand yanks me forward and I tumble into a warm body, my ass landing on their lap. The scent of leather, pine trees, and amber invades my senses, and before I can think twice, I lean farther forward to inhale the scent.

"Some people would say 'thank you' before nuzzling their savior's neck," the voice rumbles.

Snapping my eyes open, my chest flushes as I look up into the red glow of the LED-mask.

"Sorry, thank you." I breathe out, mesmerized by light.

"Not a problem, little dove." My left arm is still pressed against his pecs, and I can feel the steady beat of his heart beneath it. The commotion continues around me, but it fades to a buzz as my brain focuses on the feeling of his grip loosening and his hand slowly tracing its way up my arm. I shift on his lap, chasing his touch. His gloved hand comes to stop under my chin, tipping it slightly back. This close, I can see the faint traces of his eyes behind the red X's. I know without a doubt that if I could see them clearly, I would be drowning in them.

He leans forward, the mask grazing my jaw.

"I suggest you stay still if you're going to sit on my lap. I'd hate to ruin these pants." I freeze and he lets out a soft chuckle. Goosebumps break out over my body as his hand glides back down my neck, the leather rough against my skin.

"Stevie, oh my god, are you okay?" Deanna pushes her way through the gathering crowd, breaking my trance.

I shoot up, a slight wobble in my heels and a dizziness in my head. *What the hell was that?* It was probably only a few seconds, but it felt like time had frozen the moment he touched me.

Deanna grips my arms. "Stevie, are you okay?"

"Yeah," I shake my head, trying to dissipate the internal haze, "yeah, I'm fine."

She lets out a deep sigh, her hands coming down to hold mine as she starts to tug me away from the table. "Let's get you some water."

I flip my head back, looking into the three bright masks before settling on the red. I open my mouth to say…something, anything, but he beats me to it.

"I'll be waiting for that drink."

Heat rushes through me. I whip around, out of Deanna's grasp, and speed walk my way through the crowd, my three-inch heels twisting between the clusters of bodies. The farther away I can get from him, the more likely I am to start thinking clearly again.

It's not until I reach the small bar next to the stage that the knot in my chest starts to loosen. It's less crowded here, cooler. The flush on my skin begins to fade, and my body calms into a somewhat normal state.

"Can I get you anything?"

I thread a small smile on my face for the bartender. "One cosmopolitan and a whiskey, neat."

"Any whiskey preference?"

I only need to scan the liquor selection for a moment before homing in on the perfect choice.

"Macallan 12, please."

He nods before turning to grab the signature bottle from the top shelf. The amber liquid glistens as the shining lights from the stage shoot through it, a veritable sea of caramel. I want to ask him to pour me one as well, but I'm pretty sure that would be frowned upon given the mess I've already made. Shit. This definitely falls into Lia's category of "don't fuck up."

Groaning, I lean back on the bar just as Deanna breaks through the dance floor crowd. She tosses her empty drink tray on the bar and perches next to me, one elbow propped on the marble.

"Could you have run away any faster?" She huffs.

"Probably. You know I'm very talented in heels."

She rolls her eyes before signaling to the barback for some waters.

"I'm so sorry, Dee. I'll talk to Lia."

"It's fine, I'm her favorite niece. She won't chew me out over something like this. Plus, we were the ones who asked you for help."

"Pretty sure what I did was the opposite of helping," I pout. I hate messing up, and I hate disappointing people even more.

She just waves me off, eyes flitting over the crowd. "It's fine, hon."

I grab one of the waters from the barback, tossing it back like a large shot.

"Seriously though, Stevie. Out of every table, you just had to pick The System's. I mean, really. I thought even you would have steered clear from them." She snorts.

"The what?"

"The System, the guys in the masks." She takes a sip from her water before raising her left brow at me. "They're some of the top streamers. You've heard of The System."

"Uh, I don't think so."

"Girl, you've been playing video games since before I knew you. How have you never even heard of them?"

"I play farming sims. The only streamer I watch is that girl who also gives cozy game recommendations on You-Tube."

"Liar. I've seen you play shooting games before," she challenges. "You have *Death Valley 3* on your shelf at home."

It's finally my turn to roll my eyes at her.

"Oh my god. Sure, rarely. I don't follow any streamers or anything like that. It's just for fun. Come on, you know this."

She purses her lips at me, and I pinch the bridge of my nose. I have no idea why she is getting so hung up on this. She only started paying attention to the video game industry recently because her new girlfriend works for some big esports team. I love her to death, but Deanna has a habit of immersing herself fully into whatever her partner is into. I'll never forget the time she dated a guy on the baseball team during our junior year of college. I spent months being dragged along to games and listening to her explain the rules and run down the season stats. If I never go to another baseball game in my life, it will be too soon.

"Well, wise one, tell me. Who are they?"

The corners of Deanna's lips turn up as she clasps her hands together. "Okay, so, the guy in the green mask is Shield3d, blue mask is EnglishCoffee, and red mask—your hottie—is NightBlade32." She wiggles her eyebrows at me. "But they just go by Shield, English, and Blade."

Blade.

"They go by their gamertags?"

"Babe, no one knows what they look like, of course they go by their gamertags."

"Fair," I pause, "and he isn't my hottie."

Deanna laughs, plucking a maraschino cherry from behind the bar and popping it into her mouth. "You were literally in his lap when I arrived, Stevie."

"So? It's not like I was grinding on him." *Cause he told you not to*, says the little voice in my head.

"A wasted opportunity if you ask me."

"Well, I didn't."

The bartender returns, sliding the whiskey and cosmopolitan my way. He dips his head toward them.

"Your drinks."

"Thanks." I eye the beverages with equal parts joy and resentment. I really don't want to go back to their table after embarrassing myself, but I also don't want to pass up the chance to see Blade again. It's that feeling of having butterflies in your stomach and throat at the same time; you're not sure if you want to laugh or throw up.

Dee's voice pulls my attention back. "In any case, they're pretty elusive. They only turn on their webcams when they stream games together and are chatting."

"And that's how they became so popular? Three masked men chatting on the internet?"

"Not exactly. Blade has been around for years now. He got big because he was making content when the market wasn't so saturated," she smirks. "He's never shown his face. Ever. The most anyone has ever seen is his hands."

"His hands?"

"Yup," she pops another cherry in her mouth, "hand fetishes are a thing."

"So is a mask kink," I mutter.

"Girl, the mask kink is real as fuck, and those boys know it."

"What about the other two?" I sit up and scan through the crowd.

"Well, English got big because one, his accent, and two, he does that thing where you try to complete a game as quickly as you can."

"Oh, he's a speedrunner?" Impressive. It's a super competitive field and takes a lot of dedication, especially if you speedrun multiple games.

"Yeah, that! And then Shield kind of just appeared one day playing with Blade, the two of them crushing any game they teamed up in. He also sometimes posts himself playing those horror games you know I hate to watch."

"Guess that makes sense."

The crowd finally breaks, and I catch a glimpse of bright red, my heart jerking.

"Those cocktails are going to get watery by the way." Deanna nudges me with her elbow.

I groan, eyeing the growing condensation on the glasses.

"I'm headed back out before my aunt catches us gossiping any longer. You need to stop overthinking everything and just live. Chase doesn't dictate that pussy anymore, girl, you do." She picks up her gold tray and disappears into the crowd, leaving me alone.

Shit...I left my tray at their table. Crime scene is probably a better description of the mess I left behind. I'll need to track down a new one so I can keep serving. I don't need another reason for Lia to be mad at me tonight.

I take a deep breath, squeeze my eyes shut as hard as I can, then I let out a loud exhale. When there is no air left, I pop open my eyes and plaster on a plastic smile.

I've got this.

Chapter THREE

ALEKS

"Again, we are so sorry for the inconvenience. If there is anything we can do…"

I roll my eyes behind my mask.

Davis has been riding my ass for years, trying to get me to attend this award show. I have a feeling that if I didn't show up this year, next year he would've gone to Sydney and gotten down on his hands and knees to beg for our attendance, and I didn't have the patience for that. Davis isn't a bad guy by any means, he's just desperate. And I hate the smell of desperation. "The young woman will be heavily reprimanded, rest assured."

My head snaps up at the comment, and my fingers curl into a fist, black nails biting into the soft leather of my fingerless gloves.

"There's no need for that, Davis. It wasn't her fault."

It was that jackass, Daniel "FlyingFox" Decker. Said jackass was still milling around my table, too. Playing the woe-is-me card, letting the stream bunnies coo over him. Typical two-faced Decker.

"No, Mr. Blade, her actions were inexcusable and a poor reflection on our event brand. Really, we–" he squeaks as my hand shoots forward and squeezes his wrist. I wait a second before raising myself, standing a solid five inches above his eye level.

"I said, there is no need," I adjust my grip so my thumb lands on a pressure point. "It was not her fault."

"Of course," he cringes. "It was not her fault."

I release my grip and flop back onto my seat. "Wonderful, now if that is all?"

He nods his head and scurries off. Pathetic. But considering no bones were broken, I'm counting this as my one civil conversation that I promised Sydney.

I scan the crowd, trying to find her.

Stevie. That's what her friend called her.

The visibility in the mask sucks ass, though; everyone and everything is bathed in a red haze. It's why we don't wear them full time and especially not while we're gaming. We can't see shit. But when Stevie fell in my lap, she was close enough that the mask didn't matter. The red LED bathed her in its glow, turning her into an angel who had accidentally found her way into hell. An angel whom I wanted to corrupt. I shift in my seat. My cock is still half stiff from the feeling of her tight body flush against mine. Perky tits right at eye level, little ass rubbing across my lap. She turned what was going to be an annoying night into something much more interesting. Something actually worth my time.

"How am I supposed to drink any of this with the mask on?" Parker fiddles with the three champagne flutes in front of him.

"Stick a straw in it."

"I'm not drinking champagne through a straw. I'm not some sort of heathen." His accent thickens in disgust.

"Then I guess you're not drinking 'cause you're not taking that mask off."

There is a moment of silence as Parker laments.

"Okay, how about this. What if I tip my head upside down, tilt the mask up, and you pour the champagne into my mouth." Jackson and I turn to stare at Parker at the same time, and while he can't see our expressions, he knows the looks we are giving him. He suggests the same thing every time we go out. "Fine, fine." He leans back in his chair, crossing his arms over his chest.

I feel Stevie's presence before I see her. The little dove has managed to capture my attention more than I would like to admit.

I watch her slide through the crowd, our drinks in one hand and a new tray of champagne in the other. People make way for her without her having to utter a single word. She's like a goddess, commanding attention with her mere presence. She knows it, too. It's how she carries herself. The confidence she radiates is sexy. It makes me want to hide her away and put her on display at the same time. I want everyone to be jealous of her on my arm, but I also want to pluck out their eyes for even daring to look at her.

Her long legs eat up the distance in seconds, the short dress riding higher from the large strides. I keep up my slow perusal of her figure. She might not be able to see my eyes raking up her body, but she can feel them. It's in the way her gaze flickers down to me before settling back on Jackson. She bends down and places both drinks on the table, sliding the martini glass to Jackson.

Her voice washes over me, rich like honey. "One cosmopolitan."

"Could I have a straw?"

She pauses. "A straw?"

I swear every word out of Jackson's mouth tonight has confused the poor girl.

"Like a bar straw," Jackson nods at her. "Do you have some in that little bag?" Her brows furrow as she slides two thin, short straws from the petite fanny pack clipped around her waist.

"Sure, but we don't normally serve them with cosmos." She holds them out for him to grab and he plops them into the pink drink before raising it to the bottom of his mask. Lifting the mask a few inches and tilting his chin down, he takes a long—obnoxiously loud—sip.

"Oh." The word slips out of her plush mouth.

"Show off," Parker mutters. His full champagne flutes bubble idly in front of him, taunting him.

"Would you like a straw as well? A proper one, not a bar straw."

I lean forward, resting my elbow on the table and propping my head up to stare at him.

"Yeah, English, why don't you stick a straw in it." I wish he could see my face, but my voice is laced with so much sarcasm it doesn't make a difference.

"Pricks, the lot of you." He looks up at her, and I thank

25

fuck that he is wearing his mask because I just know he has that lazy, shit-eating grin slapped on his face right now. The one that has girls turning to putty before he even opens his damn mouth–a mouth I want to punch. "A straw would be great, love. Champagne flutes and masks don't really mesh."

"No, they don't," she holds out a straw, "but I doubt much is easy with those on."

"You would be correct." He takes the straw from her hand, fingers deliberately grazing over hers, "but there is still plenty we can do with them on." She blushes and—yeah, I definitely want to punch him.

Parker sticks the straw in the flute, bringing it to the bottom of his mask. He hesitates, his brain warring between the atrocity he is about to commit and his need to have at least an ounce of alcohol in his body to make it through this awful event. He is my best friend, but I relish his struggle at the moment.

She places the amber drink in front of me. "Your whiskey." Her syrupy voice drips over me and I struggle to pull myself away. Despite the mask, her cat-like eyes manage to zero in on my own. I don't know what is going on, but I could sit here and stare into them for the rest of the night. She's mesmerizing.

"Don't I get a straw as well?"

She slips out two more bar straws and drops them in. "Of course."

Bringing the straws to my lips, the subtle scent of the whisky drifts under the mask. My body begins to warm at the rich scent. I take a sip and recognition hits me instantly as the smooth liquid slides over my tongue. The spice heats up my throat, and a slight burn travels through my nose. It all amplifies the intoxicating feeling Stevie's mere presence has created.

"Mac 12," I say, appreciation and satisfaction in my voice at her choice. "Oaked."

"You seemed like a Macallan kind of guy." She shrugs.

I give her another once-over. At first glance, one might mistake her as just another high-class server. A more dedicated observer would be able to catalogue the glistening gems in her ears, the red soles of her heels, the practiced smile. She knows her shit because she was raised to know the best.

"Anyone with taste is a Macallan person."

She snorts lightly. "You're not helping your case."

"Fine. So, what kind of guy does that make me?"

Her lip quirks up, teasing me.

"A guy who knows what he wants, what he likes," she leans her hip on the table, "but is patient. He waits until it is the right time to strike."

Fuck. I want to grip that hip and twist her onto my lap again. But there are still too many eyes on our table. We don't do these events often, but when we do, we are careful about who we interact with and for how long. Even Sydney only attends events as necessary because of the backlash she receives. Although, she would attend every event with us if we didn't stop her. She says she doesn't care—that it's part of the job—but no one is immune to online bullying, and we can handle ourselves.

"Do you know what I want right now, Stevie?"

It's the first time I've called her by her name, and I see the surprise light up on her face.

"What?" Her eyes narrow, but there is a hint of mischief in them.

I stand up and, even though she is in heels, I still have a solid four inches on her. I place my hand on the table next to her hip and lean forward, caging her between my body and the table.

"I want to reach my hand under that dress and feel how ready you are for me."

Her eyes darken for a moment before she schools her features. "Are you always this forward with women you've just met?"

"Only the ones who seem like they can handle my games."

"And what if I don't want to play?"

A soft chuckle rolls out before I can stop it, and she uses that moment to quickly move out from under my grasp. "Well, if there isn't anything else I can get for you," she reaches for the tray of champagne, "I have to continue making my rounds." She walks away without waiting for a response. I watch her go, tracking her swaying hips as they glide through the mingling patrons. My jaw ticks as other men let their gaze linger on her, like they have a chance.

It bothers me. I don't come to these events to chase women. I just use them as an easy release. And yet, I want to hunt down this little dove until I can cage her for my own.

Why her?

"You know, she seems kind of familiar." I twist to see Parker has successfully downed two of his three champagnes.

"Familiar in an I-think-we've-fucked-before way or in

a she-might-be-a-groupie way?" Jackson's cosmo is empty, but he won't reach for another drink tonight. He has a self-imposed one-drink maximum rule when we go out to events. Which is useful because Parker has a self-imposed no-max drink rule, even though he requires an obscene amount of champagne to get drunk. I think all those rich-boy parties over the years made him basically immune to champagne.

"You better hope it's not option A." I growl.

"Wouldn't be the first time we shared a bird." Parker has the nerve to shoot finger guns at me. "But, no, neither of those options. I can't place it. Maybe she has a sibling or something."

I nod my head but turn back to the crowd. With ease, I spot her chatting up a table of female streamers as she hands them more champagne.

"You promised Sydney no sexual acts of any kind at the event." Jackson can be a real killjoy when he wants to be.

"Technically, Syd was referring to fellow streamers or industry professionals."

"Literally, her words were anyone at the VSAs." I drag my eyes away from Stevie and scowl at him. "I can feel you pouting through the mask."

"I'm scowling."

"Same shit."

I'm about to argue back when music blasts through the speakers and the overhead voice announces, *"Welcome to the eighth annual Vazer Stream Awards."* I lean back in my seat as everyone starts to applaud. *"Please welcome your host for tonight's show, Adrian Castellanos!"*

I watch as Adrian jogs onto the stage, sporting his white mask—which has been defunct for a few years now. Castle's face reveal is still one of the most-viewed reveals online; people lost their shit. Probably because the fucker looks like he stepped out of an Armani catalogue, you couldn't be mad about that. Adrian started uploading videos online a few years before I did, and I'm not ashamed to admit that I looked up to him quite a bit. We used to play together a bunch, but it fizzled out as he started sticking to just first-person shooters.

I grab my drink and take another sip, the burn comforting me for what is going to be a long night ahead.

Chapter FOUR

ALEKS

66 I'm going to kill Sydney."

When Syd mentioned that I had to accept the Golden Vazer Award, she failed to mention that there were other awards the group and I had been nominated for. Which I probably would have known if I bothered to look anything up. I've had to go on stage twice in the last hour and have yet to accept that damn Golden award.

Is it sick that The System won Best Content Organization? Yeah. Is it cool that I won Best *Death Valley* Role-Play? Yeah. Still, I would've been just as happy to accept them from my couch at home than here on stage. Instead, I've had to pull speeches out of my ass.

"Pretty sure murdering our publicist isn't in our best interest." Jackson nudges me.

"Pretty sure murdering you isn't in my best interest either, but I still dream about it."

"Love you, too."

I go to take a sip of my whiskey only to remember I finished it about three awards ago. I keep meaning to order a new one, but I'm waiting until Stevie makes her way back over during one of the breaks so I can order it from her.

"And the nominees for Best Speedrunner are CreepyP-illows, EnglishCoffee, KyleOdd, JustAGame, and Only-Van."

"I don't even care if I win this year so long as Creep doesn't." Parker huffs.

"You just hate that he's the Australian version of you." I taunt.

"No," Parker crosses his arms, "I just hate that he won Best Speedrunner at the Streamzies awards last year after I beat his time in *Dreadlander* in my livestream."

I don't bother reminding him that what they really care about are the times recorded in live tournaments versus streams. It's an even touchier subject. He can't even play in tournaments because of the mask.

"And the winner for Best Speedrunner is... JustAGame!"

"See, nothing to worry about."

I zone out as Game begins his speech and focus on Stevie instead. With everyone seated for the award show, I can spot her a lot easier. She's propped up against one of the champagne carts chatting with that friend of hers. I watch her move her hands animatedly as they laugh. She's barely paid any attention to the award show itself, so I know she isn't a stream bunny, which is a huge plus for me. Stream bunnies have lost their appeal over the years, becoming more trouble than they're worth. Plus, I hate having to wear the mask the entire time. Even though it would be easy to slip into a coat closet with one of them and be back in ten, I'd rather go through the effort to get my dick wet with my mask off elsewhere. As Aleksander, not Blade.

"We will be back after a five-minute break."

Game's speech is over, and Stevie finally turns her attention back to our table. I'd noticed her sneaking glances throughout the show, but just before every break she would dart off in a different direction. *Not this time.* I lift my empty glass and nod at her, watching as she freezes momentarily. Her lips move, and I'm pretty sure she just swore. Her friend leans close before sliding a couple of flutes onto her empty tray and nudging her in our direction. I smirk at her lazy gait and aloof eyes. The little dove doesn't like being ordered around.

She's only a few tables away when I see Daniel-fucking-Decker motion her over. Annoyance bubbles as she changes course to him.

Decker rests his hand on the back of her thigh while she hands him a flute, and my grip tightens on the empty tumbler in my hand. He is talking to her, but her lips don't move. She just gives him a tense smile and goes to move away, but Decker keeps his hand on her until she grips the tray with both hands and leans forward to hear him better. He whispers something to her, and her face sours. If I thought I wanted to punch Parker earlier for flirting with her, it is nothing compared to the damage I wish to inflict upon Decker. The jackass was the reason she fell in the first place, and she doesn't even know it. I'm about to get up and intercept when Decker releases her and leans back against his chair. He sips his champagne with a dirty smile.

Stevie's strides are quick as she makes a beeline to our table. You wouldn't be able to tell there was anything wrong if not for the way her manicured hands are angrily gripping the tray.

She tosses out an apologetic smile. "Sorry, can I—"

"Are you alright?"

"What?" Her smile freezes for a second. "Oh, no, I'm fine." She weaves around to Parker and places two new champagne flutes in front of him before plopping straws in them.

"It's like you read my mind." He immediately picks up one flute and shoves the straw under his mask.

She tilts her head towards Jackson's empty martini glass. "Another cosmo?"

Jackson silently shakes his head.

Stevie hesitates before twisting her body toward me. "Another whiskey?"

"A double."

Her nod is short, and it prickles in my chest. No matter how she tries, she can't hide the fury that is simmering behind her eyes. I have no clue what that asshole said to her, but it's set her off.

"And we are back!"

Her honey eyes rip away from my gaze as she pulls back and makes her way to the edge of the event hall. The niggling in my chest only gets stronger the farther she gets. I get up to follow her when Jackson tugs on my jacket sleeve and nods toward the stage. My eyes slip to Adrian as he brings the microphone to his mouth.

34

"I was fortunate enough to receive the Golden Vazer Award two years ago and am so excited to present that award this year to one of my good friends. The Golden Vazer is awarded to those who have created a legacy within the streaming community. They are a pillar for other streamers look up to and have used their career to shape a new path for us to follow. They have made an impact growing their brand, elevating their content to new heights, and leaving their mark on viewers."

I sit back down as I watch a video compilation of my streams and events make its way across the projector—something I'm sure Sydney approved beforehand.

"Please welcome to the stage the winner of this year's Golden Vazer Award, NightBlade32, or as we all affectionately call him, Blade!"

I really wish I had that second whiskey right about now.

I get up and hug Parker and Jackson before making my way to the stage. A few people try to clap me on the back as I pass them. I jog up the steps, and Adrian shakes my hand and claps me on the back before the woman next to him hands me the shiny award. *Finally.* I reach into my pocket for my Sydney-approved speech and look out into the crowd. I can barely see anything through the glaring stage lights directed through my mask as I rattle off my thanks. It's a little more put together than the other two speeches I've given tonight. I make sure to thank my fans before focusing on what my journey has been like as a content creator and streamer over the years. I give a shout out to Parker and Jackson—well, English and Shield. There is also a line thanking Sydney and another for our manager, Mathias.

They allowed me five minutes for this speech since it is one of the bigger awards, but I'm finished in under four. I close out the speech with my classic, "Blade, out," tagline. Freedom sings as I go to hop off the stage and return to the safety of my table. The award girl stops me, tapping my elbow and guiding me backstage instead, away from the blinding lights and the crowd. But not before I spot Daniel-fucking-Decker pulling a reluctant Stevie around the corner to the bathrooms and out of sight.

Chapter FIVE

STEVIE

Well, this is shit.

It's just my luck that there is someone here who not only knows Chase, but also knows that I broke up with him.

I stare up at the redhead as he tugs me around the corner and away from the award ceremony. I could step on his foot or pull myself out of his arm and run back, but I have no doubt in my mind that he would spend the rest of the night trying to find a way to pull me aside. I don't want to cause another commotion tonight.

"I heard Chase cheated on you again."

"I heard you've been ignoring him."

"What would he say if he saw you here tonight like this?"

Goosebumps break out over my arms as I remember

his warm, vodka-soaked breath in my ear. Gross.

"Why don't we chat in here?"

My lip curls as he proceeds to open one of the storage closets. I recognize it as the one I'd grabbed extra cocktail napkins from earlier. It's small; you wouldn't be able to fit more than three, maybe four, people in here at a time, and even that would be snug. The two yellow lights on the ceiling render the room in a somber tone. The walls are lined with wooden shelves that house various event items like tealights, straws, tablecloths, and, of course, cocktail napkins. The guy drags me fully inside before kicking the door shut.

"Look," I pause, realizing I never caught his name.

"Daniel."

"Right." I roll my wrist in his grip. "Look, Daniel. You're attractive and all, but as you pointed out, I just broke up with Chase, and I'm not really looking to get into bed with anyone else right now. So, whatever you think you're getting out of this, you're not."

It's a lie. I really want to get laid. I could use a good dicking down after all these years. Daniel's definitely attractive, but not my type at all. I would much rather go for a round with the hot masked guy instead.

"Trust me. I'm not looking for secondhand goods, Stephanie." I feel my right eyebrow twitch up at the insult. "Although, even when Chase was screwing a different girl every weekend, he constantly said you were his favorite. That he could always count on you to bend over for him."

Well, if I wasn't already planning on never getting back together with Chase, this just sealed the deal. It's one thing to talk about your sex life with your close friends, but I've never even heard of Daniel a day in my life. Which means Chase has been slutting me out to anyone who will listen. Probably acting like his penis is some magical nine-inch wand. Just wonderful.

"Well, unfortunately for Chase, I will no longer be bending over for him." I narrow my eyes at him, trying to give him my best bitch stare. "I don't know what you want, Daniel, other than to stand here and insult me about my ex, so let go of my damn wrist."

His eyes flicker to the door before he tightens his grip, the pressure painful now. Panic lances through my body. Oh, hell no. I'm not dealing with this shit. I don't think he is going to try anything shady, but I've heard one too many horror stories to risk it. I shove my free hand into his chest before bringing my shin up to collide with his balls. I hear the breath woosh out of his chest as he curls forward, and I spin my wrist out of his grasp. Free, I turn to grab the doorknob. My hand slips, fingertips brushing over it, as I feel Daniel grab my dress and pull. He mutters something, but I miss it as a shocked yelp escapes my throat.

"What the fuck?"

I'm about to have an all-out brawl with this guy in the storage closet.

I'm such a dumbass. Why did I even let him drag me this far?

Fucking Chase.

"Well, this isn't the bathroom."

Daniel and I both go still at the new voice, his hand turning slack. I turn around and come face-to-face with a bright red light. Relief floods my body, and I lurch forward to grab Blade's arm. He quickly maneuvers me behind him, and I keep clutching his bicep. His very toned, muscular bicep, from what I can feel.

"Huh, considering this isn't the bathroom, it smells like a load of bullshit in here." Blade muses. Daniel's jaw hardens as his focus switches over to Blade. "You should go back to your stream bunnies, Decker. Get them to lick your wounds."

"Why don't you take off that mask and say it to my face."

"I wouldn't want to make you feel worse about yourself when you see how handsome I am."

"I know you're ugly as shit under there."

"At least I know people follow me because I'm actually a good gamer, unlike someone who sits around shirtless eighty percent of the time."

"Fuck you, Blade." Daniel snarls before pushing past us and slamming the closet door behind him. I let go of Blade and allow myself to fall back against the door, slowly sinking to the ground, ass resting against my heels.

Blade crouches before me, silver chain swinging across his neck. My eyes trace the veins there before they get lost under his shirt. My heart is beating faster in Blade's mere presence than it was when Daniel was hounding me.

"I'm going to ask you this again, and I want the truth. Are you alright?"

His voice isn't deep, but it has this guttural tone to it. Something that draws you in, like a siren song. No wonder people don't care about seeing his face, his voice is all you need. You just want to hear more, even if it's only for a second.

"Like I said, I'm fine. Some jackass's shitty comments

aren't enough to tear down my walls."

It's the truth. Daniel never really freaked me out. He was just being rude as fuck. In fact, he only made me angry. Secondhand goods? As if. Chase was the one sticking his hot dog in various buns. I can't believe Daniel had the gall to act like my vagina wasn't good enough for him. I bet he has a pencil dick.

"Yeah, I can see that. You've got a little fire in you."

"Try a volcano."

Blade laughs, and my abdomen clenches in response.

"Why in the world did you think it was a smart idea to follow Decker out here?" I avert my gaze to the ground, but he tilts my chin until I'm forced to look at him, the red light burning my eyes.

"He seemed harmless enough."

He chuckles. "There isn't a man in that room who is harmless."

"Not even you?"

"Especially not me."

I stare into the X's, the dim lighting turning them a little more opaque as I search for a glimpse of his eyes. There is something about not knowing what his face looks like that sends tingles across my thighs. I haven't had this kind of visceral reaction to another person in years. Sure, there were guys I thought were hot while dating Chase, but there was never anyone so utterly captivating. The air conditioner turns on, and a breeze of cool air runs over my body, making me even more aware of the growing wetness below. At odds with the shiver across my body, my cheeks heat with embarrassment at my attraction.

Uneasily, I push myself off the floor to stand back

against the door, giving myself the ability to squeeze my thighs together. It's a shitty attempt to alleviate the growing pressure, and it's stupidly obvious given the fact that he is still crouching before me, his face practically in line with my pussy.

He cocks his head, looking up at me, and I squirm again. A soft chuckle bounces his shoulders, and I have to fight myself to not bite my bottom lip.

Blade stands up, his full height towering over me.

"Something wrong, little dove?"

I grit my teeth, but even I can see my chest heaving up and down as my attraction takes over my body. How the hell is he so hot? Dammit. I need to get out of here before Horny Stevie makes an appearance and does something stupid, like lick him...or suck him.

My hand fumbles for the doorknob, struggling to function because I can't take my eyes off him no matter how hard I try. Blade's hand comes to rest across mine, holding it firm against the handle. His heat transfers into me, and I melt at his rough skin over mine.

I must be drunk...on his smell or something.

"Do you want to leave, Stevie?"

I don't *want* to. What I want is to give in to Horny Stevie. Have a little fun. Be satisfied for once. Give a giant "fuck you" to Chase.

I shake my head, letting any rational thoughts fade away.

"Good." He rocks his body into mine, and I feel the hard length of him press against my belly. His other hand begins to skate down the length of my dress, resting on the bare skin of my thigh as he starts to rub slow circles.

Alright. Now I am definitely damp and one hundred percent certain that I want those hands rubbing circles a lot higher.

"This okay? Would you like me to go further?" I nod my head again, and his grip tightens. "Words, little dove."

"Yes, please, go further. Give me more."

His hand grips the side of my dress, pulling it up. He traces the top of my panties with a single finger, his nail raising goosebumps across my skin. He moves the fabric to the side and, with two fingers, slowly glides the tips along my folds, gathering my arousal.

"Fuck, you're just dripping. All for me." He grunts before ripping off his glove and dipping his fingers in.

I inhale sharply, my hand shooting forward to grasp the bicep of his arm that is keeping me upright. His fingers work in an almost lazy curling motion that has my back slowly arching off the door.

I can't believe I am doing this right now. I can't believe it feels this good. I can get myself off pretty easily, but this guy is playing my pussy like one of his games. His thumb begins rubbing my clit in time with his fingers, and all I feel is the heat pooling in my stomach turning molten. The pressure builds, and it feels like I'm floating.

"Fuck, Blade, I'm—" I can't even finish my sentence. My breath stutters.

I feel his fingers slip out a little, and I am about to protest when there is a sharp pull on my clit and my legs spasm as I moan.

His fingers resume their magic, but quicker this time. They pulse into me with a relentless rhythm. He adjusts his angle slightly, and I gasp, squeezing his bicep with a death grip.

"There, right there. Stay there."

"Do you want to come?"

"Yes." The word comes out like a hiss.

"Then beg."

I can barely process what he is saying. My whole body is focused on the tightness coiling inside, winding me higher and higher and higher. The pressure is almost painful. So close. He wants me to beg? I'll fucking beg.

"Please, Blade. Please let me come."

He pinches my clit one last time, and I break.

My brain blanks as the orgasm rips through me. Stars shoot through my tightly squeezed eyes, and I feel the strength leave my thighs. This has to be a record. Who makes a person come in just a few minutes?

"Oh my god."

I hear him chuckle, and I open my eyes to see him tilt the bottom of his mask up. He brings his other hand, still soaked with my arousal, underneath, and I watch as he sucks it clean. "Delicious."

He then bends down and slides my ruined thong down my legs. I lift my heels one by one to step out of it, and he bunches it up before slipping it into his jacket pocket.

I didn't think that would turn me on, but the possessiveness of it sparks in my chest. My gaze drops to the bulge in his pants, and a new hunger blooms in my stomach. I reach out to stroke it, feeling it twitch under my touch, but his hand comes to rest on mine.

"No need. Watching you come made this whole show worth it."

"But I want to." My voice comes out whiney, but I

don't care. I want to see him come undone, even if I can't see his face. I want that power, that feeling. I crave it.

"Stevie?" Deanna's voice fills my ears, and I freeze as I crash back to reality.

"Another time." He reaches behind me to open the door. "And I'm still waiting on that double whiskey." He exits the room just as I see Deanna round the corner. Her gaze snags on Blade before it lands on me, and her eyes widen. She rushes to me and smacks my shoulder.

"I was wondering where you were because you missed the last break, but clearly I should've just let you be."

"Sorry, things just," my brain is failing to catch up, "things just happened."

"Obviously." She reaches out to smooth my hair. "Let's try to make it seem like you weren't just freshly fucked for when we go back out there."

"We didn't fuck."

"Well, he wasn't helping you look for cocktail napkins." I snort as she repositions my dress and smooths it out. "Are you not wearing underwear?"

"Not anymore." She squeals and smacks my arm again. "Oh my god, Dee, stop. You're going to bruise me if you keep this up."

"I expect a full debrief in the morning. Brunch at Glass & Grass."

"Okay. I have yoga at ten, but let's meet after."

"Deal." She gives me another once over before linking her arm through mine and leading me back out to the floor.

ALEKS

"Sydney might just murder you."

"I pay her too much for her to murder me."

"I think she's saved up enough that she might accept the loss."

It's times like this that I hate wearing the mask because the death glare I'm giving Jackson right now would normally shut him up.

"Whatever, the ceremony is almost over." At least I hope it is. We've been here almost two hours.

"You should've seen Decker's face when he came back to his table. He was livid."

I smirk. It's a universal agreement in our group that Decker is a dick. Even if it weren't for the fact that he runs in the same circle as the Covingtons—risking Parker's identity, or that he always hits on Sydney, or that he spent weeks saying I used cheat codes to beat him in a ranked match when I fucking didn't… Basically, Decker has it out for us, and in return, we have it out for him. And him harassing Stevie is just the icing on the douchebag cake.

I can feel Decker turning back every few minutes to glare at me, something I'm sure the media has picked up on. Maybe I should send Sydney a heads up. I flip my phone over and pull up her contact right as I see Stevie making her way past the nearest champagne cart, whiskey in hand. My still-hard dick twitches at the sight of her, especially knowing that she has nothing on under that dress right now.

"In the next few minutes, we will be announcing the nominees and winners for the Best Breakout Streamer and Streamer of the Year!"

The audience goes wild, their attention wholly focused on Castle. Stevie uses that moment to breeze up to our table, a mischievous glint in her eyes.

"Double whiskey." She slides the amber tumbler into my hand, two bar straws swirling around the liquid. She reaches into her bag and pulls out a cocktail napkin, but it drops to the floor and floats under the tablecloth. "Sorry, let me grab that." She crouches down, but when her hand touches the napkin, she slides it farther under the table, her back arching to follow the momentum.

"And the nominees for Best Breakout Streamer are…"

All noise turns to a muffle as I watch in pure shock as Stevie's entire body slips under the white tablecloth.

She's not going to…

I feel her hands on my ankles before they begin to trace their way up my legs, stopping when she reaches the bulge in my pants.

She is.

I grip the table to pull my chair flush with the edge. Her dainty fingers run lazily across the fabric, the pace teasing me as I struggle not to shift in my seat. She starts to apply more pressure, and I let out a deep breath. She hasn't even unzipped me, and I'm already straining at the seams. I feel her fiddling with the button of my pants, and I'm grateful that Sydney didn't make me wear a belt.

She pulls the zipper down, and my cock pushes forward in my boxers. She proceeds to taunt me further, palming my covered dick, up and down, increasing in pressure as she reaches the tip. I shakily reach forward and bring the whiskey to the edge of my mask, tipping it up so I can take a long sip from the straw. Just as the burn begins in my throat, she reaches under the band and frees my dick. I groan as soft fingers graze over the sensitive skin.

Her thumb rolls over the bead of precum that has gathered at the tip, swirling it around. There is a pause as she removes her hand for a second before quickly replacing it, wet this time. I smirk at the thought of her on her hands and knees under the table, spitting into her palm before grabbing my cock.

I relax my body against the back of the chair, closing my eyes as I lose myself to her rhythm for the next few minutes. One hand pumps and twists along my length while the other cups my balls with light pressure. I have to ball my hands up tightly to stop myself from reaching under the table and fisting her hair, shoving those plump lips around my cock. Something tells me she would love a little pain.

"And the winner for Streamer of the Year is Celery-God!"

Everything tightens, the pressure near boiling. I'm seconds away from coming. I reach down to tap her arm, trying to give her some warning. My breathing hitches when her warm mouth closes around the tip of my cock, and I have to stifle a groan. She sucks just the tip as her hand continues to stroke at a quick, pressured pace. Her tongue flicks across my slit, and it triggers my release to shoot through me. I've never been more thankful for the mask I'm wearing as I squeeze my eyes shut, riding the high.

As she swallows the last of my release, Stevie laps at my tip, cleaning every last drop. She releases me with a pop of her lips, and I allow a true smile to form. I reach down to shove my dick back in my boxers and feel her move to zip and button my pants. There is a round of applause, and I look up to see CeleryGod making his way off the stage, award in hand. I didn't hear a word of his acceptance speech, my brain was too focused on the five-star service I was receiving. I quickly bring my hands up to join the applauding crowd.

"And that concludes this year's Vazer Stream Awards! Thank you for coming!"

Everyone begins to stand up and leave, saying short goodbyes before trying to beat the traffic out of the building. I scan the room, keeping a lookout for any of the journalists who might have their eyes on me, but most of them seem to be rushing out to see where everyone is headed next—and who with.

"Is she planning on staying under there all night?" Jackson stands up and stretches next to me.

"No, you asshole."

Parker ducks under the table to join Stevie, and I go to pinch the bridge of my nose, only to hit the mask. I feel them rustling around for a minute before they pop out next to me, Parker holding his hand out for Stevie to guide her up. She delicately smooths out the bottom of her dress.

"Just wanted to make sure her makeup didn't have that I-just-licked-dick look." Parker winks at me as he tosses a napkin onto the table. The white fabric is slightly stained with red lipstick.

Stevie doesn't even cringe at the comment. She tucks a loose strand of brown hair behind her ear before giving me a grin, her lips now a dusty red color.

"Well, I hope you all had a lovely night. I know I did." She gives a half-assed curtsey before spinning on her heels to walk away.

I stand up and grab her wrist, tugging her back to me. Her eyes flash with uncertainty, but when I bring my free hand to her chin, she leans into it, gaze softening. I search her honeyed eyes for answers.

"What's your name?"

The corners of her lips curve up in a smirk and her body relaxes as she leans out of my touch, tilting back on her heels.

"Stevie."

Brat. I know that.

"Stevie what?"

I wait for her to continue, but she just chuckles play-fully. Tilting her head up, she places a small kiss on the cheek of my mask, hand grazing dangerously close to the bottom of my jaw. Her painted nails trail briefly down the length of my neck. I'm still lost in her whiskey eyes as she quickly twists on her heels and strides away.

"Well, that's a new one." Parker links his arms through mine and Jackson's. "Come on, Syd texted that the car is waiting for us out front."

I'm in a haze as we head out of the building, barely paying attention to what is going on around us. There are a couple of flashes of light as some of the remaining paparazzi get off last minute shots. It isn't until I see our black Escalade, our driver Francis standing with the door open, that I start to come to. Jackson and Parker slide in first, and I'm about to follow behind when a small body jolts me to the side.

"Blade, hey, sorry!" I look down to see all five foot nothing of none other than Allison Lee, also known as LoveLee. I smile, even though she can't see it, and lift my hand to ruffle her mass of black hair.

"Lee, what's up?"

"I know you are probably going to say no, but…" I let out a groan, and she starts to wave her hands frantically in front of me. "But I wanted to see if I could convince you to come to the after-party."

"How do you know I'm not already headed there?"

She purses her lips dramatically and frowns, the slit in her brow crinkling. "Because you never go."

"Well, I can't be breaking my streak then, can I?" She somehow purses her lips even further, and I sigh. "Look, why don't we set up a time sometime next week, and we can all stream *Frontline Doom: Zombies*? I haven't played Zombie mode in ages."

"Lee! The car's leaving, with or without ya!" some girl

yells from far off.

"Shit, Deer will totally leave me behind. Okay, *Zombies*, deal." She reaches around my waist to give me a quick hug before bouncing off.

I slip into the car with a laugh and close it behind me.

Allison Lee began streaming a few years after me and is the only person I have really brought under my wing. Her popularity blew up three years back, and with that came a lot of scrutiny. She has a solid circle of streamers and creators she is close with now, but it was rough back then. Trolls attacked her for being an upbeat, attractive girl playing video games. She spilled onto the scene with on-line multiplayer games, a beast at what she knew and a good sport at what she sucked at. When she played well, people accused her of cheating or being carried, and when she lost, they said it was obvious she was nothing more than a pair of tits—which was stupid given that she used to wear the same black anime sweatshirt in every stream. It was a lot for her to handle, a huge mental health toll, and I made a point of streaming with her frequently so that I could tell the shit-stirrers to fuck right off.

The trolls still exist, they always will, but I hooked her up with a solid moderator whom I trust for her streams and social media. Plus, she has grown a lot since then, come into her own, and developed her own style and branched out to different games—she has an entire cozy series with her best friend and wears whatever she wants. She's like a little sister to me, and I'll probably always be protective of her.

"You better hope none of the cameras caught wind of tonight."

I stare at Jackson out of the corner of my eye.

"They were probably too focused on Decker throwing a hissy fit," Parker chimes in. "He cracked off at this poor waitress when he came back out about the wrong olives being used in his martini."

I snort and close my eyes, leaning my head back in the seat. "Whatever, it'll be fine. It's not like I'm going to be front-page news."

That's what I keep telling myself the entire ride home. But there is something in the back of my mind that has me worried.

Chapter SEVEN

STEVIE

What in the ever-loving whorehouse did I just do tonight?

I sink back against the closed door of my apartment, knees tucked against my chest, groaning. I palm my eyes until white spots appear in the blackness and it starts to hurt just a little.

I'm not ashamed that I got down and dirty with the dick of some guy I barely know—god knows I did that more than a few times in college—but the fact that I did it in such a public setting? Definitely not a norm for me. Plus, there were cameras everywhere. As discreet as I feel like I was…Ugh, whatever. It's stupid to be worrying over it when I should be rejoicing over the Michelin-starred orgasm he gave me instead. My body feels more relaxed than it has in months. They say regular orgasms improve your health; what they don't say is that getting those orgasms from someone other than yourself is exponentially better.

Chase and I had a lot of sex over the years. We couldn't keep our hands off each other in the beginning, but his fuck-to-orgasm ratio always left much to be desired. Considering how hung he is, one would think he would know how to wield it better. But no. A waste of a good dick, if you ask me. A dick I no longer plan to see again. Blade's on the other hand…

I smile to myself. The visibility was shit under the table, which shouldn't come as a surprise, but I could tell with just my hands that he was more than enough. Not too thick that I couldn't wrap my hands comfortably around it, and I'd been able to suck the tip as I swallowed him without bumping my head under the table. Would it be weird to call his dick perfectly proportioned? Probably. But it was.

I kick my legs out to unstrap my heels, shoving them to the side of my door before rolling my ankles a few times and standing up. Stretching, I pad across the hardwood floors and into my kitchen. While my apartment is technically old, my yiayia spent some money to modernize it a few years before she passed.

The walls are all white, but the crown molding is a deep forest green, which I decorated the rest of the apartment to match. Anyone who comes in here would think green is my favorite color with the way I've gone about accenting it. The living room doubles as a dining room, and you can see it from the kitchen, which has an open countertop. All the kitchen appliances were updated with the newest versions at the time, which is a godsend given how often I cook.

The apartment has two bedrooms, but I've converted the second one into my art space—it's organized chaos in there. There are a few plants scattered around, mostly different types of succulents because I am awful at remembering whether I have watered them or not. Deanna bought me a spider plant a year ago, and I killed it in two weeks. She was appalled to say the least.

I pluck out some leftover spanakopita from the fridge, transfer it onto a plate with a little bit of water, and shove it in the microwave for a few minutes. It's almost midnight, and I have to be up in six hours for my yoga class, but I haven't eaten anything since I'd arrived at the show at five.

While I wait, I strip out of my dress and throw it into my bedroom along with my bra. Sweet, sweet relief floods through me as my boobs pop free. I move to take off my underwear, realizing belatedly that they are no longer in my possession. My stomach dips, remembering Blade sliding them off and tucking them in his pocket.

Fuck, that was hot.

I turn my shower on full blast and remove my makeup while I let it heat. Once steam starts to coat the mirror, I step inside to rinse off the sweat from the night. I throw on an old cheer tee before making my way back to the kitchen to retrieve my slice of spinach heaven. I shovel half the spanakopita into my stomach before finally—reluctantly—checking my phone.

There are three messages from Deanna and…yup, twenty-two new messages from Chase, plus four missed calls. I contemplate throwing my phone across the room.

I scan his messages, but they are all basically the same thing. *I miss you. I'm sorry. It's not what you think. Noth-*

ing happened. She was just a friend. Please text me. I miss you. Steffy, please. It meant nothing. I promise it won't happen again. It was a mistake. Steffy.

I personally love how he moves back and forth between denying that anything happened and apologizing for what happened when I quite literally walked in on him cheating. His best friend had been throwing a party that night, and I initially said I couldn't make it because I was finishing an art piece for an exhibition. However, I'd managed to finish it more quickly than expected and decided to surprise him by showing up. When I'd finally made my way to the party, everyone was well on their way to being wasted. It had taken me twenty minutes to track him down only to find him in the bathroom, balls deep in Felicity Taylor's two-faced vagina. My head hurts to even think about it. It was shit enough to find him cheating, *again*, but even worse that it was Felicity. Her family, Chase's, and mine run in the same circles, and she has always been trying to one-up me. I stab the last piece of phyllo angrily before chomping at it.

I scan the rest of his messages, eyes narrowing.

Stephanie, you can't just ignore me. Come on, Steffy. Pls. I need you. You need me. U can't do better than me. You're being a child. I love you.

It's a mixture of desperation and asshole. I've never ignored him for this long before. Even the last time we broke up, when it had taken me a week before I got back with him, I'd still messaged him. My radio silence these last three days is something he isn't used to.

I click my phone off before throwing my plate into the dishwasher.

Whatever.

He'll cool off eventually.

Chapter EIGHT

ALEKS

'm front-page news.

I'm front-page news, and Sydney might just murder me.

Although, to be fair, it's not the news I was afraid of. According to all the gossip sites, Decker and I got into an argument over Allison Lee at the VSAs, and I was reportedly seen embracing her longingly before we left that night. No mention of Stevie at all. Thank god.

The elevator doors ding open, and the boys and I look up from the couch to watch Sydney power walk into the apartment. "Please confirm for me that you didn't punch Daniel Decker." Her blonde hair is pulled into a messy bun, eyes frantic under her bangs. She sits on top of the coffee table, sipping on a red juice as she swipes across her tablet. She flips it over to show me the article in question.

BLADE DECKS DECKER AT VAZER STREAM AWARDS

"That's a good one," Parker mumbles through the tea he is sipping on.

"I didn't lay a hand on him, Syd. I swear."

She nods.

"I'm also not sleeping with Allison."

She nods again, her fingers flying across her tablet and phone simultaneously.

"I might have threatened him though. Unrelated to Allison."

She freezes, sighs, and continues typing.

"Well, this doesn't seem like a me issue." Jackson goes to stand up, but Sydney shoots out her left leg to stop him.

"This is an everyone issue because the second any of you go live today, your comments will be littered with people asking about the situation. So, you're all on pause until I get this sorted. Which should only take me another five or ten minutes, depending." Her phone rings, and she moves up and into my streaming room to answer it.

I pull out my own phone and shoot a quick message to Allison to see how she's doing. While I'm not worried about the rumors on my behalf and the comments in my streams, I know the ones she's getting are a million times worse. The last time there was a rumor about the two of us, she had death threats sent to her apartment. The damage control was a nightmare.

This is why I hate events. Because of the mask, everyone pays attention to every little thing I do in the hopes that I will somehow slip up and give something away. Like I might breathe wrong and accidentally exhale my real name. It's stressful.

In the beginning, though, it was fun. A year after I started streaming and making content, my channel took off. The fame was shiny and new. I was barely eighteen, and while there were a bunch of popular content creators in the gaming space, there weren't a lot of major streamers. Even fewer of us were what people referred to as "faceless gamers." It was sick to be the center of attention, to feel like people cared about who I was, that they thought I was cool, that they wanted to be me. I got invited to events, conventions, and clubs, left, right, and center. I drank it all in, fucking different stream bunnies wherever I went, filling my body with whatever liquor I could get my hands on. It felt like the life.

Then I started getting dubbed the bad boy of streaming, and people were wanting to know exactly who was behind the mask. They got restless. Then they got invasive. People began trying to follow me home. They would stake out where I lived. I was afraid to leave my home, didn't know who I could trust. But then I started getting swatted, and it freaked me the fuck out. I finally told my manager it was enough. At that point, Parker, Jackson, and I had been running The System for a year, and it was going well. I moved in with them and hired a new driver who would switch cars for every event and take different routes back to our apartment. I also found out that the key is to live in an enormous apartment complex. When over four hundred people live in a building, it's hard to track who might be whom.

"It's all done!" Sydney returns with a triumphant smile. "You're all streaming with Allison this afternoon.

I don't care what your previous plans were, adapt them. We've got a blanket statement going out on her account and yours, Aleks. Your moderators are also being briefed as we speak. You will address the rumors at the start of the stream, and that's it. The hug picture is unavoidable since there is video as well, so we will be sticking with the 'she's like a kid sister' storyline that we've used in the past. Everyone good?"

The three of us nod like trained dogs.

"Perfect. Now someone better turn on that TV and get a trashy, reality dating show on the screen so I can relax." She plops down on the sofa and props her legs across Parker's lap, sipping on the remains of her juice.

"I'm heading to the gym." I announce. There's too much energy buzzing around me right now to focus on anything else, and I need some way to distract myself before the stream later.

My mind keeps wandering to Stevie's face as she smirked and walked away from me last night. It's frustrating how I can't seem to get her out of my head. I've fucked and forgotten girls I've known for longer than her. She's this haze sitting in the back of my mind, fogging my thoughts.

I head into my room quickly to throw on my workout clothes before grabbing a bottle of water and pre-workout from the fridge. I'm almost in the elevator when Jackson stops me.

"Want me to join you?"

"Didn't you already work out this morning?"

Even on nights where we stream until 2 a.m., Jackson will still get up to head to the gym at six thirty on the dot.

"Yeah, but you're currently wearing your shirt inside out, so I'd rather come down and make sure you don't accidentally drop a dumbbell on your foot."

I pull at the collar of my shirt and swear before tugging it off and putting it back on again.

"I'll be fine. I just need to blow off a little steam."

"Thought last night would've settled that."

Last night is why I'm in this fucking spiral.

Jackson crosses his arms when I don't say anything. "I'm serious, Aleks. I'll meet you down there and spot you."

He's not going to let this go. Protective grump.

"Fine, whatever." I get in the elevator and punch the button for the tenth floor, watching Jackson dart into his room as the doors close. I lean against the side wall, sipping on my pre-workout as I watch the numbers slowly count down. If I'm lucky, the gym will be empty. It's highly unlikely given that it is Sunday morning, but a guy can hope.

When I step out of the elevator, I'm immediately greeted by that classic gym smell. I let it roll over me, getting me in the headspace.

Swiping a towel from the entry, I make my way into the workout area and onto an empty treadmill to warm up. Sliding on my headphones, I blast my workout playlist, hardcore EDM filling my ears.

Two hours later, I'm finishing up my arm circuit with Jackson, adrenaline and endorphins rushing through me. I feel a million times better. Until I catch the flash of a brunette walking into the gym and stop mid-rep. It's not Stevie. But for the split second that I thought it was her, hope sparked in my chest.

I'm so fucked.

hope sparked in my chest.
I'm so fucked.

Chapter NINE

STEVIE

I pull into the parking lot by Glass & Grass with a sigh. I tossed and turned all night for no goddamned reason, causing me to miss my first alarm. Which meant I had no time to make coffee before yoga. Ok, realistically, I could have made a coffee, but I decided my time was better spent putting on mascara and doing my brows.

I eye myself in the rearview mirror.

While I feel like death, at least I don't look it.

I swipe a fresh coat of lip gloss on before shoving the tube in my purse and getting out of my car. There is a cool breeze today, and I take a second to embrace it before making my way to the restaurant.

I adore this place. The interior is decked out in neon yellow motivational signs, hanging glass sculptures, and copious numbers of plants. The food is great, the drinks are strong for the price you pay, and they make my favorite coffee in the entire world: a maple bourbon latte. It is pure heaven. I hate sugary drinks, and ninety percent of the time when you order a flavored coffee, it tastes like someone spilled half the syrup bottle in it. But not this one. Nope, it has a slightly sweet taste with a smoky undertone. Perfection.

Deanna is parked at one of the half booth tables, obviously having taken the plush booth side for herself. Her full concentration is on the phone in front of her, her thick braids curtaining her face.

"Is the world falling apart?" I ask Dee as I slide onto the white seat across from her. She glances up and blows me a kiss.

"You have no idea. Hang on, let me show you." Her pink acrylics fly across the screen before she slides her phone across the table.

FIST FIGHT AT VSAs: STREAMERS BATTLE IT OUT OVER A WOMAN

My stomach drops.

"Oh no. Oh please, no." I snatch the phone up and scroll through the article, speed reading as fast as I can.

All I can think about is that my mother is going to be embarrassed and furious. She is going to force me to start attending women's luncheons and join more charity committees to repair the family's image. Then, she'll set me up on a bunch of dates with boring business heirs to get me to settle down. Or worse, she'll have me marry Chase to save face.

It's not until I've read it three times and zoomed in on every photo that the nausea begins to dissipate.

"I hate you." I shove her phone back across the table and cross my arms. "You knew I'd think that was about me."

Deanna snorts. "Because I wish it was."

"Oh yeah? What do you wish it said? *Waitress Receives Finger Treatment from Famous Streamer at Awards Ceremony?*"

"I mean, I was thinking of something a little punchier like, *Bad Boy Streamer Bangs One Out at VSAs.*"

"That just makes it sound like he got himself off."

We pause our conversation as the waitress swings past to grab our orders. Deanna gets a mimosa and blueberry crumble baked oatmeal while I order my maple bourbon coffee and a poached egg avocado toast. I'm trying to find a way to tell her I jerked him off under the table without her making a huge fuss about it, but there is no scenario in my head where that doesn't happen. I wait until the waitress has brought our drinks so that there is no risk of someone overhearing.

I take a sip of the mapley goodness, humming in delight as the warmth spreads throughout me. There is nothing quite like that first sip of coffee.

"So, are you going to give me all the details, or am I going to have to pull them out of you?" Deanna slurps loudly on her mimosa.

"Maybe I don't kiss and tell."

She gives me a short laugh. "Bullshit. First off, there is no way you kissed unless he took off his mask, and sorry, babe, I love you, but even I know you aren't special enough for that to be the case."

"Ouch," I bring my hand to my chest and give her a

fake pained expression.

"Second," she points a finger at me, "I spent all of Freshman year listening to you provide excessively detailed recaps of your sexual adventures, so don't try to bullshit me now."

"Fine, fine," I concede. She stares at me and raises a single eyebrow, waiting. "He fingered me in the closet after I kneed that Decker dude in the balls for trying to corner me, and then I went back to the event floor and jerked him off under the table." The words tumble out of my mouth like my tongue is on fire.

Deanna proceeds to choke on her mimosa.

"You did what?"

"I kneed Daniel Decker in the balls."

"You know that is not what I was referring to."

I give her an awkward smile before taking another sip of coffee. Maybe I should've gotten some Baileys in this…

"I got down on my knees, crawled under the table, gave him a hand job, and swallowed him clean."

She blinks a few times before letting out a snort.

"Well, I wasn't expecting that." She tilts her head. "Also, why a hand job? That's so…high school."

I roll my eyes. "I'm sorry. Next time I'll make sure the event has tables high enough so that they can accommodate dick sucking."

"Was it big? Wait, no, rewind. The closet. Was he good?"

"That man can make a girl come with his fingers like Mozart can play the piano. Flawlessly." I can't stop the smile from spreading out on my face. "You know how you hear people talk about seeing stars? It was like that. Totally mind-blowing."

"See, I knew this was what you needed. You get a solid orgasm, and you are glowing."

The waitress drops off our food, and we eat in silence for a few minutes, hunger winning out over any potential conversation. The satisfying crunch of the freshly toasted sourdough is music to my ears. Good friends, good food, good coffee, and a good orgasm. All a girl needs.

"I still can't believe you snuck under the table to give him a handy. That was ballsy as hell."

"More like risky as hell. I blame the orgasm brain." I curl my hands into fists and stack them on one another. "It was like this big by the way."

She tilts her head. "Not bad."

I scoff at her, taking another large bite of my toast. We polish off the rest of our food, mindlessly chatting about the rest of the event. My mind keeps slipping back to Blade, and it frustrates me because it's not like I'll ever see him again. It was one night, but I'm treating it like forbidden fruit I want a second bite of. Plus, if the articles are true, he already has other drama going on with streamers, and I don't need that in my life. It was bad enough that I got close to being front-page news, the last thing I need is to actually be front-page news and have my family see it.

Deanna and I split the bill, promising to meet up again later in the week when our schedules aren't so busy. I pop a quick kiss on her cheek and head out to my car. I'm a few feet away when my eyes catch on something pink on my windshield.

There is a rose stuck under the left wiper blade. A single pink rose.

I hate roses.

Chase, however, thinks pink roses are a timeless symbol of love. I pick up the flower with the very tips of my thumb and pointer finger, like it's poisonous.

What in the ever-loving shit is this?

I whip my head around, scanning the parking lot for Chase's BMW. How did he know I was here? Sure, Deanna and I frequent Glass & Grass at least once a week... but he couldn't have known I would be here today. I didn't post about it on social media, and a quick scan of Deanna's socials show she hasn't either.

Paranoid, I scan the backseat and trunk of my car through the windows, just to make sure he didn't do something stupid like break in as well. Chase isn't the brightest guy I've met, but he is resourceful, has a lot of money, and is used to getting what he wants. I quickly slip inside and lock the doors after throwing the rose on the ground.

Not wanting to stick around, I turn on my car and head back home, blasting my favorite playlist in an attempt to block out any thoughts. For thirty minutes, I scream lyrics into the void. It's not until I scan into my apartment complex that the tension in my shoulders finally drops. I'm checking my mailbox when my phone starts vibrating in the side pocket of my leggings, and I freeze. If it's Chase, I'm not sure if I should answer or not. On one hand, I don't want to give in to him, on the other hand, I want to rip him a new one for basically stalking me.

I slip my phone out and peek at the caller ID.

Mother.

I kind of wish it was Chase instead.

"Mother, hello, to what do I—"

"Stephanie Andwell, do you want to embarrass this family?"

"Pardon?" I can hear her heels clacking on the floor in the background.

"I just had lunch with Marisol Broadshire, and she informed me that you and Chauncy have not only broken up again, but that you have been acting like a complete child and are ignoring his calls?"

I gag a little at my mother's use of Chase's given name.

"Well, if you must know, I caught him with—"

"The Taylors are hosting their annual party in a few weeks, and I expect you to have this situation sorted before then. *Katalavaineis?*"

Do I understand? Seriously. I don't even want to touch the irony of that sentence with a ten-foot pole. *Sort the situation.* I scoff. Yeah, like I'm so excited to reconcile with my ex-boyfriend so we can attend a party hosted by the family of the latest girl he cheated on me with. A real hoot. Let me just go pick up my rose-tinted glasses while I'm at it, maybe a dunce hat as well.

"Stephanie, did you just scoff at me? Since when did you become so disrespectful?" She tsks. "This is what happens when you spend all that time inhaling paint fumes."

I don't bother reminding her that her friends have bid on my pieces before. That they've paid me tens of thousands of dollars just to hang my work in their homes. Instead, I tune her out as I walk the five flights up to my apartment. There is an elevator, but it is atrociously slow, so I only use it when I have groceries or large packages. She is still droning on, slipping into Greek every once in a while, by the time I reach my door and unlock it. Dumping my purse on the table, I toe off my sneakers and flop onto my couch.

"I'll have your father wire you extra money to pick out a dress. Vittoria is wearing red, so please do not clash with her like last time."

Vittoria is my older brother's fiancée, and my mother is in love with her. I don't blame her; I adore Vittoria, too. She works as a neonatal nurse practitioner and is literal sunshine. She met my brother when he was a resident at her hospital. Now Michail works as a facial plastic surgeon at his own private practice, which my mother also loves for obvious reasons. Practically free Botox at her disposal and a heavily discounted face lift she will deny she had if you ask her. Really. She won't even admit it to me, and I saw her the weekend after with her face covered in gauze.

My mother and I weren't always at odds. We had a pretty good relationship when I was young. I was her little star. Her *asteraki*. I loved going to parties with her and getting dressed up. I still do. But I'm no longer her prized daughter to show off unless I'm attached to Chase's arm or the arm of an equally outstanding man. It's frustrating. It's almost worse that she was so amazing and attentive growing up because I know what her love feels like. Not that she doesn't love me, but her judgement always comes first. I had my role in the family, and I've ignored it. Apparently, I'm choosing to be selfish by pursuing my own dreams. My choices are disrespecting how hard my yiayia and papou worked to make it in America. My chest goes hollow, and my eyes begin to prickle. I know it's not true. My grandparents only ever wanted me to be happy—it's why yiayia left me this place. I squeeze my eyes shut for a few seconds, focusing on my breathing.

"Stephanie?"

"Yes, Mother. I won't clash with Vittoria, and I'll be on my best behavior."

"And Chauncy. Every relationship has its hiccups, but that is no reason to throw away the last five years of your life. You aren't getting any younger."

I'm twenty-five, not fifty-five.

"Love you, Mother. Talk soon. Bye!"

I hang up before she can say anything else. It's a little rude and she'll berate me for it later, but there was no way she was hanging up first unless I conceded to trying to get back with Chase. Not happening.

I don't even miss him. Which is weird. You would think after years of dating that I would. I went back to him three times, for Christ's sake. One would assume I was borderline codependent on him because of that. I probably was, in the beginning. I started dating him my junior year of college after a nasty breakup. He was my rock. Now he is nothing but a leech, sapping my strength instead.

I roll off the couch and snatch my laptop from the coffee table, opening it to run through my emails. There is a slight chill in my apartment, so I grab my knitted blanket and curl back up on the couch for a long evening.

My mind can't focus though, eyes glazing over every word. I groan, throwing my head farther back on the arm rest.

Tentatively, I open a new tab and type in Night-Blade32. The first few things to pop up are the articles from the VSAs, the gossip blogs going off about his supposed fight as well as acclaimed ravings about his Golden

Vazer Award. I scroll down a little and find the link to his streaming channel.

I'm shocked a little when the screen opens up and shows that he is currently live, playing *Frontline Doom* with some other streamers, it sounds like. His voice filters out of my laptop straight into my veins.

"Oh, fuck you. You did not just steal that ammo drop."

"Ha ha. Snoozers are losers, mate." A British voice joins in; it must be the platinum blond champagne guy.

Blade's face isn't on screen–not that I expected it to be. But weirdly enough there is a live video in the corner of his hands on the keyboard and mouse. He is wearing the leather fingerless gloves again, the kind bikers wear. His black nail polish glints as his hands flicker across his red LED keyboard.

"Blade, I need back up here. Empire Zombies are breaking through." A female voice breaks through my thoughts.

"Sure, Lee. Not going to be much help, though, with just my machete and shotgun, since dickwad over here stole the rifle ammo."

"Oh, yeah, blame me." There is a pause in conversation, and I watch Blade's character run across the screen, machete swinging in hand. "Plus, don't act like the machete isn't your favorite weapon, you baby," the English guy taunts.

"You're the ammo hoarder, that makes you the baby, baby."

I bark out a small laugh. I can't believe I've never watched them before. They're hilarious together. It's no wonder they're popular.

I grew up playing video games with Michail. We used to play some of the earlier versions of *Frontline Doom* ourselves until he got "too old" for games. In recent years, I've just defaulted to those cozy farming games in my spare time when I'm not painting or sketching. As therapeutic as my art can be, there are times when I want to throw my brushes against the wall. Playing video games helps with the art block. I get to sit there and create little farms instead of staring at a landscape that just won't turn the right shade of green.

My eyes flick to the corner screen again, watching Blade's fingers swiftly tap the keys rhythmically as he massacres the Zombies on screen. Suddenly, I feel the ghost of his hands trailing up my thighs, the slight squeeze of my hip.

"You guys see that?" He is speaking directly to us, his fans, subscribers, viewers. "A horde kill." His deep chuckle reverberates through my speakers, the same chuckle he gave me last night. My stomach flips low, pussy melting at the memory. My fingers twitch, inching away from my laptop, skimming the top of my blanket before dipping under. Tentatively, I cup my heat, middle finger tracing up my slit through my leggings.

"Alright, let's go again." His deep voice urges me on. My mind hazes out, unable to discern reality from memory. I slip my hand under the band of my leggings and thong, fingers slowly swiping over my slick. I bite my lip, heart rate climbing.

I'm in the privacy of my own apartment, but I feel like I'm on full display. Like what I'm doing is a dirty little secret, something forbidden, taboo. I can't help it. I'm so turned on right now. I want more. I want him.

I curl my fingers inside and a sigh releases. I imagine it's his fingers. Moving faster. His strong arms keeping me caged against the door again, body pressing against mine. His words encouraging me on, praising me, taunting me, telling me to beg.

Inside, the wave begins to crest. My release builds and my mind flashes to his breath on my skin. Whispers in my ear. Without a second thought, I pinch my clit. It's not the same as when he did it, but fuck, it feels good. So good that with a second tug, it pushes me over. Euphoria floods my body, pleasure radiating through my veins as I moan his name like a prayer.

I lie there for a moment in peace before I start registering the stream again, various voices floating in and out of my consciousness. I bolt upright and slam the laptop shut with my free hand. I shove the blanket off my body and attempt to stand, but my legs are still a little weak from the orgasm. I clutch the arm rest, taking a deep breath.

I feel like I just blacked out. As if someone else took control of my body. I've never done anything like that before. Sure, I've gotten off to porn here and there, but it never really did much for me. That? That was something else entirely.

Shakily, I make my way into my bedroom and over to my bathroom, turning the shower on full blast. Cold water. That'll help everything.

Shucking off my clothes, I step under the icy spray, letting it wash everything away…but still I hear his voice in the back of my mind. His laugh tattooed on my heart.

I'm so fucked.

Chapter TEN

ALEKS

I take out the enemy with a quick headshot before reloading my pistol. I have five minutes to get the stolen vehicle to the transfer point before the mission is a failure.

Normally, not an issue, except it's a damn van with the worst handling known to man. And if I crash into anything too hard, the stupid thing blows up. I guess that makes it more realistic. I'm carrying a literal truckload of explosives. Sometimes, I miss the days when there was a little more leeway, when I could run over a couple dozen pedestrians before the police really got upset and put a warrant out for me.

I swerve between the oncoming cars, my fingers twitching left and right to maneuver it as smoothly as possible. Red dots pop up on my digital map, alerting me that potential enemies are closing in. I have two more minutes to make it to the drop point.

I've only hit a few cars in the process, the damage meter is still low. But these damn enemy gangs are closing in, and I can't have them reaming my ass.

In a last-ditch effort, I deploy one of my EMP bombs, effectively freezing them all. But it doesn't stop the helicopter closing in. Shit, I'm so close.

300 meters away.

200 meters away.

I hit a fire hydrant, and the damage meter turns red.

100 meters away.

30 meters away.

MISSION COMPLETE.

I roll out of the car, abandoning it to its post, and make a run for the nearest building, climbing the ladder and a few pipes until I make it to the roof. Safe.

I let out a sigh of relief, pushing away from my desk and letting my chair roll me away from the screen. I failed that mission twice last night while streaming, and it sucked. Granted, it was my first time playing the new *Death Valley 5* DLC, but still.

I wasn't the best because I failed, I was the best because I won.

Sometimes, I feel like the creative directors of *Death Valley* watch my channels to try to find ways to make new missions that specifically cater to my weaknesses. Patience in video games is one of said weaknesses.

It's been a week and the drama from the VSAs has finally died down. Sure, I had to play nice and make sure I was participating in more group streams than normal instead of just doing my own thing, but I could play nice for

Sydney if it kept everyone safe and happy.

Plus, I had the sweet, sweet memories of a feisty brunette to keep me company during my social isolation. Company in my mind, in my shower, in my bed. Fuck, just thinking of her gets me heated again. Maybe I should go out with the guys this weekend. Get a little relief from something other than my own hand.

My phone begins to buzz, and I swipe to answer the incoming call.

"What's up, loser?"

"Nice to talk to you, too, asshole." Jackson's voice comes through a little far off. He must be calling me from his car speaker. "You're not practicing right now, are you?"

"Nah, I just finished. I'm taking a break before tonight's stream. Why?"

"*Devil Nun 5* just came out."

Fucking Devil Nun. I should've known it was that time of the year. Jackson is obsessed with the franchise. I have seen every single installment, and I have hated every single one.

"Ask your sister."

"She's thirteen. I'm not bringing a thirteen-year-old to *Devil Nun 5*. Plus, it's our tradition."

Tradition my ass. He has been dragging me to every single Devil Nun movie since we were in high school because no one else in their right mind wants to watch a series about a freaking devil nun. There's even a video game series for it on PlayStation, and Jackson owns a signed limited-edition copy. As his resident best friend, I've gotten suckered into being his movie buddy. I forced Parker to go with us to the premiere of *Devil Nun 4*, but he literally ran out of the theatre in the first thirty minutes and drove home without us out of spite. We had to call Francis to give us a ride to the apartment at three in the morning. The whole ordeal was a nightmare.

"I'll buy you ice cream afterward. Come on, Aleks."

Why do all my friends try to bribe me with food?

"I can buy my own ice cream."

"Yes, but the theatre is next to that place that does the brownie batter one you like."

My stomach rumbles. Crap, I haven't eaten anything for hours. Gaming brain.

"Fine, but I also want chocolate pretzels for the movie." I reluctantly push out of the comfort of my gaming chair. I head into my bedroom and sift through the pile of jackets haphazardly thrown in the corner before tugging on my leather jacket.

"You've got yourself a deal. I'll see you there in thirty. The movie starts at three."

"Yeah, yeah. I'll see you there."

I hang up the call before shoving my phone, wallet, headphones, and bike keys into my pocket. I slip into a pair of combat boots and grab my bike helmet from the hallway before taking the elevator down to the garage.

I fucking love the private garage. The apartment building has a larger one on the floor above that is for the other residents in the building, but this one is just ours. Parker has five cars down here and three bikes, including a gorgeous Aprilia that I've been dying to get my hands on. I'm a little more reasonable with just one car and three bikes. Although Jackson says we are both ridiculous. He just has his one Jeep, which isn't even down here right now.

I run my hand over my Kawasaki Ninja H2 with a smile. It's the most recent bike I've purchased, and it's a beast on the road.

My grandfather used to ride motorcycles, and my grandmother held onto his favorite bike after he passed. When I was fifteen, I got it into my head to refurbish it. I was a bored kid with no friends and just video games to pass the time. The bike intrigued me. It was a fucking messy experience and took way longer than it should have. But I was proud as hell after the year of hard work. My grandmother was reluctant to let me get my license, but I was a sixteen-year-old kid who spent ninety percent of his free time playing games in his bedroom, so she saw it as a way for me to get fresh air. My eyes slip to the bike. A Triumph TR6. It's a classic. I still ride it occasionally, but it's been hard ever since my grandmother passed. Losing her was the hardest thing I've ever experienced even though I knew it was coming. The cancer was something no one could stop.

My chest drops at the memories, and I quickly put in my wireless headphones, turning on my indie rock playlist to shake my body out of the somber waters that are beginning to churn. I tug on my helmet and swing onto my bike. I turn on the engine and the resounding rumble courses through my body, centering me. When I'm on my bike, everything makes sense.

I rev the engine one more time before kicking my leg up and ripping up the garage levels until I break into the sunlight. The heat beats through my leather jacket instantly, but the breeze quickly whips around me as I gain speed on the open road. My heart lightens with each mile, and

I feel myself smiling even though I'm about to spend the next few hours in pure torture.

"That was a solid eight out of ten. Not as good as *Devil Nun 3* but definitely better than *Devil Nun 4*." Jackson is all amped up as we exit the theatre.

The movie was awful. As it always is. I have no idea how they are still making movies. The whole franchise follows nuns in different parts of the world becoming possessed by the devil and then wreaking havoc until some group of people comes in to stop them. It's quite literally same shit, different country. How each movie lasts almost three hours is beyond me.

I loop my arm around Jackson's shoulders as I wheel him in the direction of the ice cream shop next door.

"Yes, yes. I'm glad you enjoyed it. Now you owe me an entire tub of brownie batter."

The bell above the door chimes as we enter the shop. The AC is so strong inside that it gives me the chills. The store is empty save for the two employees who are chatting in the corner.

"I never said I'd buy you an entire tub."

"You never said you wouldn't either." I grin at him.

Jackson gives me a side-eye expression, mouth flat. He shakes me off his shoulder and walks up to the counter.

"Two pints please. One brownie batter and one vanilla bean."

I scowl at Jackson as I shift my helmet, which I've

been carrying under my left arm, and place it on the counter next to him. One of the employees moves to begin packing a container while the other rings him up.

"A quart is only two dollars more." I challenge him. I don't really care about getting more ice cream. He already bought me three bags of chocolate pretzels for the movie. One for each hour. I just enjoy annoying him.

He hands his card over to the employee while looking me dead in the eye. "You'll survive."

Killjoy.

My phone goes off, and I pull it out to see a reminder from Sydney that my stream starts in a little over an hour. We're only twenty minutes from home. Less for me technically since I rode here on my bike and can weave through the traffic. It leaves us plenty of time.

Jackson grabs the bag with the two pints of ice cream from the second employee, and we file out of the store toward the parking lot. We're only twenty feet away from where Jackson parked when I see a white Mercedes Benz back out of its spot, right into the rear of Jackson's army green Wrangler.

I stop and stare slack-jawed at the cars. Jackson, on the other hand, starts running, ice cream bag swinging in his hand. The driver hasn't exited the vehicle. They haven't driven off either.

I jog to catch up with Jackson, who is busy inspecting the back of his car. The Mercedes drives forward a few feet before the engine cuts off. The door opens, and when I see the woman step out, I almost drop my helmet.

Well, hello.

The evening sun casts the woman before me in an amber glow. The same woman who has been invading my thoughts for the last week. Stevie is wearing a short, flowy white dress with heels; her hair hangs in loose waves down her back. The innocent angel look is so at odds with the woman in the tight black dress who fisted my cock around hundreds of people.

Her expression is one of pure anxiety, caramel eyes spilling over with guilt.

"I am so sorry!"

Jackson looks back at her, and I see him do a double take before he folds his arms over his chest. The entire display makes him look like a giant, grumpy bear, and I see more fear leak into Stevie's eyes. I weave behind Jackson to look at how much damage she could've caused.

Huh. Jackson's Wrangler is perfectly fine. The Mercedes has a nasty dent in its trunk, though. It looks like she hit the tire on the back of the Jeep straight on. I spin back to Jackson and raise my brow at him.

"I'll pay for any damages. I really didn't mean to. I was just so distracted by some bad news, and I…" she trails off, bringing her hand up to her forehead. "Here let me grab my license."

"It's fine. You didn't even damage it."

Stevie isn't listening to Jackson, though. She starts rummaging through her designer handbag, brows pinched. The entire thing drops out of her hands and spills onto the asphalt. She just stares at it, her shoulders slumping in defeat.

"How does this day just keep getting worse?"

My heart cracks at her small voice. I bend down, resting my helmet next to me while I collect the spilled items.

How the hell does she have this much stuff in such a small bag?

Stevie crouches down next to me.

"Thank you."

When her eyes meet mine, I see a split second of arousal seep in as she gives me a once over, her lips parting ever so slightly. But she is quick to school her features. We both reach for her sunglasses at the same time, and my hand brushes over hers. She stills before pulling her hand back.

"I'm Aleksander. The grump over there is Jackson."

I hand her the sunglasses, and she gives me a small smile.

"I'm Stevie."

"Well, Stevie. You really don't have to worry about damage except to your own car. His is fine."

"Seriously?" She looks at me with a wary expression before she picks up her handbag, stands, and moves to inspect the cars. She lets out a small groan when she sees her crushed trunk.

"At least it's still drivable," Jackson offers.

Stevie laughs, and a strange feeling of relief fills my veins.

"I suppose you're right. Are you sure you don't need me to give you my insurance or anything?"

Jackson shakes his head, "No, you're all good on my end."

She bites her lip, and fuck, it makes her look sexy.

"Alright, well, I'm going to head off then. Sorry, again, Jackson."

She turns and gives me a small wave of her hand before disappearing into her vehicle and driving off. My hands clench around my helmet. Fuck. I really wanted to ask for her number. But, why? It's not like I can date her. Not with my lifestyle. None of us can have girlfriends, not without risking our identities.

"Pretty sure this ice cream has melted." Jackson lifts the plastic bag.

I shrug. "Probably, but nothing the freezer can't fix."

"That was the girl, though, wasn't it?"

Ah. I was wondering if he would bring that up.

"What girl?"

"Dude." He levels me with his *"I'm so sick of your shit"* look.

"Yeah, yeah. It was."

"That's so weird." He crinkles his brows. "The girl who backed into my car fisted you under a table at an award ceremony."

"I mean, that sounds pretty hot to me."

Jackson just rolls his eyes as he opens the passenger door and throws the ice cream onto the seat.

"It's not like she recognized us."

"I would have given her a prize if she had been able to." He snorts.

"Maybe if she'd seen my dick." I give him a wink.

"Sometimes you're just as bad as Parker." He rounds the car and gets into the driver's side. "I'll see you at home." Jackson shuts the door and starts the engine. I give him a salute before making the trek over to my bike on the other side of the lot.

My phone pings with a thirty-minute reminder for my stream. *Damnit.* I shove my helmet on and quickly start up my bike. I tear out of the parking lot and onto the highway at breakneck speed.

The cooling night air flies around me as I weave my way between the growing traffic. All the while I try to forget about the brown-haired beauty who is taking up residence in my mind.

Chapter ELEVEN

STEVIE

"What if I pour this entire bottle of wine into a bowl and drown myself in it."

"While death by wine sounds like a classy way to go, I'm going to advise against it."

I pout at Deanna's face on the screen before propping my phone against the unopened bottle of red wine and resting my forehead on the cool counter. I take a deep breath before letting out an extremely unattractive groan of frustration.

It was a shit day.

A really, really shit day.

I got rejected for another exhibition. I was so freaking sure that they were going to accept my art this time around. The curator had been talking me up for the last few weeks, asking me to submit pieces and crooning over how amazing they were. Instead, she called me this morning to inform me they had gone with another artist.

It was annoying as hell. It's not like I haven't gotten rejected before. And it's not like I haven't been featured in other exhibitions. My pieces sell steadily throughout the year, that isn't an issue. I know I'm good at what I do, and I love it with my whole heart. My work bleeds my soul. People see that. Even if they didn't, it wouldn't stop me from creating my art. But I really wanted this gallery. Annalise Owens, the curator, was known for bringing in the best. She was only rivaled by Caleb Hayes. Getting my art into their galleries would be the sign to my parents that what I was doing was real.

Instead, I got rejected by Annalise and spent four hours avoiding reality by playing *Cherry Farm*. When I finally decided to be a human again, I realized I was out of wine. So, I went to go pick some up only to crash my car. The Jeep wasn't even moving. It was parked. I hit a freaking stationary vehicle. Who does something as stupid as that?

I let out my hundredth groan of the day.

"You know what you should do tomorrow?" Deanna's voice filters back in.

"Drown myself in a bottle of wine?"

"No. You should go buy an extremely hot as hell dress for the Taylors' ball. Retail therapy and revenge always go hand in hand. Nothing like trying on pretty dresses to put you in a good mood, and then you can top it off by knowing that you are going to look seventeen times better than the Taylor tramp."

I lift my head up from the counter.

"I always look better than Felicity."

"That's the spirit, girl."

I smile at her. I can always count on Deanna for a pep talk.

I push away from the island and slip off the bar stool. Grabbing my phone—and abandoning the wine—I pad over to the couch and sink into the corner, knees to chest. There is something about being curled in a ball that just makes everything feel better.

"Anyway, enough about my sorrows. What are your plans this weekend?"

"Maya is back in town, so we have a dinner date planned."

"Jealous."

"Yup, and lots of sex."

"Wow, thanks. Way to rub it in."

"Oh, I'm going to be rubbing many things."

My jaw falls open. "You did not just say that."

She smirks at me from the screen. I swear, she has the wit of a teenage boy. And I love it.

"You really should find a nice one-night stand."

"What do you want me to do? Go to a bar by myself and sit there until a man approaches me?"

"Well, my first thought was a dating app, but that works, too."

"Ew, and be subjected to unsolicited dick pics? No thanks."

Maybe I should've gotten that guy's number today...

"What guy?" I look down and see Deanna shoving her face unnecessarily close to the camera.

"What?"

"What guy's number?"

Shit. I must've said that out loud.

"No one. Really. Just the friend of the guy whose car I almost totaled."

"Oooh," she crows. "And he was hot?"

"I guess."

"He must have been super-hot for you to be this evasive about it."

"I'm not being evasive."

Great. I can feel my cheeks heating at the complete lie.

I most certainly was not expecting to meet a dreamboat in a mall parking lot. His friend was attractive, too, but Aleksander? His features were begging to be drawn. My soul is calling me into my art room to find the right colors to capture his sultry green gaze and caramel hair.

Pair all that with the leather jacket and motorcycle helmet, and he was a walking bad decision, no doubt about it. I'm pretty sure my brain glitched for a half second before rebooting. I should've listened to Horny Stevie and gotten his number before she drove off. Although, I probably seemed like a hot mess to him.

"Stevie?"

"Ok, fine. Yes, he was hot. Like super, mega bad boy vibe hot. But I didn't get his number, and I doubt I'll see him again."

"Well, that's a lost opportunity. What happened to my confident best friend?"

"She lost her game after her ex sucked the life out of her."

"Your actions at the VSAs say otherwise."

I laugh at her, "Now *that* would have been an amazing one-night stand."

I wonder if Blade keeps the mask on during sex. If he took it off, the person would know his identity, right? Maybe they sign an NDA. Although, sex with the mask on isn't exactly a turn-off. God, what I would do for anything to spice up my sex life right now. Chase basically turned everything into store-brand vanilla ice cream, not even the fancy kind.

"Yet another example of a missed opportunity."

"Come on, Dee."

"I'm just saying."

Maybe she's right. I need to stop letting every opportunity pass me by. I'm not held back by Chase anymore. I can do whatever and whoever I want. Plus, I can't keep waiting to get back in the saddle. I haven't been on a first date in years.

"Fine. The next hot guy I meet, I'll take the chance." I promise it not only to her but also myself. No more sitting in the passenger seat.

"That's what I like to hear." She yawns. "I'm heading to bed. I'm running on like four hours of sleep."

"Alright. Love you."

"Love you, too."

The screen goes dark, and I stretch. All this talk about hot men has my mind spinning in five different directions. It's only nine at night, but my body is wired. Blade's red mask flashes in my mind again, and suddenly, I know exactly what to do.

I slink off the couch and head back to the kitchen to pour myself a glass of red wine. I pad into my art room and settle the glass on my table—which used to be white but is now stained with charcoal and oil paint—before pulling out a new canvas to set on my easel. Taking a sip of red wine, I let the rich taste float over my tongue while I stare at the blank beauty before me. An image flashes in my mind. One of pure darkness with slashes of red and white. I smile to myself before squeezing out a tube of black oil paint.

My mind becomes lost in the process, my body moving on its own as it bleeds to get the image onto the canvas. It feels like a dance. My head and my hand are partners, working together to create a masterpiece of the heart.

It's not until I pad into the kitchen for some water that I realize it's almost three in the morning. I debate pausing and heading to bed. But there is something in my core that tells me to keep going. That there is something about this piece that is special.

Fuck it. I head back into my art room, the smell of fresh paint wrapping me in a hug. I pick up my brush and allow the vision to dance with every stroke until the birds begin their morning call.

Chapter TWELVE

STEVIE

'm going to show up to the Taylors' annual ball naked.

Maybe I'll purchase some diamond nipple tassels; that will class up the whole naked look. Definitely give Felicity a run for her money.

This is the third department store I have gone to, and if I don't find a dress here, I'm giving up. Don't get me wrong, I adore shopping. I appreciate nice things, and I'm a firm believer that when you look good, you feel good. But when you are actively looking for a specific outfit and can't find it despite wandering around department stores for five hours, it sucks ass.

I drift through a handful of designer racks, trailing my hands across various dresses. My eyes snag on a black Jason Wu tulle gown, and my fingers twitch to take it off the rack. It takes all my power to turn away and walk to the next rack. As much as I would love to wear it, I need something that stands out more. I have no doubt in my mind that Felicity is going to put her absolute best foot forward for this damn ball since she will finally have Chase to tote around on her arm.

I catch a flash of gold and pause, pulling the gown from the rack. It's a gold-toned, sequin-embellished fishtail dress. In other words, it's gorgeous.

I peek at the price tag.

Forty-three hundred dollars.

My lips purse. It's a little pricier than I wanted for this event, but money is nothing if it means I look better than everyone else. Plus, Father had wired six thousand for the dress, so this leaves me with some cushion to buy a hot pair of stilettos with which I can stomp all over Felicity.

Okay, my bitterness toward her might just border on plain hatred at this point.

There is just something about someone who makes it their entire life's mission to outdo you when you have never been anything but nice to them that just sends you a little over the edge. I tried being her friend, invited her to events, and even hung out with her. She used every little thing against me, turned every situation into an opportunity to climb the ladder above me. Her personality is toxic. Thankfully, I've always been able to outmaneuver her. Well, until she finally managed to sleep with Chase. I really didn't think that would happen. An oversight on my behalf that Chase wouldn't someday give in to her open legs.

Which is why I need to kick ass at this party.

Now, I just have to pray that this dress fits me. As gorgeous as a dress looks on the hanger, you never know how that's going to translate on your body.

I turn to look for the dressing room and bump into a hard body. A strong, tattooed hand comes down to steady me.

"Well, isn't this a surprise."

My body shivers as the voice runs over me, and I look up into a pair of deep emerald eyes. His mouth is broken out in a smile, and I feel mine pulling to match.

"Aleksander."

Somehow, Aleksander's grin gets even wider after I say his name, his left dimple becoming more pronounced. It's an adorable smile, completely at odds with the rest of his look. He is wearing a plain black tee that shows off his tattooed, muscular arms—arms I am becoming unnaturally obsessed with—ripped black jeans, and cobalt Odissea sneakers. He looks hot again. Of course.

This guy oozes sex appeal in the way you only read about in books or see in movies. He could probably knock me up with a single look. Utterly mesmerizing.

"Stevie."

Oh, thank god, he remembers my name.

"That's quite the dress you've got there."

I bristle at the comment, shoulder raising. "What? Too much?"

"Not at all. It seems like a showstopper."

The tension melts away with relief at his response. I'm so used to my mother telling me that my dress choices are "too loud," that my brain instantly reverts to that expectation.

"Thank you, I have an event coming up. I was just

about to try it on." I pause. *Screw it.* "Would you mind giving me a second opinion?"

Surprise flashes in his eyes before a lopsided grin steals onto his face.

"I would be honored." He winks at me before guiding me over to the dressing rooms I had been searching for.

I peek at him from the corner of my eye. His arms are sexy as hell, veins peeking out from the taut muscles. The leather jacket he wore the other day hid the strength he was packing underneath…that and the extra tattoos. They look like the patchwork kind; a bunch of different small tattoos dot his arms. I can see an intricate sword tattoo that disappears under the sleeve of his T-shirt. The linework is gorgeous. Tattoo artists truly are in a league of their own.

My eyes snag on a small scar by his eyebrow before tracing down his sharp jawline. He wears a small black hoop through his left lobe with a chain that is cuffed to the top of his ear. God. He really is dangerously handsome. With his soft, fluffy hair, he gives off boy-next-door meets delinquent-skater-boy vibes. Like he is the kind of guy who would rail you in the backseat of his car before heading inside the house to charm the pants off your parents at dinner. Well, maybe not my parents. They'd probably have a heart attack at the sight of him.

My abdomen clenches.

Great, now I'm picturing him railing me in the backseat of a car.

"Are you getting your car fixed?"

I startle at his question. "My car?"

He laughs at me. "Yeah, the car you crashed."

Right. Right.

"I'm bringing it in to get repaired soon. It's a pain, but they should give me a loan car while they fix it." In all honesty, I haven't called the dealership yet and I'm dreading it. Paying to fix cars is one of the worst things in the world. It costs a stupid amount of money.

"That's good." He hums.

We finally make it to the changing rooms and the woman managing it gives me a smile that could reach the moon with how large it is.

"Hi, just one item today?" She chirps.

"Just the one."

"Perfect, you can use the room over here." She gestures behind her.

Aleksander gives my shoulder a small squeeze. "I'll just wait outside. Let me know when you're ready."

"Thanks, Aleksander."

"Just Aleks is fine." He winks.

"Alright, Aleks." My mouth tips into a small smile before I follow the employee. She leads me around the corner to a dressing room, unlocking the door for me. "Would you like me to get you a pair of heels to try on with the dress so you can check the length?"

"That would be helpful, thank you. I'm an eight and a half."

"Of course. I'll be right back."

I shut the door and lock it, dropping my forehead against it briefly. I need to get my brain out of the gutter. My body is already heating up just from being near him, it's ridiculous. I didn't think I was this dick deprived.

I drop my handbag on the stool in the corner before toeing off my platform sandals. I slip out of my high-waist linen pants just as a pair of nude heels slide under the door.

"Here are the shoes. I'm Luisa, by the way. Give me a shout if you need anything else."

"Thank you!"

I throw my black crop-top onto the stool and hang my nude lace bra over one of the hooks. Standing in just my thong, I unzip the dress, excitement bubbling through my veins.

Something tells me that it's going to be perfect.

I step into it, shimmying the dress up over my hips and slipping my arms through the holes. A quick glance in the mirror confirms my suspicions. Oh yeah, this is going to be flawless.

I reach around and bend my arm so I can zip up the dress. I get halfway before it snags. I pinch my shoulders together and manage to get the zipper up another inch...but it halts again. I look over my shoulder to stare at my back in the mirror. I'm close. There's barely two inches of zipper left. I try shifting the angle of my shoulders, contorting my arms to get the zipper the rest of the way, but it's just not budging.

Huffing, I stick my head out the door, searching for Luisa, but the hallway is empty.

"Luisa." I call her name in a loud whisper and wait.

I bite my bottom lip after a few moments of silence have passed. The woman is nowhere in sight, and I'm not about to start shouting for her. That's just embarrassing. But is it more embarrassing than what I am about to do? Debatable.

"Aleks?"

There's no response.

"Aleks." I whisper his name louder.

"Yeah?" His tall frame pokes around the corner.

"I can't get the zipper up."

His eyes crinkle, and it makes his dimple even more pronounced.

"I've got you." Those three words release a handful of butterflies from my stomach.

I open the door wide and spin around so my back faces him.

"Thank you," I mutter.

I watch him in the reflection of the mirror as he walks up behind me. I feel his hands grasp the top of my dress, the tips of his fingers brushing against my skin, and I have to stop my body from shivering at his touch. I should not be having such a visceral reaction to a guy I barely know.

He zips those last two inches with ease.

"All done." His hands come up to rest on my shoulders, and they give me a light squeeze. I watch as he tips his head and lowers his jaw to my left ear. His light stubble grazes the base of my neck, and this time I can't help the shiver that comes over my body. The corner of his lip tweaks up in response to my reaction.

"You look devastating." His voice comes out low and deep. "Like a goddess dripping in gold, and I'm just an unworthy mortal blinded by your beauty."

My throat goes dry, and I fight the smile threatening to spill out. I've never been complimented in such a poetic way before. It feels like a flower is blossoming in my chest, drinking in his words to feed itself.

I do look hot. Maybe even goddess level.

The dress fits me like a glove, the fishtail shape giving

me the illusion of full hips. The gold tones of the dress compliment my olive skin and dark hair. The same hair Aleks is now sweeping off my shoulder.

"You look like sin," his lips brush against my ear, sending a bolt straight to my core. "I have no doubt in my mind that you are going to tempt every person at that event of yours."

"Aleks." His name comes out as a whisper, almost reverent.

He squeezes my shoulders once more, lingering this time, before turning to stand in front of me. He sandwiches himself between me and the mirror before dropping to his knees.

I suck in a deep breath at the sight. This devious man on his knees before me.

"Enjoying the view?" He smirks.

He lifts the hem of my dress, and my heart stops. I swallow deeply, not letting my eyes leave his field of green for a second. Anticipation threads its way through my skin.

"Let me help you put these on." He reaches for the heels Luisa brought and brings them to my feet.

My heart jolts before setting back on course, and an inferno blazes its way across my cheeks. For the love of all that is sane in this world. My imagination is having a field day today. Horny Stevie needs to go into time out. Did I really think that he was about to get down and dirty in the middle of a luxury department store's dressing room?

Okay, yes. That is exactly what I thought.

It's not like I wasn't fingered in a closet a week ago with another virtual stranger.

Shit. Am I starting a pattern? I can't even tell if it's a

good or bad one. Whatever pattern it is, it isn't stopping my pussy from pulsing slightly. I can't even clutch my thighs to stop the ache without him noticing.

"What are you thinking about up there?" I blink back down at Aleks as he slips my feet into the heels. "Something dirty I hope."

I'm absolutely boiling, a mixture of lust, confusion, and embarrassment simmering beneath my skin. His fingertips are burning into my ankle, branding me with want. Everything feels too damn close, too sensitive. I need space. I can't breathe. I take a sudden step back, shoulders crashing into someone. The thin heels do nothing to support me. I feel my balance slip backward, but Aleks shoots up and grabs my wrist, pulling me into his body.

"I'm sensing a pattern here with how clumsy you are. You need someone watching out for you."

I look up into his eyes, my free hand flattening against his warm chest. His eyes flicker to my mouth, and my eyes flash down as he bites his bottom lip. My own tongue darts out to swipe along my lips, want hot on my breath. His bright eyes darken to a jungle green, and I'm hypnotized by their depth.

"So sorry about that! How's the dress?"

Chapter THIRTEEN

ALEKS

This woman cannot read a room.

I curb a groan as Stevie pushes off me, the haze clearing from her eyes, as she spins to face the sales associate with a bright smile.

"It's perfect, thank you."

The woman hums in delight, fluttering around Stevie for a few seconds, assessing her from various angles.

"I couldn't agree more. It's like it was made for you. I can get a garment bag ready and ring you up out front when you're done."

"That would be perfect, thank you. I'll be out shortly."

The woman lingers for a moment, and I'm three seconds away from barking at her to take the hint and leave.

"Alright. I'll get it all started." She nods, eyes slipping to me briefly before leaving us.

Finally.

I rake my gaze over Stevie again. She is beautiful. I was more than ready to kneel at her feet and worship her. A mortal before a goddess. Stevie has an undeniable beauty, the kind that lures you in like a siren call and doesn't let go. When her tongue flicked out, I had to restrain myself from tangling it with my own. I was seconds away from pushing her against the wall and attacking those plush lips. Honestly, it's a crime that I have yet to kiss her. The temptation is killing me, making my dick throb.

"Do you mind helping me out of my dress?"

"Not at all."

I unzip the dress more slowly than necessary, all the way to the base of her back, and allow my thumb to slip and brush a sliver of exposed flesh. She sucks in a small breath at the contact, shoulders tensing. I can smell her arousal building from here, the memory of her release on my tongue rushing through my mind. I swallow deeply.

"I'll wait for you outside."

Confusion and want swirl in her eyes as I shut the door, placing a barrier between us. It takes all my mental strength to drag myself out of the dressing room and back into the department store. Every inch of my body is screaming to be touching her. But I don't want to scare her off. She has no idea I'm Blade. That I had her sweet body falling to pieces around my fingers mere days ago. Right now, I'm just the friend of the guy whose car she backed into.

It was pure luck that I spotted Stevie earlier as she rode the escalator to the women's floor. I'd been with Parker in the men's shoe section, watching him try on twenty different pairs of dress shoes for some family event.

The little asshole got me here on the false pretense of running a quick errand before picking up some wood-oven pizza from my favorite restaurant. Quick being a complete lie as I'd been here for over two hours and was five minutes away from strangling him with a shoelace. Luckily, Stevie saved me from committing manslaughter.

"Hey, thanks for waiting," Stevie slips next to me, gold dress pooling in her arms, "you really didn't have to."

"It was not without an ulterior motive."

"Oh?" Her brow quirks up as she passes me on her way to the checkout desk. "And what might that motive be?"

"Asking you for your number."

"What number? Apartment number? Phone number? Body count number?"

Always a bit of a brat, this one.

"Social security, actually. I was really hoping to steal your identity and open multiple credit cards in your name so that I could fund my addiction to Cadbury chocolate."

I watch as her steps falter slightly and she lets out a short laugh.

"Cadbury chocolate?"

"Yup. It's an English brand of chocolate. Once you try it, all the American stuff tastes like crap. I get special limited-edition flavors shipped in from the UK or Australia sometimes. Costs a pretty penny."

She pauses and turns her head to stare at me for a few seconds. Her warm brown eyes narrow as she assesses me, trying to tell if I'm lying. It is the cutest thing I've ever seen. How this woman manages to be sexy as sin one minute and cute as fuck the next, I'll never know.

"That statement is so oddly specific. I can't tell if you

are bullshitting me or not."

I give her a smirk. My chocolate addiction is a real thing. I've loved the stuff since I was a kid, but the Cadbury obsession is one Parker regrets creating after bringing me to spend Christmas with his family years ago. I force him to bring me back an entire bag of the stuff whenever he travels home.

"I guess you'll just have to give me your social security number to find out."

She rolls her eyes as she turns back to finish making her way to Luisa. I stand off to the side as she pays. When she finishes, she turns and holds her hand out to me, palm up. Which is a little weird, but I high-five her anyway.

"No, dumbass, your phone. Or did you really want my social security number?"

I am a dumbass.

An actual idiot.

This woman. She brings out every part of me.

Pulling my phone from my jeans pocket, I unlock it and open it to the contacts app before slipping it into her hand. I'm careful to watch as she types that no weird texts or notifications pop up. I had two phones at one point, one for Aleksander and one for Blade. But it became such a pain in the ass, I reverted back to one phone and just got a second e-SIM for it. Which means that any number of things could pop up, especially stream notifications or Discord messages.

I hate handing people my phone. When your life is based online, it breeds a certain level of anxiety around privacy.

"Here, I texted myself, but," she scans me up and

down, "we'll see if you actually text me."

I take the phone back, glancing at the screen.

Stevie Andwell.

"I guess we will."

"On second thought, maybe I should just wear a blue tie. It's kind of my thing."

"I don't care what color the tie is, it'll all look the same against your pale neck when I'm strangling you with it."

"I said I was sorry!"

I shoot Parker another glare before going back to the game on my phone. Even though my career is PC based, I spend my free time outside of training, streaming, and filming by playing on my consoles or my phone. It's a way to keep my brain working and hand-eye coordination up without feeling burnt out over the same games over and over. It's like ordering takeout from a different cuisine: you love food altogether, but you need to switch it up, otherwise you'll get sick of the same thing.

My phone vibrates from a text notification, and my heart pauses for a second before realizing it's from Sydney and not Stevie.

Stevie left right after buying her dress; apparently, the store she wanted to buy shoes from was far away, and she wanted to get there before traffic hit. I was tempted to try to find a way to get her to stay, but begging a girl is not really my style.

SYD

Your interview's confirmed. Sent you the calendar invite.

Don't decline it.

I groan. I know Syd wouldn't have agreed to the interview if she didn't think it was worth the opportunity, but it's still a pain. Hopefully it's an online interview and not something at a coffee shop. I did that once, and it was awful.

"Oh yeah, the blue is proper good."

I glance up to see Parker admiring the shit out of himself in the mirror. The guy is like a damned peacock half the time – he buys more clothes than Jackson and me combined. I've never met a guy who is so optimistic and nerdy but also full of himself and bleeding money.

"Have you made a decision, Mr. Covington?"

The sales associate has popped back around. The old guy has been watching Parker like a hawk. He could smell the sales commission from a mile away. I have to give him credit, he picked the best mark.

"Yes, I'll be taking this tie. You can add it to the same tab as earlier with the cufflinks and shoes, and then I'll be done."

He hands the tie over to the associate.

"Wonderful choice. I'll get the payment processed. The tie is two hundred and forty dollars which brings your total to one thousand seven hundred and forty-five. Just to confirm."

"Perfectly well, John."

The old man shuffles off with excitement, and I stare at

Parker as he shrugs his bomber jacket back on.

"What's the tie made of? The emperor's holy silk?"

"It's Gucci, you ass."

"Oh, of course. How uncultured of me."

"Mate, you act like you don't make double the rest of us."

"Not true if you add in your inheritance."

He just sighs in response and starts walking away from me to the sales desk. He knows I'm right. The Covingtons are stupid rich. I could stream for another ten years and still not be worth half as much as he is right now.

"Plus, having money doesn't mean I can tell a brand from a mile away."

"True, you can buy fame, but you can't buy culture."

I gasp and fake grasp my chest. "Ouch. I'll have you know I have never bought followers, Mr. Covington."

"You know I hate it when you call me that." He throws his Black Card on the desk and turns to me. "Where did you go earlier, anyway?"

"I just saw something that caught my eye."

Jackson's penchant for pineapple on pizza is a choice, to say the least.

I stack the four boxes of pizza on my lap before buckling my seatbelt. Parker took his Ferrari 812 Superfast GTS out today, which means there is no backseat I can throw the pizzas in—not that Parker would let me do that in any of his cars. He complains that the smell of pizza leaks into the leather and that he would sooner put the pizza in its own Uber than let that happen. While I agree with him on the leather thing, the Uber part is a little out there. Which is why all four pizzas are now uncomfortably warming up my thighs.

Parker presses the button that rolls the roof off as he starts up the engine. It revs to life, and we grin at each other as he roars out of the parking lot at a speed that is inappropriate for the space.

The warm spring air blasts around us, and I close my eyes, enjoying the feel of the car purring around me and the bass thumping into me. Out of everyone, Parker is the best to drive with. He doesn't pussyfoot when it comes to how loud he plays music and isn't afraid to go way above the speed limit when he can.

We both have an appreciation for fast cars and killer bikes. His family has a track in Italy that he brought me out to one fall where we raced a bunch of new models his family friend was testing out. One of the best life experiences ever. If there's anything I'll spend money on after PC hardware and video game merch, it's motorcycles.

Sydney, however, refuses to ride with either of us. When she can, she'll only let Jackson drive. The few times she gets tricked into driving with Parker or me, she screams like a banshee the entire time.

I feel my phone buzz in my pocket and shift to pull it out from underneath the pizzas.

Stevie.

Finally.

I tamp down the smile I feel forming at the edges. The last thing I need is Parker looking over and asking me any questions. He is already suspicious about the mall, and as carefree as Parker may seem, he has a sly streak hidden beneath that golden boy exterior.

I shot her a text while we were waiting for pizza to see if she'd be down to meet up tomorrow to grab a bite or coffee. I'm not one to play games and wait twenty-four hours to text her or some bullshit. If I'm interested, I'm interested. If I'm not, then I just let it fizzle out. The good thing is I never give out my number as Blade, so I never have to worry about those one-night stands trying to contact me. Aleksander, however, sometimes makes the drunken mistake of handing over his number, which does result in a problem at times.

ALEKS

Hey, u free tomorrow?

STEVIE

I might be...

ALEKS

Would u be free for the best muffin ever

STEVIE

That's pretty big talk

ALEKS

I know other things that are big

111

STEVIE

Omg.

ALEKS

I'm taking that as a yes. I'll pick u up at 12?

STEVIE

Yes...buuut I'll drive myself

ALEKS

Where's the fun in that?

STEVIE

Safety.

You could be a serial killer and murder me in my home 💀

OR what if I have an awful time and need to escape? Can't do that if you drive me

ALEKS

Baby I'm always a good time

STEVIE

ALEKS

Fine. There's a place called Terrestrial Coffee

STEVIE

ok 😊 I'll see you there

ALEKS

Sounds good

I don't give off axe murderer vibes FYI

STEVIE

true, it's more psychopathic serial killer

I snort, shutting my phone off and sliding it under my leg before turning to look out the window. I release the huge grin I've been holding back, letting it spread across my face.

Date one scored.

Just you wait, Stevie. I'm going to give you the best ride of your life.

Chapter FOURTEEN

STEVIE

"Don't be nervous, Stevie. You're hot as hell."

I smile at myself in the little mirror of my visor, trying to pep myself up. This is the first time I've gone on a first date in years. I've been sitting in my car for five minutes, convincing myself to get the hell out. I'm not late, but I will be if I don't get out now.

It took me over an hour to decide on an outfit. *Over an hour.* I had picked out an outfit last night while lying in bed and it had seemed perfect in my mind, but when I tried it on after yoga this morning…it was all wrong. I immediately threw it off and the next thing I knew, half my walk-in closet was spilled on the floor.

I settled on a cute pair of light-wash jeans and a white crochet halter top with some clear heels. I couldn't find my nipple pasties, so I'm just free-titting it. The weather has been warming up, so I should be safe. Although, if I catch even a whiff of a breeze, I'm a little worried about how obvious my nips are going to be through the crochet—it's an adorable flower pattern, but it doesn't leave much to the imagination.

Oh well. It's cute with a dash of sexy, which feels perfect for the occasion. Plus, I love how I look. I give my shoulders a roll before snatching my purse from the passenger seat and slipping out of the car. I tap the handle to lock it before taking a picture of the parking spot, so I remember where it is.

Tossing my keys into my purse, I make my way out of the lot and walk the two blocks to the café. It's a cute place that I haven't been to before and definitely not the sort of place I would've pegged him to pick. He gave off more indie, grunge coffee shop vibes, not minimalistic, plant-parent coffee shop vibes.

The exterior of the café is all floor-to-ceiling glass with a quaint, neon green sign, so I can already see inside to the all-black interior with a copious number of hanging plants and retro light fittings that create a yellow haze. I'm not the best at recognizing plants, but I can at least tell there are several large monstera plants dotted all over the place. If they make good coffee, I might just have to add this as a new go-to coffee shop.

I pull the door open and step inside, greeted with the smell of freshly roasted coffee and the lightly sweet scent of fresh-baked pastries. Just the smell of caffeine wakes me up a little. There are a couple of tables free, but I can spot some cream C-shaped couches in the back of the shop that look too inviting to pass up.

I don't know whether I should claim a couch now or wait here for Aleks so he can find me easier.

I take another glance at my phone but don't have any new messages from him. It's five past twelve. Five minutes late isn't bad, but...wouldn't he let me know if he was running late?

He wouldn't stand me up, would he?

Catching myself swaying back and forth on the balls of my feet, I shake out my hands and wander closer to the large marble counter to distract myself with the various pastries enclosed in glass. The flaky golden crust of the maple croissant looks really inviting, but so does the gooey carrot cake muffin. I bite my bottom lip when I spot a matcha macaron as well. This place seems to have it all.

Looking up at the drinks, my upper lip curls momentarily when I spot a lavender latte. Too damn sweet. I've made that mistake one too many times. A pistachio latte, though? That could be promising. Or maybe I should just go with a black coffee, save myself the risk of not liking what I pick and pretending to sip it during the entire date.

This is a date, right?

Shit.

Is it just a hang out, a meet-up? People grab drinks all the time at bars, and those aren't technically dates... wouldn't grabbing coffee fall into the same category?

The sound of a loud engine pulling up outside startles me from my thoughts, and I turn to look out the windows and see a sleek black motorcycle stop in front of the shop. The guy on it seamlessly swings off before lifting off his red helmet.

My breathing stops as I watch Aleks shake his head

before running his hand through his hair. My eyes zero in on the way his biceps flex at the action. He is wearing another tight T-shirt today, and I am not complaining. I almost want to petition that he only wears T-shirts with tight sleeves. That or he can go just plain shirtless. Although, a sleeveless tee would be sexy, too. Maybe then I could see how far his tattoos reach.

I watch him check his phone with a frown before jogging to the door. We make eye contact, and he gives me an apologetic smile.

"Hey, sorry I'm late. There was a crash on the highway."

There is a light sheen of sweat on his neck that shouldn't look sexy but really is when paired with the prominent vein peeking through. I want to lick it.

Oh my god, Horny Stevie can't be making an appearance already. The man has been in my vicinity for negative five seconds.

"Totally fine, you'll just have to buy my coffee to make up for it."

He chuckles deeply, and it niggles something in my chest. "I was always going to buy you coffee and some food. Take your pick."

I nod, trying to stifle my small smile. "Alright, let's see."

I order the pistachio latte with an extra shot of espresso and the maple croissant. Aleks, to my surprise, orders a mocha whipped coffee with oat milk and the vegan double-chocolate muffin warmed up. I would've bet money on him ordering a black coffee, and I would have lost every cent.

"Are you vegan?" I query him.

"No, but my friend is and this is her favorite place. She introduced me and my friends to it because she loves this muffin and swears by it. I was hesitant at first because, well, it's a *vegan* muffin. But it's really freaking good."

She?

"Oh, that's cool."

Is she just a female friend, or is she something more? Obviously not someone's girlfriend or he would have referred to her in that way. I'm concocting an image of a total knockout in my mind. Aleks is hot; there's no way his "friends" aren't hot as well. Also, guys rarely have female friends they haven't contemplated banging at least once. Just look at Chase.

Dammit, I'm getting jealous over a girl I know absolutely nothing about. Horny Stevie has turned into Green-Eyed Monster Stevie. Stupid.

"Do you want to save us a seat in the back while I wait for the drinks and food? They have these super comfortable couches."

"Yeah, you got it." I make sure to give him a smile before heading deeper into the café.

I can't let one little comment ruminate. That's just ridiculous. He isn't mine or anything.

Yet.

There are a few of the C-shaped couches free, but there is one snuggled farther to the back, hidden by one of the large monstera plants, that calls to me. I weave my way through the other patrons dotted about and slide onto the couch.

I instantly sink into the insanely soft fabric. Oh my god,

I never want to leave this couch. Honestly, it seems like a risky choice for a coffee shop to invest in cream fabric, though. I imagine people spill coffee on these regularly.

"You picked my favorite seat."

Aleks slides the tray with our drinks and food onto the table, plucking the mug with my drink off and placing it in front of me, along with the plate hosting my croissant. He slides his own glass of coffee and plate to the center of the table before entering the couch from the opposite side, placing his helmet next to him. He shifts closer to the middle of the C, and I feel the couch dip slightly as he positions himself nearer to me.

"I did? Great minds think alike."

"Yup, I like that it feels a little more private. Especially when it gets busier in here."

He's right. The monstera gives the illusion that we are hidden from everyone else. It didn't even occur to me how intimate it would feel back here. But it does feel like we are in our own little world, tucked into this corner.

I pick up the gold mug, blowing on it softly before taking a sip. The nutty taste melts onto my tongue. There's also a sweet undernote of cinnamon, and once I've swallowed, there is a little kick from the extra shot of espresso in the back of my throat. It's an amazing combination. As good as my maple bourbon latte? Debatable. But it's damn close.

"What's the verdict? Did I bring you to a good place?" Aleks props his right elbow on the table and leans his chin into his palm while sipping his coffee with his left hand. My eyes slip, once again, to the veins running down his inner forearm. They shift slightly as he brings the glass to his lips, and the sleeve of his T-shirt tightens around his bicep. The muscle flexes effortlessly, making the small emblem tattoo ripple.

This man is going to think I have an arm fetish soon.

"I can't give it a rating before trying the pastry first." I tell him.

He gestures towards the croissant with his coffee hand, raising his brows.

I tamp down a smile as I tear off a piece of croissant. The pastry flakes off beautifully, like you would see in a commercial. Popping it into my mouth, I can't help the small moan that rumbles in my throat. Maple is my favorite flavor of anything, but pair it with a fresh, high-quality croissant, and you have pure heaven.

"I take that as a positive response."

"It's amazing. You did well. I'd give this place a solid B-plus."

"Ouch, not an A?"

"The latte is good but not as good as my favorite place. The croissant, though, is heavenly."

"I don't know. This muffin is pretty A-plus." He peels down the wrapping and takes a large bite of the gooey chocolate muffin.

"Mmm—fuck, I love this."

My ovaries burst a little at the noise he makes.

Is there anything this guy does that isn't sexual?

He uses his thumb to sweep a stray crumb from the corner of his lip and sucks it off the pad.

Nope.

Everything he does is sexual.

I reach for my mug and take a massive gulp so my

mouth doesn't just hang open.

"I haven't had this in a hot minute. Sydney, that's the friend, has been salty with me and the guys lately and won't bring them when she comes over. She just keeps shoving these health juices down our throats. Don't tell her, but they are kind of growing on me." He shoots me a cheeky smirk, and sparkles erupt in my chest. Aleks lifts his muffin in my direction. "Want to try some?"

"Sure." I'm still drunk on the sparkles, so my mouth speaks without my brain processing.

Crap.

Why'd I say that? I don't even like chocolate.

He uses a plastic fork to take a chunk off the muffin and holds it out to me. I tuck my hair behind my ear as I dip my head and take the bite.

The richness coats my tongue as the melted chocolate spreads. It's not great. Way too much chocolate taste. Which is the whole point of a double chocolate muffin, so I can't really get mad at it for that. The gooiness is sticking to my tastebuds, but I make sure to school my features.

"It's pretty good," I offer. I'm not going to rave about it; he will be able to tell I'm lying if I go that far.

I realize the fork hasn't moved and look up. His deep green eyes are staring at me intently, or more specifically, my lips. They flicker up to my eyes briefly before settling back down. My body is starting to warm from the attention, and I can't stop myself from quickly licking my lips.

"Damn."

The word is soft as it falls from his lips.

I sit up straight, putting some distance between us, trying to calm my beating heart. I take a massive gulp of coffee, the nuttiness washing out the thick chocolate.

"So, tell me about yourself, Mr. Aleks Knight. What do you do?" My voice comes out a little breathy, and I stuff another piece of croissant into my mouth to keep from word vomiting.

He drops the fork on the table and shifts around. I catch him readjusting himself and drag my eyes away from his crotch before he sees me. It's bad enough he probably knows I'm obsessed with his arms, the last thing I need is for him to think I'm also obsessed with his dick.

He takes a long sip of his coffee and clears his throat.

"I work with computers, which means I get to work from home most of the time. But I have a lot of late nights and long hours."

"Really? How late?"

"I'll be working past midnight a few days a week, even weekends."

"Wow, that sucks."

"What about you? What does Stevie Andwell get up to?"

"I'm an artist."

I wait to see what his reaction is. Everyone is different. But more often than not, people look at me with thinly veiled sympathy. They don't see it as a real job, just something I'm playing at. They think I'm childish and living out some lofty dream. *"Oh, look at the little rich girl fiddling with her paints."* It's annoying and belittling.

"Really? That's awesome. You must be amazing at it. Do you have any pictures?"

My heart blooms, and I smile up at him, unable to stop myself.

"Yeah." I pull out my phone and open the album I have photos of my art pieces saved in. I keep records of all my work, especially since once they are sold, I rarely get to see them again. Aleks takes my phone, and I watch his features as he scrolls through the images. My nerves begin to wiggle under my skin like worms as I wait to see what he thinks. Finally, he smiles, his dimple lighting up his face as he turns to me.

"These are phenomenal, Stevie. You're really talented."

"Thank you." I feel like I have freaking heart-shaped eyes right now.

"How did you get started?"

I sink back against the couch and angle my body toward him.

"I was always a hands-on child, doodling and drawing all the time. It drove my nannies crazy because I would attack any surface I got my hands on. When I began taking art class at school, I fell in love with it. I started painting and sketching whenever I could. I'm a mixed media artist, so I don't just stick to one form, but I tend to gravitate toward oil and graphite pieces. I adore working with charcoal, but those are more like passion projects because they don't sell as well.

"I knew I wanted to go to college, so I majored in fine arts. It wasn't exactly what my parents wanted, but it was a degree, and it ended up being really fun. It helped me realize that I needed to be an artist, no matter what it took." I leave out the part about how it was actually my mother who was furious at my choice. She thought being an arts major was a waste of time. *Pointless.* That I should've been spending my time finding a husband and producing babies. Of course, her tune changed when I met Chase junior year.

I take a quick sip of my coffee before bringing my gaze back to him. "Honestly, though, I was worried about becoming a full-time artist. That it would put too much pressure on something I loved and turn it into something I hated."

Something flashes across Aleks' eyes, but it's too fast for me to fully understand what it is, so I keep going.

"But when I started having my pieces featured in exhibitions and had strangers coming up to me telling me how much they loved my art, I knew I couldn't back away from it. I want to share my art with the world, these small pieces of my soul. Sure, it hurts when people reject them because it's like they are rejecting a part of me. But it's worth the risk to find that one person who also resonates with my work. I sold my first piece when I was a senior in college, and I just haven't stopped."

I'm also lucky enough that I have an inheritance that allows me to pursue my passion. Sure, my pieces sell enough now that I could easily sustain myself without the cushion. But I could never have gotten to where I am without it.

"Wow. That's amazing. Not everyone gets to follow their dreams."

"What about you? Is what you do your dream job?"

His expression softens. "Yeah, it's the ultimate dream. I couldn't breathe without it."

I smile up at him. "I feel that."

"You know, it's sexy to hear you talk about something you love." He gives me a lopsided smile and places his hand over mine. It's a little cold from holding his coffee, but I'm warming up with the heat currently working its way through my body.

The sparkles explode in my chest again. I try to say something, anything, but nothing comes out. I just stare at him, dumbly. My eyes flick from his gaze down to his lips and back up again. I watch him make the same move. He swallows thickly, his Adam's apple bobbing. I can feel my heartbeat quickening in my chest; I'm both nervous and turned on. The butterflies trapped in my ribcage are making a slow decent to my abdomen and then lower...

He turns my hand over and, holding my gaze, slowly lowers his lips to my wrist. They graze the sensitive skin softly, the lightest touch. His lower lip drags up, and I can't do anything but just sit and watch. His gaze flicks away to my chest, and I feel the quick inhale of his breath on my wrist as I watch his eyes darken. My arms pebble in response.

Pebble...

Fuck.

My nipples.

There is no way to look down subtly, so I don't even try to hide it.

Sure enough, the girls have made an appearance. If he didn't know I was turned on before, this certainly informed him. I'm pretty sure the left one is trying to poke through the middle of one of the flowers.

Instinctively, my free hand comes up to shield my boobs. I try to remove my other hand from his grip, but he holds tight, pulling me toward him instead and resting his other hand on my thigh.

He leans forward, bringing his head next to mine and whispering in my ear.

"Nothing to be ashamed of, baby. In fact, it's quite hot. But why don't we get out of here before I ravage you? I would hate to get banned from this place."

He gives my thigh a slight squeeze, and I melt, feeling my core pulse with need.

"Where are you thinking?"

Honestly, he could say his place, and my mind is such a hazy mess that I would probably agree to it.

"Why don't we go for a ride on my bike? See where we end up."

"Really?"

I turn my head toward his in excitement, not realizing just how close our faces would be. He is inches away, our noses almost touching, our breaths intermingling. His eyes pour into my soul, and I let myself get lost in the forest.

"Fuck, come on."

He pulls back quickly, and I feel the loss of his warmth. He gathers our empty plates and coffees and shifts off the couch, presumably to return them somewhere. I'm still sitting like some lovestruck dummy. I feel like the spinning wheel of death, just trying to load and failing.

I slide off the couch and roll my shoulders a few times, trying to recalibrate myself. I do a little two-to-one breathing, channeling this morning's yoga class. I am not about to scare this guy away by coming off as obsessed already.

I'm not even obsessed.

I'm just... attracted to him.

Really attracted to him.

Aleks rounds the corner, hands empty, and winks at

me. He picks up his helmet and holds his free hand out to me. I return his smile, slipping my purse over my body and placing my hand in his.

"Ready?"

He gives my hand a quick squeeze, and my smile grows even larger.

"Ready."

Chapter FIFTEEN

ALEKS

"**B**ut if I wear your helmet, what will you wear?"

I laugh as I place the helmet on her and tighten the strap. It's a little big but better than nothing.

"I've driven plenty of times without a helmet."

Actually, that's not true. I'm pretty fucking diligent about wearing my helmet. We aren't referred to as organ donors for no reason. Parker and I got into a stupid accident once, racing each other at night. We totaled our bikes, fractured our ribs, got concussions, and ended up with matching scars on our temples. We were lucky we didn't fuck up our hands. It was one time, but we made sure never to screw shit up like that again.

Still, I'd rather her wear the helmet than me, and letting her think I'm more carefree about it is the only way

I'll placate her. I do, however, grab my sunglasses and throw them on.

I swing onto the bike and gesture to the space behind me. I picked my BMW K1600GT this morning since it has a pillion seat. I had a gut feeling that she would be joining me. That or just plain cockiness that I'd get her on the back of my bike at some point today.

"You can hold onto me to get on, but it's just like a regular bicycle, only there are footrests."

She grips my shoulders as she gets on, and I mean *grips*, like she is afraid she is going to topple off.

I feel her settle behind me and start to rethink this idea. She begins to wriggle as she tries to get comfortable on the seat. Her hands slide from my shoulders to my ribs. It isn't meant to be sexual, but everything right now feels that way. I can feel the heat of her against me and clench my jaw. We haven't even taken off yet, and I'm beginning to lose control again.

I was five seconds away from pulling her onto my lap and making out with her in the café. I was so close to tasting those plush lips. But I knew that if I started, I would have basically been humping her on the couch, and that would have gotten us kicked out very quickly. Sydney loves that place too much for me to do that.

"Ready?"

"As I'll ever be." She pauses. "I can't fall off right?"

"Have you ever ridden on the back of a jet ski?"

"Yeah."

"Did you fall off?"

"Once."

Well…fuck. Not exactly the way I wanted this to go.

129

"Once out of how many times?"

"Hundreds, probably. We go every summer."

"Then just think of this as the same. Hold on tight, shift your weight a little when you feel it, and keep your feet planted."

I feel her take a deep inhale and exhale against my back.

"Alright, I'm ready."

"Then here we go, baby."

I take off out of the parking lot and onto the street at a reasonable speed, mainly to let her get adjusted. After a few minutes, we swing onto the highway, and I start to speed up. If I was alone, I would've ramped up all the way at once, but she might impale me with her nails if I do that. My speed creeps up from fifty to sixty and finally seventy miles per hour. Once we get a little farther out, I'll be able to go ninety, and that's when I really fly. There is an old highway no one uses anymore; if you follow it long enough, it takes you to an overlook with a view of the ocean.

Stevie's grip begins to tighten as my speed continues to creep up. It's early afternoon, yet there aren't too many cars out, so I'm able to zip my way between the vehicles. Sliding from one lane to the next, the sun is beating down on us. With the speed I'm flying at, it forces the air to whip by us, cooling our skin. My hair rustles against the wind, and I let the freedom take over. I'd forgotten how nice it felt to ride without a helmet.

After thirty minutes, we finally arrive at the turn off, and my speed slows. I pull down a couple of streets before the highway entrance starts to appear in the distance.

I can feel her moving as she turns to look around us, but she doesn't say anything. She does, however, keep fucking shifting. Each time she moves, I can feel her pussy grinding against my ass. That, on top of her tits pressing up against my back whenever I speed up, is getting to be a smidge distracting.

My brain is trying to focus on the road, but my dick is centered on her.

I really want to show her the highway and the view, but if she keeps moving, we're not going to make it. I slow down a bit so it's easier for her to hear me.

"Stevie."

"Yes?"

"I'm going to need you to stay still for this next bit and just hold me. I promise it's worth it."

"What do you mean?"

She shifts a-fucking-gain.

"That. That is what I mean."

"What?"

She leans in to hear me better, and her tits squish against my shoulders and I about fucking lose it.

"Stephanie. If you keep grinding your pussy against my ass, I'm going to turn around and fuck you on this bike faster than you can say 'oh.'"

"Oh."

This woman.

"If you can wait just ten minutes, it'll be worth it."

Although, I'm beginning to doubt that myself. I'd rather be buried deep in her than admiring a view I've seen a thousand times. But getting to see Stevie experience it for the first time? Yeah, that'll be something.

"Okay, I promise. Just let me readjust one last time."

I groan, deep and loud, and she just chuckles at me. She starts to shift herself forward and repositions her hands. I feel them drift farther up my chest and hold my breath. She travels just far enough to find a surprise and pauses, pulling back.

"Was that—" she cuts herself off, her hand tentatively reaching back out. "Is this a nipple piercing?" She starts toying with it, and now we have a whole new issue.

"Sure is," I ground out. "But, again, I'm going to have to ask you to explore it later."

"Right, sorry." Her arms return to my ribs, and she squeezes tightly. "Okay, I'm ready. Show me what you got."

I smirk, not giving her any warning as I push my speed quickly. The six-cylinder in-line engine purrs under us as I gain traction during that first mile. I lean forward, closer to the handlebars. Stevie's body follows my movement, her head turning so the helmet rests on my back, allowing her to watch the scenery we pass.

I love this feeling. It is pure freedom and adrenaline, threading through your veins. Traveling at a hundred miles an hour, completely uninhibited, the highway your playground. Riding on the precipice of death, teasing the Underworld to swallow you with the slightest misstep. You feel euphoric, a high like no other.

I swerve us around the corner, tilting low to the asphalt, and a laugh rips itself from my body. My stomach dips from the motion, the same feeling you get when a plane lands or a roller coaster drops—it is my favorite feeling in the world. One I am addicted to.

When I exit the curve and straighten, I hear Stevie let out a whoop and feel her laughter rumble against my back. I grin, loving that she is loving this, too. You never know how someone is going to react being on the back of your bike. But when they also become one with you? That is something special.

I knew this girl was going to ruin me, but I think she is going to be my complete destruction. And I will happily let my castle crumble around me if it makes her happy.

The end of the highway crests, and I start pulling back on my speed. The highway used to go on for miles, but after it was abandoned, some asshole decided to do his own DIY project on it and tore up a bunch of the pavement. Now, there is a solid mile that is a mixture of weeds, grass, and bumpy asphalt before it starts up again. You could technically keep going, but it gets a little unsafe. Plus, the real view is here anyway.

I pull us to a stop and turn the engine off. Taking my sunglasses off, I place them on the dashboard and turn to her.

"You're going to need to get off first."

"Right."

Giving my shoulders her death-grip again, she swings herself off and almost crumples. Shit, I forgot to warn her. I quickly jump off and prop myself under her shoulder.

"Holy fuck, my legs hurt," she groans.

"Yeah, you were probably clenching your thighs together for like thirty minutes straight. It does a number on you."

"It feels like I've just been banged within an inch of my life."

133

Well, that gets my dick stirring again.

I shift so I'm in front of her but she can still lean on me. Reaching up, I unclasp the helmet and slide it off. Her beautiful maple eyes meet mine, and damn, I missed looking in them. Still holding her, I lean past her to settle the helmet on the bike while she weakly attempts to smooth her hair.

"Come on, there's a bench over there we can sit on."

"Nuh-uh." She shakes her head. "Not gonna make it. My thighs feel like death."

"It's just a few feet away."

"I'll crawl."

"As much as I'd love to see you on your knees—" She glares at me. "—I have an alternative."

"What do you—" she cuts off with a shriek as I reach down to hook her legs around my waist and hoist her up. She immediately loops her arms around my neck.

"What are you doing?"

"Carrying you."

"Couldn't you have done a princess carry?"

"I could have. I also could have tossed you over my shoulder like a sack of potatoes."

She pouts her lips, and I toss her up a bit higher so her heat isn't as close to my groin. Which means her tits are now eye level. I just can't catch a break, and I'm trying damn hard to be somewhat respectful.

I guide us over to the bench, struggling to watch where I'm going and not search for a glimpse of her nipples through the holes in her top. I saw the flimsy little bow she tied to keep the top up, and it would have been so easy to lean over and use my teeth to untie it. To watch it tumble down and reveal the tops of her creamy breasts.

Restraint, Knight. Restraint.

I bend down on one knee and place her on the bench, my hands slowly grazing down the back of her thighs in the process. I hold her gaze for a second, heat filling her eyes, before standing up and turning around to face the view.

I close my eyes and take a deep breath. The air has a slightly salty taste up here, and I love it. Opening my eyes, I stare out at the scenery in front of me. You can still see the highway and suburbs below the edge of the hill, but beyond that is the unrivaled view of the ocean. Miles and miles of glistening blue open water. Waves crashing against the sand, little dots of humans milling about, a few boats chugging along.

"Wow, this is gorgeous."

"Worth it?"

"One hundred percent."

I smile to myself before turning back and plopping myself on the bench next to her. She's taken off her purse and hung it over the armrest. It's a rickety old bench. I tried to fix it up a while back, but it's not really my forte. People have scribbled their initials into it and carved their names; there's also the occasional Sharpie graffiti.

She leans her head on my shoulder, and I tilt my head to lean back on her. It's a bit of an odd angle, but I don't dare move an inch.

We sit there for a few minutes in silence. It's something I've never done before. Normally people feel the need to just keep talking, to fill in any blank spaces. I'm always talking to myself for work, commentating, making sure that something is always flowing no matter what I'm play-ing. Silence isn't something I get a lot of, not even in my own mind. But this, right here and now? It's comfortable.

It also freaks me out.

"So, is this where you bring all the girls?"

I let out a deep laugh.

"Yeah, right before I kill them and stash their bodies in the mountain."

"I had a feeling that was the case. To think, I'm going to die a virgin."

I sit up straight.

"What?"

"I'm kidding, I'm kidding. God, the look on your face." She doubles over with laughter.

"You're such a brat."

She has the gall to wink at me in response, and I just scoff.

"Really, it's a gorgeous view. Thank you for bringing me here."

"It's not a big deal."

Although, I really haven't brought anyone else up here other than the guys before. It's our place where we can just get away from it all. Decompress and let our minds blank. Sometimes we bring beers or a joint, but more often than not it's just me coming up here alone after a tough tourna-ment or a hectic stream schedule.

"Why did you bring me here, then, out of all the places you could think of?"

"What do you mean?"

"Well, you could've just as easily taken me back to your place. We didn't really settle on a location."

That's true. Except we don't bring girls back to our place. Ever. We would run too high a risk of them figuring out what our real professions are—even if we took down the giant The System poster and stashed our awards. On the flip side, it would just be plain dumb to bring a girl back to our place in our masks. Stalker Fan 101 says not to do that.

Our setup has proven to be an issue on a few occasions. For some reason, girls prefer to head to a guy's place over bringing them to theirs. I've had to shell out a few hundred every once in a while to grab a hotel room, which makes me feel a little seedy. It's why I've ramped it down over the last few years. Just the occasional quickie in a convention bathroom or a girl on her knees in some back room. Classy? Not really. A safe stress reliever? Totally.

I look at Stevie again. She's leaning forward, elbows on her knees and chin resting in the palms of her hands, as she stares out at the open landscape. I'm once again struck by how many sides to her there are. From the sultry cocktail waitress to the innocent angel to the carefree woman next to me now. She's like a flower that never stops blooming.

"If I'd brought you right to my place, wouldn't I have seemed like a presumptuous douche?"

"Well, hanging out at someone's apartment doesn't equal consent."

"True." I lean back on the bench, spreading my arms across the top. "You know, there was a reason why I wanted to come here."

She turns to me, cocking an eyebrow. "Really?"

"Really."

She sits up, angling her body slightly toward mine before resting against the back of the bench lightly. The tips of my right fingers are millimeters from her shoulder.

"And what's that reason?"

I smile at her, letting my hand drop slightly so my fingers graze against her bare shoulder. I move them back and forth, holding eye contact with her the entire time. I watch her pupils dilate, little by little, with each stroke. I can't stop myself from biting my lip before slipping my hand onto the slope of her shoulder, my thumb lightly gliding up the length of her neck. Her lips part ever so slightly, and that's the moment I'm done.

My hand moves up to cradle the base of her neck, and I pull her toward me, leaving barely an inch between our lips. Our breathing blends for a few seconds, my chest thumping with anticipation. I graze my lips against hers, a preview, before dipping down to her neck. I drag my bottom lip up her neck until I reach her ear, lingering a moment before capturing her lobe and giving it a soft tug. The quiet gasp that leaves her shoots right into my hardening cock. I smile to myself before finally, *finally*, giving in to what I've been dying to do since the moment I laid eyes on her.

Her lips melt against mine, the kiss soft as we slowly move against each other. She tastes like an angel, her feathery lips bringing me to the gates of heaven. I have never wanted a kiss this much in my life, and the satisfaction of finally tasting it is euphoric. It's everything I imagined and more. My tongue teases her lips apart, and I take my time exploring her as she sighs into me, knowing I could spend all day like this.

I pull back, looking at her. Her golden eyes are dripping with lust. I'm about to drag her into another kiss when her hand suddenly shoots up and grasps my jaw, pulling me hungrily into a new kiss. It's fervent, desperate, delicious. A complete switch from the soft, lazy perusal of before. But I match her one for one, devouring her with equal ferocity. My little angel wants to dance with the devil.

Suddenly, she's swinging one of her legs over my body, straddling my lap. I feel her against my dick and groan. Like the tease she is, she starts moving her hips slowly over me, and it feels so damn good. I can't help it when both my hands travel to her hips, pushing her down harder.

"Fuck, Stevie."

I give her lip a sharp nibble, and she moans into it, fingers tightening around my jaw. I knew she'd like to flirt with pain. This woman is perfection. I push her down on me harder, feeling her slide back and forth on my cock with more friction. But I'm a hungry man, and I let one of my hands travel up past her hip, along the lines of her body, until I reach the soft fabric at the bottom of her top.

My hand palms her through the fabric, and it's a tease. I get touches of her bare skin between the holes in the fabric, and my dick twitches when I get her nipple to finally poke through one of them. My thumb circles the hard peak while I make the tough decision to tear myself away from her lips and take her nipple into my mouth.

Her head lolls back, along with the rest of her body, and I have to grip her hips again to prevent her from accidentally sliding back.

"You feel so good."

Those four words are like magic to my ears.

I bring her back to my lips, kissing her like she is my first breath of air and without her, I'll die. Her tongue spears into my mouth, and I match her, twining us together. I tap on the back of her neck where the strings to her top are tied.

"Can I?" The words are breathy against her lips.

She gives me a hum and nods her head before kissing me again.

I tug on the string, feeling it unravel, and guide my hands along her collarbones slowly before dipping to peel her top down, freeing her breasts. I feel her smile against my lips as I run my fingers across the sides of her breasts. I pull back from her kisses to admire the goddess in front of me.

The setting sun is hitting her with its amber glow, bathing her in its grace. Her tan body shines in the rays as she leans back slightly, her chest raising and perking her tits up. I grab them both in my hands, the soft mounds sitting perfectly cupped in my palms. I give them a squeeze and rock my hips up because, fuck, they feel perfect. I've been dying to get my hands on them since she wore that tight little black number at the VSAs.

I give her nipples a small twist, and she gasps, eyes flashing open to stare at me. I smirk and lean down to suck on her left tit. I place kiss upon kiss before circling my tongue around her nipple, flicking the soft bud. Her hips continue to rock over my dick in a lazy rhythm, building the pressure higher and higher. I move on to her other breast, laving it with the same attention.

She reaches down and grips my chin, guiding me back up to her lips. Taking control. It's not normally a position

I prefer, but with her, it's sexy. She wants what she wants, and right now she wants me. As she kisses me, her breasts press against my chest, and I become desperate to feel her skin on mine. Reaching back, I grab the neck of my shirt and pull it off my head, throwing it next to us on the bench.

She pauses, placing her small hands on my pecs.

"Wow, your tattoos are gorgeous."

Her hands run over the various tattoos on my chest before moving onto the ones on my biceps and then traveling down to hold my hands. She turns them over to study the words inked on the top. The word "Good" is printed on the top of my right hand, and "Game" is on the left. I fucking love them, even though they're the reason why I'm stuck wearing gloves as Blade all the time.

"Why 'Good Game'?" She asks.

"It's a gaming thing. I got them when I was seventeen." I try to act chill about it in the hopes that she doesn't ask further. It's not like I can tell her that I got the tattoos to commemorate my streaming career.

Instead, I pull her back to me, enveloping her lips in a heavy kiss. My hand threads into the hair at the base of her neck, gripping it with a slight tug, and she lets out a small sigh. My other hand rests on the small of her back, pressing her closer to me. Her breasts slide against my bare chest, and I savor the contact, her hardened peaks rubbing across my skin. I'm desperate for her. I want to taste, suck, and lick every inch of her.

She pulls away and I growl, but she just smiles before dipping her head and licking the barbell in my left nipple.

"Fuck, Stevie."

My hips buck up in response to her hot tongue sliding

over the sensitive skin. It sends a shot of electricity right to my dick, and I grind my hips into her harder. I feel her lips curve into a smirk a second before I feel one of her hands slip between us. Her hand runs over my hard length, which is straining against my jeans. I don't think it is possible for my dick to get any harder than it is right now, but fuck, she feels amazing.

I pull her into another fervent kiss, sucking hard on her bottom lip. She gives my dick a squeeze, and I bite down. The slight tang of blood spreads, and it just spurs me on further. Her hand moves to the button of my jeans, and all I can think is, *yes, yes, yes.*

A deep groan spills out of me as she starts to tug down the zipper, relieving some of the ache she has built within me.

And that's when I hear a car speeding quickly up the road, its engine roaring obscenely loud. Sounds like it's been heavily modified, and not in a good way.

Stevie gasps, her hands flying off my dick and up to clutch her top to her chest in an attempt to shield herself.

The engine roars again in the distance with a piercing screech—like the car is attempting a round of donuts—and the sudden noise shocks me, making me pause, delaying my reaction time. So much so that when Stevie goes to push us apart, I fail to grab her and she quickly goes tumbling off my lap and onto the ground. Her eyes go round as she stares at me from below. She didn't even attempt to break her fall, too afraid to let go of her shirt. She doesn't even bother to retie her top or brush herself off, she just scrambles to her feet and does this little crouch-run to my bike, mumbling, "fuck, fuck, fuck," the entire time.

I'd laugh at how cute it is if I wasn't still in a half-delirious state. My dick is raging against itself at the tease show it just experienced.

My heart rate is sky high, and I just slump against the hard back of the bench, its wood digging into my skin, and let my head hang back for a few seconds. The engine gets loud enough that I know they are probably only a minute or two out. I snatch my shirt and tug it back on. I push up from the bench just as the car comes into view.

They swerve hard when they reach the top, their half circle burning rubber. *Tsk.* What a waste.

Three guys file out of the car, giving each other pats on the back and talking loudly. I don't pay attention to what they're saying and grab my helmet and Stevie's purse from the bench before making my way to her. Her cheeks are still flushed red, the blush leaking down her neck to her chest.

"Are you okay?"

I hand her purse over.

"Yeah, sorry," she takes the purse from me and slips it over her head. "I just wasn't expecting that. Thank you."

"No worries." I reach forward to brush some of the gravel off her arms, and she shivers in response.

"I—" she pauses, playing with the strap of her purse, "it's not like I didn't want to, like…" She trails off and somehow her blush deepens. She was five seconds away from whipping my dick out for all of California to see, but now she gets shy. She really is the cutest thing ever.

"Stevie, it's fine. I know." I use my free hand to grab one of hers and give it a squeeze. She looks up at me with doe eyes, worry bleeding through them.

Fuck that. She shouldn't be embarrassed.

I bring her hand up to my lips and give it a kiss. "I'll just have to wait until next time to learn if your pussy tastes as sweet as your lips do." Technically, it's a lie since I've had her arousal slick around my fingers. But it is true that I haven't had the honor of drinking her pussy in, having her suffocate my face with every fiber of her being.

Her eyes widen further at the comment, but a smile breaks out across her lips, and mine raise to match.

"You're absolutely adorable, Stevie."

"Thank you, you aren't half bad yourself."

I laugh, tugging her into my body for a small hug.

"Alright, let's get you home."

"Are you sure you can ride with—" She bumps her hip into my still-hard dick, and I groan. "—that."

"I drove here with it half-hard already; just try not to wiggle as much."

She chuckles at me as I hand her the helmet to put on and slip onto the bike.

"I can't guarantee anything."

She swings on behind me, with more ease than before but still with a tight grip on my shoulder.

"Where did you leave your car?"

"In the parking ramp by Credence Mall, fourth floor. But you don't have to take me there, you can just drop me by the café."

I shake my head and turn to look at her over my shoulder. "Now what kind of gentleman would I be if I didn't see you home safely?"

I can't see her lips with the helmet on, but her eyes smile through the visor.

144

"I didn't realize you were a gentleman," she teases.

"You're right. I'm not. If it were my choice, I would've kept you pinned down to that bench no matter who came rolling up this highway. I would've let your moans and screams of pleasure fill the air for anyone who dared come near so they knew your pussy belongs to me."

"Oh."

I just smirk in response. For all the sass she throws my way and as much as she likes to be a flirtatious tease, she gets flustered whenever I throw it back. I live for it.

"Come on, babe. I want to get you back before it gets dark. You holding on tight?"

Her arms readjust slightly and tighten under my ribs.

"Yup, I'm ready."

I turn the engine on and kick my bike to life. Revving the engine, I take one last look at the view before speeding back down the highway. Stevie screams a little at the quick intake of speed, and all I can think about is that I was so close to having her screams of pleasure in the palm of my hand.

I drive up to the fourth story of the parking structure, slowing down so she can direct me to her car. Her left hand gives my ribs a death grip as her other hand comes up to point in a vague direction on our left, so I slow to a stop. When the engine turns off, she slings herself off the bike with grace. Damn, she got a handle on that quickly.

She unhooks the helmet and slips it off, handing it to

me before rubbing her thighs.

"Ugh, my legs still hurt like a bitch."

I laugh, relieved to hear her joke. She didn't say much on the ride back, and I was worried the whole thing might have spooked her. Even though she was more than happy to get down with Blade, the mask tends to give people the confidence to do things they normally wouldn't—including myself. When push comes to shove, most people get thrown off. The thrill of public play turns to pure fear or embarrassment. I'm glad that's not the case for her.

"It'll be like that for another day or so. You don't realize the strain until it's too late."

"Worth it, though." She gives me a lop-sided grin.

"I can think of some other ways it would've been worth it." I wink at her.

She lets out a light laugh, her eyes shining. I'm tempted to pull her back to me again.

"Well, this is my rental." She gestures to the black Mercedes behind her. "Thank you, for inviting me out today. It was amazing."

"This date was definitely the highlight of my week."

"Date?" Her brows raise as mine furrow.

"Well, yeah. A date."

She cocks her head for a second like she is contemplating something.

Fuck. If she didn't think this was a date, then what did she think it was?

I haven't been on an actual date in a few years. Have things changed? Great. If she thought this was just us hanging out then…wait, but who hangs out and gets half naked? Well, I've fucked girls and didn't call that a date…

Dammit. I'm getting in my head.

"Thank god," she presses a hand to her chest and chuckles, "I thought it was a date as well." My chest lightens with relief as I stare into her smile. "Thank you for a fun first date."

"No kiss before you leave?" I raise my brows suggestively up and down.

She smirks back at me before blowing me a kiss. "Bye, Aleks."

She wiggles her manicured fingers at me and turns to her car.

Little tease.

"Bye, Stevie."

She goes to slip into the car but pauses, grabbing something off the windshield before descending inside and shutting the door. Her car rumbles to life, and she turns to give me a little wave through the back window. I wave back before sliding down my visor, releasing my break, and taking off.

I'm leaving her behind, but the memory of today is stained in my mind forever, just like the taste of her on my lips.

Chapter SIXTEEN

STEVIE

I have to be dreaming right now.

The paint brush in my hand drops to the ground, splattering flecks of blue onto the sheet below me.

"Ms. Andwell, are you still there?"

"Yes, I'm here. Sorry." I turn up the volume on my headphones so I can hear the person on the other side of the line. I must have misheard them.

"We would like to formally include you in our exhibition next weekend. Would you be able to bring your piece over this afternoon? Mr. Hayes would like to inspect it again before we figure out where it would fit in the layout."

Okay, so I didn't mishear her. Holy crap.

"Yes, I can bring it over this afternoon."

"Wonderful, we shall see you then."

"Okay. Thank you so much."

The woman hangs up the phone without further delay, and the music I had been blaring starts back up. I stand in complete shock, staring at the canvas piece I was just working on. The bright colors of the sea blur in my vision.

Caleb Hayes is going to feature my art.

It was a total shot in the dark when I submitted my newest piece for the Hayes Art Gallery's upcoming artist exhibition. They were specifically looking for artists whose pieces fit their theme of "Devil's Night." The piece I had crafted during my all-nighter a week ago was practically singing to be featured. Eleven hours straight I had worked on it. And now, it would be an exhibition piece.

My phone pings, and I quickly wipe my hands on my apron before picking it up.

It's a good morning text from Aleksander. It's one in the afternoon, and yet *this* is morning for him. We started texting each other good morning and good night a few days ago. It quickly became clear that while I may have a few long nights here and there when I get particularly sucked into an art piece, Aleksander always has late nights. It's a miracle if he responds to my morning texts before twelve.

I smile and shoot him a text back, letting him know I just got some great news. My phone instantly lights up with a call. I tap on my headphones to answer it so I can clean up my room while chatting to him. I need to head off to the gallery as soon as I can, but I can't leave open paint about.

"Hey, babe. What's the news?" His morning voice is gravelly, and my body shivers at the deep tone.

"Hey, sleepyhead," I tease. "I just heard back from an art gallery."

"Oh? And what did they say?"

"They're featuring one of my pieces next week." I pick up my brushes and bring them into the bathroom. I soap them up and work my fingers through the bristles to rub out the paint. I run them under some warm water and dry them off. Then, I swirl them in a fresh jar of mineral spirits to get any of the remaining paint off before running them under the warm water again. Oil-based paints are a pain to clean, but I've lost too many brushes from half-assing the process.

"Seriously? That's amazing, Stevie. Congratulations."

"Thanks, I bring them my piece later today."

"Damn, I would say we should go out to celebrate, but I have to work tonight."

"Don't worry about it." I shove the phone between my ear and shoulder as I wash my hands to remove residual paint.

"Any chance I can see a sneak peek of this piece."

"You can see it next week at the exhibition." I untie my apron and throw it on my table before bouncing over to my bedroom. I'm riding a wave of happiness right now.

"Are you asking me on a second date, Stephanie Andwell?"

"Well, I'll be preoccupied for most of the night with buyers and investors…but yes, Aleksander. I'm asking you on a date."

"Send me the details, and I'll be there."

I smile. "Alright, I have to get ready to head to the gallery, but I'll text you later."

"Sounds great, bye."

"Bye."

I quickly touch up my makeup, dabbing on a little more blush and swiping on some gloss. I tear off my art clothes, which consist of an old cheer T-shirt and jean shorts, and throw them onto the floor of my closet. I exchange them for a tight, sleeveless, black turtleneck dress, Gucci brand tights, and knee-high black boots. I give myself a quick twirl in the mirror and fluff up my hair.

I then take the time to prep my painting for transport. I place it face down onto a few sheets of wax paper. I begin rolling the painting around a roller as loosely as possible from the short edge, ensuring there are no lines or bends. I tape it and then roll it again in some bubble wrap before popping it into a tube.

Once everything is secured, I grab my handbag and exit the building.

My heel taps nervously against the marble tiles. I've been wandering around the Hayes Art Gallery since handing off my tube to Caleb Hayes' assistant thirty minutes ago. I can't even focus on any of the pieces. My stomach is churning with nerves. It's not like he is going to renege on his offer after looking at the piece again. Right?

Goddammit. Why can't they just put me out of my misery? This sucks.

"Ms. Andwell?"

My head whips around at the deep voice. A tall man with perfectly styled dark hair and a thick beard is waiting behind me. Caleb Hayes is giving off real Chris Evans vibes in his tightly pressed grey suit. He looks even better than he does online.

"Yes. That's me."

He holds his hand out and gives mine a quick, firm shake.

"Caleb Hayes. It's a pleasure to officially meet you."

"That should be my line, Mr. Hayes."

"Please, just call me Caleb. I have a feeling that after this exhibition, we are going to be working together fairly often." My heart shines at the comment, at the implication. "I took another look at your work, and I would like to make it the centerpiece reveal for the exhibition, if that works for you?"

I lose every ounce of decorum in my body. "Are you serious? I would love that."

He smiles at me. "Wonderful. Now, there is just one slight issue."

"What is it?"

"Your piece. When you submitted it, you left it untitled. I am going to need a name for the exhibition. Did you have one in mind?"

At the time? No. I had no clue what I wanted to name it. But right now, the answer seems so obvious.

"The Game."

Chapter
SEVENTEEN

STEVIE

I stare up at the piece that Hayes centered in the middle of the room.

The Game.

It's a swath of drowning black; swirls of obsidian draw unsuspecting onlookers to it. Cutting through the darkness is a slash of glowing red. A mask flipping over and over until it crashes in the middle, breaking. With each turn of the mask, the expression changes from one of happiness to one of sadness. I'd modeled the mask after the ones The System wears.

"Stevie. You absolutely killed this, girl." Deanna gives me a tight squeeze from behind. The place is packed. There are at least two hundred people here, and we're only in the first hour of the exhibition. My brother stopped by right when it opened, but he could only spare a few minutes before he had to leave for a surgery that couldn't be rescheduled. It doesn't bother me; I've been busy, anyway. Hayes has been trotting me around to various collectors and buyers. The introductions have been invaluable. Even if no one purchases my piece tonight, just being here was enough.

I watch as a couple walks up to *The Game*. Their heads tilt as they stare at it, exchanging words that I can't hear. When the woman smiles as she gestures across the painting, satisfaction rolls through me.

I turn to Dee with a massive smile. "Thanks, it's everything I could've wanted."

"When's that man of yours supposed to show up?"

"I told you he would be here around eight. He had to rearrange his work schedule, and it's the earliest he could swing." Aleks apologized for a solid fifteen minutes on the phone this morning. Even though I told him it wasn't a big deal because I'd be busy for the first hour or so, he still felt awful about not being here as soon as it started.

"Well, it's five to eight."

I roll my eyes at Dee. Always one to be punctual.

"Which means, he still has five minutes to get here."

"Well, if he isn't here in five minutes, I'm deducting five points from my assessment of him."

"If I'm five minutes early, do I gain five points?" I spin on my heels, almost tipping over, at the sound of Aleks' voice. I'm immediately greeted by a bouquet of purple irises. Aleks holds them out toward me with a warm smile. "Congratulations."

"Thank you." I take the flowers from his hands, sniffing their sweet scent. They're stunning. I don't think I've ever been given irises before, but they have now become my favorite flower.

I hand the bouquet to Deanna before launching myself at Aleks to give him a giant hug. His arms squeeze me back, and I sink into him. It's odd how comforting his presence is…it's like a missing piece clicking into place. Even though we call all the time and text every day, this is the first time I've seen him since our date.

Aleks releases me, and his hungry gaze rakes over my figure.

"You look stunning. Just as much a piece of art as the rest of the room."

"Says the man who walked in here looking like a complete snack."

Seriously. I don't know how he keeps getting hotter and hotter every time I see him. Aleksander in an all-black suit is delicious.

Deanna not so subtly coughs.

"Aleks, this is my best friend, Deanna."

He holds out his hand to her. "Pleasure to meet you."

She shakes it, her eyes slowly assessing him. It feels like minutes pass even though it's only mere seconds. Finally, her award-winning smile flashes out.

"I approve," she declares. "And you do get an extra five points. But for the flowers."

Aleks laughs at her, and the tightness in my shoulders eases. It was one thing to go on a date with him to the coffee shop and ride around on his bike. It's another to bring him into my world. Seeing him not only with Deanna but also surrounded by art…it's special. I'm still worried about letting him see such a vulnerable part of myself so early on.

But if I learned anything from my mistakes with Chase, it's that it is important that I invest my time in someone who accepts every part of me no matter what. If he didn't get along with Dee or hated being at the exhibition, it would show me now that I should back off before my heart gets any more invested.

"So, where's your piece? I'm dying to see it." Aleks loops his arm around my waist and pulls me into him.

"It's over there." I point to the growing crowd of people. I'm still shocked by how much attention it is getting. I've done exhibitions and shows before where people have fawned over my art but never to this level. I can't tell whether it's me or the fact that this is Caleb's gallery.

"Do you want me to go see it myself, or do you want to join me?"

It's a kind question. Depending on the piece, I don't always want to be there. I feel like my presence can hinder a person's experience. But I need to see Aleks' reaction even though the butterflies in my stomach are getting restless.

"I'll take you over."

"And I'll put your flowers somewhere safe." Deanna nods at us before dipping into the crowd and disappearing.

I lead Aleks over to the centerpiece, weaving us through the group of people until we are in the front. "It's called *The Game*." I watch him from the corner of my eye. Analyzing every twitch as he looks up at the darkness before him.

Aleks' arm drops from my waist and his mouth parts. I see his brows furrow before he takes a step forward, standing as close as he can get to the piece. He says nothing. The butterflies are beginning to wage an all-out war inside me. I think they might be eating each other. I yearn to stand next to him, but I let him be. Whatever the painting is telling him, it's his to feel. I don't want to interrupt.

When several minutes pass, I begin to worry. The butterflies are basically exploding inside me now. Screw it. I reach forward and tug on his elbow before taking a step to meet him.

He jerks at the contact with a sharp breath. When he looks down at me, all I see is a barrage of emotions swimming across his emerald eyes. There are too many to pinpoint exactly what he is feeling.

"Everything alright?"

"Yeah, sorry. I just got into my head. It's an amazing piece, Stevie. It just…" he trails off. "It just took me by surprise."

"I understand that. Painting it took me by surprise. The piece practically yelled at me to be painted. I stood in my room for eleven hours straight from start to finish."

"Seriously?"

"Mhm," I hum.

"What does it mean?"

"That depends. What does it mean to you?" I never tell anyone what a piece means to me first. Everyone has their own interpretation. What a painting means today could mean something entirely different a year from now. It all depends on where you are in life as to what message it will give you. Sure, there are literal ways to interpret a piece. But at the heart of it, it's everchanging.

"Breaking point." Aleks' voice is soft.

"What?"

"The piece, it represents a person's breaking point."

Interesting. To me, it represented inner turmoil. Some-one who is stuck between two doors and has to make a decision.

His hand reaches forward toward the piece, but he stops himself. Which is good because the security guard is giving him some weird looks. "It's a phenomenal piece, Stevie. Truly." This time, when he turns to me, I see relief in his expression. It's almost like the painting sucked away whatever demons had floated to the surface. He holds my hand and brings it to his lips, placing a delicate kiss in the center. "Thank you for sharing this with me."

A flood bursts in my chest. I don't know why, but my heart feels like it's cracking apart and mending together at the same time.

"I'm glad you could see it."

He matches my smile, his dimples on full display. I'm hit with the urge to kiss him. To let him feel all my emo-tions without a word. Aleks' gaze heats in response and the yearning amps up. I move my hand to his cheek, running my thumb across his jaw.

"Hi, sorry to interrupt." My bubble shatters as Caleb steps up to us. "Do you mind if I steal her away for a few minutes? We have quite the bidding war going on for her piece."

Aleks looks like he certainly does mind, but he just gives Hayes a lazy smile.

"Of course not. Everyone deserves the chance to meet my girl, see how amazing she and her art are." He gestures around the room. "I'm just going to look around the ex-hibit myself."

"Wonderful."

Hayes rests his hand on my elbow and steers me away. Disappointment ripples through me, but I plaster a smile on my face.

It takes another hour before I'm able to escape the barrage of people Caleb insists on introducing me to. My mind is spinning with all the new names, and I'm exhausted. Grateful. But exhausted. At this point, all I want to do is just hang out with Aleks. Deanna already texted me letting me know she had to head home but that she left my flowers with coat check.

I finally spot Aleks out of the corner of my eye and wave him over. I drink him in, appreciating the way he commands the attention of those around him without even trying.

Damn. This man is *my* date.

Aleks hands me a flute of champagne when he reaches me, and I all but snatch it from his grasp. "Thank you, I needed this." I take a quick sip and let the bubbles wash away some of the tension.

He leans in and places a kiss on my cheek. But he doesn't move away. Instead, he inches farther forward, his lips grazing my ear.

"I just spent the last hour watching you being paraded around on the arm of another man. He was acting like you're some shiny trophy when you're a queen. My queen."

I choke on the bubbles.

"I'm a patient man, Stevie. But I'm no gentlemen." His breath is hot on my ear. "For the rest of tonight, you're mine."

My core clenches, and I squeeze my thighs together

to alleviate the growing want. He leans back and smiles at me. At first glance, it looks sweet. But I see it for what it really is. It's the smile of a predator playing with its prey.

Two can play that game.

This time, I lean forward. I bring my lips to his ear with the piercing in it and let my lips brush against his lobe.

"You're forgetting that I invited you here as my arm candy. We play by my rules." I tug on the chain of his ear piercing, and he shivers. "I am the queen, after all."

He rests his hand on the small of my back and pulls me closer to him. My hips are flush against his, and I feel his growing need. My stomach flips, and I lean back to look at him. Aleks' eyes have grown so dark, you can barely even tell they're green. He wets his lips, and my eyes dart down to follow the movement before I find myself automatically repeating the same thing. Aleks leans forward, his lips a mere breath away.

"Stephanie, there you are."

My insides die. Hayes' voice spears through our lust-filled world. Aleks clenches his jaw. He doesn't even bother hiding his frustration at this point. He tugs me to his side and levels Caleb with a death stare.

"Can we help you?"

Hayes is either oblivious to the growl in Aleks' tone or he just doesn't care because he steamrolls on.

"Yes, I have fabulous news. Your piece has sold."

"Seriously?" I gape.

"Seriously. I just got the final bid numbers from my assistant. You should be very proud of yourself, Stephanie."

It takes every ounce of restraint in my body not to squeal like a child going down a slide right now. "Thank you so much. This is the best news I could've hoped for."

"Of course." He clinks his champagne flute against my own. I'd forgotten about it. "I see a long career for you if this is anything to go by. Congratulations, and I look forward to your next piece." He takes a quick sip before leaving us. I down my flute, letting the fizz mix with the happy bubbles popping inside me. This is a dream come true.

"You're amazing, baby." Aleks gives my waist a squeeze, and I see my happiness reflected back in his own eyes.

"I can't even begin to believe it. I've never had a bidding war last all night. And now, Hayes wants to work with me again. This is the best day ever."

"What if I could make it even better?" Aleks whispers in my ear. It sends a bolt through me, reigniting the want of only a few moments ago.

"I'd say that sounds like a great idea." I lean my forehead against his, letting myself melt into the moment. "Did you drive here or take your bike?"

He shakes his head. "I had a buddy drop me off."

"Well. I'm still in my rental since my car is getting fixed." I lean back and throw him a coy smile. "Would you be opposed to riding back with me?"

He matches me, tossing out a flirty grin. "Not at all."

"Perfect," I wriggle myself out of his embrace and hold his hand. "Let's get out of here."

Chapter EIGHTEEN

ALEKS

I need her.

Stevie and I crash into the door of her apartment.

"Shh," she hisses. "You're going to wake up my entire floor."

"They'll be grateful for the free show."

"They're all over the age of seventy. I'm pretty sure you'll be giving them a heart attack instead."

I laugh at her but push off the door so she can unlock it. The second it's open, I scoop her into my arms and carry her inside. She squeals as I kick the door shut behind me.

I go to move her onto the couch, but she shakes her head and points to an open door. I walk into her bedroom and drop her on the bed.

She smiles before curling one finger at me. "Off with your shirt."

I grin back, tossing my jacket to the side before slowly undoing every button on my shirt. Her hungry gaze watches me the entire time, and my thickening cock twitches in anticipation. When I get to the last button and drop the shirt to the floor, she stands up and pushes me onto the bed. I lean back and watch as she tortures me back. She bites her lip as she reaches around to unzip her dress. I watch as the black fabric drops to the ground and her perky tits bounce free. She stands before me in nothing but a pair of lacy black underwear and her stilettos.

She's going to ruin me.

Stevie walks forward and kneels on the bed before crawling her way up to me. She straddles my hips and runs her hands across my body. I watch her with rapt attention. Mesmerized.

She grips the hair at the base of my neck, tugging on it, and I grin.

"I like it a little rough."

Her smile turns wicked, and she grips harder in response. "So do I."

We are inches apart, her breath melding with mine. I lick my lips a split second before her fingers press on them. Slowly her fingers drag down, her long nails tugging. The second they release, I dip forward, capturing her fingers in my mouth. I give her a small bite mixed with a low suck, pulling a gasp from her.

"Are you ready, baby?"

"Show me what you got." She grinds down on me without warning, and this time I can't stop the groan pouring from my throat.

Fucking hell. This woman.

I capture her mouth in a bruising kiss. There's nothing kind about it. It's desperate, vicious. I bite down, tugging her into me, and she moans. My lips are hot and demanding, but she pushes back, drinking me in like I'm her lifeline. My hands tangle in her hair, and I pull just enough. Stevie returns in kind, finally with more strength, and the pain urges me on. Our tongues dance, and she grinds into me with each marriage of our lips. I can feel her wetness seeping through her panties onto the front of my pants. The back-and-forth pumps more and more blood to my cock. I already know it's seeping with precum.

Holding the back of her head, I flip us around, laying her across the sheets. Her legs splay wide, leaving me access to prop my bulging length against her heat. I lean down, nuzzling her neck before licking my way back up to her ear. She arches into me, and I trace my hand to her pussy, circling it once before gripping her panties.

I gather the fabric in the front, bunching it in my hands, and then I rip. The delicate, lacy material gives little resistance.

She hisses at the slight pain.

"I liked those, asshole."

"I like you better without them."

I toss them to the side before kissing a path down her stomach to her center. She is glistening for me. Flattening my tongue, I give her one long lick. I groan at the taste of her honey sweetness. I push inside her tight hole and flick my tongue in quick motions. I lap at her arousal, letting it completely coat me. I move one of my hands to play with her clit, rubbing it in slow circles. She moans at the dual sensation.

"Oh god. Don't stop."

She lifts her hips, burying me further into her sweetness. It spurs me on. I drink her in, savoring every drop like I'm a pilgrim who's been lost in the desert for days and she is the mirage that's appeared before me. Stevie's knees start to open and close on me, slowly crushing me with desperation as her orgasm crawls up. I move to her clit and begin to circle it with my tongue.

"More," she pleads.

I insert two fingers and curl them deeply. Her body quivers as her orgasm crests, legs shaking as she tries to keep them from caging me in. Her moan turns into a scream as I continue to worship that same spot. Just as her knees clamp around me again, I pull back.

"I—what the fuck, Aleksander!" she screeches.

"Just getting you prepped, babe."

"Nooo," she whines.

Her hand flicks down to finish the job I started, but I bat it away.

"Ah, ah, ah. Good girls wait. I want to feel you coming while you milk my cock."

She bolts up, hands fumbling for a second until she grips my hips. A Cheshire grin spreads as she strokes my aching cock through my pants. "Alright then, bad boy. Show me what you got."

She undoes the button and zipper with deft quickness before tugging my pants down my thighs. She reaches for my boxers next but pauses to squeeze my cock with one hand and balls with the other. Stars burst in my vision.

"Fuck, Stevie, you can't do that. I'm already close."

"Karma," she taunts as she proceeds to repeat the

movement, and I whip my hand out to hold her off. The damn thing is about to have a stroke if it doesn't get inside her soon.

"Seriously. I refuse to come before getting to feel that sweet pussy clenching around me."

Not trusting her to not try something, I step out of my pants and boxers myself. I grab my condom from my pocket before throwing my pants to the side.

Stevie lays her naked body back on the sheets, propping one leg up and resting her arms above her head. The girl knows her angles. She looks like an absolute meal, and I'm a starving man about to indulge in his feast.

Positioning myself between her legs, I grab my dick and slide the tip over her arousal.

We both groan at the contact.

It's goddamned torture to feel her like this.

I roll the condom on before I do something stupid. Then, I line myself up with her center and slowly push in. Her tight heat welcomes me, and I groan at the feeling as she sucks me in. Every inch is intoxicating. She hums with pleasure the moment I'm fully seated in her.

"Holy crap. I love the feeling of you inside me. I'm so fucking full." She clenches her pussy, and I have to pause, gathering my sanity to slow my blow. The mouth on this girl.

I start to slowly pump in and out, increasing my pace with each thrust. I grip the thigh of the leg she has propped up and push her knee toward her chest, the new angle letting me reach even deeper. My tip grazes her cervix, and I can feel the veins in my neck straining as I hold myself back.

"Unf. That's it." Her hand comes up to replace mine as she brings her knees flush against her breast. I sink in farther with the next thrust, and she cries out. I'm impossibly deep within her. My self-control snaps.

I start pounding into her, her tits bouncing with each thrust. The pace is feral. Her brows furrow and eyes squeeze shut while her mouth opens in a silent plea. The speed makes it difficult for her to do anything but let out breathy moans. I flatten my palm against her belly, and her eyes open wide.

She takes in a gulp of air. "Oh, god. That's it. Faster."

"You're doing so well," I tell her. "You take my dick so good."

She grins, her back arching off the bed momentarily before sinking back down. The new angle pushes me in even deeper, and I roll my hips into her. I look between us, watching my dick thrust in and out of her pussy. It shines with the slickness of her want. It's a goddamned vision. I want it burned in my memory.

Just as I start to lose myself in her pussy, her arms come up to circle my back, nails digging in. The sharpness heightens my arousal, and my breath becomes ragged as sweat drips down my body. I lean down on one arm to frame her head, and I bring the other between us and start rubbing her clit.

Her leg spasms, her pussy clenching. She's close.

I'm fucking close. My cock is thickening, and there is nothing I can do to stop it.

"Shit, Stevie."

"I need to come, Aleks," she begs. "I need to."

"Come with me, then, little dove."

167

Her eyes widen in confusion momentarily, but they glaze back over when I lean down and suck on her ear before giving it a tug. She gasps right before she comes undone with a scream. Her pussy milks me, clamping in tight pulses. The last thread of my control breaks. I come in hot, jerking spurts.

"Oh, fuck," I moan.

My vision burns up. My soul leaves my body. I make it to fucking Elysium. It's an out-of-body experience. I haven't come that hard in...ever.

My body slumps down onto hers, my breathing trying to even out. The sweat on our bodies is cold and mixes as our chests beat against one another.

"Sorry if I'm crushing you."

"You just murdered my pussy, this is nothing."

I laugh at her. Only she would make a joke.

I don't dare release myself from her yet. Her pussy is still silently clenching against my cock. It's all so sensitive. When Stevie's breathing finally begins to slow, I reluctantly pull out of her and dispose of the condom.

"Hey. I wanted you to stay in longer."

This fucking woman is going to be the death of me.

"Next time," I promise her. "Next time we'll fall asleep like that."

"It's a deal." She pushes up on the back of her arms and grins at me. Her hair is a total mess, but she couldn't be more perfect.

"Alright. Let me just get you cleaned up."

I'm about to go in search of something to wipe her off when a better idea forms. I kneel on the bed before her and butterfly her legs apart. I lean forward, licking up her thighs, drinking in the remains of her arousal.

She draws in a short breath before slapping me lightly on my shoulder.

"Aleks!" It's a teasing laugh, no real threat present.

"What? Just cleaning you up."

"With your tongue, really?"

"I never let dessert go to waste."

Once she's all cleaned up, I lick my lips and place a kiss on her thigh. She stares down at me dreamily before reaching forward and dragging me into a kiss. The taste of her mixes with the taste of us.

She runs her hands over my face, her fingers pausing when they get to my scar.

"How did you get this?"

"I got into a motorcycle accident with one of my best friends. We were speed racing on this track and ended up crashing. Somehow, we ended up with matching scars."

"Oh my god, you crashed and that's the only scar you got?"

I laugh at her. "No, we broke a couple of ribs, too. It was a whole ordeal. Everyone got so mad at us."

"I can only expect. It didn't make you afraid to ride again. After the crash?"

I shake my head. "Nah. It just taught me that I needed to be a lot smarter and get a lot better. We all make mistakes. If we don't learn from them, we can't grow. If I didn't get back on the bike after one accident, then I would've been giving up something I loved out of fear. That's no way to live life." I run my hand along her arm, tracing it up and down. "What about you? Have you ever broken any bones?"

"Nope. But I did sprain my wrist my freshmen year of high school when I was on the cheer team."

"You seem like you'd be a cheerleader."

She smacks me on the arm. "What's that supposed to mean?"

"Just that you're super flexible."

"Mhm," she hums.

We spend the rest of the night talking. Swapping stories and telling each other what our favorite season is (mine, fall; hers, spring), the best movie we've seen (mine, the entire Fast & The Furious franchise [which she called a cheat]; hers, Legally Blonde), our most embarrassing moment (mine, when my grandmother walked in on me fondling Mary Steven's boobs in the seventh grade; hers, when her skirt ripped mid-stunt during a cheer competition senior year).

It's not until the red, rising sun starts to peek through her curtains that we begin to doze off, her soft body curling further into mine. I lose myself to the warmth of her… and begin to worry that I might be losing my heart as well.

Fri, June 2 at 9:03am

STEVIE
Good morning 🙂

Fri, June 2 at 12:11pm

ALEKS
morning babe :)

STEVIE
12pm isn't reeeally morning anymore

ALEKS
technicalities

STEVIE

ALEKS
wow

guess I'm not bringing someone coffee...

STEVIE

wait! Noooo I'm sorry

I meant

omg! That's so early for you!! Amazing babe!!!!

ALEKS

haha I'll see u in a bit

STEVIE

okay 🖤

Tues, June 13 at 22:58pm

STEVIE

Just getting ready for bed 😴

ALEKS

Still working over here

STEVIE

eww

ALEKS

Send me a pic to get me through the night
;)

STEVIE

Ha. No.

ALEKS

Ur no fun

STEVIE

Fineee Here

ALEKS

Babe. That's a cup of tea

STEVIE

it is

ALEKS

I meant a sexy pic

STEVIE

Did you???

well…you didn't specify…

ALEKS

Really

STEVIE

😘

ALEKS

Haha good night babe

STEVIE

Night 🖤🖤

Chapter NINETEEN

STEVIE

Another rose.

Another. Damn. Rose.

I can't even decide if I am creeped out, annoyed, or just mad at this point. All the emotions are coalescing into one.

The last rose was left on my rental car after my first date with Aleks. How he even found it in the parking structure is one thing. The fact that he knew the rental was mine is a whole other issue. There had been a lull in rose deliveries since then, so I thought maybe he'd stopped. Clearly not.

He is still calling me every few days, but I just let it go to voicemail. Now, I'm seriously wondering if I should just pick up the next time and tell him to back off.

Then again, I know Chase. I know him too well.

That will only spur him on, give him satisfaction, let him know he still has access to me. He isn't dangerous. Sure, most people would think this weird rose-stalking situation would turn into something more sinister. Like maybe he would snatch me up in the parking lot after Sunday yoga class, throw me in his trunk until he can take me to one of his remote vacation houses—probably the one in Colorado—before locking me there forever.

But that's not Chase.

His infatuation with me is having me on his arm like a trophy. He wants me because I am useful to him and his reputation. He wants me because he no longer has me. Chase might be a sweet talker, a charmer, but it was me who helped him keep so many of his clients. I was the one making friends with the wives and girlfriends, getting us invitations to their private parties. Chase doesn't want to lose that. I could care less.

What I need is for him to find a new shiny toy.

As much as I hate Felicity Taylor, I really wish she would fit the bill.

Sighing, I pick up the stupid thing and throw it, a little aggressively, into the trash can next to me. The young girl behind the counter gives me a concerned look before continuing to serve the customer in front of her.

Today, the rose was taped to my take-out juice order. He must be tracking my credit card or something. I'm not sure how he would have access to it, but Chase has enough money that I suppose anything is possible. I stab a reusable straw through my green tonic and take a long sip, the tang of ginger curbing my annoyance. It was a great day until this point. I was excited to go hang out with Dee. Now,

Chase's ugly shadow looms over it. Asshole.

I fiddle with the take-out bag, which contains another green tonic for Deanna plus a vitality juice for me, as I try to take my phone out of my pocket, all while walking toward the exit. A clear recipe for disaster when I look up just in time to bump into a petite blonde.

My drinks remain intact, but hers goes sloshing onto the ground, the red color seeping onto the floor like a bloody massacre.

"Oh my god, I'm so sorry. Are you alright?"

An employee rushes over with a mop to clean the spillage in record time, all the while the girl just looks up at me with a bewildered expression.

Her gray eyes blink beneath her bangs before she lets out the loudest laugh I've heard in a long time. Tears start seeping out of the corners of her eyes, and I begin to wonder if I have somehow broken her in the process.

"No, you're fine. It's completely my fault for just stopping midstride." She waves her phone around. "I just got an emergency work notification which has me on the verge of murdering my employer, so it is only right that I now look like I have committed one."

I look down and notice that her white pumps are now painted in the red juice; my Gucci sneakers somehow spared.

"Shit, here, let me help."

I guide her over to one of the closest tables, depositing my juices on it before grabbing the napkins in the bag and attempting to clean her shoes with them.

It's not doing a great job. A faint pink residue remains on the otherwise pristine patent leather.

"What the hell was in that drink?" I mutter to myself.
"Beetroot."

"Ah. The most dangerous yet delicious vegetable."

"It's lovely to meet someone who understands the appeal and thrill of beets."

I laugh with her now, getting up from my crouch and joining her at the table. She has one of those small, round faces that look angelic in nature, like those "no-makeup makeup" models you see online.

"I'm Sydney." She reaches out her hand, and I take it.
"Stevie."

"Well, Stevie, while it is sad to lose a juice, I am glad you managed to distract me long enough to calm my murderous rage to more of a potential accidental homicide."

I smile at her for a second, before cringing.

"Seriously, though. Can I get you another juice? Or shoes? I was also totally distracted."

"Oh, don't worry about the shoes," she waves me off. "I'll make my employer buy me a new pair. He is the main reason this all happened anyway. And I already had a second juice, and technically a third and fourth." She pulls out an identical red drink from her own white take-out bag. "I was planning on bringing it back for the guys, but one of them is now on my shit list, so I'll just have his." She then proceeds to take a long, loud sip as if to prove her point to me.

She's sweet. I think. Murder jokes aside.

I eye the time on my phone. I still have a good twenty minutes before I need to meet up with Deanna.

"So, why is this guy on your shit list?"

"Oh, god." She rolls her eyes. "it's a whole story."

I take another sip of my drink and lean forward on the table.

"Basically, I work as a publicist for these three guys. I was able to get this amazing partnership for them, one that they all agreed on." She leans in to whisper, "They're easier when they work together." She shifts back. "Anyway, the photoshoot for the collaboration was today, and one of them didn't go. Just didn't show up." She slams her juice on the table. "I knew I should've ridden there with them myself. But no, they assured me it was fine. To trust them. 'Don't worry, Syd,' they said. 'We won't screw up.' Liars."

"No way, did he tell you why he didn't show up?"

She scoffs before taking an angry sip of her juice. "Yeah, his excuse was that the other two were already going, so it should be fine. Like he isn't the main face of the damn group."

"Oof, so now what?"

"Now I need to find a separate time to get him to do the shoot individually. Which he will probably try and skip out on again." She groans. "Men. They act like little boys sometimes, I swear."

"At least it's the weekend so you get to relax."

"Ha, there's no relaxing when you work PR for these guys."

"Wait, really?"

"Yeah. I mean, you just never know when a fire is going to break out. I could be on a cruise ship to the Bahamas and find out one of them had public sex in a fountain, or I could be sitting at home for five days and not hear a peep."

I'm beginning to seriously wonder just who these guys are that she represents. Public sex in a fountain? Sounds like some weird rock star shit.

"Seems like you could use a spa day at least."

She snorts. "The last time I got a massage, the masseuse had to turn off my phone because it wouldn't stop vibrating with notifications. He said it ruined the vibes."

As if on cue, her phone begins to chime.

"Dammit. This is the brand. It was really nice to meet you, Stevie." She reaches into her pocket and pulls out a business card. "Here's my number. Text me if you want to grab another juice sometime!"

She whisks out of the store in record time, dress ruffling behind her. I barely even blink before she's gone. No evidence she was even there other than a ring of red liquid on the table and her business card.

Sydney Lake

Public Relations Manager

Still no insight into what sort of clients she handles, but in California it could be anything.

I stuff the card into my handbag before dumping my empty juice into the trash can and carrying the remaining two out. I keep an eye out this time for my surroundings, careful not to cause another commotion as I make my way through the parking lot.

Sydney was sweet, though. I don't have many girlfriends. Deanna is the only one I really have other than my cousin Trinity. But she's been living in Milan these last three years as a catwalk model. She is totally killing it, making one hell of a name for herself, but it does mean I only get to video call with her every couple of months. It would be nice to have someone else to hang out with.

I balance my juices on the hood of my car, searching

around for any latent roses. It's ridiculous that this has become a habit now. But after weeks of random roses popping up, I just can't help it.

Suddenly, my neck prickles with awareness. I whip my head around, scanning for the cause. My eyes dart around the parking lot, but there's no sign of Chase. Paranoia drips in my stomach. I snatch my juices off the hood and hastily shuffle into my car. I lock it immediately.

Deanna's family's house is only a fifteen-minute drive and located within a gated community. A gated community that I know Chase has no connections with. Sure, he could bribe the security guards or gate attendants, but I know none of his friends or acquaintances reside here. Plus, Chase hates Dee. He always has. Something he has against the nouveau riche, apparently. Deanna hates him as well, but that's just because she thinks he is an ass. Which I can't help but agree with nowadays.

I start the engine and peel out of the parking lot quickly. One of my favorite songs blasts through the speakers. I try to focus on it...but I just can't shake the feeling that someone was watching me.

"We're going out tonight."

"What?"

"To a club."

"No."

I'm curled up in the hanging chair located in Deanna's living room. While she still lives at home with her parents, Dee lives in a small two-story cottage on the back of their property. It's probably around two-thousand square feet, and she doesn't have to pay shit on it. In other words, heaven.

"You told that girl earlier that she deserves to relax."

"So?"

"Well, I'm telling you, you need a night out."

"I don't see how the two are connected."

"They're connected because most of the time people don't know when they've hit their stress level and need a moment to reset and recharge. Or in your case, let loose. Not until someone else points it out to them."

"So, you're telling me I'm too stressed and need to go clubbing to relax? Clubs are not relaxing, Dee."

"Dancing is! Dancing is like a massage for your brain."

I give her a skeptical look. Mostly because I kind of agree with her and don't know how else to respond without being roped in.

"When was the last time you went clubbing?"

I groan, knowing my answer is going to cost me a point in this battle. "Like, four-ish months ago."

It's a guess. Chase didn't like when I went clubbing without him, and all the clubs he dragged me to were… awful. Sure, he and his friends were dropping twenty thousand on table service, but I'd just be stuck sitting there while he hung out with his friends and—now that I think about it—probably got his dick sucked by random girls in the back room. All the while I just sat there like a naïve girlfriend drinking glass after glass of Dom Perignon Luminous Brut Champagne. Which, for the record, tastes like any other vintage of Dom. I'm pretty sure the extra price just comes from the glowing green label.

It was boring. I never got to dance. Never got to properly show off my cute club outfits. Eventually, I just stopped going. It was more fun just staying in than subjecting myself to those nights out.

"Four? Well, it's settled. Now we have to go clubbing. Get that ass shaking a little bit."

I snort at her.

"Look, Maya told me about a new club that just opened by the same owners as The Blue Petal. She still out of town, but she said we can put the drinks on her team's table; we won't even need to tempt unsuspecting men into getting us cocktails. No strings. Just you, me, booze, and music."

Dammit. She knows I love The Blue Petal. It's not the ritziest club in California, but it has some of the best music. And when it comes to a club, music is key. If I can't sing and dance, I might as well just be at a cocktail lounge or a bar somewhere.

"What's it called?"

A smile breaks out on her face. She knows she has me hooked.

"Yes!" She gives herself a fist bump. "It's called Electric Tyger. It'll only be like a thirty, maybe forty-minute ride from here. We should get there just before midnight."

She disappears into her room, and I proceed to swing back and forth in the chair, listening to her prattle on.

"I'm pretty sure you left some of your outfits here from the last time we went clubbing, back in the stone ages, ya know?"

"Or I could just drive home and grab some and be back in like thirty? It's only two, we have plenty of time."

She pokes her head around the corner, her new white braids swaying back and forth.

"And trust that you will return? Hell no. I'm keeping you trapped here until we leave."

She does have a point. But she also has me excited, and I haven't been excited to go out since the night I helped her at the VSA's, and technically that was a work obligation... even if I was the furthest from professional.

My core clenches at the memory of that night. I'm not ashamed to admit that I've looked Blade up a few more times since that night. I get little notification bells when he goes live or uploads a video. There's something comforting about his voice. Although, part of me wonders if it's a little obsessive.

I haven't gotten off again from watching him, though. Not that the temptation hasn't been there, but...I just couldn't do it. Not with the way things are going with Aleks. Shit. What does it say about me? That I'm hot over two different guys in the span of a month right after getting out of a five year relationship?

Nothing. Actually. It says nothing about me. Sex is healthy. Pleasure is healthy.

"We don't slut shame in this house."

"No, we don't. But why do you bring that up?" Deanna drops a handful of clothes at my feet and gives me a quizzical look.

"What?"

"You said we don't slut shame."

"Oh, no I was just...did I?"

She laughs and drops a few heels into the pile of clothes.

"Your mind riding the dick train again?"

I give her a small grin and drop out of the chair onto the floor.

"I'm riding first class, currently," I tease.

"Only the best for my girl. Now, go through the shit you've left at my place and find a hot fit for tonight." She gestures to the mishmash of clothing I'm currently perched in front of. "I expect you to make your way into the cockpit tonight." She gives me a wink.

"Cockpits are in planes, not trains."

"Tom-ay-to, tom-ah-to." Deanna rolls her eyes and walks off into her room, leaving me to scavenge. I sift through the clothes for a few minutes before finding an old gem. A two-piece miniskirt and crop top set that I haven't worn since last spring. The fabric is soft black satin. The miniskirt has a high waist and a small slit; the top has a built-in bra with a satin cowl neck draped over, and the straps are lined with diamantes, matching the hem of the skirt. The exact outfit I need for tonight. I grin to myself as I gather the clothes in my arms and clutch them to my chest.

It's going to be a hot-girl night.

Chapter TWENTY

ALEKS

"I'm pretty sure that girl just flashed us her tits."

I *know* that girl just flashed us her tits because she yelled my name as she did it. I'm more surprised that I could hear her over the music than at the show she tried to give me.

The club is hot and sweaty. We're in the VIP section at our own table, which is located on the second level of the club. It overlooks the general dance floor and main bar, as well as a couple of the cheaper tables customers can reserve. Cheaper, meaning they go for around two or three grand. This new place isn't as upper level as The Blue Petal, where the minimum starts at five grand, but it isn't as basic as Horizon, where the tables start at five hundred dollars.

Orange neon lights flash around the black interior of

the club before switching to a blinding white. I have to give the owners credit; they really went all out with the vibe of this place. There is a giant LED tiger set up behind the DJ booth, and sprinkled around the walls of the club are neon claw marks. There is smoke that feeds in from the vents on the upper level where we are, dousing the VIP area in a slight haze. They've even got a couple of custom glasses with neon orange bases here in VIP, and I'm pretty sure I saw a bottle of tequila that was neon as well. Our VIP wristbands are also bright orange, but the stamp to get in is a black light-sensitive lightning bolt.

Everyone turned out tonight even though Electric Tyger has only been open a few days. They had their soft launch last Saturday and have had a solid lineup of events and DJs throughout the week. For Saturday, they've brought out one of the top female DJs making the rounds in Cali nightlife currently, ATHENA. Her transitions have been smooth, and her mixes are sick. The bass of the EDM music flooding through the speakers bounces off my skin, a steady hum bumping through me. We're not close enough to her setup to feel it more than that, but I wish we were, so the music would be pounding in my chest.

I go to run my hand through my hair only to smack it against the top of my mask. I sigh. Wearing the masks in public isn't easy in the first place, but wearing them in a club? Way worse. Sweat pools under the plastic and the haze from the smoke machines makes our vision through the LED lights horrible. It's easier to look out onto the clear dance floor below than look three feet in front of me. At least the orange neon lights don't make a difference, although I'm sure it looks a little weird to Jackson and

Parker through their mask colors.

"Could you at least pretend you're having fun?"

Allison Lee leans over Jackson so she can yell the words at me over the music. The two tiny braids framing her face sway as she bops her head, straight black hair swishing behind. I lift my gloved hand and start fist bumping to the music for a few beats, just to have her laugh in my face and settle back in against the black leather booth that cocoons our table. If we'd had it our way, the boys and I would have just hit up a bar near our place or gone to one of the clubs Parker's friends own. Unfortunately, all the top streamers in Cali, currently, were invited out tonight. We have three of the six tables in VIP all to ourselves for the night, bottle service and more included. I have absolutely zero interest in touching any of the cocaine that is currently being passed, and I keep having to reject random vapes being thrown my way.

Turns out the owners are big investors in esports and are looking to expand their horizons to streaming. Which is why the three of us are sitting shoulder to shoulder in this club, struggling to breathe in these masks and unable to even indulge in the free booze because of them. No cocktail straws tonight.

"I'm going to take some shots in the bathroom. Want to join me?"

Parker flashes a handle of Don Julio in my face.

I don't really want to take shots in the bathroom. I do, however, want alcohol. I also don't trust Parker to make his way to and from the bathroom in one piece. The guy is smart, probably smarter than Jackson and I combined, but he has a habit of being too nice. Someone will probably ask to take a swig of his handle, and the next thing I know, he'll be up on a table with a bunch of chicks who have downed the whole thing, and his pictures will be all over the internet, some stupid hashtag trending. Sydney would have a conniption. She's already livid that I bailed on the photoshoot this morning. I don't need more reasons for her to be mad at me, and she would for sure blame anything that goes wrong tonight on me just out of spite.

"Sure."

We push up from the couch, but Jackson catches my wrist. I flick my thumb towards the bathroom, and he nods before going back to monitor Allison and her friends— ever the protector.

We shoulder our way through the bodies lingering in VIP. There are probably a solid forty streamers here, some I recognize, others I don't. We flash our wristbands to the security guard outside the men's bathroom before heading in. There are only three stalls here in addition to the five urinals. After checking that no one else is inside, I pop back out and slip the guard a hundred to hold anyone else from entering.

Parker has already peeled off his mask, the blue lights reflecting off the sink he rested it on. I tug off my own, relief hitting me as the cooler air in the bathroom melts onto my sweaty skin.

"Hell, I can breathe again," I moan.

Parker laughs, his steel-blue eyes glinting as he pulls two shot glasses out of his pants pocket. I raise my eyebrow at him.

"They're sanitary, I promise. Got them fresh from the lad at the bar," he drawls. Parker's enough of a princess that I believe him. He tears off the plastic and pops off the lid before tipping the amber liquid into the shot glasses, filling them close to the rim.

"Cheers."

I roll my eyes at him before reaching for my shot glass and clinking it with his. "Cheers," I say back before downing the liquid. The heat burns down my throat, settling in my chest. I hand the empty glass back to Parker before turning to the mirror. The mask mixing with the heat of the club has my hair sticking to my skin. I give it a quick shake, running my hand through it before turning to my outfit. It's hot as balls, so I unbutton all but the last four buttons on my red shirt, tucking one side into my ripped black jeans and rolling the sleeves to my elbow.

"Very fuckboi, I like it," Parker croons over my shoulder.

I give him a light elbow back into his bare chest. "Like you can say anything."

His floral blue short-sleeve shirt has been open all night, which he paired with a pair of white jeans. White jeans. In a club.

"It's what the ladies like." He winks at me. "We have to give them a show."

He says that, and yet the likelihood of him bringing a girl home is astronomically lower than Jackson and me. The kid acts like he is a baller, but he's a romantic at heart. He'll flirt with every girl, but he'll never go any further. Jackson, on the other hand, will probably head somewhere else after this and find someone warm for the night. Me? Depending on the night, I would've headed downstairs to find some girl to bring up to this bathroom for an hour and called it. But now, the idea makes me sick. It turns the tequila in my stomach. My head has been taken over by a slinky brunette. She's eaten her way into my mind, burrowed herself so deep that I don't know how to get her out.

I shot her our nightly good night text earlier but haven't heard back yet, which is weird. She's normally in bed way before me. God, I sound like a simp.

Parker hands me another shot, and I down it before tossing it back his way. He catches it against his own empty glass and clinks them against the handle.

"One more for the road? Doubt we'll be able to get in here again before we need to leave."

I eye my phone. It's just hit midnight, which means everyone who isn't here is about to be. How have we only been here an hour? It feels like a lifetime, and we can't leave until at least one.

"Fuck it, why not?"

He shoots me his trademark grin and fills up our shots. I've honestly never met someone who can hold their liquor like Parker. The guy isn't even as built as Jackson and me, but damn he is a machine. I wouldn't be surprised if a quarter of his blood was actually champagne at this point.

I down the final shot, the collective warmth of all the tequila building deep in me. I feel a bit looser now, though I doubt any of the alcohol has made it into my bloodstream already.

"Alright, back to battle," I joke.

"After you, Captain," he tosses back, pocketing the shot glasses in his jeans again. We reach for our masks and, reluctantly, put them back on. I love the damn things, but I also hate them. The world plunges into red, and I give my body a shake, becoming Blade once again.

We push out of the bathroom only to be greeted by someone yelling in our faces.

"What do you mean it's occupied? Do you know who I am? I'm Daniel-fucking-Decker."

Hell.

My mood instantly plummets as I stare at the disgruntled redhead in front of me, his hair gelled within an inch of its life, gold watch glinting in the lights as he flicks his fist holding a vape toward us.

I know, logically, that there is no way he will just let us pass him without a fight, but still I try. I weave past the security guard, Parker on my tail. I make it past Decker when his hand shoots out and grips Parker's shoulder before snatching the tequila from his hands.

"Seriously? What were you two doing in there? Making out and taking shots? Guess that makes sense. You guys are probably all screwing each other. Not like you can get any chicks with those freakish masks on."

My patience hangs by a thread. It's always hanging by a thread when it comes to Decker.

I spin back around and rip the tequila from him, tucking it under my arm.

"So, what if we are? Got something against that, Decker? Afraid of a little dick? Although, in English's case, little is a bit offensive," I lean closer, "or maybe you're just projecting?"

He pushes back from me, spluttering.

"The hell do you mean?"

"I've gone a couple rounds before, wouldn't mind showing you the ropes." I wish I could wink at him right now. Damn mask.

"Fuck you, Blade." He shoulders past Parker and me, heading into the bathroom.

"Only if you ask nicely enough," I throw back. Decker slams the door behind him, and Parker slings an arm around my neck.

"Love you, mate. But if you fucked Decker, I would really have to reevaluate our friendship."

I laugh and drag him along with me back through the growing crowd to our table.

"I'd sooner dip my dick in acid than Decker's ass."

We make it to the table and claim our spots next to Jackson again. The VIP area has gotten noticeably busier since we left. I count a few more familiar faces, including Allison's best friend, Deer—her pink hair stands out at the edge of our booth. I slide the Don Julio to them.

"All yours."

Lee tosses me a giant smile. "Always the gentlemen."

Jackson pours them both a shot from the glasses piled on our table. They down them quicker than Parker and I did, Lee scrunching up her face while Deer laughs at her.

"You need to get better at that."

Lee sticks her tongue out at her best friend.

I twist away from them. Looking over the edge, the dance floor is rife with moving bodies. I watch the different colors bleed as everyone grinds on each other. Groups of girls bounce up and down, their heels slamming into the floor as their curves sway to the music. Men on the outskirts eye them while throwing back shots and chugging beers, but bouncers watch them in turn. It's a recipe for controlled debauchery. Sin and pleasure seeps into the air, every moving body drunk off the taste. It's a riot to watch.

My veins warm up as my body loosens. The shots are working their way through my system, and my foot starts to tap to the bass pounding through the venue. I'm about to turn back around when two girls catch my eye. I don't know how I pick them out from up here, but my eyes zero in on them.

They're holding each other's hands as they weave through the throng of bodies to the bar. The girl with the purple dress and mocha skin pushes her way through the waiting customers to the front of the bar, waving her fingers to one of the bartenders. A guy walks over, depositing two shots in front of her and then motions up to the VIP section, handing her two wristbands. I watch as she looks up, almost exactly at me, and smiles. She flicks her white braids over her shoulders and shimmies back out of the crowd to the brunette, handing her the shot. The brunette turns around to her friend, accepting the liquor with confidence. She throws her head back, and when I see her face, the club falls away.

Stevie.

Her olive skin is deliciously on display, gleaming under the neon lights. I wish I wasn't wearing the mask so I could see her better. She tugs her friend onto the dance floor, laughing. Her hips sway to the music, skirt swishing around the tops of her thighs. They move farther into the throng of bodies, but now that I've seen her, there's no way I'll lose her.

She holds her friend's hands, bouncing up and down to the music, screaming along to the lyrics. Happiness bleeds from her body, and I feel a smile curl on my own lips.

She's infectious. I wish I could text her, tell her to come up here. But I'm not Aleksander. I'm Blade.

I'm not stupid enough to go down there myself. I'd be mobbed in minutes. Everyone knows we're here tonight. Not just streamers, but The System, LoveLee, FlyingFox— as much as I despise him, the people love Decker. All the big names are out, everyone is watching. If I was worried she'd be a target at the VSAs, it would be even more so tonight. The space is too small, the eyes too wary. Fuck. I really wish we'd just come here normally.

I watch as some guys make their way to the girls, dancing around them, attempting to grind. Stevie and her friend flip, dancing back-to-back as they face the men. Appeasing them, but not giving in. Smart girls. One of the guys grabs Stevie's hand, pulling her in to dance. It looks like she laughs, but I can't tell if it's real or not.

Heat bubbles under my skin as I watch him twirl her around.

Her friend pulls her back though, out of his grip. I watch, transfixed, as they dance on each other, basically grinding to the music. Stevie dips down, disappearing from my sight for a second, before she bops back up. She's a goddess to the grind, a minx to the music. My body twitches, desperate to be in her grace.

She lifts one of her legs, hooking it around her friend's hip before dipping backward. Her bare stomach stretches and glows in the orange light. My cock stiffens at the sight. The guys around them watch with rapt attention. Fucking hell. If they thought this show would dissuade them, it's had the opposite effect.

Her friend leans forward, whispering in her ear. She

pulls the wristbands the bartender gave her out of her boobs, attaching one to Stevie's wrist before her own. The girls smile to each other before Stevie grabs her friend's wrist and pulls her through the bulge of bodies. I watch as they weave their way through to the bottom of the stairs.

They brandish their wristbands like Cartier bracelets before the security guard gives them a nod and pulls back the rope for them to walk up. They grasp each other's hands again, giggling as they jog their way up the steps.

I turn back to the table now.

Waiting. Watching. Expecting.

I can't see the door from where I currently am, and it's pissing me off.

I lean forward a little, a sliver of the doorway entering my peripheral view.

Stevie saunters in, arm still linked in her friend's. Her friend lifts her hand, motioning to the table on the far right, just opposite and to the side of where we sit. I watch as they stride over, nothing but pleasure dripping from their skin.

I hold contact with Stevie, pleading that she turns my way. They pass the table, and I track as her gait doesn't break, not even for a second. She's on a mission.

They reach their table, and her shoulders drop, relief entering her body. Her friend reaches forward to pour them another shot. Their alcohol is crap compared to ours. Still good, don't get me wrong, but not nearly as good. She downs the shot, not a grimace in sight. There isn't much room left at their table. Her friend squeezes in next to a guy with a bleached fade, and Stevie deposits herself onto her lap.

"Will someone take Deer to grab a drink?" Lee's voice breaks through my fixation.

"What?"

Allison's brows furrow at me for a second before she flicks her attention to Jackson.

"Shield, do you mind taking Deer to the bar? She's going to get trampled otherwise."

"Hey, why not me?" Parker leans excessively over the table.

"Because you'll get distracted on your way."

"Fair nuff, babe." Parker leans back, resting against my shoulder. I can feel his knee twitching, tapping up and down. He's a bundle of energy, waiting to explode.

Jackson edges out of the table, holding his hand out for Deer. Her eyes flick to Allison for a second before she takes it and follows him to the VIP bar. It's smaller than the main one, but just as crowded because there's only one bartender.

We've hung out with Deer a few times, but I don't know her too well. I think the only personal thing I know about her is that she is half Irish and moved here as a kid, which is why her accent isn't that strong. She's only been in the gaming community for a few years, and just started gaining notoriety over the last year. She sits in the cozy gaming community and focuses a lot on creating video content, only live-streaming twice a week. Our paths don't cross too often even though Lee's invited her to a few of our *Frontline Doom* sessions.

"Well, well, well. If it isn't the Holy Vagina."

Decker's voice is so obnoxious, you couldn't miss it even with the loud music. Our entire group tunes its attention to him, and my insides turn to ice when I realize he has made his way over to Stevie's table. My hands fist, the leather of the gloves tightening.

Stevie's expression turns from a smile to a sneer in mere seconds, and I watch as her friend tightens her grip on Stevie's hip.

"I'm sorry, I forgot your name."

There's no way she's forgotten Decker's name, but it pisses him off all the same. Which was clearly her goal. I'm just not sure how smart it was.

He leans forward, pushing one of his hands onto the table in front of her, and my body jolts forward at the same time. Parker's hand grips my thigh, pulling me back. He tilts his mask, and I settle back. For now.

"Daniel Decker."

Why the douchebag always insists on repeating his full name, I'll never know. Should've just made that his gamertag at this point.

"Right, David."

"Daniel." He growls out.

"Whatever." She stands up now, her heels bringing her equal to his six-foot stature. "I'm here with my friends. I have no interest in whatever you or Chase or whoever has going on, alright?"

"Don't be a tease, Stephanie." Her fingers twitch at the use of her full name.

"Thought you weren't interested in second-hand goods, Darren."

Now I know she is getting his name wrong on purpose.

He steps closer to her, basically standing nose to nose, and I shoot out of my seat, Parker and Lee following suit.

"I'm not. No matter how hot the goods might look." His hand trails over the back of her hand, but she rips it from his touch. A wolfish grin breaks out on Decker's face. "I bet you don't even know how many women he screwed while he was with you. How many nights you were parading around on his arm while he was banging chicks in the bathroom when your back was turned."

Her eyes flash. I push out from the table, but I'm not quick enough. Stevie grabs a drink from the table and sloshes it onto Decker's face. Within the next second, he has his hand pulled back to slap her. *Fuck.* I shove past Lee, stumbling forward, but his hand is quicker.

The slap rings out, but it's not Stevie's cheek he comes into contact with. A flash of pink hair has taken Stevie's place, and I see Deer clutching her cheek. How she got there that fast, I'll never know. His eyes widen as he stares at her, shock turning to fear.

"Don't make a scene, Decker. You're already on thin ice," she warns.

His gaze becomes molten. "Fuck you, Deer. And fuck your family."

He shoves her out of his way, but Jackson is there in a swift step to catch her before she tips over, guarding her in his arms.

Decker rears his hand again, but this time I'm there. My leg sweeps out in the small space, catching his knees, and I watch as Decker goes down. It's not graceful. He bangs his chin on the table on the way, the sound of his jaw clacking resounding through the room as his ass hits the floor. I stand over him, foot on his hand. I bend forward, bringing my mask to his ear.

"I suggest you back the fuck out of here now Decker before I stomp my foot over your hand so hard, you can kiss your career goodbye."

"Always coming to her rescue aren't you, Blade."

I pull back and look at him, assessing.

"I'm serious, Decker. Get the fuck up and get out of here. If I see you bothering her or anyone else, I will have you by the balls."

He pushes off the ground, standing chest to chest with me. Unfortunately for him, he is still a solid four inches shorter.

"Why don't you say that without the mask on, big guy? I'm beginning to think you're all talk. Maybe without that mask, you'll realize how little you have."

It's an empty threat. The whining of an insecure man.

"Seems like you're the one who is afraid of what will happen once the mask is off."

Jackson and Parker position themselves behind me. The three of us together, side by side. Decker's eyes flick to them.

"Tsk. Whatever. This place is lame. Clearly. Have fun with that second-rate pussy."

"Thought you said it was holy?" Parker muses.

I'm going to murder him.

"*Go fuck yourself* with a crumpet, English." Decker gives us the bird before stalking off through the crowd, a few of his friends trailing behind him.

"You know, that was a pretty good insult. I have to give him that."

I turn to Parker and smack him on the side of his mask. "Don't poke the bear, you asshole."

"Oh, come on, he's more of an angry raccoon."

"That doesn't make it any better," Jackson drawls.

A round of laughter spills around us, and my attention flicks back to Stevie, her friend, and Deer. They're clutching their stomachs, doubled over, as laughter flows uncontrollably from their mouths. Jackson still has his arm protectively over Deer.

Finally, Stevie looks up, her eyes clashing with mine.

Chapter
TWENTY-ONE

STEVIE

The music bleeds away as I stare into the glowing red mask.

He's here.

He's here, and I don't even know what just happened.

My mind is still a jumble from how quickly everything escalated. One minute, Deanna and I are having the time of our lives, and the next, that asshat from the VSAs turns up and starts spouting a bunch of utter bullshit. Goddamned Chase and his entitled friends. They were always known for causing unnecessary drama just because they thought they owned everything and everyone.

"Are you alright?"

My eyes snap away from Blade to the pink-haired girl in front of me. She can't be more than five feet, and yet she threw herself right in front of me.

"Am I alright? I should be asking you. Is your cheek okay?"

She just waves her hands around. "Don't worry about it, just looking out for a fellow girl." Her forehead crinkles, "I thought he'd back off if I got involved. He can't afford to screw me over right now, but...I guess I miscalculated a little."

Her cheek is slightly pink from the slap, but it's hard to tell since she is wearing so much blush. Now that I get a better look at her without the chaos of everything around us...

Holy crap.

Pink hair. White eyeliner. Body glitter. Inch-long nails. Bubble-gum dress.

She's TheCozyDeer.

I'm freaking obsessed with her videos. She is *the* cozy game and life-sim content creator right now. I play her streams and videos in the background while I paint. I live and die by her recommendations; she's never wrong.

And she just took a slap for me.

What in the multiverse is going on?

Concern pools in her eyes. "Wait, seriously, are you alright?" She leans forward, loosely holding my wrist.

"Yeah. Sorry, no, I'm fine. I just..." Crap. I don't want to seem like a total fangirl and scare her off, but I don't know how else to explain my dumbstruck state. "I just didn't realize you were, well, you."

Her eyes soften, the worry disappearing, and a small laugh lilts out of her.

"Oh! You're completely fine." She leans backward into the green mask's protective hold—Shield, I think.

"Thank you, though. He is my ex's friend, and…well that pretty much sums it up, honestly."

She shakes her head, "No, trust me. I understand." There is a sadness that swirls through her gaze, but in a flash, it's gone.

"Deer!" A petite girl with silky black hair pushes through the crowd and tumbles into our group. She tugs Deer out of the guy's grip, porcelain hands running over her to check for any injuries. "Why would you do that? Are you okay?"

Deer squeezes her friend's hand reassuringly. "I'm fine, Al. It was just Decker."

"And you!" The girl pokes Shield in the chest. "You should've stopped her. What's the point in having these big muscles if you don't use them."

"Chill, Lee. I might be muscley, but Deer is quick as a fox. Slipped right under the crowd."

They continue to bicker back and forth, but I feel the heat of Blade's gaze burning into my skin. I peek to my right, and sure enough, he is leaning against the pillar, arms folded, watching silently.

"Not to be the responsible one, but we should probably take this back over to our table. We're gathering quite the crowd here." His deep voice carries over the group, commanding their attention without needing to raise it any louder.

"Nope. I want to dance. Rid my body of the bad energy Decker brought." Lee grabs Deer's hands. "Come on, dance with me. Pleeeease."

Lee proceeds to twirl her around, and she laughs. "Fine, but only if they join us."

Deer nods her head toward me. I look back at Deanna, who hasn't said a word this entire time. Her steely black eyes flick over the group, assessing, before a wolfish grin spills out.

"We'd love to."

Lee squeals before taking off through the crowd, and the guys yell after her to be careful. Deer tugs me forward, and I grip Deanna's hand to pull her through the crowd with me. A glance back gives me one last look at Blade before I lose track of him in the throng of bodies as we exit VIP to the general dance floor. My body is tossed between jostling bodies while we try to follow Lee's snaking path. Her sparkly mini dress is the only way we are able to track her.

Sweat beads on my skin as the sticky heat from the dance floor surrounds me. I'm elbowed a few times, and someone steps on my foot at least twice before Deer pulls us to an abrupt stop. I look up, coming face-to-face with a giant neon tiger, and grin. Lee led us all the way to the front of the DJ booth.

Despite the muggy air clinging to my body, a shiver racks down my spine. My gaze lifts from the crowd, searching the balcony.

There.

Blade's telltale red mask glows like a beacon guiding me to danger. It's hypnotizing. There's a part of me that is drawn to him, no matter how I try to deny it. My body aches at the distance. He looks even hotter than when I saw him at the VSAs. The way his muscles flexed and glistened in the lights as he cornered Decker should be considered a sin. Even now, I want to trail my fingers down his abs.

What were the freaking odds that he would be at the same club? I really thought the chances of us crossing paths again were slim to none. And yet, here we are, just a few weeks later.

I'm jostled out of my trance when some random bumps against me. I force myself to rip my gaze away from Blade to the women in front of me.

Lee shoves her fist into the air. "Alright, ladies. Fuck Decker. Let's have some fun!"

"Fuck Decker!" Deer chants back.

"Fuck Decker!" Deanna and I join in after.

We all raise our fists in the air as the beat drops. The four of us move seamlessly to the music, our bodies twisting and turning in time with the beat. I let the bass reverberate through my body, my skin jumping at the force. My head and body move as one, blending into the sounds beating through the speakers. All the want and temptation that has been building inside me fuels my movements. I let the music fill me, power me. Euphoria creeps into my soul, and I know I'm grinning hard as hell right now.

An EDM remix of a popular song comes on, and the four of us squeal before singing along with the lyrics. Well, shouting might be a little more accurate than singing.

The margaritas Deanna made at her place and the shots we took here are finally making their way through my body. My muscles loosen as the liquor warms my blood. I let myself slip into the feeling. Everything around me becomes a blur of orange and white as I lose myself to the music, lights, bodies, heat. My ass drops to the floor, bouncing on my heels, as I shout along to the song. Deer follows my movement down and bops her pink hair wildly to the beat. Deanna grabs my hand and pulls me up into a spin, and I laugh against her. All my worries feel like they were blown into a balloon and thrown into the sky. My eyes shut as I allow all my inhibitions to be free.

I feel a trail of hands on my hips, ghosting the line between my skirt and my skin. A warm body presses up against mine. My eyes pop open in shock, and I make eye contact with Deanna. She just smiles and winks before turning her back to me, dancing with Deer and Lee. Confusion bubbles over the shock, but as I twist my head around, both disappear as lust takes over.

Shining red X's tower above me, and the club's neon lights bounce off the black mask. It all mixes into one addictive, hazy glow. Unable to stop myself, my hand reaches up, caressing the bottom of the mask. The hard plastic is slippery under my sweaty touch. This close, I can see the faint trace of his eyes behind the mask, staring right at me.

"Blade," I breathe.

The music is so loud, and my voice is so soft, but still, I can see his eyes crinkle in response.

"Hello, little dove."

Even with the base pumping through my veins, I feel his chest rumble against my shoulders as he speaks to me. I smile up at him. Genuine happiness floods my system, desire simmering beneath it. The deep growl of his voice is comforting in a way I can't quite pinpoint.

His hands skim down my hips, over the soft fabric, and back up to the bare skin of my ribs. I sink into his touch, leaning my head back on him. My body pushes up against his. The bare skin on my back sticks against his chest.

I allow the music to take over me again, but with more

heat this time. My hips dip and sway in time with the beat. I don't push, letting my ass barely graze over his groin. Just the touch of temptation.

His hands move to grip my hips tighter. I flick my head to the side briefly, catching his eyes with a smile, before covering his hands with my own. Taking back some of the control. Continuing to move to the music the way I want to.

He pulls me closer to his body, forcing my movements to grind against his hips. I feel his length against my ass and grin to myself. The bass drops again, and I drop with it, bending in half, pushing my ass right up to his body. I rock side to side against him, dipping briefly as the beat sways.

The song changes, and I bring my body back up, raising my arm to curl behind me and loop around the back of his neck. My back arches slightly in the new position, and my fingertips dance against the straps of his mask. I'm flirting with temptation, and it has my core clenching.

I allow my nails to dance a little in his hair, scratching slightly. He releases his tight hold of my hips and trails his large fingers up my bare ribs. They pause momentarily under my breasts. With both hands, he skims four fingers from the center of my chest out, scraping his nails lightly as they round my ribs and then move down my hips. It sends a shiver up my body, and when he repeats the motion, my pussy drips.

I'm living for this. Loving this.

He begins a soft trail up my arms. His touch is feather-light, but his nails have a slight bite.

When he reaches my hands, he grips them in his own.

We stay like that for a few beats, connected. My grinding gets slower, more languid, as I become one with his body. The slower pace means I feel how hard he is. Another zing travels right to my lower stomach. The lingering pulse causes my tiny thong to dampen significantly.

He pries my hands away from his neck and guides them down my own body. He starts with my shoulders, moving to my collar bones. His fingers remained laced through mine as he grazes over my breasts, purposely running across my stiff nipples. He moves us down my bare stomach, reaching the band of my skirt at my belly button. He pauses then and then rips my arms back over my head, spinning me around to face him. My eyes fly open as he pulls me chest to chest.

I stare up at him, stunned arousal coursing through me. He lets go of my hands and cups my face. He traces along my jaw before stopping to press his thumb against my lips. I wind my arms back around his neck, my gaze transfixed on his. The lust is hazing my vision, the red X's hypnotizing me. All I see, all I feel, all I hear is red.

He presses on my lower lip, dragging his thumb down until my lip pops back up.

I'm so wound up right now. I can feel my arousal sticking between my thighs. I don't even give it a second thought as I bring my right knee up to loop my leg around his hips. His hands move to spread across my back, just below my shoulder blades, to pull me tight around him. I sigh in relief as the air cools my raging heat.

That is until I realize my center is pressed right up against his dick in this new position. Shit. Shit, shitty, shit-shit.

He moves one of his hands to grip my ass. When the bass drops again, he lifts me slightly to grind farther onto his dick. I can't stop my eyes from squeezing shut, but I do bite my lip to stop my moan from slipping out.

"Are you wet for me, again, baby?"

It's the first thing he has said to me over the past…God knows how many minutes now. There's something about the way he says it, something in his voice, that sounds familiar. Whatever it is, it sends flutters right to my pussy.

The hand on my ass moves to slip between us, and I panic for a second, knowing exactly where this is going. Embarrassed by what he is going to find. But the feeling is fleeting as I remember my mantra from earlier tonight. I can enjoy myself as much as I want. Just because Chase chastised me for my wants doesn't mean that I was in the wrong—he was.

With my leg looped around him, the slit in my skirt has risen significantly. He rests his hand on my thigh for a second, giving it a small squeeze, and I tighten my arms around his neck. Then his hand dips between our bodies, and with his whole hand, he cups my heat, squeezing it so the palm of his hand grinds my clit. I'm so ready, so strung up, that the one movement causes my whole body to spasm.

"Fuck."

The word leaves my mouth without me even registering it.

"Can I?" His voice is low, his fingers grazing back and forth against the damp fabric.

I nod my head frantically, and then I remember the last time we were in this position.

"Yes. Please, yes." The words leave me like a supplication.

His chest shakes with a small chuckle. I preen at the compliment, all the while he swiftly moves my thong to the side.

He doesn't push in right away. Instead, he lets his fingers glaze against my slick pussy, coating himself in my potent arousal. I hear him groan under the music right before he slips two fingers inside me. Desire pools in my stomach at the feel of him filling me. It builds as he moves his fingers inside me, alternating between curling and scissoring. The hand supporting my back moves to my ass so he can hike me higher, plunging me deeper on his fingers, pulling me flush against his body. I moan at the new position, his fingers hitting me at just the right spot, my orgasm building faster than the beat around us. My eyes flutter shut.

"I'm so fucking hard for you, Stevie."

My mind flickers to Aleks for some reason. The words bring me back to the other week. It's almost a sense of déjà vu. But my body ignores the confusion. Instead, it replaces Blade with Aleks' hot gaze. The memories take over, and I find myself grinding even harder against Blade's palm. Desperate for release. He picks up his pace then. Using the bass of the music to rub my clit in time with it.

"Come for me."

My eyes pop open at the command.

Everything blends together.

The neon lights. The bass. His mask. His hot skin. My orgasm.

He pinches my clit, that same damn motion that got me

last time, and I fall.

The world drops under me. My eyes roll back, and my mouth opens in a silent scream as my release tumbles out of me. The orgasm shuts my body down while pure pleasure races through my veins. My legs turn numb, and Blade quickly shifts the hand coated in my arousal to grab my leg as it begins to slip. I feel my slickness on the back of my thigh as he grips it tight.

"Want to move this elsewhere?"

I'm still swimming in my post-orgasm haze, but I still manage to get some words out.

"I would love to."

"Can you stand?"

Probably not, but I still nod in return. He slowly releases his grip on my thigh. My heel hits the floor, and I give myself a moment to stand there, the orgasm running through my body still leaving my knees a little jiggly.

As my senses begin to return, the music amplifies and the lights brighten. A quick assessment of my surroundings shows Deanna and the girls dancing in a weird semicircle. I soon realize the way they're positioned hides Blade and me from prying eyes. Kind of. Blade's tall as hell.

God damnit. I did it again. Public play without a care in the world.

What was I becoming?

An exhibitionist it seemed like.

Blade tugs on my hand, bringing my brain back to Earth.

"Follow me."

I give Deanna a quick tap on her shoulder. She turns around, and when her eyes meet mine, they light up with a devious glint, her smile turning serpentine.

"Having fun?" she teases.

I laugh. Even in this heat and with the flush of my orgasm still coursing through me, I feel my cheeks reddening.

"I'm heading out. Is that alright with you? Will you be okay?"

She nods. "Totally, I've got Deer and Lee. Don't worry about me. Just worry about getting that dick."

I roll my eyes.

"Just remember to use protection."

"Oh my god, I'm leaving. Text me when you get home."

"You too," she winks, "if you make it home."

I turn back to Blade.

"Still good?" he asks.

"Yup, lead the way, sir."

His body stiffens for a second, grip tightening, before he laughs and leads me through the sway of moving bodies. The crowd has thickened since we got down here, sweat dripping off skin, liquor filling the air.

We spill out of the dance floor crowd. The air lightens a little in the general access area, but it doesn't do anything to curb the growing want for more in my body. He speeds us around the tables, bypassing VIP. Blade takes us the opposite way to the entrance. My four-inch heels give me enough height that I can see pretty well over the general crowd to the back exit he seems to be spearing toward.

We are only a few feet away when a hand grabs my wrist, wrenching me back. I slip out of Blade's grip, which had loosened.

I spin around, face to face with none other than Daniel Decker. Again.

The guy is a cockroach.

He pulls me to his body quickly, leaning down to my ear.

"You should be careful of the company you're keeping, Stephanie. It'll put a target on your back."

It's a warning. I just can't tell whether he means it to be malicious or not.

He lets go of me right as Blade pulls me behind his body.

Decker brings his hands up, a surrender.

A growl builds in Blade's chest. I rest my hands on his back.

"Come on, let's go."

He spins back around, guiding me past the two security guards and out the back entrance.

I have no clue what time it is, but the night air is sweet relief against my flushed skin. I tilt my head up to the sky, taking in a deep breath of fresh air. Or as fresh as the air can be in the city.

A white Lincoln MKT pulls up in front of us, and I stare at the limo.

"Wait, where are we going?"

"Do you trust me, Stevie?"

I eye him for a second. I've met him twice. We've barely had a full conversation, and yet…there's something in him that calls to me. A connection I can't pinpoint, but can't deny.

"Yes."

Chapter
TWENTY-TWO

ALEKS

Thank, fuck.

I open the door and hold my palm up for Stevie to grip as she dips into the car. I eye her ass as she bends to scoot onto the leather seats. My throbbing dick twitches. I swear, my hard on is about ready to break out of my pants.

I make a quick assessment of our surroundings, confirming that there is no one else back here before slipping into the vehicle myself. Technically, the boys and I came here together and picked up Lee on our way. But if they want to leave before I'm done, they can just use one of Lee's drivers. I couldn't give a rat's ass how they get home. It's my night to be selfish.

I sidle in next to Stevie on the leather, shutting the door. The inside of the limo is dark, save for the lights lining the roof. She instantly hooks one of her legs over mine, her warmth joining mine. I live for the connection, the touch.

I tap on the divider twice, signaling to Francis, our driver, that we are good to go.

I'm not driving us anywhere specific. Just around in various circles until we decide. If we even do. My focus right now is on Stevie. Well, Stevie and myself.

Heat floods my dick in anticipation.

The car takes off, and I reach into the nearby fridge compartment to pull out some bottled water and pass one to her before taking a sip myself.

The club was hot as balls.

"Thanks." She downs the bottle in what feels like five seconds, and I just stare at her, blinking. "Guess I was a little thirsty." She laughs, and it is such a sweet sound. I wish I could take her home, hold her in my arms, wake up to her in the morning. But I can't jeopardize The System. As connected to her as I feel, I won't put us in danger because of that.

I lean over her and pull out one of the ties we keep stashed in the car for emergency events. This car is stocked with everything, honestly. Sydney foresees every possible scenario, every way we could possibly fuck something up, and plans for it—or she tries to. We each have three changes of clothes in the trunk, protein bars up front, a shaving kit, everything.

Stevie eyes the black tie, brow raised.

"Still trust me?" My voice comes out deep and raspy as I try to keep my desperation at bay.

She smiles. "Enough to see where this goes."

"Turn around for me." It's a small command, nothing

too strong.

Her leg slips off mine as she spins so her back faces me. My jaw clenches at the loss of her touch, but I swallow it down as I move to tie the tie around her eyes. It's not perfect. Not what I would've chosen to use if I'd had the time to actually prepare, but it'll do. She lifts her hair off her smooth neck, giving me better access to tie it. It takes all my restraint not to lean down and taste her.

Once it's secure, I guide her back around to face me.

"How does that feel?"

"A little tight, but it's good."

I hold up one of my hands.

"How many fingers am I holding up?"

She snorts, "Um, I don't know, four?"

I am holding up four fingers…

I can't tell if we are just always on the same wavelength or if it's some weird coincidence. I know she can't see my fingers, so I just brush it off.

Adrenaline pumps through my veins as I reach up to take off my mask. My fingers fumble a little, nervously twitching. With a deep breath, I pull it off.

My eyes blink a few times, readjusting to the light. It's dark in the limo, but the LED lights lining the roof bathe it in a slight purple glow. I toss the mask on the seats across from us.

Stevie is a dream in front of me. I catalogue every inch of her, memorizing her lines. Her brown hair is a mess of waves around her face, and the black tie brings focus to her pink, pouty lips. Her skin is still slightly flushed from the club, and her chest rises and falls in pace with my own heartbeat.

"Can I—" she stops, pressing her lips together.

"Can you what?"

"No, nothing. It's stupid."

I grab her hand, bringing it to my lips, and she sucks in a breath. "Nothing you could ever say would be stupid."

She bites her lip, and I want to lean over and suck it into my own.

"Can I touch your face?"

My heart stutters, fear lancing through it.

Normally, my response would be no, but...

I grab her hands and guide them to my cheeks.

The second her hands make contact, she smiles. I let go, and she starts her slow perusal. Her touch is light as her thumbs run over my brows. She pauses when she reaches the scar on my temple, fingertips tracing it while her brows furrow. She rounds my jaw and brings her hands to cup under my ears. I feel her still as her knuckle grazes my piercing. She rolls the stud, and I shiver.

She runs her hands through my hair next, and I lean into her touch, my guard lowering with each passing second.

Fuck. I know what this feeling is. I don't *want* to know what this feeling is.

She grips the hair at the base of my neck, tugging on it, and I grin.

"I like it a little rough," I tease her.

She freezes, and my brain flashes back to the other week. When I said the exact same thing to her as Aleks. Crap. I don't think I can do this. Not if she doesn't know who I am. It doesn't feel right.

God-fucking-dammit.

The car swerves suddenly before righting itself, and we go sliding off the seats onto the floor.

"Francis. The fuck?" I yell.

"Sorry, sir!" he yells back. "A couple of kids ran into the street."

Stevie's body shakes with laughter under me. I push off her and help her back onto the seat before sitting next to her. I hold her hands and realize just how clammy mine have become.

"Hey, I'm sorry. I don't think I can do this."

She sucks in a deep breath before a single, sharp laugh spills out. "Oh my god. I was literally about to say the same thing."

Relief and rejection mix within me. I'm glad she feels the same way. But I'm also a little offended she doesn't want to have sex with Blade. It's a weird feeling. Fucking hell. This shit is getting too confusing. I don't know if I can keep this up. I just want to be with her. Why does it have to be so hard?

My phone starts pinging from somewhere on the ground. I swear I put the damn thing on 'do not disturb.' It's not even a regular notification tone, either. It's a full-on siren alert.

"Someone's looking for you," Stevie muses.

I flip it over to see a 'Find My Phone' alert going off. Unlocking the phone, I see a dozen missed calls and texts from Parker and Jackson asking where I am and where the car is. Needy little shits.

I shoot them both a text letting them know I'm using the car to take Stevie home and that they have to sort their own shit out.

219

"All good?"

"Yeah. The guys are just heading home and wondering where I was. I let them know I was dropping you off."

"That would require me telling you where I live, and for all I know you could come murder me in my sleep."

"I am not abandoning you to some street corner."

"I never said that," she smirks. "I'm staying at my friend's tonight. You can drop me at hers."

I squeeze her tightly in my arms for a few seconds before loosening my grip. I place a kiss on the side of her head and let out a sigh.

"Alright, sounds good. Let me just get my mask back on."

I pick up my mask and pause. I give Stevie one last once over, drinking her in before I strap the mask back on, my world turning back to red. I tug my gloves out from where I stashed them in my back pocket earlier and slip them back on. All evidence of Aleksander is hidden.

I reach forward and untie the tie, letting it slip from her face.

She blinks a few times, her honeyed eyes readjusting.

She shimmies to the front of the limo and gives Francis her friend's address through the divider and then bends down to retrieve her purse from somewhere.

She looks at me with a melancholy smile and places a kiss on my mask.

It's a kiss that speaks a thousand words, but she just says two.

"Thank you."

Chapter
TWENTY-THREE

STEVIE

I look hot as fuck.

I twirl in the mirror again, admiring myself as the train follows my movements. The gold embellishments glitter in the light. I toe on my classic nude Louboutin heels and give myself one last check, making sure that my makeup isn't shiny and that my hair hasn't shifted.

I even went over to Deanna's before she left for work to have her put my hair in an elaborate half-up Dutch braid crown. There are a handful of bobby pins sticking uncomfortably into my skull, but it's worth it.

My makeup is subtle, a brown eye with smudged black liner and a nude-pink lip. The overall look is giving a Greek goddess vibe, just like Aleks remarked the first time he saw the dress.

I snap a quick selfie in the mirror and send it to him

with a wink emoji.

He replies instantly.

ALEKS

You look hot, baby

I think I just came

I snort, rolling my eyes before clicking it off.

After our night together, things shifted. They feel easier.

He brought over tacos for lunch this week while I was deep in the painting groove. It was super sweet. He sat with me while I painted and just played a game on his phone, chattering away every once in a while. But even when we didn't speak, it was a comfortable silence. Something I've never experienced before. Just being around him brings me peace, and the little things he does make my heart flutter more than any grand gesture. I used to think I was Chase's princess, but Aleks has shown me what it is like to truly be treated like a queen. We plan to meet up tomorrow; he took the night off and has some cute dinner planned. He's been super hush about it, and it's adorable.

Guilt slithers into my stomach as I remember my night with Blade a week ago. I had a major debrief with Deanna the following morning, who basically told me that I should embrace my pussy power. But what I'd concluded was that I was all-in on Aleksander. Even if we weren't technically exclusive, it felt wrong. Plus, something else seemed entirely off about the whole situation. The entire time I was with Blade, my mind kept wandering to Aleks. And it wasn't in some "oh, I can't stop thinking about him" kind of way but more of a "this reminds me of him" way…

My phone buzzes, and I pick it up to see three notifications. A bell alerting me that Blade has started a livestream, a text from Deanna imploring me to spill my drink on Felicity if the chance arises, and an update from the driver my father ordered letting me know he is a few minutes out.

I tuck my phone into my purse and swing by my fridge to pull out an old handle of Fireball. Too lazy to grab a shot glass, I take a swig right from the bottle. The spicy liquor goes down easily, instantly warming my insides and leaving a deep cinnamon taste behind. A little liquid courage is needed before I spend the rest of my night around my insufferable ex and hawkish mother.

Throwing the bottle back into the fridge, I grab my purse and make sure my invitation is inside along with my lipstick, ID, and credit card. A glance at my phone confirms that my driver is downstairs, so I open my door to leave and stop.

There's a bouquet of pink roses.

Of course.

Lifting them, a note falls to the ground. I pick it up, opening it to read the message within.

Until tonight xo

Lovely.

I turn back into my apartment, throwing them in the trash.

I give myself a smile in the mirror next to my door.

It looks fake.

I try again, imagining my heel digging into Chase's

back.

That's it. Perfection.

The car rolls to a stop in the oval driveway outside the Taylors' residence. Well, one of their many residences. They decided to host their party at their Orange County mansion this year. The location is more convenient than their Napa or Palm Springs house, meaning I can actually go home after the event instead of staying at a nearby hotel or with my parents in the Hills.

Rolling my shoulders, I take the driver's hand and step out of the car and into the snake pit.

A camera flashes.

There are a handful of photographers stationed around the entrance, capturing everyone as they arrive and head into the party. They'll probably move inside once the event starts, documenting everything for the Taylors to brag about later.

I make my way up the steps and am greeted by one of the security guards at the double-door. I pull my invitation from my clutch, flashing it. He crosses my name off the list before gesturing inside.

"Enjoy your evening, Miss Andwell."

Unlikely.

I enter the foyer, stepping onto the white marble floor. A server offers me a flute of champagne, which I graciously accept but refrain from taking a sip of, knowing I can't begin drinking until the toast is called.

I take in the foyer. There are two large marble pillars on either side, framing the double staircase leading to the second floor. A large raindrop crystal chandelier makes its statement in the middle of the room. The Orange County mansion is one of the Taylors' newer constructions; they purchased it only a few years back for a good sixty million, if I remember correctly. Felicity bragged about it because it isn't too far from one of the Broadshires' homes.

Instantly, I feel eyes on me. I make sure to straighten my spine and keep my expression one of neutral content. Scanning the crowd, I clock a large number of familiar faces. A few smile my way as our eyes make contact, and I make sure to smile and dip my head back.

There are probably fifty people already here, the foyer seeming a little crowded. The Taylors must be waiting for everyone to arrive before giving the toast and allowing guests to mill about the house.

The chattering of conversation rises over a live string quartet, maybe a piano as well. Where the musicians are set up, I have no clue. Probably farther into the house. Knowing the Taylors, the event will spill into their immaculately manicured backyard as the evening progresses.

I spot my mother, father, brother, and Vittoria by the left side set of stairs, near one of the main pillars. A glance up confirms Mr. and Mrs. Taylor positioned on the second-story balcony. I accidentally make eye contact with Annabelle, and she leans in to whisper something to her husband.

He immediately raises his champagne flute, giving it a clink.

Ah, so they weren't waiting for everyone to arrive.

They were waiting for me.

Aren't I special.

"Thank you all for gathering here today for our annual ball. We are excited to kick off the summer with the celebration of the year," Henry Taylor drawls.

Celebration of the year is big talk. Especially considering a lot of the people in this room also hold annual parties and celebrations. People of higher status than the Taylors. It's an interesting angle for them to pull.

"We hope you will enjoy the champagne throughout the party, and please feel free to stop by the outdoor bar for cocktails—including a custom event cocktail created by my lovely daughter, Felicity, and her new beau, Chauncy Broadshire."

My eyes twitch as I try to prevent them from rolling at the obvious display.

I had a feeling they would try to peacock this event, I just didn't realize how blatantly. I mean, Chase and I have only been broken up a few weeks; Felicity is playing a dangerous game. I don't plan to get back with Chase, but she doesn't know that, and a three-week "break" for us is nothing new in the grand scheme of things. What is interesting is that Chase would go along with this all while still trying to win me back. Quite stupid, if you ask me.

Felicity and Chase appear at the foot of the right side staircase. Felicity's auburn hair is slicked into a high ponytail, a diamond cuff around the base. She is wearing the new Danielle Frankel Nina gown; the basque waist accentuates her slim build, and the white satin highlights her snowy skin. The pleated gown trails behind her as she holds Chase's arm up the stairs.

I'm not a bitch, I'll admit that she looks pretty. The issue, however, is she also looks like a freaking bride. I'm ninety percent sure it was designed as a wedding dress, which, in turn, makes it tacky and cringey.

They reach the top of the stairs, and even from down here I can see the way her manicured claws are digging into Chase's suit jacket. He looks good. His blond hair has been trimmed slightly, and his black suit hugs his body in all the right ways. I'm not ashamed to say that. I didn't date him for five years because I thought he was unattractive. It's just that the attraction isn't the same anymore. I can admire that he is good looking, but my body doesn't react to him like it used to. I don't feel that rush of lust. He just looks like every other rich country club kid. Boring.

"Thank you, everyone, for joining us tonight! We hope you love the fun drink Chasey and I came up with," she leans into him and locks eyes with me. I have to tamper back a laugh. She should just pee on him and stake her territory while she's at it.

"Please allow the party to commence," Henry's voice rings out. "Tonight's feast is brought to you by Chef Gauthier and his team at House Charles. Hors d'oeuvres are being passed around by waitstaff, and our meal shall commence in the great room at twenty-one hours."

He could've just said nine o'clock.

Henry lifts his champagne and takes a sip. Everyone else follows suit, including myself. I make the conscious decision not to down the first flute all at once. I've apparently got two hours until the meal is even served. What a pain.

The crowd starts thinning out as people begin to make

their way through the foyer into the rest of the mansion. I can see a patio leading outdoors, where it seems a majority of guests are moving toward. A handful of people are making their way up the staircases, probably to kiss ass with the Taylors. Not something I need to do.

Knowing I need to let my parents know I've shown up, I make my way toward the pillar they are still mingling near.

"Having fun yet?"

I twist to my right. Tristan Taylor leans against the wall, foot propped behind him, empty champagne flute dangling from his grip.

"I'm surprised to see you here, seeing as you didn't make a grand entrance with the rest of your family."

I file this tidbit of information in my back pocket. There must be some tension between the Taylors and their youngest child.

"Oh, you know me. Thought I would do my family a favor and make my appearance. I just finished my finals, figured I could spare the time to come down from Stanford."

"How gracious of you." I go to walk off when he pushes off the wall and comes to stand by me, boyish glint in his eyes.

"What do you think of the happy couple?"

I narrow my eyes. I'm not sure what Tristan's game is. I never interacted with him much. With him being several years younger, he ran in a different circle than his older sister and myself.

"I wish them the best."

"Looks more like you hope they choke on the froufrou

drink they're calling a cocktail."

"Tristan, darling," I touch his shoulder, giving him a tight smile, "I couldn't care less about them. They could streak naked around the foyer or announce this is their surprise engagement party. Either way, I'd have no interest."

"Then let me give you a piece of advice: be careful. You are still a livewire in their relationship, and you don't want to get electrocuted." He pointedly looks me up and down. "Have fun, Stephanie. You look amazing."

He walks away, and I watch him with narrowed eyes.

Another warning.

I'm so sick of warnings.

A glance around the room confirms that my family has moved on. *Great.* Now I'm going to have to track them down somewhere on this twenty thousand-square-foot property.

I walk through the foyer between the two staircases, heels clacking beneath me, into the open kitchen and living room—well, one of their living rooms, I guess. I make small talk with a few people I cross paths with, asking how they are, if their children are well, what they've been up to. Everyone compliments my dress, and each time it feels like a win in my corner. No one has said a word about Chase and me being broken up, so it's off to a good start at least.

I keep my smile plastered on my face but finish off the rest of my champagne. This is why I stopped coming to these events. They're no fun when you have no one to hang out with. The few society friends—which is a loose term—that I have are already busy jet-setting across Europe for the summer.

My mind flickers to Tristan for a second, but I dismiss it. I am not spending my evening with an eighteen-year-old boy to survive—that's just sad.

I shield my eyes as I make my way onto the crowded patio. The setting sun coats everything in a soft light, and I let the rays warm up my skin. It's a gorgeous backyard, I'll give the Taylors that. A fire pit sits to my right with two circular couches surrounding it. To my left is an enormous bar area, where I'm guessing the signature cocktail is being served. Stairs in front of me lead down to a large garden surrounding a swimming pool, hot tub, and volleyball court, perfectly tapered bushes lining the way.

"Stephanie! There you are."

My mother loops her arm in mine, dragging me in the direction of the stairs before veering right. My father is standing on the edge of the patio by the firepit. He stares out over the garden, nursing what is probably an old fashioned.

"Hello, dear." She plops a kiss on my cheek before releasing me to stand next to my father.

"Hello, pumpkin." My father gives me a quick hug, careful not to spill his drink. "You look beautiful. The most gorgeous woman here, after your mother, of course."

"Jameson," my mother taps my father's arm lightly.

"Thank you, Dad."

"It is a lovely dress, a classy cut, Stephanie. But it is a little," my mother's lips purse as she tries to find the right word, "loud."

"Yes, well, at least it's not a wedding dress."

My mother whips her head around, staring at the people around us. "Stephanie, lower your voice. *Theo mou,*" she scolds.

"Stevie! You look *bellissima*! Like a celebrity." Vittoria sidles up with Michail on her arm, her black locks contrasting beautifully against her red dress and tan skin.

"As do you, that color is gorgeous on you."

My brother disentangles himself from his fiancée, enveloping me in a large, crushing hug.

"Good to see you, little one."

"And you."

My mother begins chatting with Michail and Vittoria about their upcoming wedding plans, and I tune out. I go to sip my champagne only to realize it's still empty. A loss, truly.

A waitress slips past with a tray of oysters and horseradish. I slip one off, swallowing it down, appreciating the saltiness, before placing the empty shell back on the tray. Another waiter follows close behind her with more champagne, and I smile, replacing my flute. Oysters and champagne, the best combination. *This* I miss.

My mother gasps, and I switch my ears back to the conversation.

"The Covingtons are here."

"The Covingtons?" Vittoria questions.

I stare at the beautiful blond family that just walked in. I know of the Covingtons, but I've never crossed paths with them. They're old English wealth but are making modern waves. I'm pretty sure the mother comes from some royal lineage, a marquess maybe. They're part of the upper echelon, so I'm surprised to see them here of all places. They outrank the Taylors, hell, they outrank ninety-nine percent of the families here. I'm not sure what their reasoning is for being here, but it is going to be something that Felicity lords over the rest of us now.

"The older man is Patrick Covington, head of the Covington Hotel conglomerate. Jameson and I stay in their hotel whenever we travel to Paris. Children, you remember their flagship hotel in London; we stayed there when you were in middle school."

"I remember the fountain in the lobby." It was a gorgeous fountain with an angel in the center and cherubs lining the sides—the sort of thing a young girl coos over. We traveled so much as children that the odds of me remembering one hotel versus another are very slim, but that fountain I remember.

"The mother is Pricilla. Her grandfather was knighted by the Queen and then granted barony; God rest her soul."

Ah, a baron. Close enough.

"Then there's the elder daughters, Paige and Phoebe, and the son, Parker. He is the heir to *everything*, but rumors say he is dabbling in his own ventures. He's the same age as you, Stephanie, handsome as well." My mother raises her eyebrow at me, like I wouldn't have picked up on her point without it. "You know, I always thought you could do better than Chauncy."

I can't stop the soft scoff that releases from me.

That's not what she's been saying every time we've talked on the phone since the breakup, but alright.

They're a tall, attractive family. The sisters are night and day, one in a dusty pink tulle gown, the other in a strapless, fitted black gown. Parker has every girl's eye on him. The guy looks like he belongs on a magazine cover. The navy-blue suit he is sporting is tailored to perfection, a stark blue tie resting against his white shirt. Everyone says British men are sexier, and they are correct. The other men at this event don't hold a candle to him. But as attractive as he might be, my mind is trapped on a devilish, tattooed brunette.

We make eye contact, and he looks at me with surprise before smiling and waving, cuff links glinting in the sunlight. Reflex has me waving back with an equal smile, but I can't stop my brows from pinching in slight confusion. His eyes startle and panic flashes across his face as he turns away to speak with one of his sisters.

Strange.

My mother grips my arm. "Stephanie, since when are you acquainted with the Covington heir?"

Since never.

But I can't really say that, so I just shrug.

"I was about to ask the same thing. I wasn't aware you knew Parker."

A chill runs down my spine. I'd know that voice anywhere. His presence presses against my back without even touching me. My brother tries to discreetly move our parents a few steps away in an attempt to give us privacy. I spin around, cocking my right brow while looking my ex-boyfriend up and down.

"Chase."

"Steffy."

My jaw clenches at the use of my pet name. Chase wanted to call me something no one else did as a token of his adoration. At first, it seemed cute. But as time drew on, the playful tone shifted. He has this way of saying it that makes me feel like a child, like I'm beneath him.

"You look beautiful tonight."

"Mmm, your date doesn't look half bad herself."

I take a sip of champagne, watching as he huffs, jaw ticking up slightly with frustration.

"It's not that serious, Steffy, you know that. I only came with her because you haven't been answering my calls. You've completely shut me out."

"Well, I'm serious. I told you I was done, and I meant it."

"You're throwing away years, Stephanie. Years."

"No, Chase. I *wasted* years, and I won't waste any more, not for a man who never saw me for me. I'm not some pet you can train and take out whenever you like; I'm my own person."

"Stop being dramatic, Steffy. Do you think you're worth anything without me?"

"I know what I'm worth, *Chasey*, and you can't afford it."

Whether the use of his new girlfriend's pet name bothers him or not, I don't know. What I do know is that Felicity has spotted us chatting, her glare hot on me. I lean into Chase, watching Felicity stalk over in her shiny stilettos.

"Also, you can stop with the flowers, Chase. It's not doing you any favors; it's just getting creepy."

His eyes narrow, but he loses his chance to respond.

"Chasey!" Felicity's voice is shrill as she loops her arm through Chase's, drawing him back from me. "Stevie, hi, you're looking," she pauses, giving me a once over, "shiny."

"Felicity." My lips might be smiling, but I can't stop the slight spread of venom from creeping into my eyes.

Insults teeter on the tip of my tongue, but I bite them all back. "Thank you."

She didn't mean it as a compliment. I know that. She knows that. Her nose twitches in annoyance at my lack of reaction. She's quick to recover though.

"I didn't see you come in," *lie*, "did you bring a date?"

She makes a show of widening her eyes dramatically to look around for some invisible boyfriend, lips slightly pouted.

"Nope, just myself."

"Oh, I'm so sorry about that. It must be hard to see that your ex has moved on." She reaches out and touches my hand in a move of faux sympathy.

I let my smile drop into a fake look of confusion.

"Oh, Felicity. Why would I be upset? You're the one who had to steal someone's boyfriend because you couldn't land one on your own."

"Well, at least I'm not on some slutty rebound tour," she bites back. My eyes narrow at her over the top of my glass.

"What do you mean?"

Her smile turns smug, and she presses her chest out with the confidence of someone who is about to spill a dirty secret. "Our mutual friend said you've been spreading your legs for strangers. I know you're hurt over Chase dumping you for an upgrade, but you really should be careful. You don't want to catch an STI."

Mutual friend, my ass. I bet it was fucking Daniel Decker. I didn't realize how entrenched he was in Chase's social life. He's even spent time with Felicity. I've clearly been missing something, and I don't like being in the dark.

"Upgrade? Ha. Honey, you're the backup." Felicity's expression sours as I drain the last of my champagne. I use the empty flute to point towards Chase, holding her eyes the entire time. "Plus, my sex life was pretty boring these last few years. I've been needing to spice it up now that I'm free. You'll understand quickly."

"Really, Stephanie. Talking about our private affairs in public?" Chase's tone is dripping with disappointment. "Why must you be so unladylike at times?"

My heart pangs with shame at the deprecatory comment. Stomach swirling, my body naturally reacts to his words like it was trained to from years of pleasing him. I try to tamp down the nausea. Felicity is the one who started it, and he didn't chastise her.

My grip tightens on the stem of the champagne flute as I fight for something to say back. Felicity whiffs the second of weakness, eyes lighting with fire as she opens glossy lips to release a snarky comment.

"Stevie, love. Look at you, popular as ever." An English accent breaks through the silence, and a strong arm loops around my shoulders. Felicity's fire is doused instantly. "I've barely had a chance to talk with you all night."

Parker Covington is a sight to behold. If I thought he was attractive from far away, he is even more spectacular up close. His crystal blue eyes glitter with trouble as he smiles at my ex. Unlike the rest of his blond family, Parker's hair seems to be dyed a bright platinum, close cropped on the sides and longer on top. With his high cheekbones and sharp jawline, he looks like a British version of Apollo. There is a small scar on his temple, but it's so faded it almost blends right into his pale skin. Weirdly, it looks a

"Parker Covington." He holds out his hand, and Felicity is quick to grasp it.

"Felicity Taylor, I'm so glad you could make it."

"Yes, well, Dad didn't give us much of a choice. Business deals and all."

"Oh, um, still, it's cool to have you here. You should come out with us more often. I can give you my number so you can stay in the loop for all the up-and-coming events."

Lord, she is laying it on thick.

"Thanks, I'll keep it in mind."

Chase steps forward, displeased with his date fawning over a man who is currently draped over his ex-girlfriend. I couldn't have painted a better scenario myself.

"Chase Broadshire."

The men grip hands but exchange no further words. Chase eyes Parker with a wary gaze, focusing on the way his arm hangs lazily around me.

"You look ravishing tonight, by the way, darling." Parker winks at me, and I smile at the compliment, giving him a laugh. He nods his head back toward Chase. "She's quite the catch, wouldn't you say?"

Parker Covington is sly. He looks like the golden boy everyone wants to be with, but I see the mischief that lurks under his skin.

Chase's nostrils flare slightly, and he speaks through his teeth. "Yes, she is."

Felicity's eyes spark with displeasure, and she returns her vice-like grip to Chase's arm. Parker ignores them both, returning his full attention to me and plucking my empty flute out of my hand.

"Care for another drink?"

"I would adore one."

As Parker goes to steer us away, Chase attempts to step forward to stop us. Felicity, however, tightens her grip to keep him back, and mutters something low in his ear. Chase's upper lip curls slightly, but he relaxes into Felicity's hold. Parker manages to glide us a few steps from the happy couple, but we are halted again when we land in the path of my mother's sharp gaze.

"Stephanie, don't you want to introduce us to your new friend?"

A small, quiet groan leaves my lips. Parker gives my shoulder a squeeze before redirecting us toward the railing my mother and father are leaning against. Vittoria and Michail have gone elsewhere, leaving me to deal with them.

"Parker Covington, lovely to meet you, Mrs. Andwell." He disentangles himself from me, grabbing my mother's hand and leaning down to place a kiss on it.

"Please, call me Cassia," she croons.

My father steps forward, and Parker grips his hand in a healthy shake, exchanging pleasantries.

"Well, I hate to cut our introductions short, but Stevie and I were about to take a walk in the garden, if that's alright."

I can tell my mother wants to inundate Parker with questions, desperate to make a connection with him. But another part of her is trying to scheme a way to get me to become the next Mrs. Covington, and that part wins out.

"Of course, take care of my daughter."

Parker holds my hand, all but running us to the stairs in a desperate attempt to avoid being pulled into any further conversations. My tight dress doesn't allow me much movement, so Parker slows as we walk down the stairs. I wonder if he regrets coming to my rescue.

We descend the last step, and Parker swipes a champagne flute off a nearby waiter, passing it to me before grabbing one himself, downing it in record time, and picking up two more. I laugh at the sight.

"I don't think they're going to run out of champagne anytime soon," I quip.

"Yes, but my sanity might."

I tilt my head in agreement, taking in a healthy gulp of bubbles.

We walk in comfortable silence, and I let the cooling breeze ground me. My mind calms the farther we get from the bustle of the party. When we reach the garden, Parker drops down onto a small bench surrounded by forget-me-nots. He places one of his champagne flutes on the ground next to him before leaning back and nursing the remaining flute. I stare at him, something nagging in the back of my brain. It might be the alcohol catching up to me, but this entire scene gives me a weird sense of déjà vu.

"Have we met before?"

He pauses mid champagne sip, gaze flicking over to me before focusing ahead.

"Nope."

I walk over and sit next to him, crossing my legs and leaning back. My near-empty champagne flute dangles from my hand.

"Really, because it seems like you know me."

"I don't."

"Then how did you know my name? Why did you

wave to me?"

"Coincidence." His Adam's apple bobs up and down as he swallows thickly. He sits up and drains the last of his champagne before placing the empty flute on the ground. His hand clenches before he runs it through his thick hair.

I finish off my glass, analyzing him.

Something's off.

I just don't know what it is, and it's bothering me.

His phone chimes, and he pulls it out of his pocket. I sneak a glance and see a notification alert that looks familiar. It's one that's been popping up on my phone every other night.

Jigsaw pieces begin falling into place. The puzzle isn't complete, but I can make an educated guess of what the image is supposed to be.

It's a longshot. A little out there. But it might just be right.

The only issue is…if I'm right about this…it means I might be right about something else.

"Parker—"

He stands up abruptly, shoving his phone back in his pocket and picking up his remaining champagne flute.

"Great chatting, Stevie, but I have to take care of something."

What the hell.

He gets a few steps before I call out.

"English."

His steps falter, and he whips back around, fear bleeding into those baby blues. He chugs his champagne, then tosses the flute into a bush with complete disregard. I stand up to yell at him, but he takes off in a bolt.

Oh, no you don't, buddy.

I start to run after him, my heels pounding into the stone, but I'm nowhere near as quick in this damn dress. I hike it up, attempting to give myself a little more movement. We get to the stairs, and he begins taking them two at a time.

Ligo. Skata.

I bounce up behind him, the people coming down the opposite side give us bewildered looks. Parker spills onto the patio and starts to shoulder his way through the mingling guests. I cross over the last step and knock into a body. I almost go falling back, right down the staircase, to my death. But the person reaches out and pulls me back.

"If it isn't Stephanie Andwell."

Oh, fuck me with me a pogo stick.

"Daniel Decker."

"Having fun, are we?"

I shake out of his grip, "I'm in a rush, Decker."

"Decker? Seems like those guys are rubbing off on you, Andwell."

Running off on me is more like it. I scan the crowd and spot Parker's stark hair disappearing inside the house. Shit, I'm going to lose him.

"Seriously, I need to go."

He steps aside and gestures in front of him. I eye him warily, surprised at how quickly he relented.

"Thanks," I mutter, stepping past him and then breaking into a jog. I try to move through the crowd as gracefully as possible. The last thing I need to do is bowl over some state judge or CEO.

I make it inside and see Parker through the archway,

standing in the foyer. He gives one of his sisters a kiss on the cheek before slipping out the double doors.

He is not seriously trying to leave, is he?

I jog after him, hiking my dress even higher. There's barely anyone in this part of the house anymore. I speed down the staircase just as a black Tesla Model X pulls up. I push myself faster. Parker hasn't seen me yet; he probably thinks he lost me back on the staircase.

He waits for his driver to step out and lift the door open for him. The delay gives me the edge I need. Parker slides into the car, and I push past his driver, shouting a quick sorry as I dive in after him.

This was not my best idea.

I don't make it fully inside. My body gets caught on Parker, my knees smashing on his thighs. The top half of my body jerks and slams onto the floor between the two seats. My heels kick up in the air, and my purse goes flying somewhere into the third row of seats in the back.

"Owww," I moan.

"Bloody hell, Stevie. Are you mad?"

I scramble my legs forward and off his body, squishing myself on the floor. Pushing up, I corner myself onto the white leather seat next to his. My heart feels like it is beating in my head. I smooth the tendrils of loose hair back from my face as I attempt to catch my breath.

"Sir?"

Parker's driver is looking at him with concern, probably wondering if he needs to call security to get the crazy lady out of the car. Parker leans forward, looking past his driver before snapping his body up. He tries to crush himself flat against the seat.

"Close the door *now*, Francis, and get us out of here quick."

Another puzzle piece slots into place at the name of the driver.

Francis stands back, the door automatically lowering as he walks to the driver's side. I lean forward to peer out Parker's window, trying to see what spooked him more than me flinging myself into his car.

Decker stands in the entrance chatting with Parker's sister. I have no doubt in my mind that he is going to go back into that party and let everyone know we left together. Gossiping jerk.

The car rumbles to life, and we drive in silence for a few minutes, soft music trickling from the speakers.

It's a Friday night, so the streets are packed with cars. I'm not sure what time it is, but it has to be before nine since we never did get to eat dinner. Dammit, the food and booze are the only good reasons to go to these events.

The car windows are a deep black, probably tinted. I stare out at the moving cars, blurs of light against the dark night. We get stuck in a pocket of traffic, and I slip from my seat, reaching around in the back until I locate my purse. Settling back against the soft leather of my chair, I take out my phone and swipe it open, eyes dipping briefly to the broody man next to me.

Parker's giving me the silent treatment.

Parker is also driving me god knows where.

I pull open the streaming app; a little red circle shows Blade is still live. I click on the search bar and type in EnglishCoffee. I tap on the account, opening his page. The most recent stream was yesterday. I press my volume all

243

the way up and click on the stream recording. It takes a second to load before the crisp accent blares out from my phone.

"Hello, hello, hello. How are we doing, my little Coffee Makers?"

Parker jumps in my periphery.

"We just got a new patch update for Legends of Destiny, so I figured we would give it another shot since the buggy release. Then, we will jump on with the lads and play a little FrozeLine later, how does that sound?"

We stare at each other before he lunges over, ripping the phone from my hands and shutting the screen. The voice cuts out.

"I'm right, aren't I?"

He folds his arms and stares forward.

If he wants to deny it, he isn't doing a good job. At all.

"You know, the silent treatment just incriminates yourself further."

"I have no idea what you're talking about."

I pinch the bridge of my nose.

"Seriously?"

This is like pulling teeth.

I can't blame him. If I'm right, and I'm pretty damn sure I'm right, I've just discovered something no one is supposed to know. The information I'm sitting on is worth thousands of dollars. Maybe even hundreds of thousands to the right bidder.

Not that I would sell this information. I don't care about that. I don't care if Parker is English or if English is Parker. It's all the same to me. What does make a difference is the little seedling that has been growing in my stomach ever since that night at the club. This niggling sensation that maybe there is something more to Alek's job than he has been letting on.

My cell phone rings. Parker stares at the foreign sound in his hand. He tosses the phone back to me, and I see a call from my mother.

I send it to voicemail.

Parker's phone rings, but he answers it.

"Sorry, I had to leave, something came up. Yes, I know. I know. *I know.* It is an emergency. No, she—Alright, I'll be home Sunday night." He hangs up with a sigh.

"Fuck. Me." Parker runs his hands down his face.

"Sorry to interrupt, Mr. Covington, but I need to know where I'm headed."

Parker peeks out from between his fingers and groans, mumbling his words.

"The apartment."

I see the driver's eyes widen in the rearview mirror.

"The apartment?"

"Yes, Francis. The apartment."

"Are you sure?"

"Unfortunately, yes. I have to do some damage control."

Pretty sure I'm the damage.

"Alright, it'll take a bit longer, probably an hour from now. We have a tail."

"Of course, we do."

Parker reaches under the seat in front of him, rummaging for a minute until he pulls out a silver flask. He opens it, taking a large gulp before holding it out to me.

"You're going to need it for the night we have ahead."

His laugh is bitter.

I accept the flask and take a small sip, the heat of whiskey burning my throat.

For the first time since I took off running after Parker, worry filters into my system, and I begin to wonder if I made a mistake. I don't think I'm wrong about Parker secretly being one of the biggest streamers of our generation, but I do think I might have made a mistake in confirming it. Because it seems like whatever is waiting at *the apartment* is not going to be good.

We pull into a private underground parking lot beneath a dazzling glass apartment complex. Francis parks the car next to a black Escalade, gets out, and opens the door for me. I take his hand and step out onto the concrete. Parker doesn't wait, jumping out my side as well.

I wobble on my feet slightly, all the alcohol catching up to me over the long drive. Parker doesn't look any better. He runs his hands through his hair for the thousandth time, then twists the hoops in his ears. I've come to recognize it's his nervous twitch.

"Alright, Stevie. Let's see how bad this can get."

He tugs at his tie, loosening it, before throwing an arm around my shoulders.

"Bye, Francis." He dramatically salutes.

"Thank you!" I add on.

Francis' parting words are a mere "good luck," but they feel like a death sentence.

Parker steers us toward a set of elevators, but my eyes are darting around the private lot. There is a row of luxury cars, Porsches, Maseratis, Ferraris, plus a stray Jeep. My eyes snag on a set of motorcycles, and I halt. Parker continues walking forward, and we jerk against each other.

"Having second thoughts? Sorry, love, you can't really back out now."

"No. No, it's not that," I stare at the black motorcycle, my tipsy brain trying to put the wires together and failing. "You know what, it's nothing."

Parker hits the elevator button, and my heart rate spikes.

I'm nervous. I have no idea what is waiting up there for me.

The doors ding open, and Parker hits the PH button before leaning us against the back of the elevator. I watch as the number crawls higher and higher, heart in my throat.

Oh god, I'm going to throw up.

Okay, I won't, but these damn nerves feel like it. Like I have a swarm of bees in my chest fighting to find their way out. The buzzing is insane.

My ears pop as we pass the fiftieth floor, and it dulls my senses, bringing in a sliver of calm.

Finally, the elevator pings. A robotic voice announces, "Penthouse."

Parker pushes off the wall, bringing me with him. He hasn't let go of me this entire time. I appreciate it because I'm not sure I could stand on my own with the nerves and liquor trembling under my skin. I'd rather go into whatever is awaiting us as somewhat of a team. I steel my eyes ahead as the doors open.

My first thought is that this apartment is gorgeous.

It's modern, with sleek white walls and gray marble tiles. The elevator opens into a small hallway with a closet, but a bunch of men's shoes are strewn all over the floor in front of it–complete disregard for said closet. The opposite wall is lined with four neon art pieces, an X, O, triangle, and square. We step out of the elevator, and my heels clink on the tiles, alarmingly loud.

"Parker?" a female voice rings out.

"Hey, dude, thought you were crashing at your parent's?" a male voice joins in.

We round the corner and enter the main living space. It has a completely open layout with floor-to-ceiling windows lining the entire right wall where the kitchen and dining table are. There looks to be a small outdoor space with a balcony that runs along the right side as well. There are two hallways, one to my left and another between the kitchen and living room. Straight ahead is a gorgeous black L-shaped couch facing what seems to be a ninety-eight-inch flatscreen mounted above an electric fireplace. The wall ahead is lined with various gaming memorabilia, but my eyes snag on the giant poster of The System.

Oh shit. He brought me to their apartment.

There is a giant golden-skinned guy sprawled out against the couch, snacking on a bag of popcorn. When his eyes meet mine, a handful of popcorn drops onto his chest. My own purse falls to the ground as I realize I'm staring at the guy whose car I crashed into. Jackson pushes himself up with lightning speed.

"The fuck, Parker?" His voice is a roar.

"Boys, it's almost midnight, can we keep it down." A

petite blonde girl closes the fridge and turns around. Like a scene on repeat, when her stormy eyes meet mine, the bottle she is holding drops. "Crap!" She jumps back as it clangs loudly on the tiles.

Her gaze narrows as it zips to the blond man draped over my body.

"Parker. What in the ever-loving-god is going on here?" She grips her temples, closing her eyes. "I must be seeing things, because out of all the stupid things you have ever done, this is worse than all of them combined." She's quiet for a few seconds. Then, her controls snaps. Her eyes flash open and pure anger streams out. "Are you freaking kidding me?" she screeches.

I stare at her, something seeming familiar. This entire interaction has sobered me up a little, and I fight through the bubbly haze. The wires connect, and my mouth pops open.

"Sydney?"

She gives me a double take, recognition setting in.

"Stevie?"

A war of emotions seems to run through her, from shock to confusion to fury. She stalks over to me, and I back up farther into Parker. In my heels, she's a solid six inches shorter than me, but it doesn't make her any less intimidating in this moment.

"Were you following me?" She points a finger at me. "Were you at the juice bar to get closer to them? What are you? A reporter? A groupie? A stalker?"

Irritation growls in my gut, and I push her finger away.

"Are you serious? No. Why on earth would I even do that?"

The idea sounds beyond ridiculous.

Until I remember who these guys are, and the frustration fizzles out. I'm standing here like some foreign code in their system. They don't know whether I'm here to ruin them or not. Of course they'd be distrustful.

"One of you better start explaining right now, or I'm calling security *and* our lawyers." Sydney's cold stare pierces through me.

Panic begins to take over. I've made a huge mistake. My heart rate is increasing, anxiety working its way through my body. I start fidgeting then, my fingers curling in on themselves, opening, and then curling again. I repeat the motion over and over.

"Look," Parker holds his free hand out, "I didn't fuck up, not really."

"Doesn't look that way, my guy." Jackson gets off the couch and comes to tower behind Sydney.

"Parker, I am actually going to murder you." Sydney props her hand on her hip, "In fact, I'm going to have to murder *both* of you. I can't even begin to fathom the scenario that would warrant you doing something so risky."

I hear something rattle. My eyes dart left, down the hallway. One of the doors opens and out steps a bedraggled guy in a hoodie, messy brown hair peeking out. Everyone is still fighting.

"Seriously, you guys. I just got off a four-hour stream. Unless someone is dying, can you shut the fuck up?" His voice is laced with exhaustion.

The new guy stands tall, lifting his head. Green eyes meet mine, and the world stops.

It just.

Stops.

I was right.

Black dots fill my vision as my breathing quickens, body shaking. The sounds of everyone arguing begin to dull.

I watch as Aleks' lips move, forming one word.

My name.

And then, I pass out.

Chapter
TWENTY-FOUR

ALEKS

I need to start planning Parker's funeral since he is a dead man.

Actually, I don't even have to worry about murdering him since it looks like Sydney will be doing it for me. She won't even make it a quick death. That girl looks like she is going to strap him to a chair and tear his toenails off one by one. Maybe she'll castrate him too, play ping-pong with his balls.

Instinct has me rushing forward to grab Stevie as she crumples in Parker's arms.

The last sixty seconds play on loop in my mind as a stare down at her.

I was pissed, walking out of my streaming room to a bunch of people shouting. When I saw her, everything came to a halt. I thought I was momentarily hallucinating. Stevie looked like an absolute vision in her tight gold gown. The light sparkling off the dress turned her ethereal. Transcendent. Until reality came crashing down.

I lift her out of Parker's arms into a princess carry. Everyone is staring at her with mixed emotions, anger and concern bleeding together. Ignoring them, I walk her over to my bedroom, kneeing open the door. I lay her on my bed and untangle her hair from her face. Worry needles its way into my chest as I stare at her.

Seventeen thousand emotions are running through me, but Stevie's safety is at the forefront.

Running my thumb over her wrist, I check her pulse. Her heartbeat is steadying out, and it seems like her breathing is relatively normal. I reach down and slip off her heels, placing them on the floor next to the bed. I give my room a quick once over, but it's relatively clean minus a collection of empty glasses strewn about and my pile of jackets in the corner. I push off the bed and leave her to rest while I go back out to deal with the shitshow.

"Alright, everyone shut the fuck up and go sit on the couch."

The three of them turn to look at me, and I cross my arms. In the distraction, Parker all but sprints away from Sydney and throws himself protectively into the corner of the couch, hugging a pillow to his chest.

Sydney huffs at me before trudging over and perching herself on the arm of the couch farthest from Parker. Jackson follows me over and sits down on the cushion next to Sydney. I lower myself to the coffee table so I'm facing them all.

I can see the wheels turning in Sydney's mind. She's

working at a mile a minute, running through thousands of scenarios, planning hundreds of defense measures, trying to solve a puzzle she only has half the pieces to.

"Parker." I turn to him, and he stares at me with big blue puppy-dog eyes. Fucking hell. "Care to explain how you ended up bringing Stevie back to our apartment?"

"Wait, you all know her?" Sydney cuts in.

Jackson just laughs, giving me a look that says, *"all you, dude."*

"We met her at the VSAs, she was a server. Then we saw her again when we went to Electric Tyger. She hung out with us a little bit."

"Yeah, if you call grinding on her ass in the club 'hanging out.'"

Jackson has the gall to use air quotes.

"So, she *is* a groupie. Goddammit." Sydney whips out her phone.

"No!" Parker and I shout, me lunging forward to rip Syd's phone from her hand.

"Can you just listen to us for a second?" I plead. I might be pissed as hell at Parker for giving away our apartment location and bringing Stevie back here without any safety measures, but there is a kernel of sick happiness there as well.

Sydney narrows her gaze on me. Her bloodhound abilities rise as she studies me.

"You're not telling me something. This seems like more than a two-hit wonder."

Great. I'm really not sure how I'm going to get out of this unscathed. Parker and I might both be at equal risk of murder when this is all over. Although, my death at least might be a little swifter. Maybe.

"I might have run into Stevie a few times as Aleks, not Blade."

"What's a few times?"

"Like…four or five?"

"*Four or five* is a pattern, Aleksander." She tilts her head. "Are you seeing her?"

"Not technically."

"Meaning?"

"We went on two dates..."

"I knew it!" Parker shouts, throwing his pillow at me. "You've been proper chuffed lately, texting all the time. Nice one, mate."

"Not. The fucking. Time." I grind at him through closed teeth.

"Aleksander Knight. As your publicist, I need to know these things. I can't do my job if you keep me in the shadows. How you all failed to mention this woman hasn't escaped me. Aleks is not the only one in trouble here. You all are."

"Oh, come on, what have I done?" Jackson throws his arms up.

"Don't play pretend with me, Jackson Lau. Parker here might have had a hunch about Aleksander sneaking off, but I'll bet a month's worth of salary that you knew, without a doubt. I bet you even covered for him."

Jackson purses his lips, looking in the opposite direction of Syd.

"Alright, we'll deal with this later. What I want to know is how she ended up here."

We all turn to Parker. He just stares at us with wide

eyes, holding his hands out in front of his body.

"Now, now. Let's not all gang up on Parker, okay?"

I grab the pillow he tossed at me and throw it back, whacking him.

"Stop screwing around."

"Fine, fine. She was at the party I went to tonight." He points to me. "Remember when I told you she seemed familiar? It's because she is an Andwell. Her family runs in all the high society circles here. Now, don't get me wrong. I didn't know she was an Andwell until I got to the party and saw her. By then I'd already waved to her."

"And she had no clue who you were or how you knew her." Sydney sighs.

"No…"

"Which made her suspicious."

"Kind of? She was getting into it with her ex and his new girlfriend, so I stepped in, took her to get some champagne and get away from the crowd. Those events are breeding grounds for twisted emotions. I don't know how she did it, but she started piecing things together. She guessed who I was, and I just kind of…bolted."

"You bolted." Sydney stares at him in disbelief. "Are you serious?"

"Of course! And then the crazy chick ran after me, right through the party in her damn heels. All but threw herself into the car."

"Crazy isn't a nice word to use, English."

We all whip our heads around to stare at the tall brunette leaning against the wall in the hallway.

"And I didn't throw myself into the car, I dove, gracefully."

"If a stone is graceful," Parker scoffs.

She ignores us, padding into the kitchen, dress swishing as it drags around her. We watch as she begins to open random cupboards until she locates a glass and fills it up with water from the fridge dispenser. She takes a sip, eying me over the rim. Normally, she bleeds her emotions, but right now, I can't read a thing.

She is stone cold.

"I can't believe you just told her who you were," Sydney groans.

"Actually, Parker never verbally admitted he was English. Just ran like his ass was on fire." She sits on one of the stools at the island. Everyone is twisted on the couch to watch her. "I highly suggest you never try to rob a bank or anything, you'd be god-awful."

"Alright, so if he never told you…then why the hell did you bring her here?"

"Because she knew," Parker whines. "She was in the car, and she knew. I figured, *what the hell*, why not just bring her back and let us deal with it together."

We collectively groan.

"Alright, I'm giving our lawyers a call, getting an NDA drawn up. Then I'm going to make sure no cameras caught your little escapade." Sydney arches around, "you have no issue signing an NDA, Stevie, do you?"

"Depends on the terms," Stevie shrugs.

"Fair." Syd swipes open her phone, grabbing her tablet from the coffee table and heading onto the balcony to make the call.

The four of us stare at each other. The room is silent save for the slight murmur of the TV from whatever show

Jackson was watching.

I stand up and start to make my way to Stevie, cautiously. She's like a panther on the loose, lazily prowling, and I'm a hunter, trying not to scare her off.

"Are you feeling okay?"

She just shrugs again.

"Since we're all fully stuck in this situation, I suppose we should reintroduce ourselves." Jackson pushes off the couch and strolls over, sticking his hand out for her. "Jackson Lau, also known as Shield3d, the green mask of The System. I'm a Sagittarius, I enjoy working out, and I would do anything for my younger siblings."

His hand rests in the air for a few seconds after he finishes, long enough that I begin to doubt she is going to shake it. Just when I see Jackson twitch, Stevie's hand glides forward and gives him a small shake.

She's still silent. Watching.

Parker jogs over. He has too much energy for someone who was just on the chopping block. But then again, that's Parker for you.

"Parker Covington, also beloved by the name English-Coffee. Acclaimed speedrunner, British billionaire, and vehicle enthusiast. I hate coffee, but I love champagne."

Stevie's mask starts to slip, the corner of her mouth twitching up. I feel a pang of jealousy toward my best friend. When she puts her hand in his, he bends down and drops a kiss on it. "Enchanté, mademoiselle."

Her mask fully drops then, a snort tumbling out of her.

"You're a loser, Parker."

"A rich and attractive loser," he winks.

I take a small step forward, and her eyes whip to mine.

The laughter fading.

My throat is dry, but I power forward, putting my hand out to her.

"Aleksander Knight, also known as NightBlade32." I scratch the back of my neck, stalling. "I like gaming, bikes, and anything chocolate. I hate events, and I hate that I made you hate me."

She drops my gaze, but I keep my hand straight. I'll keep my hand hovering here for as long as it takes. Hell, I'll drop to my knees if I need to.

Stevie slips off the stool, gold material pooling around her feet. Her lithe hand caresses mine.

"Stephanie Andwell." She looks into my eyes, burning into my soul. "I love art, action movies, and anything maple-syrup flavored. I hate pink roses and that I'm still trapped in this dress, but I don't hate you."

My body relaxes, hope blooming.

"Want to change into one of my shirts?"

She eyes me warily for a second, nibbling on her lower lip. My heart pauses as it waits.

"Sure."

One word, and my heart starts beating again. She hasn't released my hand, so I hold it tighter, bringing her to my room. I rifle through my closet, grabbing an old gaming tournament T-shirt and a pair of basketball shorts she can tie up. She takes them from me, tossing them on my bed. Then, she turns her back to me, swiping her hair to the side, revealing a smooth triangle of skin.

I watch as she reaches up and unzips the top of her dress, the gold fabric splitting away, revealing her tan back in tantalizing segments. I'm mesmerized by her movements.

She reaches the base of her back, then shrugs each of her arms out of the dress. The fabric collects at her waist, and I stare at her state of undress, my cock twitching.

She leans forward, tugging at the fabric on her hips, shimmying out of it. Once it's over her hips, her ass sits on display for me. She's leaning far enough forward that I can see the outline of her pussy. Fuck, she's not wearing any underwear.

I move forward as she proceeds to drop the dress to the ground, the shimmering fabric reflecting the LED lights in my room.

I run a finger over her hip, and she swats it away, half turning her body to me.

"I don't hate you, but I'm still mad at you."

"I know."

She holds up the T-shirt and shorts, assessing them briefly before tossing them back on the bed. Instead, she shoulders past me, one of her breasts grazing my arm. She walks, completely naked, to my closet and rummages through it herself. My length thickens at the sight, want needling under my skin. I have to readjust myself for some relief.

She pulls out a large The System T-shirt and shrugs it over her head. It reaches her mid thigh, the sleeves hitting her elbows. She looks at herself in my mirror and smiles, satisfied. Then she moseys back to my bed, lifting the covers and crawling inside.

I move to sit on the edge of the bed, and it dips below my weight.

"I couldn't tell you, Stevie."

"I know."

She brings her knees to her chest, resting her chin on them.

"I know, and that makes it more frustrating. Because I can't really be mad at you for not telling me. We're not even officially dating; why would you have told me this secret. A secret that virtually no one knows. One people would pay for. One, it seems, Sydney would murder to keep."

I keep silent, not interrupting. I let her talk it through, feel out her emotions.

"But I still feel lied to, and I'm still hurt. I feel like I was tricked, like I was played with. I was vulnerable with you in two different ways. I was falling for one guy while lusting over another, telling myself to not feel guilty over it, only to learn they're one and the same." Her brows scrunch then. "Actually, I suppose that is kind of a win-win situation."

She shoves her forehead against her knees and lets out a long, loud groan.

"Why does this have to be so goddamn confusing?"

She stays like that for a minute before I scoot forward and rub my hand up and down her back. I still don't say anything, letting her soak it all in. Giving her what little comfort I can without words.

I want to say everything. I want to tell her it was all real. Everything she experienced with Aleks, everything with Blade, they were both me. That I came *this close* to bringing her back here the night at the club, saying fuck it all, just like Parker did. To showing her the truth because I wanted to let her in.

Because in the short period of time that I've known her, she has completely crushed my world and rebuilt it around herself. My universe doesn't revolve around the sun, it revolves around Stevie. Seeing her smile is like the stars lighting up the night sky. She's the moon and I'm the tide; she pulls me in when she's near, and when she's away, I crave her touch.

She lifts her head, the mascara around her caramel eyes smudged.

"What happens now, Blade?"

"Now, you decide how we move on, little dove."

Her brows pinch together. I grab her hands, pulling them away from her knees, holding them in my own.

"You swept into my life one night and disappeared without a trace. Everywhere I went, I searched for your face. For the chance that the fates would cause our paths to cross again. It drove me nuts, Stevie. And then it happened: I found you again, and again, and again." I squeeze her hands. "Whether it was Blade or Aleksander, it was me. It was real, every text, every touch, every kiss, everything."

She blushes then, and I smile. I live for her blushes, for when she gets shy or nervous.

"I wish I could have told you, but I had to think about more than myself. The System is my everything, *our* everything. It's what we all rely on. As selfish as I can be at times, I know where the line is."

She squeezes my hand.

"I want to be with you, Stevie. I want to see where this can go. I trust you, and maybe that's silly after only knowing you for two months. But every morning I look forward to those little texts you send, and I can't imagine a world where they just stop."

She bites her lip, eyes glistening.

"I trust you, too. And I would never betray your secret, or either of the guys'. NDA or not, that's just not me." She lets out a stuttering breath, her voice small. "I want to see where this can go, too. I'm scared, don't get me wrong. You're the gaming world's number one heartthrob—"

"Actually, I'm only in the top five."

"Oh my god." She shoves me back. "I'm serious. It's like dating an actor, something I swore to myself I would never do. But…I can't imagine going to bed without seeing your goodnight texts. It would feel like a hole in my life. So, I'm trusting you, Aleksander Knight. I'm giving you my heart. I just ask that you take care of it."

"I'd sooner rip my own heart out than shatter yours, Stephanie Andwell."

I hold her chin, eyes flicking to her soft lips. She smiles, and it's the confirmation I need. I start softly, a bare brushing of lips. Then I drink her in slowly.

Kissing Stevie is like drowning in an ocean. The pressure builds around you, dulling every sense as it burns you from the inside out. Just when you think it's the end, when you begin to run out of breath, you gasp that one last time and slip into euphoric oblivion. It's a heady bliss.

She tastes like all that is right in the world. I could kiss her for days, lose myself in her lips.

She sighs into me, and I take her breath like it's my own.

Her legs fall open, and I maneuver my body between them. I hold her head, devouring her with kisses while laying her flat against the bed. I lift up, gripping the comforter and ripping it to the side to reveal her body, not letting my lips leave hers for one moment.

Stevie is my sin and my salvation. She tastes like an angel, but kisses like the devil. Her nails rake into my back, and I roll my body against hers, groaning as my stiff cock rubs against her through the fabric of my sweatpants. She's hot already, and it spurs me on.

I'm starving for her, desperate to feel her skin on mine. I slide and kick off my sweatpants, my cock springing free. We continue our assault of tongues and lips, drinking each other in. The emotions of the night make everything taste sweeter.

Her legs come up to hook around my back, and I grind into her sweet heat, my cock sliding through the folds of her wet pussy. I coat myself in her, growing harder and harder with each pass. Her hips lift higher, and the tip of my cock slips against her opening.

We both groan at the sensation.

It's a fucking tease but in the best way possible. We're not edging, we're not having sex, it's everything but.

Reluctantly, I pull away from her lips. I reach behind my neck and pull off my hoodie, tossing it onto the ground. Stevie crosses her arms, peeling off the T-shirt, letting it fall to the wayside.

She just gets sexier and sexier every time I see her. I worship her body, starting with her breasts. I palm them, rubbing her nipples in circles, kissing her soft lips at the same time. Just as she begins to squirm against me, I give her nipples a tug. She sucks in a breath, but I feel her smile against my lips.

My cock is drenched in her arousal, and I'm not sure how much longer I can go without being inside her. I'm so lost in my thoughts of her body, that Stevie uses the distraction to flip us over.

I must look shocked because she giggles.

"I'm all for a good time, Aleks. But I'm tired of waiting. I want you inside me now. I'm fucking starving, and I need my fill of cock." She dips down, sucking on my nipple piercing, tongue twisting the barbell before impaling herself on my cock in one swift motion.

I slide right into her, and with her on top, she controls just how deep I go. She drives herself right down to my base, so I'm completely buried in her.

"Fuck, Stevie," I growl.

My mind becomes a blank space as she finds her rhythm, grinding on me. She leans forward a bit, and her eyes squeeze shut as I feel her pussy clench around me. She's just as wound up as I am, running too close to the sun.

"Eyes on me, baby."

Her eyes slowly open, and she gives me a wicked grin.

I rock my hips into hers, matching her rhythm. Our bodies slap together, a mess of sweat and a tangle of limbs. Her movements begin to stutter, and her hands hit the mattress as she grips the sheets tightly.

"Fuck, it's right there. Right fucking there."

She chases her orgasm, using me for her pleasure. It's sexy as fuck as her tits bounce up and down in time with her rhythm. She reaches down to play with her clit, and I watch, mesmerized, as her eyes tip back in her head.

She gasps, and I feel her break. Her pussy pulses,

squeezing rhythmically around my cock. I watch the pleasure rush over her face, her mouth popping open before she bites her lips, a high moan escaping, nonetheless. She falls against my body, breathing heavily. Our sweat mixes, and our bodies continue to burn.

But I don't let her rest. I flip us around, my cock still fully seated within her. I draw my dick out slowly, before plunging it back in. She cries out as I repeat the motion, over and over, her eyes squeezing shut.

"Ohmigod, it's too much. I can't. Aleks!"

"Yes, you can. Come on, baby. Show me how good you take my cock."

She's beyond sensitive, still coming down from her high, but I'm building it back up. When I feel her clench around me, I start pistoning into her. Deep, strong strokes. I'm right on the edge, my balls tightening within an inch of their lives, desperate to give me release. She cries out, a smaller release this time as she quivers around my cock.

I let go then, falling with her, filling her up. My hot release spills inside her, and I chase the euphoria with a few last jerks, groaning.

My energy is completely spent. I pull out of her, my dick slick with both of our arousals. I look down and watch as some of my cum leaks out of her, satisfaction purring in my chest. I place a kiss on her stomach as I use my fingers to push it back in. The post-nut clarity brings me to another level; I feel like I could do anything.

Until the clarity makes one thing very fucking clear.

I freeze.

"Shit. Shit!"

I sit up on my knees. Stevie stares at me with confusion, propping herself up on her elbows.

"What's wrong?"

"I forgot the condom."

I'm such an idiot. I've never forgotten it before. It's the one thing I'm really good at remembering when it comes to sex, or at least I thought it was. Then again, I haven't had repeat sex with a person in years. That already says so much about how serious I am about Stevie.

She blinks at me for a few seconds. Then she purses her lips to the side, humming. Her eyes flick to mine and away, then they flick back and away again.

"Well. I have an IUD, and I'm clean. I got tested when I broke up with my ex. I will, however, need to go pee so I don't get a UTI."

Shame floods my body then.

"I haven't been tested in a while." I'm honest with her. I'm not going to sit here and say I was magically tested recently when I haven't been. I think the last time was six months ago. It's out of pure laziness, and now I'm kicking myself.

She sits up, putting a hand on my shoulder and giving me a smile.

"Hey, it's fine. We'll figure it out." She places a kiss on my cheek and slips off the bed. But I remain stewing with guilt and frustration. She leans down, cupping my cheek. "Aleksander, I'm serious. Get out of your head and come join me in the shower. As sexy as it is to have your scent all over me, I need to wash this sweat off or I'll never sleep."

"Oh, are you sleeping over now?" I tease.

I watch as she shrugs her shoulders and slips into the bathroom, "I plan on sleeping here. Whether that's in your bed or someone else's is up to you to decide."

A bolt of possessiveness runs through me at the thought of her in Parker's or Jackson's bed.

I jump out of the bed and run into the bathroom to join her as I hear the shower turn on. I let myself get lost in taking care of her, allowing the fears to drain away. I soap up her soft body inch by inch. She's careful to keep her hair out of the water, even though I sprinkle her with a few drops here and there—which earns me some stern glares. She runs her hands up and down my body in return. I bend, allowing her to wash my hair, humming as she massages my scalp. I might never let my hair be washed again if it's not by her. This feels too good.

I let her use my big fluffy towel to dry while I shake off and pad into my room to replace my sheets with a new ones. We tumble into bed together, exhausted, but even my dreams are filled with thoughts of her.

Chapter
TWENTY-FIVE

STEVIE

The smell of fresh coffee mixed with a light sweetness pulls me from my dreams. I crack my eyes open, but the room is still completely dark save for the LED lights Aleks has lining his ceiling.

I'm hugging him like a tree, one arm strewn across his chest with a leg thrown over his body, his hand holding onto my calf. My ear is connected to his chest, and I can hear the steady *thump, thump, thump* as his chest rises with soft breaths. He looks so much younger when he sleeps, vulnerable. I memorize the lines of his face, the slope of his nose, the curve of his lashes. My eyes catch on the scar on his temple, and my hand flutters up to touch it.

Oh. *That's* what bothered me. I noticed the scar when we were together after the gallery exhibit, and when I touched it the night with Blade, my brain realized the same thing. I also bet Parker is the friend he crashed with. His scar had seemed too familiar.

I know if I explained this situation to anyone else, they'd think I was nuts. Trusting a guy who had been lying to me, living a double life. One who let me fall for both versions of himself.

But I'm sick of listening to everyone else.

My heart was falling for Aleks as it was lusting over Blade. Now, it has both in one hot, tattooed package. I basically won the boyfriend lottery, and I'm not giving up my prize. I spent too many years unhappy. Playing the perfect girlfriend for Chase and my mother and telling myself it was enough, when in reality, I was starving. I'd become an empty shell that was putting on a show so no one saw the hollowness within. In the short time I've been with Aleks, he has filled me with so much light, scaring the darkness away. More than anything, I feel like my true self around him. He lets me feel seen, adored. And I deserve that.

Aleks is sleeping like the dead. He's so out of it that I'm not even worried about jostling him awake as I disentangle my body from his. I slip out of the bed, and he groans, rolling onto his side.

I search the floor for the T-shirt I grabbed last night. It's a gray acid wash shirt with The System written in metal-band font. I'd kill for this in a crop-top version. I wonder if he has others that I could try cutting up.

I tug it over my head, padding into the bathroom to assess my current state. Which looks…not awful. Not great. But not awful.

I got all my makeup off in the shower with a cleanser and used Aleks' surprisingly expensive moisturizer before heading to bed. He felt the need to defend his masculinity by reiterating multiple times that Parker had bought all the skincare products for him. I kept telling him I didn't care who bought it, just that I'm impressed he has more than a two-in-one shampoo and conditioner.

My hair, however, looks like a rat's nest. I tugged out the bobby pins keeping the Dutch braids secure behind my head and let them loose before I went to bed, but the back of my head is still a mess of knots. I attempt to run my hands through it, fingers snagging. After a few minutes, it looks mildly better—like a rat's vacation home. I wet my hands with some water, running it through my hair, smoothing it down, then I grab some mouthwash, swishing it around and spitting it out. The minty taste burns my mouth, making everything feel astronomically cleaner. I give myself a wide grin in the mirror.

Well, that's as good as it's going to get.

Opening the bedroom door, I find a set of folded clothes along with my purse. I crouch down, setting them apart. It's a pair of women's workout shorts, a tank top, and underwear. I throw the underwear and workout shorts on. I don't bother with the tank top. The T-shirt I'm wearing smells like Aleks—there's a slight motor oil scent mixed with his pine body wash—so there's no chance in hell I'm trading it out.

My eyes are instantly assaulted by the bright morning light leaking in through the windows as I walk into the living space. God, Aleks' blackout curtains must be worth a fortune if they stopped this from coming into his bat cave.

Jackson has his back to me in the kitchen, his black hair tied in a half bun, sweatpants slung low on his hips.

271

I'm surprised to see a large black tiger tattoo spilling down his back. His muscles contract and ripple as he cooks what smells like eggs on the stove. The guy is absolutely ripped. I have a feeling if he turned around, he would be sporting an eight-pack or something.

I don't want to startle him, so I throw out a tentative, "Morning."

He twists his head around and smiles at me. "Morning, just getting some brunch ready. Figured you all could use it after the night you had."

My cheeks warm up, and it's not from the heat of the kitchen. Oh god, they probably all heard us having sex. They were right here in the living room. Only a couple feet away.

He smirks at me. "I was more so referencing the fact that you all skipped out on dinner, but I guess you probably need the energy for other activities as well."

"Right. Dinner."

Shit, I haven't texted anyone since my disappearing act. I pull my phone out of my purse only to see that it's dead. Double shit.

I spot a charging cable hanging from the island and plug it in before standing next to Jackson. He opens the oven and pulls out a small tray of bacon. The scent wafts through the kitchen, and my stomach growls. I'm not even the biggest fan of bacon, but something about the smell just tells your body it's time to eat. It's a comforting smell, bringing back memories of early childhood mornings by the beach in the summer. Jackson tongs the strips into a dish that has a variety of cooked eggs in it before covering it with a lid.

"Can I help?"

I hate that I'm just standing here, doing nothing.

"Sure. Can you grab some condiments from the fridge and put them on the island? I already have the plates set up there. I'm just going to get the waffles ready, and then we'll wake up the sleeping beauties."

"Wow, waffles? You're going all out." I pull open the fridge and start pulling out various condiments from the side compartment. It's more stocked than I would expect for a guys' fridge. There is actual food in here, not just energy drinks, beer, and take-out boxes.

"Trust me, it's not like this every weekend. I like to leave them to fend for themselves occasionally. It humbles them."

"Hey, now, don't lump me in with Parker. At least I can cook for myself. Parker starves if there's no food."

I turn around, drinking in Aleks' disheveled form. He is just wearing a pair of gray sweatpants, tattoos on display and nipple piercing glinting in the sunlight. I lick my lips.

"My eyes are up here, babe." He winks.

I scoff, turning back around. I locate a bottle of maple syrup in the back of the fridge along with some whipped cream and smile triumphantly.

Aleks comes up behind me, looping his arms around my waist.

"You look sexy in my shirt," he whispers in my ear. It sends a shiver down my spine. "Even sexier knowing there's nothing underneath."

"Sorry to disappoint but I'm all covered up. There was a set of clothes left for me."

"Tsk," he lets go of me, "Sydney." He reaches around

me, pulling out some milk and chocolate syrup, and plops them on the table before skirting around me to fiddle with an elaborate espresso machine.

I sit on a stool at the island, observing Jackson and Aleks. They are fit as hell, all lean muscles and tight asses. This entire apartment is full of attractive guys. If anyone knew The System were this hot under their masks, they'd have a heart attack.

Aleks parks himself next to me at the island, handing me a cup of coffee.

"Sorry, we don't have any creamer. Jackson and I are the only ones who drink coffee, and he likes it black."

"Then how do you like it?" I've only ever seen him drink mocha lattes.

Jackson deposits a plate stacked with fresh, crispy waffles in front of me, and I light up at the smell, my mouth watering. "Oh, you're about to find out. And I'm going to apologize in advance for the absolute atrocity you're about to see."

He walks off, banging on a door in the hallway next to the kitchen, barking at Parker to wake up. All the while, I watch as Aleks pours himself half a glass of milk, squeezing in the chocolate syrup and mixing it. It seems like he is just making chocolate milk. Then, I watch as he pours two shots of espresso into it, stirs, and takes a sip.

His sip is obnoxiously loud, and he looks right at Jackson. "Yum."

"Okay, that's not *that* weird." It's just a shoddy version of a mocha latte if you think about it. Like the Dollar Tree version.

"God, you two are made for each other, then." Jackson

takes his seat at the end of the island, next to Aleks. "This guy has the biggest sweet tooth." He juts his thumb into Aleks' shoulder before plating breakfast for himself from the array before us.

"I don't like all sweets, I just like chocolate," Aleks volleys back, snatching up the waffle Jackson was in the process of picking up. Jackson swats it out of his hand, and the waffle goes slapping onto the marble.

I laugh at them, sipping my coffee. It's a comforting environment. It's been forever since I've been around this.

I grab two waffles after they've finished fighting over them, dousing mine in maple syrup, letting it fill up the little squares. I'm about to reach for the whipped cream when Aleks snatches it out of my hand.

"Hey!"

He just smirks at me, shaking it and spraying it over my waffles. I watch as he draws a little whipped cream heart, my own heart doing a flip at the cheesy display of affection.

"Aww." I lean forward, giving him a peck.

"Well, I feel very single."

Parker's morning voice is deeper than normal. It makes his accent thicker somehow. He drops into the stool next to me, grabbing a slice of watermelon before his ass even hits the seat. He is wearing nothing other than a pair of blue trunks. I'm beginning to think everything this guy owns is blue. That, and that the men of this apartment have an aversion to clothing.

I cut a piece of my waffle, bringing it to my mouth and releasing a sigh of pleasure as the tastes bloom on my tongue. It is pure crispy perfection. The maple syrup perfectly coats it, and the little pockets of whip cream cut through the sweetness.

"This is so good, Jackson. Thank you."

"See, at least someone here has manners."

Parker and Aleks mumble out thank yous as they continue to eat their fill of Jackson's brunch feast. Parker skips the waffles, piling his plate with eggs, bacon, and watermelon. Aleks stacks his waffle with eggs and maple syrup. Everyone's relatively silent as they eat, the guys chatting here and there about some gaming stuff I don't totally grasp. Some of it I can piece together from listening to Blade's streams and just minor gaming knowledge, but when they start talking stats, it goes right over my head.

The elevator dings, and Sydney's voice rings out. "I brought juice and an NDA." She strolls into the room. Her hair is styled in a fishtail braid, lashes coated with a layer of mascara, but a darkness hangs under her eyes. I feel bad. She was still on the phone when we went to bed last night, sorting everything out.

Sydney rounds the kitchen and leans across the opposite side of the island, dropping a white bag on the top. She runs her eyes over the three men with a sigh.

"You boys couldn't bother putting on a *little* more clothing this morning?"

She rummages through the bag, taking out four red juices and a green one. She slides the green juice my way. "I hope I got it right. I was eighty percent certain that you were drinking the Green Beam when we met."

I smile at her, touched by the gesture. "I was, thank you."

She slides a red drink to each guy, Parker and Jackson

groaning.

"Don't whine, you need your vegetables."

Aleks, however, sips on his happily between bites of waffle.

When I finish my food, stomach stuffed with maple waffle goodness, I force myself to get up and bring my plate to the sink to rinse it off.

"None of that, Stevie." Jackson chastises, coming up beside me. "Parker and Aleks know the rules. I cooked, they clean."

"No good deed comes free," Parker complains, pushing away from the island. He and Aleks collect the empty dishes while Jackson packs the few remaining leftovers into containers.

Sydney passes me a heavy document. "Here's the NDA for you to look over."

It's thicker than I expected, which is a touch concerning.

"Do you want my sister to take a look at it for you?" Parker calls over the running tap water. "She primarily works in real estate law, but Paige is a gun at all things."

I've read my fair share of NDAs, even signed a couple here and there. I contemplate sending it to our family lawyer to look over, but then I'd risk my parents finding out I used them for something. They'd want to know what it was for. Obviously, I could lie, but that would be an extra headache that I don't need. This NDA is also way longer than the previous ones I've dealt with. Another pair of eyes would be useful.

"Yeah, actually, that would be great."

He nods. "Alright, Syd will get our lawyers to send her

a copy."

"Thanks. I'm still going to try to give it a read myself." I park myself on the black leather couch, curling my feet under me as I start to leaf through it. It seems standard, but there is a lot of legal jargon I don't understand.

I do understand that I can't breathe a word about their identities. I can't come to the apartment unless I'm driven by Francis or an approved security member. I make a face when I see that even our dates have to be preapproved. It kind of blows, but I suck it up.

I breathe a sigh of relief when I read that the contract is void if the boys decide to reveal their identities themselves or if a third party unrelated to me does—like a media outlet.

However, when I see my compensation for the NDA, I still. The number isn't small, even by my count. My gut sours. It makes me uncomfortable, taking money from them for a secret I had no plan in revealing anyway. I contemplate whether I should ask Paige to get it removed. I don't even need the money, anyway.

"Sorry, by the way." Sydney startles me out of my thoughts, and I cock my head to the side.

"For what?"

She takes a seat next to me, "Yelling last night. Emotions were high and, well, I should've been more level-headed. It was unprofessional of me."

I close the NDA, placing it on the table to give her my full attention.

"Sydney, you were just protecting them. I don't blame you at all. You're a good person."

"Thanks." She gives me a small smile, tugging her

blonde braid to the side as she leans back against the cushions. Sydney looks at me for a moment, biting her lip before blowing out a breath.

"You know, after I met you, I kind of hoped you would text me."

Oh shit. I never texted her. It totally slipped my mind between everything else going on.

The guilt must show on my face because she starts waving her hands around.

"Crap, that sounded desperate. It's not like you were obligated to text me."

"No!" I grab her hands. "I was going to. I swear. I thought you were awesome. Things, life, just totally took over my brain." I smile at her. "You seem like an amazing friend. I'd want you in my corner any day, prepared to commit homicide."

Laughter fills her gray eyes. "Parker says I listen to too many true-crime podcasts."

"I blame Deer and Lee for that; they totally got you into it," Parker shouts.

"Whatever." She rolls her eyes before smiling at me. "Friends?"

It's an easy decision.

"Friends."

I spend the rest of the day hanging out in the apartment.

Sydney leaves shortly after brunch, but I end up gaming with the guys. I was a little anxious, knowing they'd all be so much better than me because they do this professionally. Aleks promised they'd take it easy on me, let me have some time to learn the controls and rules, feel it out. But after a couple of rounds, I started to get the hang of it and began winning. They all doubled down at that point, crushing me back for every win and more. I was getting decimated. It was nothing that a little bit of pouting at Aleks couldn't fix though. He was more than happy to help me out and nuke the guys—even though it was a PvP game, no teams involved. Jackson switched us to a racing kart game after that, eliciting a groan from Aleks. Apparently, he hates any game where he has to drive a car, let alone one where the entire point is to race against your friends on various maps. The fact that I managed to place higher than him nine times out of ten kind of spoke to his hatred. That, and him throwing his controller across the room at one point.

I, however, feel like a race kart badass.

"Who would've thought that I would be better than NightBlade32 at a video game?" I tease him as we lounge on the couch, my head on his chest. Jackson and Parker left to get some food before they stream tonight, but Aleks still has our dinner date set.

His chest rumbles with laughter. I feel it reverberating deep within him, my head bouncing with his movement.

"Jackson knows I hate that game."

"Don't lie, you love it."

"I'd love it a hell of a lot more if I was good at it." He runs his fingers lazily up and down my arm. That, paired with the evening sunlight filtering in through the windows, has me dozing off, eyelids fluttering shut, full of content.

"Did you have fun today?"

"Mhm," I hum.

"Really?" There's something off. A note of nervousness in his voice.

My eyes reluctantly peel open. "Really. Some of the most fun I've had in forever." I hold his gaze and watch as vulnerability peeks through.

"Aleksander, I'm serious. I haven't played video games with people since I was a kid. Michail, my brother, grew out of them when I was still in elementary school, so I just learned to play on my own or not at all. It was freeing to just let loose and play for the day. I'd missed it."

I watch as his smile returns, confidence building back up. So, I decide to let him in further.

"And waking up this morning to that brunch? God, I haven't had a meal like that in ages. Surrounded by people and having fun, being at ease and not having to worry about being proper or putting on a show." I snuggle in closer to his chest. "We stopped having family breakfasts on the weekend when I was in middle school. My parents were just too busy, and Michail was in high school with all his extracurriculars," I tell him. "But we'd stopped having family dinners way before that. Now, we only meet up once a month at a restaurant, and that's only if Michail and Vittoria's schedules align. It's something at least." I shrug. It sucks, but I've come to terms with it. I want to spend more time with them, but I never really had much of them growing up anyway. It was my grandparents who spent the most time with Michail and me.

"I know what you mean. I'm an only child, but I lost my parents in a plane crash when I was five. Granny raised me, but she passed a few years ago." I hear the hurt in his voice, the loss. I hug him tighter. "She was an amazing woman, made the best chocolate chip cookies, and always looked out for me even when I was getting in trouble. We didn't have much other than each other, which didn't bother me because she smothered me with love. But it meant that I never had those big family Thanksgivings or Christmases. We'd come back from school break and have to write little essays on what we spent our vacation doing, and mine were always simple compared to others. It wasn't until I met Jackson in high school that I really had any friends. His family is massive, and they make the most out of every holiday. It showed me how different life could be. You should come to their next Lunar New Year celebration; it's the best."

My body glows at his mention of the future.

"When I met Parker, my world grew even more. His parents spend most of the year at their home in Kensington if they aren't working in London, so he flies out for major holidays. I alternate between his family and Jackson's, depending on what's going on."

"That sounds like so much fun."

He grins, "They're my brothers. Their families have basically adopted me at this point. Although Jackson's mom still thinks I'm a delinquent teenager."

"Aren't you?"

He tickles me, and I squeal, rolling off the couch and onto the rug. He continues his assault, and I attempt to crawl away.

We are basically wrestling in the middle of the floor when Sydney steps out of the elevator again, phone to ear, chattering away with someone. She's holding a garment bag and pauses, staring at us on the ground. We pause before falling into another fit of laughter.

"Yeah, Paige, hold on one second, I'll get her." She taps her phone and then proceeds to kick Aleks with her heel. "Alright, lovebirds, I need you to sober up on your drunk love for a minute. I have Paige on the phone for the NDA."

I scramble to my feet, accepting the phone from Sydney. I hit the unmute button. "Hi, this is Stevie."

"Stevie! Hi, how are you?" Paige's soft British accent fills my ear.

"Good, thanks! You?"

"I'm well. Sorry, I didn't get a chance to introduce myself at the party last night. My brother whisked you off before I was able to."

I cringe at the memory. *Whisked* is definitely not the term neither Parker nor myself would use to explain the absolute shitshow we created. My mother had been pissed at the commotion I'd caused until she'd learned I'd left with the elusive Covington heir. Then her tone shifted, merely asking that I use a little more decorum in the future. Chase only left me one text, wishing me well with my new beau. I couldn't tell if it was sarcastic or not. But I wasn't going to correct anyone, not while it benefited me.

"Right, yes. I'm sure we will have more opportunities in the future." I don't know what else to say.

"I looked over the NDA. It's not dissimilar to the ones we all signed. Just with a few more clauses pertaining to the nature of your romantic relationship. I made a few small alterations there, just so you'd have a little more freedom, but otherwise you're in good shape to sign away."

"Wait, you signed an NDA? You're his sister." The idea sounds ridiculous.

"Oh, Stevie, if you knew the number of NDAs our family has signed and had people sign over the years, your head would spin," she laughs.

"Alright, well, thank you, Paige. I really appreciate it."

"No worries. You can just sign the NDA digitally; I sent the link to Sydney's phone. Give everyone my love, and I hope to see you soon."

"Of course, me too." She hangs up, and I see the message pop up with the NDA. I give it a scroll, but I trust Paige. I sign my name at the bottom and confirm everything, sending a copy to my own email.

"All done," I announce.

"Fab!" Sydney claps her hands. I look up and notice Aleks has left the room. "Here, let's trade." She holds out her palm for her phone, and I pass it over. She gives me the garment bag in return.

"What's this?"

"You have a date in an hour, don't you?"

"What?"

An hour?

I snatch her hand back, tapping on the screen of her phone. It's already six. I didn't even realize how late it had gotten. I don't have anything with me. My heart drops.

"Yeah, I had a feeling you'd spaced on the time. Come on, let's go get ready."

"But I don't have any clothes."

"Which is why Aleksander sent me to pick up a dress for you. I might be their publicist, but I'm also basically their glorified PA from time to time. Now, go grab your heels and purse from last night. We only have," she pauses, "fifty-five minutes now."

"Wait, where are we going?"

"My place. I live on the fourteenth floor. Come on."

She snaps her fingers, and I jump into motion, rushing around the apartment, picking up my loose belongings.

I dip into Aleks' room and hear the shower running. I pick up my heels off the floor before stopping to take a quick peek at the dress in the bag. Unzipping it halfway, I stare at the soft red fabric. The temptation is too strong. I lay it on the bed and unzip it fully. Before me lies a beautiful red viscose dress, with a side slit and thick black straps holding it all together up top. I tug at the label, eyes widening at the Dolce & Gabbana branding.

"Stephanie!" Sydney yells.

My back stiffens like a kid being caught with their hand in the candy jar. I quickly zip the dress back up. "Coming! I'm coming!"

"Not yet, but later." Aleks winks at me from the bathroom door frame, naked body dripping with water. He didn't even bother putting on a towel.

I stare at him, hunger clawing deep in my core. Sydney yells again, and Aleks laughs at me as I stumble out of the room, but excitement bubbles in my chest.

I couldn't be happier.

Chapter
TWENTY-SIX

ALEKS

Stevie bats my hand away for the twentieth time.

"Aleksander, I'm serious. Stop trying to feel me up. I won't have you ruining this dress by putting your hand up it."

"But the slit is so accessible."

"Yeah, and I'm sure that's why you picked it."

I grin at her.

Not only that, but I made sure it was a dress that Stevie would struggle wearing underwear with. The material is soft and clings to her body. She looks killer in red, like the Queen of Hearts. Plus, I love seeing her in my color.

I trickle my fingers along her thigh again, and she grabs my hands.

"I'm going to move seats in a second. Then you won't be able to touch any part of me."

We are huddled in the back row of seats of the Tesla, but if she moves to the second row, she'll be in her own seat. Not completely unreachable, but I won't be able to sit next to her.

"Fine. But you'll pay for this later."

"I like a good punishment," she smirks.

My dick twitches, and I rearrange it quickly.

"We're here, sir." Francis announces, tapping the button on the touchpad to open the falcon doors. They lift, and I push out of my seat, crouching to walk to the doors and stepping out. I turn back, holding out a hand for Stevie to help her down.

"Thanks, Francis. I'll text you when we're ready to leave."

"Sounds good, sir." The doors descend, and he takes off.

I hold out my elbow for Stevie, but she bypasses it, grasping my hand and threading our fingers together. I lead her inside the restaurant, giving the hostess my name. The woman taps a few buttons, confirming the reservation before leading us to our table. I pull out Stevie's chair, and she quirks an eyebrow, the corner of her lip pulling up in a small smile before sitting down.

"That was awfully gentlemanlike of you," she teases.

"You're forgetting that I tried to have a quickie in the car ride over" I muse, moving my seat from the opposite side of the table so I'm next to her. If the servers have an issue with me reconfiguring their placements, I don't care. This way, I can rest my hand on her bare knee.

"Touché."

We scan the QR code at the table, scrolling through the

drink menu.

"Cocktails or wine?" I ask her.

She puckers her lips, shifting them side to side as she assesses the menu. I've come to learn it's what she does when she's thinking hard, trying to make a decision.

"What cuisine is this place?"

"Greek."

Her eyes flash up, and she whips her head around, searching the restaurant for…honestly, I have no clue.

"Wait, what? What's this place called?"

"Moira"

"Moira? Wait, this place just opened. My mother mentioned it."

Score one for Aleksander.

Not going to lie, I was nervous picking this place. I had a feeling she would scrutinize any Greek restaurant I picked unless it was her favorite but thought I'd take a chance with this one since it was just opened by the granddaughter of the most notorious chef in Sifnos. There were a lot of high expectations surrounding it; I just hope it lives up to the hype.

"Did I tell you I was half Greek?"

"No, but the internet did."

She laughs at me, and I nudge her knee with my own, "What, are you trying to tell me you didn't look me up?"

"Not really." She starts studying the wine menu with renewed interest.

I nudge her knee again. "What does that mean, huh?"

"Nothing. I just, like, watched a stream here and there."

I'm about to push her further because there's something under that, but our waitress interrupts. She inquires whether we want still or sparkling water and if we have decided on drinks.

"We should go with a white wine," Stevie suggests, "the Gavalas."

"Sounds good to me, I trust your choice."

She beams at me while the waitress rattles off some of the specials. Stevie's ears prick up when she mentions some honey ricotta cake, her eyes practically turning into little hearts.

"Oh! We have to get that for dessert, Aleks."

I can't help but grin back. I definitely made the right choice picking this restaurant. Stevie has a field day after the waitress leaves, scrolling through the menu, rattling off different dishes and speaking mostly to herself. I'd done my own research on the restaurant, which dishes would be the best, but I'm throwing it all out the window. Watching Stevie live her best foodie life is way more enjoyable.

"Do you want to order for us both?" I ask her.

"Really? You'd be alright with that?"

"Of course, why wouldn't I be?"

She shrugs. "Chase never let me order. He picked everything, from the wine to whether we got dessert or not."

"Well, Chase sounds like an asshole and a dumbass." He looked like one, too, from the pictures I found online. My internet deep dive might have been a little too deep— but Parker has quite the connections when it comes to information gathering. "Order whatever you want. If you want to taste everything on the menu, order everything on the menu. I don't care how much it costs. Even if we can't finish it, we'll give the leftovers to the boys."

Her bottom lip pops out, kitten eyes staring up at me

through thick lashes.

"You're the best, you know that?"

"I have a few awards that say so."

She rolls her eyes, smiling at me.

"I'm serious, Stevie, order whatever you want. It's your night."

The waitress returns with our bottle of wine. She shows us the label before pouring a small amount into a wine glass, and I motion for her to pass it to Stevie. She gives it a sniff before taking a sip and nodding her approval. The waitress proceeds to fill our glasses, leaving the bottle in a stainless-steel wine chiller.

Stevie fires off various dishes to the waitress. I have only a vague understanding of what she ordered, but I'm pumped. This is probably the most fun I've had at a restaurant since the Lau's invited me out to yum cha for the first time in high school.

Stevie raises her wine glass. "To an amazing day and unforgettable night."

I raise mine in suit. "To an amazing day, unforgettable night, and a beautiful woman."

We clink our glasses and take a sip. The crisp wine brightens my tongue.

Our appetizers come out in record speed, and Stevie wastes no time in plating me various spreads and cheeses to try—including some special Siphnian cheese that she had a feeling I wouldn't love...and didn't.

"It's not to everyone's liking, don't worry about it. Here, this is garides saganaki; it's to die for." She spoons a mixture of shrimp covered in a tomato sauce and crumbled feta onto my plate, and then passes me a piece of crusty bread. I scoop everything onto the bread and take a bite. It's delicious. The fresh lemon juice cuts through the salty feta cheese and savory tomatoes. The shrimp are plump and a direct contrast to the crunchy bread. It's out of this world. I can't stop myself from going back to the skillet for seconds and thirds.

Our mains come out next, and I eye the clay pot meat dish with interest, the seafood pasta looking somewhat familiar.

"What's that?"

"Mastelo! It's a hallmark dish in Sifnos. Braised lamb in a tomato sauce with dill, cooked in a clay pot. I have a feeling it'll be your favorite. The other dish is astakomakaronada. You can't go wrong with a fresh Greek lobster pasta. Plus, I'm a seafood girl."

I cut into a piece of lamb, watching as it tears away like butter. Fuck, this is going to be good. The flavors burst in my mouth, the lush sauce coating my tongue as the meat melts. The fresh dill springs through the richness, tying everything together. Damn, this restaurant is amazing.

Stevie twirls her pasta, humming with pleasure as she bites into it.

"This has been the best dinner ever, and we haven't even gotten to the melopita. I know you prefer chocolate desserts, but everyone loves the honey cake." Her eyes crinkle. "Thank you for bringing me here."

Her excitement is utterly infectious. When she smiles, her entire being glows, and she hasn't stopped smiling this entire time. I wouldn't be surprised if she complained that her cheeks hurt tomorrow.

"I love your smile."

The compliment blurts out of me, and I reach for my wine, downing the rest of the glass then reaching to fill ours both up again, finishing the bottle.

I look up, and Stevie is trying her hardest not to smile, but she breaks into a full-blown grin.

"Thank you. That's so sweet."

I groan.

"What?" she asks.

"I'm acting like an all-out sap," I complain.

"No! It's cute."

"I'm supposed to be hot, mysterious, sexy. Not cute. NightBlade32 is not cute."

"No," she tips her wine glass toward me, "but Aleksander Knight just might be."

I give her a dead stare. "That doesn't make it any better."

She just winks at me before taking a sip of wine. I huff but let it drop.

Guess I'll just have to come to terms with the fact that when it comes to Stephanie Andwell, the playbook doesn't exist; there are no rules.

She's the king on this chessboard, and I'm just a pawn charged with protecting her.

We are waiting for dessert, Stevie filling me in on an art piece she is working on, when she halts her sentence midway, eyes widening like a deer in headlights.

She immediately whips her head away from me, duck-

"Stevie?"

"Shhhh," she hisses, one hand coming up to shield the side of her face.

I go to turn my head, but she grips my thigh. "Don't you even *think* about looking, Aleksander. Just lean forward and block me, okay?"

I pitch forward, folding my arms across the table, effectively sheltering Stevie with my chest.

"You want to give me a clue here, babe?"

"Decker and my ex just walked in."

Well, now I really want to turn around. Neither of them should recognize me. I've never met Decker as Aleksander, but I also don't want to risk it. The dude has a vendetta against me, and if Stevie was able to clock Parker after a few meetings, there is a chance Decker could do the same. I might hate the guy, but I don't underestimate him—Decker is smart, sly, a Grade-A manipulator. I might be able to beat him most of the time, but that's only because I know not to undervalue his abilities.

Chase, on the other hand, I would love to see. I want him to witness what he gave up, what he lost. How stupid he was for it, but how grateful I am because now she is mine.

I see our waitress exit the kitchen with our melopita and curse.

"Shit, the dessert's coming. Want me to get it to go? Grab the check?"

"Ugh. Why couldn't the assholes have waited until *after* dessert."

The waitress gets closer.

"Stevie," I warn her.

"Yes, yes, to go. Dammit." Her voice is laced with bitterness.

I shoot off a quick text to Francis letting him know we need to be picked up. *Now.*

I angle my body even farther away from the main entrance, facing the waitress. I'm quick to put out my hand to stop her. "Sorry, we are going to need this to go. Can we have the check? ASAP." My attempt at a casual smile doesn't stop the tension from holding in my eyes.

"Oh, sure, not a problem. I'll be right back."

The waitress twists around and almost bumps into none other than Daniel-fucking-Decker, who is deep in conversation with the blond man behind him. She pulls back, offering her sincerest apologies. Decker's mask is nothing other than perfection as he smiles at her, touching her shoulder to steady her, telling her it's fine. She apologizes again before stepping around him and back to the kitchen.

"Face me," I whisper to Stevie. In one swift movement, she dips her body, leaning her opposite elbow on the table to face me. She angles her head away by resting it on the tips of her fingers, making it look lazy even though she is tense as fuck.

Decker rolls his eyes once the waitress disappears. Then his eyes slip to me, giving me a pointed once over before continuing on. Chase passes behind him, only sparing me a quick glance. I see the second his eyes slip to Stevie, gaze a little more assessing as he scans her body like the slime he is. My heart rate is a million beats per minute. His eyebrows raise in appreciation before he takes a step away. I let out a breath but suck it back when Chase suddenly halts. He flips around, bending his body low to the table.

"Steffy?"

Fuck.

I look down at her, and she holds my gaze. I watch as the anxiety switches to steel, her eyes narrowing to catlike, a mask of unaffected seduction slipping on. I match her stroke for stroke, making the switch from Aleksander to Blade. I roll my shoulders back, leaning lazily against the back of my chair, legs spread farther apart.

Stevie slowly swivels her tilted head on her fingertips, looking him up and down before letting a saccharine smile spill onto her face. She pushes off her fingertips and moves her left hand off my thigh and rests her chin in it, crooking her elbow on the table.

"Chasey," she drips, "fancy seeing you here." Her voice registers a few octaves higher than usual.

Chase gives me a better look this time. No dismissive glance. He completely judges me, his eyes flicking around my face and body, cataloging every inch. I watch his lip curl as he records my tattoos.

"Yes, well, you know I have a soft spot for Greek food."

"Then I hope you enjoy your meal—" Stevie points to an empty table in the corner of the room. "—all the way over there."

She gives him a quick, fake smile before casting him off with her hand. Chase's jaw ticks at the movement.

"If it isn't Lady Andwell!" Decker slings his arm around Chase, feline grin on his face.

His eyes flick to me. Decker doesn't take as long as Chase did to stare me down, but he doesn't have to. Decker's a gamer; his mind works more quickly, catalogs details with speed. Not as fast as me, *never* as fast as me, but better than your average guy.

"Well, this doesn't look like Lord Covington. Making the rounds are we, Stephanie?"

The taunt lies between us, and my anger bubbles at the tainted comment. Unfortunately, it spurs the flames within Chase again.

"A bit of a downgrade, Steffy. Really, hanging with the riff raff? At least Parker had decorum. This guy is," Chase pauses, "unruly. What would your mother think?"

I'm right fucking here, but alright.

"Well, my mother loved you, so I don't exactly trust her taste in my boyfriends."

I see the shock slap Chase in the face and smirk. It doesn't escape me that she just claimed me as her boyfriend. It's not a conversation we've officially had, but it feels unspoken after the day we've experienced. And fuck if I don't want her to be my girlfriend.

I place my hand on Stevie's thigh, gripping it and pulling her chair toward me. We sit side by side now, her skin flush against mine. She brings that same thigh up, hooking it over my own, connecting us as one unit.

Chase watches the motion, my tattooed hand tracing the bare skin of his ex's thigh.

"Daniel Decker." Decker reaches his hand out to me.

"Aleks." I'm careful to keep my voice neutral; if there's one thing Decker will recognize, it'll be that.

I don't bother leaning forward, just hold my hand out and make Decker shift his stance to grip it. "Just Aleks?" He squeezes my hand.

"Just Aleks." I don't squeeze back harder, just apply pressure with my thumb onto the soft skin between his thumb and forefinger. Decker grits his jaw, pulling his hand back with a small shake.

Chase steps forward. "Stephanie, I told you. I'm not that serious about Fel. If this is all some ploy to—"

"Chase, stop." She sits up straight now. "I told you last night, I'm done. I would've thought not responding to your texts or calls or stupid flowers would've confirmed that. I don't want to have to block you, but I will. Hell, I'll get a restraining order if I must. I'm not someone's toy they can keep in a drawer to play with when they feel like it. I'm the first choice, the *only* choice." She levels him with her stare. "I'm done, Chauncy Broadshire." Her tone carries finality.

"What could he possibly offer you that I can't?" Chase snarls.

"Better orgasms and a bigger dick for one." I toss out, giving him a shark smile.

"That's two things, hun." Stevie brings her hand to my cheek, giving it a little pat. I nip at her hand before diving in to kiss her cheek as she laughs.

"Steffy." Chase's voice is small and pitiful.

She ignores him, staring only into my eyes, mischief and heat blazing across them.

He grabs her shoulder, tugging her back. Attempting to pull her attention, his voice more forceful, "Stephanie."

It takes a split second for me to flip the tiny dessert fork in my hand and reach over to press it against his skin.

"I suggest you take your hand off my girlfriend. Unless you want me to pierce this dessert fork through it." My voice is a deep growl as I tap the fork against his skin.

297

"But I would rather not get blood on the dress I bought her before I get the chance to rip it off."

He reels his hand back, as if the fork burned him. He sneers down at me. Decker wears an amused smile, but his eyes narrow in on my hand twirling the fork.

"You're insane," Chase spits.

"Insane about her," I wink.

The waitress comes back at that moment, shuffling around Decker to place the take-out bag on the table and hand me the check. I don't even glance at it, just hold out my Black Card for her. She taps it against the POS device, handing it back to me to input the tip before scuttling away.

Decker and Chase eye the Black Card as I slip it back into my pocket. Judgmental dicks.

"Well, gentlemen, this has been fun, but we have a long night of sex ahead." I slip my arm around Stevie's waist as we stand up, resting it on her hip.

"I'd say it was a pleasure, but it wasn't." She gives them a tight smile. "I'm happy, and I will do anything to keep that. If you want any sort of civility between us, you'll leave me be."

I grab the take-out bag, and we leave without deigning to wait for a response. But I make sure to loop my free arm around Stevie's waist, resting my hand on her ass and giving it a squeeze as we walk out the door.

Francis pulls up, the doors winging open before he even stalls the engine. I hold Stevie's hand as she steps inside then follow behind. We settle against the back seats again, Stevie curling into my body. I hug her against my chest as we take off.

We drive in silence for a few miles, just the soft lull of

the radio guiding us.

"What destination, Mr. Knight?" Francis asks.

I squeeze Stevie's shoulder. "Where to, little dove?"

She looks up at me, exhaustion lining her eyes. The encounter zapped all her energy. It makes me pissed. My bright and beautiful flower is wilting. I want to go back there and put that tiny fucking fork through the both of them. But the last thing I needed was a public fight ending up on the internet, my photo plastered with Decker's and Stevie's in the same image. Only a handful of photos of me exist online as it is.

"Can we just go back to your place? I just...I want to be away right now."

"Of course."

"Can we eat the melopita while watching the new Vin Diesel movie?"

"Of course."

"Can I have that T-shirt I wore today?"

"Have or wear?"

"Both." She grins up at me.

I smile at her, fucking relieved to see some of the sunshine peeking through. "We'll see."

She pouts, and I kiss her on the forehead. She nuzzles against me, eyes fluttering shut. I hold her tighter, like if I keep her close to me, I can protect her from the world.

I might play the hero in video games, but I'll be the villain in life if it keeps her safe.

Chapter
TWENTY-SEVEN

STEVIE

I don't hear from Chase after our run-in at Moira. There are no more pink roses left in odd places, no text messages, no calls. He goes radio silent for the first time since we've met.

It still feels like someone is watching me, but I think it's my paranoia from just being too used to him reaching out. It's only been two weeks, and it's strange to be living a life that is so completely Chase-free.

Instead, my days are filled by Aleks. I still text him good morning, and he still texts me good night—even though he stays up for hours after, streaming. I don't tell him, but sometimes I just lie in bed listening to his solo streams during the week until I drift off to sleep or I play his pre-recorded videos while painting just to hear his voice.

We take every moment together we can get. It's a head spin. We are running fast and hot now that everything is on the table, but I'm prepared to burn.

Aleks started switching up his streaming schedule slightly so we could see each other more. Thanks to Paige's amendments to the NDA, the boys are allowed to drive me to the apartment complex, not just Francis. But Francis mostly drives me anyway since the boys usually only use him to drive them places when it is The System-related, and Francis told me he is excited to feel more useful again.

The old man melts my heart.

Deanna knows I'm officially dating Aleks, but that's all she knows. There was no way of hiding that from her, not with how preoccupied I've been with him. She is determined to set up a time for us to go on a double date. Unfortunately, Maya and Alek's schedules constantly clash. The world of esports stops for no one, especially when it comes to her team.

The System was invited to the opening ceremony for the next *Gods League* Champion Series in a few weeks, which Sydney is insisting they attend. Aleks was bitter about it until I mentioned Maya's team would take part and that she would have a ticket for me to attend with Deanna.

We'll have to sneak around if we want to see each other, but that makes it all the more fun. I love every moment I spend with Aleksander, whether it's going out on dates, lounging on his couch with his friends, or fucking on his kitchen island.

I should probably be a little worried that I'm getting invested too quickly. That, if it doesn't work out, the fall is going to be so much worse than it ever was with Chase.

That I won't be able to pick myself back up.

I shake the thoughts from my brain and finish getting ready. I'm spending the night at the apartment, and I went all out getting a little surprise for Aleks after listening to one of his streams the other week. I slip the last of my belongings into my overnight bag as a text from Parker pings through, letting me know he is downstairs.

I lock up and bound my way down the stairs, not bothering to wait for the elevator. Parker's electric blue Porsche rumbles out front. I slip inside and go to throw my bag into the back when I startle at Sydney's hunched form.

"Hey," she smiles begrudgingly.

"Uh, hey. Whatcha doing back there?"

"*Someone* here insisted on driving to our boxing class earlier and failed to mention a third person would be joining us later."

"Sydney, love, you're five foot. You fit perfectly fine back there," Parker chimes in.

"I'm five five."

"Same thing. Now, buckle up, I don't want to hit Friday night traffic."

I clip in the blue seatbelt as Parker turns up the music so the bass reverberates through the leather. Having driven with Parker a few times now, I know to grip the safety handle as he takes off, his car speeding from zero to ninety in no time.

I adore driving with Parker. It's a thrill. He's a demon in the streets, maneuvering the car seamlessly between other vehicles at a speed that shouldn't be possible. Or legal for that matter. Although, I have a feeling Parker could get out of any speeding ticket.

Sydney does not share my thrill. Expletives pour out of her while her white knuckles grip for dear life on our headrests. I think it's the first time I've heard her swear.

Parker swings into the private underground lot in record time. Even Aleks doesn't get me here as quickly on his bike—but I think he is purposely driving more slowly so as not to throw me off.

Parker pulls in next to his Ferrari—which is also blue—and shuts off the engine. He swings out of the car and tilts his seat down so Sydney can get out. She glares at him as she takes his hand and contorts her body out of the car. I get out and wait for them at the elevator while they retrieve their boxing gear from the trunk.

We get in the elevator, Sydney getting off on her floor while Parker and I ride all the way to the top.

I slip into Aleks' bedroom at the end of the hallway, dropping my bag on the floor. I pull out my phone, opening Aleks' livestream. He's been streaming for two hours already and has another two to go. He wasn't expecting me here until ten.

He's in the middle of a game with three guys I haven't seen before plus Jackson. They're playing *FrozeLine*, a game I seriously suck at despite Aleks trying to teach me…but which is perfect for tonight.

I pull out the lingerie from my bag, grinning. The lingerie set is based on one of the characters Aleks plays in *FrozeLine*. It cost me a pretty penny because it had to be custom ordered, but it even came with the mini angel wings. The silky white and purple miniskirt has built-in crotchless panties; the whole thing only covers a third of my ass. The bra was the expensive part. It is white lace with an elaborate purple jewel design. The set mimics a version of the dress the character wears. I take off my current clothes, replacing them with the outfit. I slip on a pair of ultra-sheer, thigh-high white stockings with a white satin band. Then, I tie two mini pigtails near the front of my head, puffing them up a little so they sit on the rest of my wavy hair. Once I'm pleased with my look, I check Aleks' stream again. There are only a few minutes before the current round ends, which is perfect.

I peek my head out of his door, making sure that Parker isn't lurking about. Since I know Jackson is streaming with Aleks, I don't have to worry about him popping out either—his bedroom and streaming room are opposite Aleks'.

I make the quick slide to the door next to Aleks' bedroom, which leads into his streaming room. I switch off the hall light, then I open the door slowly. Light is still leaking in from the living space, but I make sure the door only opens wide enough for me to squeeze my body through before closing it.

The room is bathed in a deep red glow from the LED lights he has set up plus the giant neon red sign of his gamertag on the wall. Aleks is still fully immersed in the game. I can't hear what is going on save for the fast clicking of the keyboard and tapping of the mouse.

"Someone better come into combat here before I get fucking destroyed," he growls into his headset.

I get down on all fours, crawling my way slowly to his setup. I get behind his chair and sneak one of my hands forward slowly.

"Oh! What's up! Nice, Hunter. Alright, let's—" He

Good GAME

swears when I brush my hand over his thigh.

Aleks looks down at my hand and then flicks his head to me. His eyes are bewildered until he registers me kneeling there and smiles, lust dilating his pupils when he clocks my outfit.

"Fuck, shit, yeah, I'm behind you." He whips back around, fingers gliding along the keyboard. "No, it was nothing."

I stand up and pepper his neck with soft, small kisses, all the while tracing my nails along his inner thigh. I let my finger brush over his cock, and he curses again. He is only streaming his voice today, so he's just wearing a pair of red sweatpants, no shirt, no gloves. I stand behind him and scratch my nails along his bare chest. I lick my finger and slide it over his pierced nipple. He sucks in a breath, shifting in his seat. My stomach fizzes as the edges of arousal begin licking at me. Toying with Aleks while watching him play is making me wet already.

"Shit," he mutters before barking orders into the mic. "Hey, don't engage. They're in a choke point." My eyes flick to the screen, and I watch as one of his teammates goes down in front of him before Aleks takes out one of his enemies.

His black desk is L-shaped with a heightened shelf on one side where his three monitors sit, streaming mic hanging to the right. His glowing custom PC sits underneath, to the right of his feet. I move his closed laptop and perch my ass on the left side of the desk, lifting one of my legs up so my pussy is on display.

I'm so glad I went with the crotchless set.

Aleks flicks his eyes to me and stills. I give him a

305

sweet smile, squeezing my breasts before running two fingers over myself, gathering the glistening wetness that has pooled. Damn, it feels good. His chest rises with an intake of breath as he grows hungry, eyes darkening. It feeds the beast within me, Horny Stevie waking up and getting ready to play.

Aleks' jaw clicks and eyes narrow as he flips back to the game.

"Who is holding mid?" he calls into his headset. "Nice, nice, nice. I got them down over here, two remaining." His commanding voice washes over my skin, warming me.

I slip my fingers inside myself with a groan. Fuck, I didn't realize I was this sensitive already. It's like my body is trained to react instantly to Blade. It knows him and begins winding itself up without me even having to try. He truly owns this pussy.

I shift my hips and curl my fingers until I find the spot I know gets me going. I drop my head back against the wall, losing myself to the feeling and drinking in his voice.

"Fuck, that looks good."

I crack open my eyes and catch Aleks staring at me.

The beast inside roars at the attraction. It spurs on my movements. I move faster, thighs locking up at the building sensation. I keep my eyes on Aleks the entire time even though I want to squeeze them shut. The pressure waves, and I bring my other hand down to rub my clit. My body jolts at the added sensation. A soft cry escapes my lips as my raised leg slips off the desk, my orgasm tumbling with it. The endorphins rush through me, and I let them blanket my body.

Aleks swears and whips back to the game, frantically

smashing the keyboard. His mouse twitches with his fast movements.

"Oh, I'm dead. Wait, no. Yeah. No, I'm dead." Aleks swears again. "Shit, it's on you, Hunter."

He mutes his headset and mic then grips my hand, bringing my fingers to his mouth and sucking on them with a groan. It sends a zing to my clenching pussy, riling it up.

"We have two rounds left," he growls. "That gives you less than five minutes to make me come or else I'm going to punish you for making me die. I almost aced that round."

"Sounds like you need to get better at multitasking." I bat my eyelashes at him.

Honestly, I kind of want the punishment, but I also want to get him off.

The dilemmas of sex.

"Don't be a brat."

I stick my tongue out at him, and he gives my pussy a slap. A strangled gasp tears from me as my sensitive heat spasms.

"Now, get on your knees and show me how well you can suck this cock." He drops his sweatpants around his thighs, thick cock bobbing free.

I slide off the desk and crawl underneath. Aleks tracks my movement as I position myself in between his legs and look up at him. I get a flashback to the first time we met, when we were at the VSAs, except this time there is way more space under the desk and I can see his tortured expressions as he tries to remain calm. I smirk to myself; this is going to be fun.

He sits back down and unmutes his mic and headset.

"Alright, let's push out A-side this round."

I lick my tongue up the underside of his shaft, closing my lips over the top of his head, tasting the salty precum. I lap it up like milk, savoring it.

"My bad." Aleks calls out, his hips raising up and back down.

I close my hand around the top of his head, giving it a small squeeze as I bring it down his length and back up again. My hand moves easily with the mixture of my saliva and his saltiness. I add my mouth back in, sucking his smooth tip like he is a lollipop and I have a sugar addiction.

Then I go deep, taking him all the way in until he hits the back of my throat. I calm my mind, making my throat relax, then I take him even farther, bottoming out. I hear Aleks hiss above me. His entire length is in me. My eyes water and I fight the reflex to choke. Instead, I close my throat slightly around his tip and start bobbing up and down.

I cup his balls, massaging them as I speed up, wet noises filling the room as I slurp him up. One of his hands comes down momentarily, gripping my hair tightly. I smile against the pain, feeling myself getting wet again. Aleks attempts to pull me back, but I push back down, knowing he must be close.

"Aim true, aim true."

He lets go of my hair, and I release his dick from my lips. I run my thumb softly around the tip of his cock, still letting my hand work its magic below. I take him back in, hollowing out my cheeks as I suck at him as if he is my god and I'm atoning for my sins.

I let my teeth lightly graze his length.

"Fuck, I'm close." His voice is dangerously low, and it sends a shiver through my body.

I deep throat him again, tears spilling over and down my cheeks. I release his balls and reach down, touching myself. I moan against his dick as I rub my sensitive clit.

I'm jolted out of my pleasure when he grips my hair, halting my movements. I look up at him, and he smirks at me, dimple on full display.

"I won."

My shoulders slump. I'm pissed. He was so fucking close.

His self-control is unreal.

I release his dick with a wet pop and lick my lips, still staring at him. He groans, running a hand down his face. I watch his hard dick twitch and give the underside another lick. He pushes himself away from the desk and me, chair rolling back. He stands, bringing his sweatpants back over his dick. Then he sits down and rolls back to the desk.

"Alright, chat, I'm going to take a quick break before coming back to play some *Death Valley*." He pauses, reading the comments, and laughing. "Yep, yep. We'll pick up from last time, hit the casino today. I'll be back at eight forty."

I crawl out from under the desk and lean against it.

"Good game, boys. We'll link up later. Yep. Alright, see you."

He mutes everything and fiddles with a few things before ripping his headphones off, standing, and lifting me in his arms.

I squeal as he carries me to the couch in the corner, sitting down and draping me over his legs.

"Someone was a bad girl today."

"You didn't like my surprise?" I peer at him over my shoulder with big doe eyes.

He snorts. "Oh, I loved my surprise, and I think you are going to love this punishment."

I grin at him.

He plays with the wings clipped on my back before running his fingers over my ass, playing with the hem of my skirt.

"Fuck, you look sexy. I love this outfit."

I preen at the compliment, satisfaction blooming in my chest.

"But do you know what it's missing?"

I shake my head.

He slaps my ass, and I jerk with surprise.

"A little bit of color." His grin is wolfish as he looks down at me.

"Paint me red," I throw back, and his eyes darken.

"That's my girl."

He shifts me around a little so I'm positioned a bit more comfortably across his lap.

"Before we get started, I want to make sure you know your safe words."

I nod back at him.

"Green is good, yellow is on the edge, red is stop. Does that make sense?"

"Green, yellow, and red. Got it."

He strokes my head. "Good. Now I'm thinking ten spanks for the ten minutes you teased me. I want you to count each one, okay?"

"Okay."

"Good." Then, without warning, he slaps my ass. It's harder than before. A slight sting.

"One," I call out.

The second and third slaps are of the same level. The sting is growing warmer, but it's not uncomfortable.

"You were such a bad girl. Teasing me. Flashing that delectable pussy." When he spanks me the fourth time, the pain radiates across my entire ass cheek, and I suck in a breath. "Bad girls have to repent for their sins."

"Four," I grind out.

The next slap is quick and fast, and it feels like a rubber band hitting me. Heat spreads across my ass, and I hiss at the sensation. But I also feel my arousal building again, my thighs slickening as they rub together with each hit.

"Five."

"My little angel wanted to take a walk on the dark side and look where it landed you. Sweet little ass red as the devil. Are you sorry yet?"

"Never," I throw back. A peek over my shoulders shows he's staring down at me hungrily.

He massages my ass, and I relax against the soothing feeling. My emotions are running wild. A mixture of excitement, lust, and fear. It feels like I'm drunk. I've always craved pain with my pleasure. I've never been punished before, never had anyone spank my ass, but I'm already addicted.

The sixth slap jolts me out of the false sense of comfort he created, my body jerking in shock. Aleks pinches my ass, and I yelp.

"Number?" he commands.

"Six, six, sorry."

The next two spanks are harder, but I greedily accept them. My brain blanks as soon as the slaps hit, the pain shocking my system until the pleasure sinks in, blissing me out. It's like being plunged in hot water and then doused in ice. Your body is at war with the conflicting environments, and it makes everything feel heightened.

"Nine," I call out as his hand lands again. The ninth slap causes me to wince, the pain edging close to hurt. Not that my pussy registers that. I squirm against the wetness, craving more friction between my legs. Selfishly, I try grinding myself against his lap.

"Someone is getting a little greedy." His fingers dip below my ass, slipping in my wetness. "Fuck, Stevie." I look behind me and watch him suck my arousal again. "I'm addicted to the way you taste."

I hold his gaze as his hand comes down for the final time. My moan comes out like a pure scream.

"Ten. Ten. Oh my god, fuck, Aleks." He massages my ass cheek, providing some relief, before picking me up so I straddle his legs. My heat sits flush against his crotch, and I just know I'm soaking his sweatpants right now. He brings me in for a kiss, and I taste myself against his tongue.

"You did so well. I'm so proud of you."

His hands dance down my body, and I loop mine around his neck, pulling him closer to me. Our kiss deepens as I grind myself shamelessly against him. I'm so strung up, so ready to go again.

"I want you so badly," I breathe out before tugging his bottom lip between my teeth. "I want you in me. Please. I need to come again. I'm so close."

He groans, capturing my mouth with his.

"You don't have to ask me twice."

He stands, picking me up with him before laying me on my stomach on the rug below us.

"Bend over and show me that pretty pussy, baby."

I spread my arms forward, breasts pressed against the floor, arching my back as far as I can. I wiggle my ass in the air with a grin.

He tugs out of his sweatpants and kneels behind me. I look back at him, past the wings clipped to my bra. He fists his dick, staring at me through hooded eyes.

"Never fucked an angel before," he says before sliding between my folds. I moan at the sensation, his thick cock filling me up better than anything else.

After we both got retested last week, we decided as a couple to forgo the condoms. I honestly love nothing better than the feeling of him coming inside me.

He pushes into me relentlessly, his hips pounding against me. My ass is still sore from the slaps, the pain adding sensation. My orgasm wavers on the edge, feasting on the feeling, growing with every pump. His dick pistons in and out, the pressure building and falling with each movement. I cry out when he completely bottoms out, and he moans against me.

Sex with Aleks is unlike anything else. I've never felt so connected to another person. He treats my body like a temple, worshiping it like he is going to find the path to the promised land. Then he'll flip, destroying it like the devil punishing sinners in purgatory. Whether I'm his good girl or bad girl, I'm always his girl.

At this moment, I am just an angel servicing her god.

But I want *more*. I want to hit new heights. Elysium.

I roll my hips deeper, and a low growl escapes his chest. "Fuck me harder," I beg him.

His hands come down to grip my hips, and his nails dig into me as he holds me tightly. The pain sparks pleasure, and suddenly I feel my entire abdomen clench. The pressure builds to a high I've never felt before. It almost feels like I need to pee. My brain begins to short circuit as the waves continue to rise. Then his hand comes up to fist my hair, and I gasp through the sudden sting. His other hand loops around my hip and rubs at my clit, and the sensation becomes almost unbearable. The intensity of it all is too deep.

"Will my bad girl be a good girl and come around my cock?"

He pinches my clit. That goddamned move that gets me every time. Even if I wanted to, I wouldn't be able to stop the downfall. My body spasms as my orgasm erupts through me, and his name falls from my lips like a curse. Absentmindedly, I feel wetness run down my legs. My pussy clenches, milking Aleks' cock for all that it's worth. I enter the sea of bliss, letting myself get swept away in it.

"Fuck, I'm going to come," he grunts.

"Where do you want to come?"

He pulls out and stands, and I whine at the emptiness. He turns me around, placing me on my knees. I love when he moves my body, when he uses me for his pleasure.

"Let me paint that perfect face." He runs his hand up and down his shaft, looking down at me.

I tilt my chin down, peering at him up through my lashes. I poke out my tongue, spreading it flat.

"Fuck, Stevie," He groans, eyes fluttering shut momentarily before they land back on me.

I close my eyes as he comes in hot spurts, coating my face. My body lights up with pleasure, knowing that I did this to him. That I got him off, that I make him lose control.

I smile up at him while I lick my lips, drinking in his release.

"You look so pretty with my cum coating you."

He leans down, thumbing some of his cum off me then bringing it to my lips. I suck it between my lips, popping off when I finish. He grins at me before leaning in to give me a kiss.

He grabs his sweatpants and uses the fabric to wipe off the remaining cum on me.

"Come on, let's get you cleaned up." He gives me his hand and pulls me up.

We begin to head to the door when someone starts banging on it. I startle, and Aleks positions me behind his back.

Jackson opens the door, takes one look at Aleks standing there naked, swears, and slams it shut. I fall to the ground in hysterics, clutching my chest.

The door reopens, and a pair of sweatpants are flung inside before it closes again. Aleks steps into them and cracks open the door, leaning against the frame.

"Can I help you?"

"Yeah, asshole. You told your stream you would be back five minutes ago."

"Shit."

Aleks scrambles to his desk, flinging himself into his chair as he turns his mic back on.

"Sorry to keep you waiting. Shield was reciting me a love poem, and I had to let him down gently. It took a little longer than I anticipated to soothe his hurt."

Jackson rolls his eyes then spots me on the ground, trying to rein in my laughter. His eyes widen, and he brings his hands up to cover his face.

I'm still in my outfit, and I'm guessing my face looks like a complete mess. I sober myself and stand up, popping a quick kiss on Aleks' temple before slinking out the door and shutting it behind me. I give Jackson a pat on the back as I step around him to head into our bedroom.

I don't really mind that Jackson saw me in my lingerie, it's a cute as hell set. More people should see it, honestly. But I'm not going to walk around in it if it makes him uncomfortable. Plus, I have a feeling Aleks wants to keep it all to himself.

I stare at myself in the bathroom mirror. My mascara is smeared all under my eyes, and there is dried cum everywhere, even on my breasts.

It should look awful, but I feel like sex on a stick right now.

I turn the heat way up in his shower. Honestly, the reason why I stay at Aleks' half the time is because his shower is pure heaven. If I could transport it to my place, I would. There are jets along the side, and a rainfall showerhead in the center.

I tie my hair in a bun and step into the steam, letting the hot water pour down my body. The heat stings my sore ass slightly as I wash off, using his pine-scented body wash. I've never bothered bringing my own shower stuff here; I prefer to use Aleks'. It makes me smell like him. I did, however, bring all my skincare items here. I clean my face three times before I feel confident there is no makeup or cum left.

Reluctantly, I step out of the warm shower and cocoon myself in one of Aleks' fluffy towels. I dry and then turn around, standing on my tiptoes so I can admire my red ass in the mirror.

I wonder what other ways he can mark me.

Chapter
TWENTY-EIGHT

ALEKS

66 "Finally."

I roll my shoulders, tossing my headset to the side and shutting my system down for the night. It's almost eleven, and I'm starving. I streamed longer to account for the break Stevie and I took earlier. I smirk at the memory. Fuck, she was gorgeous.

I open my door and a barrage of shouting flows from the living room.

They're arguing. *Again.*

I step into the hallway, trying to discern what they could be bickering about now.

"You cheated," Jackson accuses.

"You can't even cheat at this game," Stevie throws back.

"You can cheat at any game if you try hard enough,"

Parker chimes in.

The three of them are sitting at the table we never use; it sits opposite the kitchen island, by the balcony door. Jackson is at the head, Stevie and Parker on either side of him. They're holding cards, all looking at each other with pure venom.

"You're just mad because you lost." Stevie sticks her tongue out. She's wearing another of my T-shirts, her hair in a messy bun, loose tendrils framing her face. She's always effortlessly gorgeous.

"No, I'm mad that I didn't win. Again." Jackson tosses his cards on the table and looks up, spotting me heading over. He gives me a grunt. "Your girlfriend's a cheater."

I laugh at the fact that she has managed to ruffle his feathers. Jackson likes to keep his walls up, letting only a select few in. His default is protective and grumpy. The fact that he is volleying with her means the world to me. I already knew she got along with Parker, but to see her with Jackson releases tension I didn't know I was carrying.

"Don't listen to him. Your bird's an absolute shark at cards."

"Thanks, Parker." She blows him a kiss before standing up to meet me in a hug.

"Want to join us? We're playing Bluff."

"Nah, you guys keep playing. I'm going to heat up some food and I'll watch." I give her a kiss on the top of her head before she sits back down.

I pull out some leftovers, reheating them before sitting next to Stevie.

I watch as she plays. Anyone can play Bluff so long as they can keep track of which cards they have, which they've bluffed, and what's been played. Pro card players can impart odds and statistics onto it, but you don't need that to be good. The real talent comes from how well you can lie, and Stevie has that in spades.

Jackson and Parker might be her friends now, but they can't read her like I can; they haven't been around her long enough. She gives nothing away, her tells are so small, even I take a while to recognize them. It's clear how she keeps winning. Parker and Jackson give her a run for her money though. As shit as Parker was at conning Stevie at the party, he has one hell of a poker face when he's prepared.

I watch as Stevie wins three rounds and Parker wins one. Jackson is livid at this point, but he's never had much luck with card games.

"Alright, that's it, I'm done." Jackson pushes back from the table. "I'm going to bed. Night, cheaters."

"We should play for money next time, Stevie." Parker begins collecting the cards, putting the deck back together.

"I don't know, Parker. I might just bet you for that Aprilia Aleks has been eying."

"I think the Aprilia is cursed," I mutter. "The second you bring it into a bet, everything turns to shit."

"Well, *I* think it sounds like a fun idea." Parker winks. "Next time."

"Alright." Stevie stretches her arms and nods her head at me. "Let's head to bed."

She takes my hand, and I let her lead me back to our room, leaving Parker to his own. I wash up and snuggle into bed next to her. Even though it's a king, Stevie curls up against me. I run hot, but her body is cold enough that we cancel each other out. Exhaustion looms over me after the long week, the edges of sleep crawling in.

"Can I ask you a question?" Stevie's voice breaks through.

"Sure."

"How did you get into streaming?"

Ah. My origin story.

I let my mind clear as the memories begin rolling through, a flurry of emotions linked to them.

"Well, I've been playing PC games since I was a kid. My grandmother had this big, clunky desktop, and she bought me some games in the hopes that it would keep me out of trouble. I had a knack for getting sent to detention ever since I was in elementary school. I just didn't get along with other kids."

It was never really my fault, I just had trouble concentrating in class. I was a loose cannon, never finishing tasks and causing disruptions. Other kids thought it was funny at first, but as I got older, they just found it annoying. It just seemed easier to keep to myself than to try to make friends and get made fun of instead.

"I started getting pretty serious into playing around middle school. I would look up different mods and try to create my own. The deeper I got into the community, the more I would watch gamers online. I admired the hell out of them, but I was jealous, too. They were all friends and would play with each other. They had all these subscribers in the comments supporting them. I had no one, and I wanted that. Eventually, I thought, fuck it, why not give it a shot myself? Everyone thinks I started streaming when I was seventeen, but I was actually sixteen."

"Really? That's so young."

"Yeah, looking back, I knew nothing. I spent the first year filming on and off, trying to figure out how it all worked. It was a mess, really. I met Jackson during that time. He was a grade ahead of me, but we were in the same physics class and got paired up a few times. I used to play this mobile game. Jackson saw it one day and let me know he played it, too. He made it his mission to befriend me after that even though he was older and already had a bunch of friends from the swim team. He started inviting me over, and we'd play PC games together. We didn't have anyone else, just us two. I eventually mentioned that I was looking to stream, and Jackson did this massive deep dive. Helped me figure out the best equipment, how to create VODs, everything. Even pitched in to buy the tech when I couldn't afford it. He was there when I filmed my first stream as NightBlade32, an OG, really."

"Oh, wow. Was he streaming, too?"

"No, he didn't start his own channel until a few years later. That's when he dropped out of college in his sophomore year. Which his mother blames me for even though technically he started everything *and* still got his degree later."

She laughs, her chest bubbling against mine. "Did you go to college?"

I shake my head. "I considered it, but it was during my senior year of high school that my streaming channel blew up. I had been playing *Death Valley* for years, but I began role-playing *DV3* and really found my niche in it. It's still my primary content and what I have the most fun with."

"How many years have you been streaming then?"

"Technically eleven, but I count it as ten."

She sits up, looking at me. "That's such a long time. And you've never felt burned out?"

It's a hard question to answer.

There have definitely been times over the years when I've felt burned out, when I've had to push myself to stream. When gaming felt like more of a job than something I did for enjoyment. But at the end of the day, playing games is like breathing air: I can't survive without it. It will always be a part of me.

"I have. I even stopped streaming for a month once, but I have a support system now. When my popularity first rose, it rose quickly. I tried to do everything, be friends with everyone. I felt cool for the first time. But I was young, naïve. Icarus, flying too close to the sun. Despite the warnings, I got burned. The media was in a frenzy over the 'bad boy' of gaming. Luckily, I had Parker and Jackson. The System was my haven. There wasn't so much pressure for me to be me. It went back to just me and my friends having fun. I got to solo stream whenever I felt like it, and I started playing different games. I'll always love it, even in the dark days."

I lift my head up to pop a kiss on her nose. "Plus, without it, I would have never met you, and that would've been the biggest loss. All the trophies and awards I've gotten over the years, I would trade them all for that night I met you."

"I—I don't know what to say. Thank you for sharing that with me."

"I'll share it all with you, Stevie. The good and the bad, I'm not afraid to show you all of it."

"And I'll accept it all." She caresses my cheek. "Nothing would turn me away from you, Aleks. I spent so many years in a relationship, thinking I was happy, fooling myself. I didn't realize that the way I was being loved wasn't love. Maybe at one point it was, but by the end, it was just a toxic cycle of manipulation. But being with you? God, it's like my life was in black and white, and you're introducing me to all the colors."

"Hearing that coming from an artist says a lot."

She laughs at me. "It's true. You helped me realize the sort of love I'm worth."

Love.

I push myself up, leaning on my elbow. I stare at her, bathed in the darkness, haloed by the red light, my angel living in the underworld.

"I'm falling in love with you, Stephanie Andwell."

Her eyes widen before they soften and melt. Her smile, her sunrise smile, leaks out.

"I'm falling in love with you, too, Aleksander Knight."

She pulls me in for a kiss. It's sweet like honey, sticking to my soul. We lie down against the pillows, and I pull her up against my body. She curls into my chest, and I pepper the crown of her head with kisses.

We fall asleep that way—entwined—my body protecting hers. No matter what, I will serve as her knight and slay any foes that get in our way. I will keep her safe because my heart is becoming hers.

No. That's a lie.

My heart is *already* hers.

Chapter
TWENTY-NINE

STEVIE
♪ AS THEY BLOOM BY UNLIKE PLUTO ♪

My groceries slip out of my hands, slamming onto the floor.

Pink.

Everywhere.

There are bouquets upon bouquets of pink roses in front of my door.

My entire vision is a blur of pink.

I slip to the floor, the pain in my knees registering for only a moment.

Why?

Why now?

He hasn't sent any in weeks. I haven't even heard from him. He hasn't texted me, hasn't called me. Even when I saw him at an art auction last weekend, he just gave me a bland greeting.

So, why?

I can't do anything but stare and stare and stare.

"Stephanie, dear, are you alright?"

A hand shakes me out of my trance. I look up into the soft eyes of Ms. Arkin, the sweet old woman who lives in the apartment next to mine.

"Sorry, what did you say?"

"I asked if you were alright, dear?" Concern creases her expression.

I blink at her, then look around. The spilled groceries, the perfect flowers, and me, in the middle of the hallway. It's a mess.

"Oh, yes, sorry. Just had a fright." I try to laugh it off so I don't worry her, but it clearly sounds fake.

I rush to pick up the groceries, shoving them back in my bags. Ms. Arkin crouches down and helps me, which just makes me feel worse. Once I'm standing, grocery bags repacked and in my hands, I expect her to leave. But she just watches me.

"Are you sure you're alright, Stephanie? I'm sorry to ask again, but I would be doing a disservice to your grandmother if I didn't."

I take a deep breath, plastering on an even smile. "Yes, I'm alright. I thought a spider crawled out of the flowers. Silly, really." I force my shaking hands to calm as I get my key out of my purse and unlock my door. It seems to placate her because she heads back toward her open door.

"Alright, well, I'll bring over some of my lavender cookies later, they have calming effects."

"That would be lovely." I let my smile brighten even

more and leave it there until she closes her door. Then it drops.

I stare down at the pink monstrosities again, and all I feel is anger. Pure, unadulterated anger.

Who does he think he is?

I kick one of the bouquets into my apartment.

Trying to mess with my head?

I kick another bouquet, the petals flying off.

Luring me into a false sense of peace?

I kick two bouquets this time with such force a professional soccer player would be proud.

I think fucking not.

I kick the last bouquet, my toe hitting something hard. I hear it go clanking into my apartment.

Weird.

I step inside, slamming the door closed behind me. I leave my groceries on the floor and search the ground for what could've made the noise, toeing through the strewn, bruised petals—but I find nothing. My amped up brain must have shorted out.

I stare at the broken bouquets on the floor. As offensive as they are, I can't be bothered cleaning them up. I'd set fire to them if it wouldn't burn down my apartment, and Chase doesn't deserve that satisfaction.

Dammit, I need to figure out how the hell he is getting in here and setting them up.

I pick up my groceries, noting a wet spot on the ground. Groaning, I set them down again and peer inside. Yup. My jar of olives cracked.

Sighing, I trudge with the groceries to my kitchen, emptying out the dry bag before salvaging what I can from the olive-soaked one. My head twinges, a headache forming. My entire body feels drained from that one single moment, my emotional reserves depleted.

I get everything squared away, deciding to attack my chocolate-covered pretzels—which Aleks got me addicted to—while zoning my brain out with a cozy video game. But because I can't have anything nice today, apparently, I trip over my rug, mere feet away from the couch. My arms pinwheel to correct my balance while still holding on to the bag of pretzels. I stumble a bit but remain upright.

Those flowers must be cursed.

I look back at the offending rug, ready to cuss out the inanimate object, when I spot something stuck under it. I toss the pretzels onto the couch, crouching down to stick my hand under the green woven material. My fingers close in on a rectangular chunk of plastic.

It's a flash drive with a note strung onto the end.

Dread courses through me as I open it, reading the scrawled word.

Bullseye

"What?" I mutter to myself. Frowning, I turn the flash drive over in my hand.

Obviously, there is something on the USB. However, I've watched enough TV shows to know that there could be some malware on this thing that could attack my computer. I doubt Chase has enough skill to pull that off, but it doesn't mean he couldn't hire someone to do so.

I head into my bedroom, rummaging in my closet for a specific box. My fingers close around the gray box, and I tug it out, popping off the lid. I bought a cheap laptop when I studied abroad in Aix-en-Provence, afraid that someone might steal my expensive one. I never got rid of it, just threw it into my memorabilia box when I returned.

I crawl over to an outlet, plugging the laptop in and powering it on. I snort at the screensaver that pops up, a photo of me and my friends dramatically posing outside Cezanne's studio. I type in my password three times before getting the correct one.

I thumb the flash drive, twirling it between my fingers. Stalling isn't going to change whatever is on this thing. I push it open to reveal the USB and insert it into the laptop.

The computer chirps, registering the device. When my computer doesn't have a complete meltdown from malware, I click on the drive and wait for it to open. There is just one folder. It's labeled "To Be Shared." I tap on it, and my body temperature drops.

A bunch of .jpg files pop up joined by one .mov file.

Oh god. Did Chase film us? Are these photos of me?

I never sent him any nudes…but that doesn't mean he never took any of me. He was always on his phone, and we were together for years. I didn't look for cameras hidden anywhere, but why would I? Whose natural inclination is it to even do that?

My heart thumps heavily in my chest.

Thump.

Thump.

Thump.

I double-click on the first file, holding my breath as it loads.

The image generates, and I'm…

Confused.

I tap on the right arrow, and the next image loads. Then the next. And the next. And the next.

My blood turns to ice as I see a pattern forming, a story unfolding. Some of the pictures are annotated, little notes and arrows decorating them. There are collages weaving images together, connecting threads.

Bile rises in my throat.

I get to the last image and hesitate. My finger trembles over the mousepad.

Eventually, I tap the final file. The video loads with an ugly play button front and center.

I click on it.

I watch the entire one minute and twelve seconds.

I'm glad I'm sitting.

Because my entire world just fell out from under me.

I step into the elevator sopping wet, hitting the penthouse button with my knuckle.

Francis was horrified when he pulled up to my apartment complex to find me standing on the curb in the pouring rain. It probably made matters worse that I was holding a disheveled bouquet of roses in one hand, a plastic bag full of cookies in the other, and said no words to him at all during the forty-minute drive.

I'd sat on the floor for a few hours after opening the files last night, not moving a single inch as my brain shut down. When it finally rebooted, I got up to try to do something, anything. My entire body was shaking, fifteen million thoughts running through my mind. It took a little while for me to realize that I wasn't even breathing properly. When I collapsed on the floor among the broken roses and started crying, I realized I was having a panic attack. I probably would have stayed on the floor all night, wheezing, if Ms. Arkin hadn't come knocking with her lavender cookies. I have no idea how I managed to open the door; I think I crawled.

She took one look at me and said, "Please let me take care of you." How I didn't send her running, I have no clue. That woman is too good for this world. She cleaned up my floor, tossing all the flowers and torn petals into my trash can. Made me wash my face and change clothes, sweat having soaked them. She helped me hold a glass of water until I finished it, then made me drink another before forcing me to nibble on some cookies. When my hiccupping calmed down, she tucked me into bed and recited poetry until I fell asleep.

I woke to her still in my apartment even though it was midday. She watched me choke down a bowl of cereal and change into new clothes. But she was still worried. It wasn't until I informed her that I was heading to my boyfriend's that she relented and went back to her own apartment—which is how I ended up with an extra bag of lavender cookies to share.

"Penthouse," the elevator announces.

I step out of the puddle I created and into the apartment. It's quiet. I don't hear any voices. The only reason for that would be if they were all streaming or sleeping. But it's midafternoon, so everyone should be awake.

I wait for a few minutes before knocking on everyone's doors, then cracking them open. No one's here. *Of course.* I just want to curl up and forget everything. I wish I'd never gone home, never walked up those stairs, never opened that stupid flash drive.

I stare at the room around me, at all the awards and trophies The System has won, the limited-edition gaming merch, their giant poster. The poster haunts me. They look like champions, rulers of the world. The three of them, side by side, and I've ruined it all.

My vision becomes a blur of red, blue, and green, their masks haunting me as tears spill down my cheeks. I can only tell I'm crying because they're hot against my cold, wet skin.

The elevator pings open, carrying a flood of conversation with it. My brain can't piece any of it together. It's broken.

I turn around and watch as the guys walk into the apartment, Aleks holding Parker in a headlock, Jackson shaking his head but laughing with them.

I capture this moment in my mind, burn it into my brain. Their happiness, their ease, their life still whole. Because I know the moment they see me, everything will change. The second our eyes meet, the match will be lit, and I'll be setting their world aflame.

Chapter THIRTY

ALEKS

"Ew, the elevator's wet." Sydney does a weird tiptoe into the elevator, skirting the damp circle in the middle.

Parker leans down, getting a closer look. "Doesn't look like pee."

"Who would pee in a private elevator?" I hit the buttons for Sydney's floor and our own.

"I don't know. Drunk rich people can get pretty wild. There was this lad's weekend in Windsor where—"

"Please, not the Windsor story again," I groan.

"You're just jealous you've never had sex on a horse while playing polo."

The door pings on Sydney's floor. "Oh, thank the heavens. I'm saved from this conversation." She jumps over the puddle and out the elevator. "Good job today, boys."

She waves us off as the doors close, and the elevator begins to rocket to our apartment.

"You know, the logical explanation is that it's rainwater," Jackson throws out.

"Agreed, it's pouring out." We barely missed getting drenched, our interview finishing just beforehand.

"Yeah, but rainwater is a lot less fun," Parker huffs.

"Less fun? Parker, do you have a kink you haven't told us about?" I jostle him, and he reels back.

"What? No. I am not into urolagnia."

I widen my eyes, giving him a scandalized look. "Urolagnia? Wow, you even know the proper term. You're a true believer."

He shoves me, and I grip him in a headlock.

"Let me go, asshat," he growls, trying to twist out of my hold.

"Here I am, calling it golden showers like a total noob when I should've been saying urolagnia." The elevator opens onto our floor, and I drag Parker out with me. "I feel so uncultured. Tell me, Parker, do you prefer when they pee on you or—"

"I'm going to piss on your bed, that's what I'm going to do. Then we'll see how funny this is, dickhead."

Jackson just laughs at us, shaking his head.

Parker continues to struggle out of my grip, when suddenly he slips, bringing me down with him. His elbow goes right into my stomach, and I let out a grunt.

"What the hell, dude?"

"Don't yell at me, I slipped on something."

I clutch my side, rolling off him. I land in something wet. Gross.

"Why is the floor wet?"

"See, I told you it wasn't me."

I push off the floor, my shirt stuck to my shoulder in a wet patch. There is a trail of water on the ground.

Do we have a leak somewhere? The rain isn't even that bad outside. Shit, we'll have to check all the rooms just in case, make sure none of the electronics got messed up.

"Stevie?"

I look up at Jackson and follow his line of sight.

Standing in the middle of our living room is a drenched brunette.

Stevie's hair hangs in wet strands around her face, her white tank top and tennis skirt plastered to her skin. A battered bouquet of pink roses hangs from her left hand, soaking the floor. A clear bag of some sort of cookie is gripped in her right hand. Stevie's face is twisted in anguish, and my body instantly reacts, her pain a signal to my own, activating protection mode.

I run to her, grabbing her face, searching her teary eyes. "Stevie, baby, what happened? Are you okay? Are you hurt?" I run my hands down her body, checking for any injuries. Her knees are bruised, but she otherwise appears unharmed. I pull her into a crushing hug, her body soaking mine. "Stevie, it's okay, you're safe," I murmur. She begins to sob, her body shaking against mine.

I've never seen her like this before. Never seen her cry. Never seen her so broken.

Jackson brings a towel over, and I wrap her in it.

"We need to get her out of these clothes and into a shower," he says.

I nod at him.

"Stevie, come on. You're going to catch a cold." I put my arm around her and try to persuade her to walk, but she's a blubbering mess.

"She's saying she's sorry."

I turn to Parker. "What?"

"Stevie, that's what she's saying." His expression is dead serious.

"How could you possibly know that?" Jackson asks. "She's just crying."

"Trust me." Parker walks over to Stevie. "I've been around my sisters enough times when they've had their hearts broken to understand sobbing girl talk."

He bends down to Stevie's eye level, reaching inside the towel to grab the hand that is holding the drowned flowers. "Can I have the flowers, love?"

She shakes her head, mumbling something else. He nods like he understands what she is saying.

"Well, according to Aleks, the Aprilia is cursed, so what's one more cursed object in my life?"

She releases the flowers into his hand, and when he asks for the cookies, she gives them up freely. He looks at me and nods. I scoop Stevie into my arms, towel and all, and carry her to my bathroom. I sit her on the counter so I can untie her shoes and remove her socks.

"Can you lift your arms for me, Stevie?"

She raises her arms, and I peel the soaked tank off her body, which is a lot harder than it looks. Her sobs have softened to hiccups at least.

"Alright, I'm going to need you to stand for just a second so I can get your skirt off, does that sound okay?"

She still doesn't speak, just nods. I hold her around her

ribs and lift her off the counter, onto the tiles. I don't let
go until I know she can stand on her own, then I kneel in
front of her. I go to roll her skirt down and realize that her
phone is tucked in the pocket of the built-in shorts. I tug
it out, leaving it on the counter. I check the other pocket
and pull out a zip-lock baggie. There's a small thumb drive
inside. She whimpers at the sight of it, so I quickly toss it
onto the counter.

Once she is undressed, I get her into the steaming
shower. I have all the jets on, plus the rain shower. I might
be overdoing it, but I have no clue what I'm doing. I toe
off my sneakers and go to undress when she begins sliding
down the wall to the floor of the shower. *Fuck it.* I get in,
the water drenching my jeans and silk button-down shirt.
I sit next to her and pull her into my lap. Her skin is still
so cold. I have no clue how long she was standing there,
soaked to the bone.

I'm scared.

Completely terrified.

What the hell happened?

"Please, talk to me, little dove."

She looks up at me, finally holding my gaze. I'm relieved and pained at the same time because all I see is deep
despair flooding those salted-caramel eyes. Her crying has
stopped, and she just looks dejected.

"I'm sorry, Blade." She squeezes her palms to her eyes,
curling more tightly in on herself. "I'm so fucking sorry."

I don't know what she is sorry for. A million different
scenarios run through my mind, but I force myself to stop.
There's no point speculating, no point thinking the worst.
It's Stevie, my Stevie. My little dove. My goddess. My

angel. No matter what happened, what destroyed her, we will get through it together. I don't care if she murdered someone; I'll help her hide the body. Hell, I'll take the blame. Anything to stop her pain.

Nothing she could say would make me unlove her.

Because I do. I love Stephanie Andwell.

So, I wash her up, softly soaping her body, whispering words of comfort all the while. Reminding her how special she is, what she means to me, how much I adore her. I let her know that we will get through this together. I shampoo her hair, condition it, comb it until it runs silky smooth down her back. Her skin is flushed pink by the end of it, the entire bathroom coated in a layer of steam.

I get her out of the shower and dry her, inch by inch. I even apply her face moisturizer and twist her hair up in a towel. I leave her sitting on the bathmat while I peel off my wet clothes and go in search of new clothing for the both of us. I keep the bathroom door open so I can watch her as I open one of my drawers and pull out a pair of shorts and underwear for her. Stevie started keeping stuff here last weekend, saying that it was pointless to lug her stuff back and forth. I didn't point out that she had left enough stuff at the apartment over the last three weeks that she basically had everything here already. I grab one of my sweatshirts, knowing she likes to wear them. I throw a pair of sweatpants on and bring the clothes into the bathroom.

"Can you lift your arms again?"

She shakes her head, then starts to push herself to stand. I hold onto her arm, helping her up. She peels the towel off her head, shaking her hair out. "I've got it, thank you." Her voice is small.

She holds her arms out, and I give her the sweatshirt. She slips it on, and I hand her the rest of the clothes to put on. She turns to the mirror, staring at herself, touching her puffy eyes before dropping her head and sighing.

I gather her wet hair and pull it out from under the sweatshirt. "You look fine, babe."

She snorts.

The sound relieves me. It's the first emotion she's shown other than sadness or dejection.

I feel her body stiffen. She raises her head, and her hand reaches out for the baggie with the thumb drive. She picks it up and stares at it, the plastic bag crumpling as she grips it harder. She turns to lock eyes with me, remorse written all over her face before she rests her head against my chest. I stroke her damp hair, giving her all the time she needs.

She sucks in a deep breath, her whole body lifting with the force of it, before blowing it out.

She looks at me one last time before straightening her shoulders and walking out of the bathroom.

Worry fills me again because the look she just gave me was that of someone headed into battle. Someone who doesn't plan to make it back from the war.

The guys are pacing around the living room, but they stop when they see us.

Stevie walks up to Jackson. "Do you still have your sister's laptop?"

His brow furrows. "The one with the messed-up keyboard that I replaced?"

She nods.

"Yeah."

"We need it." That's all she says. Jackson doesn't bother asking any more questions, just jogs back the way we came to grab the laptop from his room. Stevie makes her way into the kitchen, pulling out a bowl. She grabs the cookies she brought, which Parker left on the island, and opens them up, dumping them all in.

"Uh, what are the cookies for, babe?"

"They're calming cookies." She says it so matter-of-factly like calming cookies are the norm.

"Sweet." Parker picks one up. "I could use this." He pops it in his mouth.

"You're going to need more than one."

He stares at her warily, gulping the cookie down. She's acting like some Grecian oracle. Her words aren't making any sense, nothing is adding up, but you can tell that everything she is saying has a meaning and that meaning is not good.

Jackson comes back with the laptop. He sets it on the island next to Stevie, opening it up and swiveling it to her. She shakes her head, turning it back to face him. "It's not for me."

He frowns but accepts it, sitting on a stool and pulling the laptop toward himself. Parker and I seat ourselves on the stools on either side of Jackson.

Stevie's lips part and she takes in a deep breath, as if she is going to say something, but she just lets out a defeated sigh. She opens the zip-lock bag and pulls out the thumb drive, placing it on the marble and sliding it to us. We don't bother asking what she wants us to do with it. It's pretty obvious. Still, it's weird that she asked to use Jackson's sister's old laptop for it. We could've just grabbed any of ours, and they would've been better, too.

Jackson plugs the drive into the USB port, opening it up. Parker and I hover over his shoulder, reading the folder name that pops up.

"To be shared?" Parker reads out.

We look at Stevie, and she nudges the bowl of calming cookies over.

"Parker, remember when you said you had to do damage control?" It's the most words she's said at once in the last hour. Her voice is scratchy, raw, like she's been screaming for hours.

"After the party? Yeah." He begins twisting his ear piercings round and round.

"I'm sorry for being the damage. I didn't mean to cause you guys harm. I swear."

He blinks at her.

"You haven't damaged anything, Stevie. What are you talking about?"

She doesn't respond, just folds her arms around her chest protectively and looks at the ground. We all look at each other, confused. Jackson clicks on the folder. A bunch of files pop up. He looks back at Stevie again before clicking on the first image.

I'm…a little lost.

It's an image of Stevie and Blade at the VSAs. I didn't think anyone got any pictures, but it's harmless. It's a photo of us walking out from the hallway. Jackson clicks on the next image. This one is of Stevie serving all three of us at the table. The next image is of English helping Stevie out from under the table. Not exactly incriminating, but not normal either. After that is a picture of Stevie kissing

341

Blade's mask. Alright, that one's not great.

I still have no idea where this is going.

The next image is of us getting into the car. The license plate is circled, which is kind of creepy. We change plates up every few weeks though, it's already out of rotation. When Jackson gets to the next image, I frown. It's Stevie at the department store, the day I was there with Parker. The next image is the two of us together, laughing. A sourness builds in my stomach. Parker and I star in the next image, he's holding up his tie to me. There is a close-up of the two of us, little circles around our piercings, my tattoos. Parker's full name is scrawled on his close-up.

"What the hell is this?" Parker mutters.

The next set of photos are of Stevie and me on our first date. Inside the coffee shop, exiting, getting on my bike, driving off. Another image with my bike's plate circled. Shit. I don't switch that out. Why would I? It's my personal bike. The close-up reappears, this time with my full name written out. I curse, slamming my fist on the table.

The images continue. There's a photo of Stevie and Sydney at the juice shop. Sydney is circled, her name and job written next to it. There are some blurry photos of Stevie and Blade at Electric Tyger. There's an action shot of Stevie running after Parker in her golden dress. Followed by a close-up of Francis by the Tesla, circled—of course.

The next photo is of our apartment complex.

Jackson swears, but I freeze. Ice winds its way through my veins, coiling around my heart, squeezing.

Everything gets worse from there, somehow. There are photos of Parker and Francis picking up Stevie from her apartment, the license plates circled. Sydney and Parker at their boxing class. Sydney at a speedrunner event with English. Stevie and I on our date at Moira.

Parker shoves away from the table when the next image pops up. It's a side by side of Parker Covington and EnglishCoffee. Similarities circled, dates jotted down, Sydney's name underlined.

I know what's next before Jackson clicks the button.

Aleksander Knight and NightBlade32. Each of my tattoos are circled with lines linking them up, Stevie's and Parker's names underlined.

Jackson pauses, mouse hovering over the arrow to the next image. He waits a full minute before tapping the trackpad.

The image pops up, and I lose control of my emotions. Hysteria spills out of me in a round of uncontrollable laughter.

It's a blurry photo of Jackson in his Jeep entering the underground lot next to an image of Shield3d. The license plate is circled, but there's several question marks next to it. And I know why. The car is registered to me. I bought it for Jackson with the money from my first sponsored stream, a thank you.

There is no link to Jackson Lau.

He's the only person not incriminated in all this. The green enigma. Our Shield.

"What is this, Stevie? Where did it come from?"

We stare at her across the island. Her forehead is lined with worry as she nibbles on her lower lip.

"You haven't watched the video," she tells us. "It'll explain."

Jackson hits the arrow again, a video file loading. Parker sits back down as Jackson clicks play.

Static plays at first, the screen black until a digital 2-D composition of one of our masks pops up. It's orange, and the audio wave sits where a mouth would be. As the audio starts, the wave moves with it.

"Hello, Stevie and The System." The voice has been distorted. *What movie-type shit is this?*

"I hope you enjoyed my little slideshow. A detective novel, if you will. The discovery of Aleksander Knight and Parker Covington. The whole world has been wondering who you are, and here is the proof, clear as day. Undeniable. I commend you for a good game, but it's over, a KO." I grit my teeth. "Who will be the highest bidder? Will it be you? Or maybe, it's too late. Maybe little Stevie took this into her own hands." My eyes shoot to Stevie, but she just shakes her head. "I'll give you one shot. An extra HP point, you might say. Bring your highest bid to Warehouse 43 on Saturday at 7 p.m. You must all show up for the bid to be valid. That includes Shield, whom I do have to commend for escaping my radar. No funny business, no other people. Failure to comply will result in a failsafe, automatically sending the file to one of my media sources. May the best player win."

The image glitches out, and the video goes dark.

We just stare at it, the black screen screaming at us.

Jackson stands up and throws his stool to the ground. Stevie flinches, ducking behind the island.

"Saturday is tomorrow," Jackson growls.

"Yes, well, Saturday generally follows Friday," Parker drawls, but his voice is devoid of all humor.

Jackson turns to him, a murderous intent in his eyes.

It's hard for Jackson to snap, his tolerance for bullshit higher than the average person's. But when he does blow? There's no stopping him until he comes down. I put my arm up to pause him, giving him a look. Our emotions are on the fritz, we need to take a step back.

Parker pulls out his phone and brings it to his ear.

"Who are you calling?" I nod at him.

"Sydney."

Right. Shit. She's going to be pissed we didn't call her the minute we found Stevie in the apartment. But we need her, she'll know what to do. Because right now, whatever we decide won't be the right decision.

I understand everything that just happened, but my brain just won't process it. It doesn't seem real, like a deep fake or some shit.

I'm in denial. Deep, deep, deep denial.

It's not possible. Ten years. I've been Blade for ten years. And some person just appears out of thin air, having solved a puzzle I'd purposely lost the pieces to?

I was careful. We were all careful. We had a plan for everything, knew what our safety measures were. This should never have happened.

But it did. Because while I spent years perfecting the code of my life, making sure the system was flawless, I didn't account for my own backdoor. That I would create a glitch, one that opened me up to vulnerabilities. Vulnerabilities that would let someone crack the code.

The glitch could have been anyone, anything; it just happened to be Stevie in this scenario.

It would be so easy to blame her, to let her take the fall for our emotions, but that would be wrong. We all let down

345

our guards, we got comfortable. I have no regrets when it comes to Stevie. None at all.

But I have no idea what any of this means. If we can't stop the information from leaking, what does that mean for The System? What happens to us?

I walk over and sink to the floor next to Stevie, letting my armor shatter as I lean into her. She's stiff at first, but then she relaxes against me, the tension leaving her body.

"Who am I if I'm not Blade?"

"Aleksander Knight." She says it so simply.

"Aleksander Knight is nothing."

The fears that I've pushed down since I was a kid bubble their way up, the insecurities that I masked, literally, cracking through. Becoming NightBlade32 made me feel special. Everyone wants to know Blade, fuck Blade, be Blade. And I *am* Blade. I'm the source of their jealousy, their envy, and it feels fantastic to have a throne among the other gods of Olympus.

No one's ever cared about Aleksander Knight.

There's nothing special about Aleksander Knight.

A fire lights in Stevie's puffy eyes, her body coming alive for the first time in hours. "Aleksander Knight is my everything. *You* are my everything. *Eisai i psychi mou.*" Stevie reaches up and holds my face. "I know it might feel like Blade is a separate person, a persona you've built, but that is you. Aleksander Knight exists without Blade, but Blade doesn't exist without Aleksander Knight. All those trophies? All those awards? You won them. Aleksander Knight is the streaming superstar behind Blade. You are the creator, and that makes you a god."

I feel her fire warm my veins, her words recharging

me.

"I know I've been a complete mess, a zombie. I'm acting like my world is falling apart, when really, it's yours. I've been selfish, and it's because I can't bear the thought of losing you. You are the blood in my veins, my heart beats for you, but I've just injected a poison into my bloodstream, and I don't know whether it will kill us or not."

"It won't." I hold her hands. "I'll suck the poison out myself if I have to."

"I was so scared you'd hate me."

"I could never hate you. This isn't your fault."

She rests her forehead against mine. "Aleks, you *are* Blade, even without the mask."

"But will people still want Blade without the mask?"

Will they want the man behind the mystery if there is no mystery?

"I don't know, *agapi mou.*" Her honesty burns. "But I have to believe they will. Because I still want you."

I hug her to my chest.

I won't lose her, and I won't lose myself.

I'm Aleksander Knight and I'm NightBlade32. I'm one of the best. This person thinks they've got everything figured out, that they've solved the map, but they don't realize that I'm the moderator and I create my own rules.

Renewed strength flows through me like an energy potion.

Sydney comes striding out of the elevator, laptop tucked under one arm, a briefcase in the other. "Alright, hit me with it. Where's the evidence?"

We all point to the laptop still sitting open on the island.

Sydney scrolls through all the photos, jotting down her own notes as she goes. We see her face harden as the images of herself pop up, but she powers through, her mind working at its best. She watches the video over and over, listening for something.

"She's a woman on a mission," Stevie whispers.

"She's our publicist."

"It's weird, isn't it, that they couldn't figure me out?" Jackson sits next to Syd, looking over her notes.

"Not really, you can clearly tell that this person was targeting Stevie. They only ever found you guys when you were with her. Doesn't seem like they could track you otherwise. Even after they'd found the apartment, they had to rely on Stevie to know where you were because our security is so high. She was the weak link."

Stevie winces.

"Sorry, hon, just stating the facts."

"It's fine, I knew all that." She slumps against me.

"But the threat is against us, not Stevie. She was just a means to an end. Why not just send the flash drive to us?" Parker counters, swiping more tiny calming cookies from the bowl. I'm pretty sure he's eaten thirty at this point. I don't think they're helping.

"Probably because your mail gets screened. Security would have flagged this in an instant. All of management would have been called in, you boys wouldn't have had a chance to decide how to deal with anything. They used Stevie to bypass that."

"Actually, I have another reason." Stevie gets up and grabs the decrepit roses, dropping them on the island. Syd eyes them with disgust.

"What the hell happened to those?"

A bitter laugh leaves Stevie. "I did." She points at them. "I've been receiving pink roses for weeks now. Ever since Chase and I broke up. He used to get them for me all the time while we were dating. They're his thing."

"What? Why did you never mention this to me?" I shoot to my feet, and she holds her hands out defensively, trying to calm my bristling tiger.

"Because they stopped. After our date at Moira, he went radio silent. These flowers and that thumb drive are the first I've heard from him in weeks."

I'm irritated at her not telling me. Rationally, I know we had just started dating when Chase backed off, but still. Maybe if I'd known he was that obsessed, was that committed, maybe we would've caught on to this. *Maybe.*

"And you're sure this is Chase, that your ex would do this?"

"He was livid that I wouldn't take him back. Calling and texting multiple times a day. When he saw Aleks and me at Moira, I think he finally realized there was no coming back. So, he played his trump card."

Jackson frowns. "Isn't he some country club nepo baby? He seems too soft. How would he have even gotten these images?"

"I've told you multiple times, but no one listens to Parker," Parker tuts. "Rich people. They don't need to get their hands dirty when they can pay someone else. You shouldn't doubt what they're capable of."

"You're all rich," Sydney points out.

"Exactly." His expression goes dead serious.

"Alright, let's see what we can do to stop this time

bomb."

We're on the phone for hours. Sydney has to loop in our manager, who is none too happy to be called at 4 a.m. in New York. He's even less happy when he hears of the situation. Our lawyers are woken up, Paige included, to comb through our contracts. We have to go over every contingency we have in place and run through every possible scenario, from the best of the best to the worst of the worst. Parker dives into Chase's history, using his connections to dig up any clues or dirt we can use.

Stevie falls asleep around five in the morning. She tried to stay up, help out, but her battery's wasted. She dealt with this demon for an entire night without us.

I carry her to our room, tucking her into bed.

"I'm sorry, Aleks," she mumbles.

I kiss her forehead. "I told you, Stevie. Good days and bad days, we're there for each other. I'll never give up."

I'll fight tooth and nail to figure this out.

For her. For us. For the boys. For The System.

"Aleks," Parker whispers, poking his head into my room, a twisted smile on his face. "Phoebe found something."

"Oh?" My lips split into a joker's grin.

If Chase thinks he has us cornered, he has another thing coming.

I'm Aleksander Knight, and I don't lose.

It's game on.

Chapter
THIRTY-ONE

STEVIE

feel like I've been run over by a bus then hit by a train and thrown off a cliff.

Basically, I feel like trash.

At least my eyes aren't blown up anymore, the puffiness from my tears having gone down. I splash my face with more cold water. I've spent almost two days letting myself be eaten away by my emotions, surrendering to the pain, and becoming a shell of myself. I'm not going to let Chase affect me any more than he already has. I'm tougher than this, than him. I won't let this destroy me. I won't let this destroy Aleks, or any of the guys.

I open my makeup bag and begin painting on my armor. With each swipe of mascara, I strengthen. With every tap of blush, my resolve hardens. The first step to feeling good is looking good. I run a comb through my thick waves and give a half smile to myself in the mirror.

I can't keep walking around in Aleks' clothes, as much as I love them. I need to be an actual human. Opening our wardrobe, I pull my baby blue, rib-knit midi dress from its hanger. I roll the soft material onto my body, adjusting my boobs in the V neck. The straps are too thin to wear a bra with, but the slit only goes to mid-thigh, so it's still pretty casual.

I look normal, good, but I still feel the kiss of death lingering.

I need caffeine. Lots of it.

When I push open the door, I'm startled by the sheer amount of people in the apartment. There's at least twenty people milling about, but a blonde woman is in the process of ushering most of them out and into the elevator. I watch the procession until the last one leaves. They really called the cavalry in on this one.

"Well, aren't you a pretty one?" The British accent rolls over me, and I realize the woman is one of Parker's sisters, Phoebe, the one with the short hair. Her entire vibe is giving Charlize Theron with her black pantsuit, and it's pretty badass. "Come, join the party." She grabs my hand, tugging me along to the island where the guys are all sitting. Sydney, Parker's other sister Paige, and two men I don't recognize are talking out on the balcony.

"Your girlfriend's up," Phoebe announces, swinging into the kitchen. She slides a familiar take-out cup of coffee toward me as I hop onto the free stool next to Parker. I twist the green cup around and see the logo for *Glass & Grass* stamped on the side. A small spark of happiness glows in the dark waters of my chest. I sip on the cup of pure heaven. Coffee spreads into my system as I savor the mapley goodness.

"I got your favorite." Aleks leans forward on the island to talk across Parker, smiling with a touch of cockiness.

"Thank you." I return his grin and greedily devour the beverage.

"Here." Parker nudges a pastry my way. "We ordered a bunch of food earlier to refuel." My stomach growls, and I realize I haven't eaten or drunk anything since the day before. I scarf it down without a second thought.

We're all just sitting in silence, the guys tapping away on their phones. The elephant looms in the room, a dark cloud hovering at the edge of my consciousness. I swallow the last bite, and it sticks in my throat.

"So, where are we, you know, with the situation?"

"Plan A is underway; Plan B is prepped just in case," Parker's sister throws out, popping a melon ball in her mouth. The boys say nothing.

"What does that mean?"

"Means we have the situation sorted. Just need to let it play out now." She says it so nonchalantly, like the whole situation doesn't faze her.

"I'm lost."

That doesn't make any sense. How is that possible? But she doesn't offer up any additional information, just smiles and eats another damn melon ball.

"Don't worry, babe." Aleks moves to stand beside me, resting his hand on my exposed thigh. The contact calms me. "Sydney has the check and is working with the security team to make sure all is sorted for tonight. Phoebe, here, is covering everything else. We've got this. Trust me."

I purse my lips, turning everything over. I want to ask more questions, but as I look into Aleks' eyes, all I see is pure exhaustion. Dark circles having made a home beneath his dull eyes, faint stubble peeking out on his jaw. Hell, everyone looks like walking death. I might have gotten a few hours of sleep, but I don't think they've gotten any. Reluctantly, I let my questions drop.

"Alright, I trust you."

"Fabulous." Phoebe claps her hands. "Well, we have a few more hours before we need to leave. You lads should get some rest beforehand. There's nothing more you can do until then, and you all look like shit."

"Rude," Parker yawns, "but I am knackered." He slips off his stool and slinks off to his room.

Aleks squeezes my thigh. "Want to come back to bed?"

I'm tempted, but I'm too wired, so I shake my head. "I'll just stay out here, find something to distract myself with."

"Alright." Aleks leans down to give me a quick kiss before heading off with Jackson.

I shoot off a few texts to Deanna as I drain the rest of my coffee.

"Want to play *Jelly Kart*?" Phoebe asks me. "Parker said you were pretty good."

I eye the unreadable blonde as she skirts the island and heads to turn on the TV. I weigh the idea. I don't really have much else to do, and it would help turn off my brain.

"Sure." I get up to follow her, plopping myself on the couch.

"Perfect." She tosses me a controller with a kind smile, and I let the game distract me from the battle to come.

The warehouse doesn't look as creepy in person. A little less "I might murder you" than I was expecting. Then again, I doubt Chase would've picked a place that was rundown. He won't even step into a hotel unless it's four stars. The warehouse is probably all decked out inside.

We pile out of the Escalade, Francis and Phoebe remaining in the front seats. The air is cooler this close to the mountains. Aleks puts his arm around my waist, giving me a squeeze. I stare up into the red lights of his mask. The setting sun shines off it, and I can't see his eyes, but I know he is looking at me, his strength pouring into me to balance out the nerves.

"Have I told you how beautiful you look?"

"You have not."

I'd slipped into a pair of black boots that I combined with a black skirt and a red leather bandeau top. I wanted to show Chase that Aleks and I are a team, united equals. The boys each don their masks, all in black jeans and wearing shirts of their respective colors. Sydney switched into a black skirt and white silk front-tie shirt, hair pulled into a high ponytail, looking every bit their watchdog.

"Well, you look like a devilish angel."

"I was going for more of a 'rip your heart out' vibe."

"Well, you certainly have mine."

I snort at him. He's a goddamn smooth talker without missing a beat.

"Alright, if you two are done, you should head in." Phoebe rests her arm against the open window, nodding in the direction of the warehouse. "He's expecting you in five."

A stone forms in my throat, and I swallow it down, feeling it drop into the pit of my stomach. My nerves are turning into dread.

"We've got this." Parker's voice is confident.

"I know you do, little bro."

Parker takes off first, hands lazily in his pockets as he strides, Sydney and Jackson close behind him. Aleks holds my hand, linking our fingers together.

"Together."

"Together."

We take up the back, the five of us a force as we enter the final boss's lair.

The warehouse is dark, save for some glowing TV screens in the far distance. I can't make anything out. The boys' masks glow against the void. We hover near the entrance, wary of what could be farther inside. All I can hear is a faint clacking sound and some music.

Then the lights flick on all at once, and I flinch at the assaulting brightness. The warehouse walls are entirely black, the concrete floor painted white. There are boxes piled up along the two side walls, various pieces of furniture wrapped in plastic stacked around, and some framed art leaning against it all. My heart hurts a little and hopes those aren't expensive pieces because this is not the right environment in which to store them.

Now I can see that the wall opposite us houses not only a handful of mounted screens but a desk with a large chair. I can see elbows resting on the chair arms from behind. Aleks nods forward, and we make the walk across, our footsteps echoing loudly.

The closer we get, the clearer I can see the screens and the louder the music gets. There's a security feed on the left mounted screen; the screen on the right has that creepy 3D-rendered orange mask on it. The clacking sound from earlier registers as someone typing on a keyboard.

"Chase." I call out, my voice bouncing off the walls.

Once we are only a few feet away, Aleks stops. My eyes dart around the set up. In addition to the two mounted screens, there are three desktops set up on the desk, piles of paper strewn everywhere. My eyes narrow in on the video game being played on the center desktop.

"Let's start the match."

Panic lances through my stomach.

The voice isn't Chase's.

I have no idea who we are dealing with. We've just walked into enemy territory with no visibility. Whatever Plan B is, I hope it accounted for this.

"Time limit: thirty; Stock: one; Stage select: the warehouse."

The game on the screen ends, and the player in front of us emerges victorious.

"Do you accept my rules, Aleksander?"

Aleks' hand flexes around mine.

The chair swivels to face us, and my eyes widen as I fight to keep the rest of my face neutral. But it's impossible.

I stare at the cockroach in front of me. A conceited grin, blue eyes dripping with arrogance, and that hallmark, perfectly-gelled red hair.

We've just walked into the fox's den.

"Decker?" My expression falls into one of absolute incredulity.

"Daniel-fucking-Decker," the boys confirm in unison, voices laced with derision.

"I don't..." My brain is trying to rewire itself, figure out the right connections. "Did Chase set you up? Make you do this?"

"No one makes me do anything," he scoffs.

"But Chase—"

"Isn't involved in this, sweet Steffy."

No. That doesn't add up.

"But the roses?" My brain pounds as it runs through different scenarios, trying to figure out Decker's play. Why would Decker send me the roses? Those were the only things that made sense out of this whole thing. They were my clear connection to Chase.

"Think, Stephanie, when did the roses start showing up?"

"After the breakup, when Chase was trying to win me back." It was typical of Chase to do that, expected.

He shakes his head. "Think a little more specifically."

More specifically?

The first rose appeared on my car after brunch with Deanna. We'd met to debrief about the VSAs, and she freaked me out with that article.

Wait.

"After the VSAs."

"Five points to Stephanie." The asshole shoots a finger gun at me.

"What the hell. You've been following me since the VSAs?"

"Not me, my P.I."

"Same shit," I growl.

I didn't even know Decker before the VSAs. Never met him, never heard of him. Sure, he said Chase had talked about me a bunch to him, but that still doesn't fill in any more of the puzzle. I didn't even know I'd be at the VSAs until the day before when Deanna called about being short-staffed.

Aleks takes a small step forward.

"Why Stevie?"

It's the first thing any of the boys have said.

I hate that I can't see their faces, can't see how they're reacting to all of this.

"Opportunity, honestly. You guys have a habit of getting your dicks wet at those sorts of events, not that you ever take anyone home. But then I saw our sweet Steffy chatting with you, and I knew you wouldn't just let her go. She's a prize, one everyone in our circle has wanted to win. And you love to win."

If he calls me *Steffy* one more time, I'm going to punch him.

"I didn't even take her home. Barely knew who she was. You had no way of knowing I would even see her again."

"True, but my P.I. has never been able to tail your driver over the last six months, so I hedged a bet and had him tail Stephanie, leaving her little gifts just in case. Figured if it didn't pan out, she'd just attribute it to Chase. The whole thing was a gamble."

"How did you even know about the roses?" It's been bothering me.

"Come on." He rolls his eyes. "Chase has no filter. You know this. He blabs about everything. You think I've never heard him talk about getting you pink roses before? His grand gestures to win you back time and time again."

Chase really was the worst at keeping secrets; it's how I always managed to find out he was cheating. He didn't have the finesse.

Crap, that's what Jackson said last night. As if Chase could pull off something like this without tipping his hand earlier.

"So, what? You just paid some guy to follow me around, leave me creepy roses, and then what? Hope that I somehow found my way to Aleks?"

Fuck. I'd confirmed his name.

Decker smiles. "I thought there was a chance *Aleks* might try to track you down, reach out. You're an addiction like that. Although, it was slim odds. But I'd been paying my P.I. for so long and nothing was panning out. What was another few weeks tracking you in one last shot? I had the money to spare."

Lucky.

Decker got fucking lucky.

And that pisses me off all the more.

"It took a while for the pieces to line up. Covington here was my first clue, but the scales tipped that night in the club, when you took off your gloves and the tattoos matched up."

Aleks swears under his breath. But Decker keeps running his mouth, so damn proud of himself.

"It took forever to figure out where you lived. I was really hoping you'd take her home after the club. I was so damn sure. But no." He tsks. "I didn't score that until the Taylors' ball."

"The tail." Parker jogs my memory.

"But I thought Francis lost him?" He took ages getting us to the apartment.

"He did; my guy lost you after the party," Decker confirms. "Your driver is freakishly good."

"Then, how?"

"When the investigator called to let me know the tail had gone cold, I came up with the next best solution. Chase got ripping drunk after you left. It was easy to swipe his phone. You hadn't blocked him, so you were still sharing your location with him."

My stomach drops. Shit. *Shit!* I hadn't even thought to stop sharing my location. I forgot that I even was. I open my phone, pulling up Chase's contact. Sure enough, I can see his location, and he can see mine. I turn the stupid thing off.

"Again, I wasn't sure whether English would bring you back to their place or just home, especially since Blade still hadn't brought you over. Honestly, my expectations were low. So, imagine my luck when I saw you stopped elsewhere. I sent the address to the P.I., and it was smooth sailing from there."

"Not entirely," Jackson taunts.

"No. Not entirely." Decker stands up, walking right up to Jackson. "Never did figure you out." He stares at the mask, and his jaw clicks before he twists away, dropping dramatically into his chair. "But two out of three was enough." He eyes Aleks and Parker. "Not sure why you're bothering to keep those masks on, but whatever makes you more comfortable. I always knew you were nothing without them on. Spineless."

Aleks' fists curl and Parker goes to step forward, but Sydney intercepts them.

"Cut the trash talk, Decker. You've said your piece, gotten your pitiful villain monologue out of the way. All of which has just shown that, at the end of the day, you wish you were The System. You were just looking to take them down due to some deep-seated jealousy and obsession. Honestly, I could have a restraining order placed against you in a heartbeat. Your temper tantrum has created a lot of damn work for me. Unnecessary work. And I'm done."

"Alright then, Ms. Publicist. Show me the money if you're so desperate to end this."

Sydney flashes him the folded check, pinched between her second and third finger. Decker snatches it up, smiling at us as he unfolds it.

"Let's see how much you think your secret is worth."

When I thought it was Chase, I had some faith that whatever amount we offered would be enough because his main focus wasn't the boys but me. Now, knowing that it's Decker, that faith is shot like a bullet through a stained-glass window.

Decker's smug smirk flattens dead, and he slowly looks up at us, eyes full of malice.

"What the hell is this?" His voice is low as he spits out the words. "What the hell is this!" He crushes the check in his hand and throws it at the ground. It bounces a few times before tumbling to a stop before my feet.

Eyes on Decker the entire time, I crouch down and pick up the ball. I let go of Aleks' hand and uncrumple it, reading the delicately printed words.

Go fuck yourself.

I really hope there is a Plan C.

"Do you think I'm joking? That I won't send this out?" Decker's fingers crash across the keyboard as he brings up an email with a ZIP folder attached. My eyes skim across it, nausea roiling in my gut.

"No, Decker. I know you will." Aleks reaches up to remove his mask, and my hand shoots out, grasping his bicep. I desperately search through the X's for his eyes, wondering what the hell he is trying to do. Decker could have this whole place cammed up, streaming right now. I wouldn't put it past him to turn this whole thing into a show, a boost for his own channel. Besting The System is his entire goal here; he wants to feel superior. He wants the kings to bow to him, surrender their throne.

Everything halts for a beat, and then all I hear is the tearing of Velcro. My hand falls to my side as the mask slips off to reveal his deep green eyes and a sinister grin.

"You were always going to release our secret, Decker. I know your gameplay. You're as predictable as ever; it's why you'll never win against me."

Decker shoots up, his chair slamming back against the desk.

"What are you talking bout?" He points to the mask in

Aleks' hand. "You just forfeited."

"Nah, you've been ganked, mate." Parker rips off his mask.

I look at Sydney, but she's staring straight ahead. Expression completely neutral.

Something's not right.

"No, no I haven't," Decker snarls. "Time's up. Match over."

He spins around, and I cry out, lunging forward to grab him. My hand grips his shirt, but it's not quick enough. A woosh sounds out as he hits send, and I watch as the email disappears. Decker flips around, crazed triumph written over his face. "Triple kill."

Parker just laughs. "Do you really think exposing us is going to ruin us?"

"You're nothing without your masks."

"Wrong," Jackson's deep voice announces. "Without the masks, we're OP."

I hear the ripping of Velcro again, and I turn to see Jackson peeling off his mask. His expression is one of pure boredom. He sighs, running a hand through his hair.

What is going on?

Why are they all so calm?

Why does it feel like I'm in the dark?

Aleks leans forward, bringing himself to Decker's eye level. "You're playing on my server, Decker. I make the rules here."

"No, these are *my* rules. This is *my* game."

"Then why are you three steps behind?"

"I'm not," he shouts.

"Oh? Are you sure?" Aleks nudges past him and stands

in front of the desk. He begins clicking around, and I watch as he opens The System's VOD channel. My eyes fall on their latest upload, timestamped ten minutes ago. The video has twenty thousand views already.

"What the hell?" I'm the only one to speak as we all stare at the thumbnail.

It's three men, their faces blacked out with a white question mark in the center, and they're each holding a mask.

One red. One blue. One green.

NightBlade32. EnglishCoffee. Shield3d.

Aleksander Knight. Parker Covington. Jackson Lau.

The video title burns itself onto the back of my retinas.

We Are The System

"What is this?" Decker shoves Aleks out of the way, staring up at the screen.

"It's their face reveal." I don't believe the words as they spill from my lips.

They outed themselves.

They unveiled the mystery.

"Why? How?" Decker looks absolutely lost.

"Because we control our own narrative." Aleks moves to stand next to Parker and Jackson. They're a mirror of their thumbnail. Three confident kings, staring down at the courtier who thought he could usurp them.

The wires connect.

"Oh my god. You knew." A laugh leaves me. "You knew it was him." More laughter spills from my body. Decker looks at me like I'm drunk. "They've been playing you this whole time, stalling you."

I don't believe it. I don't know how they did it.

"No. No, that's not possible." Panic leaks into Decker's eyes.

"Oh, it's very possible." Parker whistles. "You should've seen half of what we were able to find." His gaze darkens, and it shocks me. "Actually, I'm sure you can imagine."

"You lost, Decker. Man up and get the fuck over it. You have no cards left." Aleks holds his hand out to me, pulling me flush against him, resting our hands on my shoulder. "And if you ever think about using Stevie again, you'll see exactly what The System is capable of. Because this? This is easy mode. But I won't hesitate to switch to permadeath."

Decker's upper lip curls, but he doesn't say anything.

"Let's move out." Jackson doesn't wait, just turns and begins walking out. Parker tucks his hands into the front pockets of his jeans and follows behind, Sydney striding beside him. I give Decker one last look as Aleks guides us out of the warehouse.

The fox thought he'd entered the chicken coop only to find himself in the lions' den.

Chapter
THIRTY-TWO

STEVIE

I sit between Aleks and Sydney in the backseat, listening to the boys relay the entire ordeal to Phoebe, who is howling with laughter.

"Oh, I wish I could've seen the little wanker's face," she hoots.

Apparently, it was Phoebe who figured out it was Decker and not Chase. The analyst, it seemed, had skills and connections that exceeded the norm.

"Why didn't you tell me?" I whisper to Aleks.

He looks down at me, an apology written in his eyes.

"Because, if you'd have known it was Decker, you would've known what we all did. That he was going to release the information, no matter what. I didn't want you to shoulder the weight of our decision to reveal ourselves before Decker could."

"I wouldn't have—" Aleks levels me with a look. "Fine, yes. I would've." There is a seed of guilt within me, threatening to grow. "It's not fair. It wasn't your choice. He forced your hand."

"That's where you're wrong, babe." He rubs my thigh, and like always, it calms me slightly. "It *was* my choice. We could've buried this if we wanted to. We spent all morning going over the logistics, what it would mean, and we all agreed on it. I made the decision to film the video and show the world who I am because *I* wanted to."

"But last night—"

"Last night, you showed me that I didn't need to be afraid anymore. That I had grown. That I am powerful in my own right. I am Blade, and I'm a fucking force, baby." He grins at me, a true smile.

"He's right." Jackson looks back at us from his seat. "We're The System, we're family, and we stand together. Anyone who threatens us will learn exactly what we are capable of to keep each other safe."

"And we are capable of so much," Phoebe grins.

"We basically threw Decker a reverse Uno," Parker pipes in. "Plus, now I can actually compete in live Speed-run tournaments. The masks were holding us back; we're going to reach a whole new level now."

Everyone seems so…happy. It's throwing me off balance. I almost feel like I've entered a parallel universe.

"As peaceful as the anonymity was, it was also suffocating. I've spent ten years on the run, basically. The three of us had each other, but we couldn't let anyone else into our lives." Aleks looks at me with pure adoration. "I have you now, and I wasn't going to keep you hidden just because it could expose my identity. That's not the relationship I want, it's not the future I want."

"Promise?"

"Promise."

He places a kiss on my forehead, and the seed of guilt dissolves.

"I already told the boys, but it's going to be a hard couple of weeks." Sydney is tapping away on her phone. She hasn't looked up from it since we got in the car, busy dealing with all the attention from the reveal. Even my phone's been blowing up, but it's just texts from Deanna screaming at me. I owe her a huge explanation and probably a nice bottle of wine. "The media is already in a frenzy over this. The boys are viral on every platform, hashtags trending, the full nine yards—and it's only been an hour."

"Everyone's debating whether they're Team Blade, Team English, or Team Shield. Although there's really no competition; we know I'm the most attractive of the group." Parker smugly scrolls through his phone.

"I'll remind you that I've ranked in the Top 10 Most Attractive Streamers more times than you have," Aleks taunts him.

"Ah, yes, but just watch, this year I'll finally rank above you."

"Want to make a bet on it?"

"The Aprilia?" Parker smirks.

"You fucking bet." Aleks grins.

They're children, I swear. I also don't understand their bets. It's always Parker betting something, but never anyone else…which isn't how a bet works.

"Anyway," Sydney cuts in, rerouting the conversation,

"once they get a whiff of you, it might get a little dicey. I don't expect a lot of issues, but you should anticipate some backlash from a few of the more intense fans. It's an unfortunate reality for a lot of girlfriends." Syd finally looks up from her phone. "But don't worry. I've got your back."

I know she does. They all do.

"I'm not worried. If I can handle the politics of the Californian elite, I'm sure I can charm the rest of the world."

This is what my mother raised me to do. I can work a room with my eyes closed. I haven't spent years battling against Felicity Taylor just to be bested by some online trolls.

Aleks pulls me into his chest, and I snuggle into him.

"That's my girl."

"Always."

Chapter
THIRTY-THREE

ALEKS

"Are you lagging or something, English? Your shots are shit."

"Well, maybe if someone wasn't camping out by the weapon drop, I could get a better fucking gun."

"I'm not camping."

I'm totally camping.

I watch as Parker's character comes ducking and rolling into the loading dock. I snipe him with a headshot. Again. He cusses me out, and I laugh back at him.

Then the screen switches perspective, and I watch as Jackson's character assassinates me with a knife.

"Asshat."

"The karma of camping," he drawls.

"Oh, yeah, that's great coming from the guy who keeps using his invisibility shield."

"Don't be bitter, it's unattractive."

While I wait to resurrect, I scan the chat. At least half of the messages are asking me to turn on the camera. BladeGurl69 is asking for "some of that eye candy," while ProFly_1 is arguing that our video was AI-generated and "there's no way all three of them could be attractive."

It's been two weeks since our reveal, our video having reached over twenty million views, but I've yet to actually stream or post any videos with my camera on. It's just not my instinct.

I have taken off my gloves, though. Baby steps.

We've had hundreds of sponsors reach out offering us new filming equipment, gaming gear, and merch. Parker was on the money when he said we would hit new levels. All of our subs went up, and my average stream views are nuts. It doesn't look like it will be slowing down any time soon. Sydney has had to hire an assistant just to help field all our social media and publicity requests. The three of us sit down for our first interview next week, and tomorrow night we'll be heading to the *Gods League* Champion Series opening event.

Four weeks ago, Stevie and I thought we would have to sneak around the event. Now, she will be riding in the limo with the rest of us.

Stevie lounges on the bean bag I bought her, sketching away in her notebook. She's been camped out at the apartment for the last four days ever since the media eventually got wind of our relationship and her place got mobbed. One of the outlets had finally gotten around to using the information Decker had scrounged up. We upped security for her, but she said it was just easier to stay here.

I stream with the boys for another hour before logging off and switching over to *Death Valley* to film some role-play content for my channel. I film around two hours' worth of content, messing around with some new people I brought into my server, then send the footage to our editor. He'll edit it into four separate videos to be posted over the next week.

It's only ten, but Stevie's knocked out on the beanbag. I go to move her sketchpad so I can carry her to bed but pause when I see what she was working on. It's a graphite half-body image of me gaming, my expression pulled into a smirk. It shocks me. Not that she sketched me, but the image itself. I'm so used to seeing myself playing in the mask that the simplicity of it just being me and my headset throws me off.

"It's rude to look at an artist's sketchbook without permission," her sleepy voice scolds.

"I think I get a pass considering I'm the subject."

"Fair." She sits up, stretching. "Do you like it?"

"I do. I've never seen myself this way before."

She tilts her head. "It's how I always see you."

"I know, but it feels different now."

She nods, looping her arms around me. I set the sketchbook down and pick her up, carrying her to the kitchen and sitting her on a stool. I pull our ice cream out of the freezer, double chocolate brownie for me, maple pecan for her. I leave them to thaw a bit as I grab some spoons from the drawer.

"You'll get used to it eventually, Aleks." She's staring at her ice cream, watching it as if that will force it to melt faster. "You've shown me time and time again that the man behind the mask is no different. That Aleksander Knight is a game-crushing, motorcycle-riding hottie all on his own."

I take the seat next to her. "You think I'm hot?"

She snorts, digging her spoon into the still frozen dessert, threatening to bend the metal. "Yeah, you're hot. Think you can use some of that hotness to melt this damn ice cream."

I dig a scoop out of mine, holding it out to her. She scrunches her nose.

"What?"

She's looking at the ice cream like it offended her.

"I have something to tell you."

"Ominous." I pop the spoon in my mouth, savoring the chocolatey goodness as it melts against my tongue. "What is it?"

"I don't really like chocolate."

I blink at her, slowly sliding the spoon from between my lips before pointing it at her. "What do you mean?"

"I mean, I don't hate it." She rubs the back of her neck avoiding my eyes. "It's not bad if it's, you know, milk chocolate or something subtle, but…"

"But?"

She covers her face with her hands, resting her elbows on the table. "But, oh my god, you overdo it on the chocolate factor. It's way too much. You keep buying those chocolate muffins, and I don't like them. They're so rich. I can't do chocolate on chocolate on chocolate." She peeks at me through her fingers.

When I don't say anything, she gives me puppy dog eyes and pouts. "I'm sorry."

I let her stew in her deception for a moment longer

before letting loose the laughter that's been building. She's priceless, I swear.

"Why are you sorry? Just means more chocolate for me." I ruffle her hair.

She sits up, eyes narrowing. "Are you sure?"

"Yes, Stevie. I'm not going to break up with you just because you don't share my chocolate addiction."

"What if I was a worm, would you break up with me then?"

"You're a loser." I spoon out some of her maple ice cream and hold it out to her. She smiles and bites it off, humming with pleasure.

"You didn't answer my question."

"No, Stevie, I wouldn't break up with you even if you were a worm."

"Everyone, Francis will be here in ten minutes, and god help me if you are all not ready and standing by this elevator." Sydney shouts from the living room. I can hear her heels clicking on the floor, pacing back and forth, no doubt.

"I'm almost done!" Stevie yells back from inside the bathroom.

Sitting on my bed, I watch her as she finishes applying her lip gloss and sprays some sort of mist on her face. She looks drop-dead gorgeous. Her dress is a red as dark as the blood running through my veins. I'm tempted to rip it off and make love to her on the bathroom counter, but I also want to kneel on the ground and kiss my way up her long, tan legs, worshiping her every inch.

I shake out my nerves, going to my bedside drawer to pull out a red velvet jewelry box. I stand behind Stevie, running one of my hands down the lace corset as she fusses with her hair in the mirror.

"How do I look?"

"Hmm." I place a kiss on her bare shoulder. "Like you're missing something."

She frowns back at me in the mirror. "Like what?"

"Like this." I hold the jewelry box in front of her and open it. A small gasp leaves her as her hand comes up to roll the delicate pendant between her fingers. It's a diamond dove attached to a gold chain. I remove it from the box, and she sweeps her hair to one side so I can clasp it around her neck. She shivers against me as I litter a dozen small kisses down the length of her neck until I reach her shoulder again.

"It's beautiful. Thank you, I love it."

She shifts to face me, her hand coming up to caress my cheek before kissing me softly. I release her lips, gazing into her eyes. She looks at me with such reverence. One look at her, and I feel powerful enough to take over the world. She is my goddess, and whether I'm a god standing beside her or a disciple at her feet, I will worship her until my dying breath—and even then, I'll follow her into the afterlife.

"You're my little dove," I whisper. "I love you."

"I love you, too. Forever and more."

I capture her lips, drinking in her sweet taste. Our tongues twist together, a dance of devotion. Her hand comes up to grasp the silver chain around my neck and she gives it a pull, dragging me closer to her. I push her flush against the counter, and her leg slips through the slit in her dress to curl around the backs of my knees. I lean into her, running my hand across her soft skin, cock growing stiffer by the minute. My fingers hover dangerously near the top of the slit, and I feel her smile against me.

"Think we have time for a quickie?" She murmurs against my lips.

I love this girl.

"Think not."

We twist our heads to see Sydney standing with her arms crossed over her silver gown. "Get that lip gloss off your face, grab your mask, and get into the elevator. I swear. I feel like a damn chaperone on a high school trip." She spins out of the room and bangs on the opposite door. "Jackson, we're leaving."

Stevie reaches up, swiping her thumb across my lips to remove the gloss that transferred over. "You know, Beach Sex is a good color on you."

"Maybe you can put more on me later tonight." I wink.

She laughs, ducking out from my grip to reapply her gloss and smooth down her hair. "You promised Sydney you'd be on your best behavior."

"True, but you didn't."

"Oh?" She throws me a mischievous grin.

"Plus, my best behavior is my worst behavior."

Stevie snorts, grabbing my hand and trailing me out of the room. "Then I guess I have to keep the bad boy in check."

Everyone is focused on The System.

The cameras flash as Jackson, Parker, and I stroll our way down the red carpet to the entrance of the convention center. They're waiting, watching, wondering. Three men, three masks, three legacies.

We stop when we get to the bottom of the stairs, and I look at my boys, taking in this final moment. Two weeks ago, we made the decision to change our futures. To embark on a new journey together, to reach new levels and dominate the world as we know it.

Jackson and Parker nod at me, and I reach up to undo my mask.

As one, we take them off.

Blade becomes Aleksander Knight, and Aleksander Knight becomes Blade.

My red world turns to one of color.

I can't understand a single word that the crowd is shouting. Everything is blinding me in pure sensory overload. Fuck. These flashing lights are twelve times brighter without the mask on.

My eyes search for Stevie, spotting her instantly. She stands to the side with Sydney and her best friend, Deanna. She looks at me with the biggest smile, and I feel her love leaking into me, holding me steady.

I reach my hand out to her, wiggling my fingers in invitation. She cocks her eyebrow, looking back at Sydney, who gives her a nod. Then, the love of my life all but runs over to me. I catch her waist with my free hand, spinning her into me. Everything else is drowned out as she looks up into my eyes.

"I'm so proud of you," she whispers. "*S'agapo.*"

I kiss her, letting the world see that she is mine and I am hers. Parker and Jackson let out whoops of cheer around us as I dip her backward and deepen our kiss. She lets out a small laugh, and I stare into her shining gaze.

Every game I play, I play to win. But I'll lose against Stevie every time if it means she wins my heart.

THE END

Exclusive
BONUS SCENE

"Aleks, babe. You have a package."

I walk through the elevator, carrying the large rectangular box. It's heavy as all hell. I can't even begin to imagine what might be inside. Actually, I can. It's probably some limited-edition gaming thing. Judging by the size, it must be a poster of some sort. I have no clue where he plans on hanging it given that the entire apartment is decked out.

"What?" Aleks' voice carries out from his streaming room.

Just great. I'm going to have to lug this damn thing the whole way. I plop the box on the ground and push it across the tiles until I get to his hallway. It takes a second to get it onto the floorboards and then over the threshold, into his streaming room.

He never stops being sexy.

Aleks sits with his red headset on, tapping away at his keyboard and mouse with complete focus. I lean against the door frame and ogle him. He is wearing nothing other than a pair of red sweatpants. His biceps flex as the game gets more intense, causing his tattoos to ripple. My eyes flick to the red mask that sits on display next to him.

It's been two months since The System's reveal and

a month since the boys officially took of their masks at the *Gods League* Championship red carpet. They haven't forgone their masks completely. The guys still wear them to events, for photo-ops, and in the occasional video. But now, at least, they have the choice to take them off. Parker, especially, loves that he can start competing in live speed-run competitions. Aleks, on the other hand, is annoyed that he lost his main excuse to avoid all the events Sydney organizes. At least now he has me to bring with him.

Aleks finishes up what looks to be a *Death Valley* mission and tugs his headphones off, laying them around his neck. He swivels around in his chair and gives me one of his sultry smiles. Butterflies flutter in my core, want bubbling. I mentally attempt to shoo them away. Last night was the first night I spent back in my own apartment in over two weeks. Which means that up until last night, I was basically banging Aleks for a straight fourteen days. My pussy needs to calm herself because she's on the verge of becoming bruised.

Hey, baby." He pushes off the chair and meets me in a crushing hug. I nuzzle against his neck, drinking in his rich amber scent. If I could bathe myself in it, I would.

"Hey, you have a package."

Aleks pulls back and looks at the package for a second before his eyes widen with delight. His smile grows so large, his dimple craters against his cheek.

"Finally."

He proceeds to pick the box up and carry it into the living room, leaning it against the couch. I follow him and perch myself on the leather arm. Aleks excitedly grabs a box cutter and proceeds to cut the cupboard with quick efficiency.

"What is it?" I wrack my brain, trying to figure out what could have him so excited.

"It's a gift. For myself and, I guess, you."

Okay. My curiosity is well peaked at this point.

He pulls out a large rectangular item covered in bubble wrap. I wait for him to unwrap it, but he pauses.

"Alright. So, remember how you lied to me for weeks that you liked chocolate when you hate it, and I didn't get mad?"

"First, I don't hate it. My veins just aren't filled with it like yours are. Second, yeah," I say warily.

"Well, I might have omitted telling you something as well. But I don't think you'll be mad…probably."

My eyes narrow in on the package. *What on god's green earth is this thing?*

"Okay. Let's see it."

He grins at me as he begins to peel off the tape. As the bubble wrap peels off, my eyes zero in on what is clearly an art frame. An oddly familiar art frame. When the wax paper falls away, my jaw drops at the painting that is revealed.

The Game.

A pang of sorrow shoots through my heart as I stare at the black beauty before me. I war between elevation and depression. I love this piece, but seeing it again? The meaning has changed for me. I hadn't been wrong when I'd initially felt turmoil from the piece. But now I understand Aleksander's visceral reaction to it. Why it represented a breaking point for him.

"How did you get your hands on it?"

"I bought it that night."

"What? You were one of the bidders?" I had no idea. It was an anonymous deal. The gallery couldn't divulge the buyer. I'd reconciled with the fact that it would be yet another one of my pieces that I'd never see again. And here it is. I can't stop the lone tear that spills across my cheek. It's neither happiness nor sadness, just an overflow of emotion. Aleks comes over and envelops me in a hug, patting my hair. I let the feelings wash over me.

"The second I saw it, I knew I had to have it."

It's the sweetest surprise I could've asked for.

"Wait." I pop out of his embrace. Jigsaw pieces fall into place as realization washes over me. "Aleksander. You spent a stupid amount of money on this piece."

He acts like Parker spends his money without a care, and yet this man paid an absurdly high price for a painting his own girlfriend painted...inspired by himself.

"I wouldn't call it stupid. It's an investment. I have a Stephanie Andwell original. It's priceless."

"You're ridiculous," I laugh.

He lifts me up and crushes his lips against mine.

"Ridiculously in love with you."

ALEKS
Four Months Earlier

"Hi, sorry to interrupt. Do you mind if I steal her away for a few minutes? We have quite the bidding war going on for her piece."

Yes. I fucking mind, you asshat. I haven't gotten a read on Caleb Hayes yet. I can't tell whether he is genuinely interested in Stevie as an artist or if he is hoping for something more. Regardless, the guy is too suave for me not to be cautious about him.

I throw him a lazy smile. "Of course not. Everyone deserves the chance to meet my girl, see how amazing she and her art are." I gesture around the room. "I'm just going to look around the exhibit myself."

"Wonderful." Hayes rests his hand on Stevie's elbow and steers her away. The possessive beast inside me batters against my ribcage. My jaw ticks as I watch her shiny figure disappear in the crowd. She looks gorgeous, as always, tonight.

Her shimmering black dress is cut mid-thigh. The front is modest, until she turns around and you get a view of her bare back. The fabric pools just above her tailbone, her tantalizing skin on full display. I'd be green with jealously over all the men staring at her if I didn't already know that she was mine.

I watch as she maneuvers through the crowd, charming each person Hayes introduces her to. She's a complete natural. I have no doubt in my mind that after tonight, Stephanie Andwell is going to be a hallmark name in the California art scene. There's no other alternative.

I turn my attention back to the piece before me. Her piece.

The Game.

Fucking hell. It took me by surprise when I saw my own mask front and center, the focal point of her piece. She doesn't even know that I'm Blade, and yet she managed to capture both him and me perfectly. It's a painful painting…but it's also beautiful. A breaking point. That's what I told her it represented. The fluctuating mask ending in a shatter couldn't be a better representation of the turmoil I'm under, hiding half of myself from Stevie. I'm worried that eventually I'm going to reach my breaking point…and I have no clue whether it will tear us apart or make us stronger. I hate the painting and I love it. It's me.

If I didn't already think that Stephanie Andwell was my other half, this cemented it for me. She's connected to me on a wavelength I couldn't even begin to describe.

I need this piece.

It takes twenty minutes for me to finally track down Hayes' assistant. The woman is slippery like an eel and just as cunning. She's weaving through investors and buyers like she is spinning gold for Rumpelstiltskin.

"Cassandra." I grip the redhaired woman's elbow before she has a chance to disappear into the crowd again. Her cold eyes rake over me, eyes narrowing as she clocks in every inch of my appearance. She's determining whether I'm worth her time. I already know what her conclusion is going to be, so I don't give her a chance. "I would like to submit a bid for *The Game*."

"We already have several interested parties, Mr.…," she trails off, raising a brow.

"Knight." I release her elbow and position myself in front of her.

"Mr. Knight." Her tone is one of utter boredom.

"I understand that. However, I have a feeling you will want to hear my price."

"Unless you can top the current bid, I don't think so." She crosses her arms.

"And the current bid is?"

"Forty thousand."

"I can offer double."

Her porcelain mask drops. "I would need some sort of proof that you would be able to purchase such an item."

"Would an endorsement from the Covington family work?"

Surprise flashes across her features. I'm not a noob. I did my research before coming here. Regardless of what the piece was, I had intended to buy it. Which is why I learned that Parker's family had invested their money in several of Hayes' pieces over the years for their hotels.

I watch as a practiced smile tilts across her face.

"Why don't you follow me, Mr. Knight. I'd love to continue this conversation in my office."

I match her back with a wolfish grin.

"Sounds wonderful, Cassandra."

READY FOR MORE OF THE SYSTEM?

Order *Forbidden Game* now for Parker and Sydney's story.
And turn the page for a **sneak peek** at chapter one ;)

Curious about how Aleks proposes to Stevie?
Download the bonus content by, visiting:
https://dl.bookfunnel.com/y4if9jg4p2

Wondering about what happened to *The Game?*
Find out where the painting ended up in a bonus chapter available in the **discreet paperback** edition!

Thank you for reading, *Good Game.*
If you enjoyed this book, I would be grateful if you could leave a review on the platform(s) of your choice. Reviews are one of the best ways to support an author!

Kisses,
Madison Fox

Forbidden GAME

THE SYSTEM
BOOK 2

SYDNEY

"Why are you naked?"

The blonde Adonis before me is lounging in bed wearing nothing more than a pair of blue Burberry trunks. He is watching a video on his laptop while he simultaneously plays a video game on his ninety-inch TV.

Parker Covington's toned body is on full display without a care in the world. Which isn't an uncommon situation. I've never met a man who wears less clothing in his own apartment than Parker. And yet, he has a closet that is three times the size of my own and filled to the brim with custom designer clothing.

"I'm not technically naked."

"That's not the point. We have to be at your photoshoot in thirty minutes. Which means we needed to leave,"

390

I check my watch, "five minutes ago, and you're not dressed."

"I have a photoshoot?" Parker runs a hand through his platinum hair.

"I texted you this morning. I even sent you a calendar invite."

I have to fight not to grind my teeth. I just saw my dentist last week, and he told me I needed a nightguard because, apparently, I grind in my sleep. I never had an issue sleeping when I was a kid. But it turns out that working for three famous video game streamers creates a little bit of stress.

"Huh, well. I do love being fashionably late. It's my brand."

Make that a lot of stress.

Each of the men I work for is difficult in their own way. Aleksander is the most popular, a natural leader, but he hates going to events and likes pissing people off. Jackson is the most well-spoken and levelheaded, but people are terrified of him because he looks like a giant grump. And Parker? Parker should be my golden goose. He is charismatic, funny, and attractive. He jumps at every opportunity I give him. He also lives in his own world and is as unpredictable as the rain in Seattle.

I walk forward and shut the laptop, looking him directly in his baby blues. "Get dressed, or I will drag you to this photoshoot as you are."

"You act like that would be a punishment," he winks. "But fine, just give me a second." Parker shifts off his Californian King and nudges past me, his hot skin brushing against my arm. Parker Covington also has very little

391

understanding of personal space. I blame it on him being British.

Unfortunately for me, all the men in The System look like they should belong on a teen drama, not streaming video games in dark rooms for hours on end each week. My radar for hot men has gotten all bent out of shape, thanks to them. It's taken four years of working for The System for me to become somewhat immune to their sculpted bodies and flirtatious jokes. Especially after The Incident.

"Alright, let's bounce." Parker fluffs the collar of his white shirt and checks himself out in the mirror approvingly. He is also wearing a pair of navy-blue chino shorts because he is incapable of not wearing blue *somewhere* on his body. I have no doubt in my mind that his entire outfit probably costs more than my biweekly paycheck.

I shoot off a quick message to our driver that we are on our way down before grabbing Parker by the elbow to usher him out of his room.

The System's penthouse apartment is stunning. Custom black tiles and pristine white walls. An open layout living room and kitchen that leads to a massive wraparound balcony. I've slowly added a few plants over the years, but the space is minimalistic, decorated mainly with limited edition gaming memorabilia, neon signs, and an iconic The System poster. I live on the tenth floor, and while it's a gorgeous apartment, it's nothing compared to theirs.

"Don't forget your mask," I remind Parker, punching the button for the elevator.

I startle when he waves the blue LED purge mask in my periphery.

"As if I would. It's only been three months, Syd. We

haven't got *that* used to life without them yet." Parker tucks the mask under his arm while he toes on a pair of loafers.

Three months. It's only been three months since Aleks, Parker, and Jackson took off their masks and revealed their identities to the world. For years, these three men rose to the top of the video game world as the most popular faceless streamers—wearing matching LED masks as part of their brand so no one knew what they looked like. Then, another streamer tried to blackmail them…and they decided they were sick of hiding. They were ready to step out of the shadows and level up their careers.

It was bittersweet.

They've all adapted differently. Parker was the easiest, Jackson the hardest, and Aleksander was in the middle. Regardless of their faces now being known, the masks are still a large part of their brand. It's my job to make sure they still take them everywhere.

The elevator arrives, and we step in. I press the button for G2 and prepare for my ears to pop during the descent. We live in the tallest apartment building in California. It was built only a few years ago and has sixty floors. I don't know what I would've done if I were afraid of heights.

"We're going to be late." I tell Parker as we rocket down to the private parking garage.

"You know, if I drove, we could get there in time."

My stomach swirls just at the mere mention of him driving. I try to avoid riding with Parker whenever possible. The man has a tendency to drive forty miles over the speed limit. How he has never gotten a speeding ticket blows my mind. If I wasn't too chicken to get my own license renewed, I could drive myself places…but the idea of being behind the wheel again sends spiders across my skin.

"Francis is perfectly capable of driving us," I tell him as the doors open. "Besides, I informed the company that we were stuck in traffic and would be a little late."

The one good thing about living in California is that you can always use traffic as an excuse. No one bats an eye.

Our driver, Francis, opens the door to the white BMW. Parker holds his hand out for me to get into the backseat, and I graciously accept it. No matter how sarcastic or boyish he can be, Parker Covington is, to his core, a gentleman.

Once we are settled, Francis begins our forty-minute drive to the studio. Parker mutters under his breath a few times at the slow pace, but I let my head lull against the headrest and shut my eyes. The exhaustion over the past few months has been unrelenting.

My phone buzzes in my pocket, and I let out a deep huff. The world never stops spinning long enough for me to breathe more than one peaceful breath. I pull my phone from my purse and swipe it open.

"This is Sydney Lake. What's the situation?"

[to be continued]
www.authormadisonfox.com/books

ACKNOWLEDGEMENTS

Honestly, I have no idea how to write one of these. At first, it seemed like this would be super easy…but it's not really. I know some people skip out on the acknowledgements, but it has always been one of my favourite things to read. And yes, I am writing this in British English because I damn well can. *[edit: I have now written this, and it ended up way longer than I expected. Turns out, I have a lot of people to thank because I'm just that sort of human.]*

I want to start by saying that I wrote this book for myself. Which sounds kind of selfish and conceited but…it's the truth. I grew up playing video games. They have always been such a massive part of my life. From when I was on a clunky 2005 desktop computer playing CD-ROMS to current days where I'm gaming on my Switch, video games have been my safety bubble. When I get super stressed with life, I know I can put on a game and completely relax my brain. I always wanted a book that featured video games as *more* than just a hobby…so I decided I would write an entire series. Taa-daa.

To every single person who has posted a picture or video of my book online…THANK YOU! As a fellow content creator, it makes my heart shine. Whether you have three followers or three million, the content you post makes a difference—never, ever, doubt that. You are a superstar.

And thank YOU, my reader. Thank you for giving my book baby a chance. For reading my very first novel. This was such a scary process, but also really exciting. Just having you read the words that I wrote means the world to me. In case no one has told you lately, you matter.

Okay, now onto my people.

First, I obviously have to thank Cat. Sure, Cat designed my absolutely killer covers (*swoon*). But what you don't know is that Cat read the very first version of Good Game...like legit, Cat read this before I had even finished the last chapter. She fell in love with Stevie and Aleks before anyone else and has been the best cheerleader I could ever ask for. I love you, my sparkly best friend.

Second, I have to thank my amazing editor Katie K! You were so amazing, and I couldn't have asked for a better person to work with. I know you had to deal with all my Australianisms...and the fact that I clearly did not know the difference between further and farther, but you were so patient with me. Also, you shipped Sydney and Parker from page two, and that makes me smile.

Thank you, Alyssa, for formatting my books. You are a superwoman, juggling seventeen different things at once.

Mum and Dad, thank you for being the reasons why I love reading. And thank you for letting me camp out for two weeks straight in your house to write eighty percent of this book. You always support me no matter what. I know that you will both be in my corner until the end of the time, and I will forever be grateful for how lucky I am to have you as parents.

Also, Dad, thanks for answering my random car and motorcycle questions.

Due to technical issues...I have to thank my little brother, Ethan. Sure, my dad played video games when I was a kid, and so did my cousins (shoutout to Elle playing The Sims of the PS1), but it is because my little brother played video games that I became so invested in them as well. We spent hours growing up playing Halo, Pokémon, and more. He is also the reason why I found out about gaming YouTubers back in the day. So, thanks lil bro… even though you suck at texting me back.

Thank you, Jen (thebookrefuge), for reading Good Game at the absolute speed of light. Even though our conversation led to me completing gutting and rewriting four chapters and then adding in another three new chapters on top of that (resulting in surprising my editor with another 8,000 words to edit…), you were a super star Beta Reader.

Thank you, Katie (katiesbooknook426). You were my very first friend I made when I joined BookTube, and so it was only right that you were one of the first people to read my book.

Thank you to Sophie and Ryan Lark for your friendship and your support. Soph, you are and always will be one of the most inspiring women I have met—sending you all the hugs.

Jeanine Bennedict. GIRLIE. You are one of the best human beings I have met. We had some random as hell voice memo exchanges, but you were the very first person who helped me figure out what the actual fuck I was even doing publishing my book. Your friendship is priceless.

Kat-freaking-Singleton. I love you.

Thank you to Carlie Jean (my vegan boo) and Cali Melle (my hockey lover) for answering my super random questions and supporting me in my debut.

Thank you, Becca, for dealing with every quarter-life crisis I had. I know I seem like a hot mess on my good days.

Ms. Arkin. I have no way of getting into contact with

you, but you were one of the best English teachers I had. You led me on my journey of writing poetry and Bellarke fanfiction.

Also, I'm thanking my Indiana college bestie, Katie. You didn't read this or anything, but you're my bestest friend who has stuck by me over the last six years no matter what. My ride-or-die.

Lastly, thank you to the super-secret, confidential-as-*fuck* project that I can't name for being the reason why I started writing this book. This project kicked my ass into gear, and I will forever be grateful for that.

**FOLLOW ME ON SOCIAL MEDIA
FOR ALL THE FUN!**

I post fun updates on my socials pertaining not only to my upcoming releases, but also my life in general and the books that I am reading. I would love to connect with you

<3

authormadisonfox.com

ABOUT THE AUTHOR

Madison Fox was born and raised in Australia but has been living in the United States for the past decade. While she still watches Australian football every Sunday, she currently resides in Nevada as a cat mum to Zelda (yes, based on the video game).

Madison has always been obsessed with books. As a child, she would stash chapter novels in her pillowcases before bedtime so she could read after her parents went to bed. Madison joined the book community in 2018 with her YouTube channel (@bymadisonfox) and has never looked back.

When Madison isn't reading or writing a new book, she can be found drowning in one of her other obsessions, such as k-dramas, manga, anime, video games, and espresso martinis.

GOOD GAME is her debut romance novel.

Milton Keynes UK
Ingram Content Group UK Ltd.
UKHW020619071223
433828UK00015B/807